Margaret Leroy

grew up in the New Forest and ﹇   ﹈
College, Oxford. She has wor﹍
playleader, shop assistant and social worker. She has written three non-fiction books, *Miscarriage*, *Pleasure* and *Some
Girls Do*, and a story for children, *Aristotle Sludge*. She has
also written widely for magazines and newspapers, and
appeared on numerous radio and television programmes.
Her first novel, *Trust*, was published in 1999 and has been
translated into five languages. *Trust*, as *Loving You*, is soon
to be a Granada TV drama, starring Niamh Cusack and
Douglas Henshall. Margaret Leroy is married with two
daughters and lives in Kingston-upon-Thames. You can
visit her website at www.margaretleroy.com.

ALYSSON'S SHOES

Margaret Leroy

Flamingo
An Imprint of HarperCollins*Publishers*

Flamingo
An Imprint of HarperCollins*Publishers*
77–85 Fulham Palace Road,
Hammersmith, London W6 8JB

Flamingo is a registered trade mark of
HarperCollins Publishers Limited

www.fireandwater.com

Published by Flamingo 2003
9 8 7 6 5 4 3 2 1

First published in Great Britain by
Flamingo 2002

Copyright © Margaret Leroy 2002

Margaret Leroy asserts the moral right to
be identified as the author of this work

Author photograph by Nikki Gibbs

ISBN 0 00 651314 X

Set in Weiss

Printed and bound in Great Britain by
Clays Ltd, St Ives plc

Acknowledgements

These people shared their knowledge with me during the writing of this book: Peter Binder, Hugh Brayne, Jeremy Cameron, Niall Campbell, David Jockelson, Patricia Law, Simon Tippet, Vicki Tippet, Christine Wright. There were also others who have chosen not to be named. I am greatly indebted to them all for their generosity.

I am also deeply grateful to Lucy Floyd for her invaluable critique of the story, to Lisa Eveleigh for her empathy and support, to Mike Fishwick for his skilful editing: and, as always, to Mick, Becky and Isabel for their love and understanding.

Chapter 1

'She's crying again. That little girl. She's always crying,' he said.

He was sitting where the corridor opens out, where there's a table-tennis table: he had his head in his hands.

'Can you hear her, Dr Craig?'

'No, Tim, I can't,' I said.

'There she is again. She cries and cries,' he said.

I stayed with him for a moment, my hand on his arm.

It was a day of fire and ice: the February sun yellow and low like pale flame, and on the tiny patches of lawn in front of the hospital where the sun rarely reaches, a crust of frost that still hadn't melted at two o'clock. But on the wards it was hot, it was always hot: a blanket of air pressed down on you, thick and heavy.

The dormitories on Derwent Ward were empty: Francine had organized a game of Trivial Pursuit in the day room, and some of the patients were at occupational therapy. It all looked very peaceful with no patients, the beds with their green-checked covers, the neat little graphs attached to the foot of the beds, all squares and right angles, all precise and contained, except on the floor in the women's dormitory, where a scratch from a bit of grit caught in a castor had traced out an extravagant arabesque. I saw that Cassie Broomfield, who had a flamboyant delusion that she was the Queen of Heaven, had added a few new postcards to the collection pinned to the head of her bed. Most were of the Pope: there was one of Jesus, with a sweet, mild-mannered Victorian mouth, a ring of pink roses round him, and eyes that seemed to follow you as you passed. A smell of disinfectant caught my throat.

I passed the interview room. I could see Sam Mehta interviewing someone: he must have expected trouble, he'd propped the door half-open. Sam had his usual lost air and lots of stubble and his shirt looked like it had been slept in: people often assumed that he was a patient. Sam was my mate on the ward – the only one I'd confide in: you have to be so careful what you say.

I left the ward, crossed the covered bridge towards the outpatient clinic. The sun seared through the glass, you had to screw up your eyes, you were walking straight into the light, but you could feel the cold. I went through the swing doors into the clinic, and past the disarranged chairs and out-of-date copies of *Prima*. The hanging baskets of ivies were all padlocked in place.

In the staff cloakroom I stood in front of the mirror for a moment. I looked OK, I thought: I'd put on more makeup than usual, and my smartest, most serious suit. I couldn't decide how to wear my hair: it's long and dark and difficult, and I never quite know what to do with it. Mac, I knew, would tell me to tie it up, though I'm never sure that suits me. But pinned-up hair does show off your cheekbones, and gives out, perhaps, some kind of subliminal message: says you're this kind of a person – definite, strong, controlled – which may or may not be true. I thought how this was a little like going on a date

2

and wondering which it should be – the crisp white shirt or the velvet bustier – what you might choose to convey. In the end I opted for the cheekbones.

I went out of the clinic and down the corridor. Outside his door, looking at the plate that said Professor Ralph Patterson, I waited for a moment. I held my hand out in front of me, saw how it trembled. I thought this was interesting: to want this thing so much it made me shake. I knew I'd be able to get some kind of consultant's post when I finished my stint as specialist registrar in the summer – but the job that was coming up would be so very prestigious. It was an academic post with a clinical component, and funded by a benefactor, Owen Fisher, an industrialist whose wife had suffered from depression; everyone referred to it as the Fisher Memorial. I'd only arranged to have an informal discussion, but I knew Ralph would find a way to tell me precisely where I stood. Distressing scenarios flitted through my head. That there'd be a little hesitancy about him, a subtle subtext that hinted, You're not quite right for us. Or it might emerge with horrible clarity that he favoured Dominic Braisby, who was a lecturer attached to Dr Sutton's firm and the most obvious in-house competition: Dominic was a serial seducer of lissom paramedics, and very confident and assured, though I felt that academically I probably had the edge.

I pushed these thoughts away, took a deep breath, put out my hand and knocked.

'Tessa. How nice to see you.'

He has this very English look, tall and bony and cerebral, and one of those upper-class accents that always suggest old port and leather armchairs. I wonder sometimes what it's like to be that kind of a person: not to have to struggle.

He waved towards a chair. I sat.

The psychiatric unit is on the fourth floor of the hospital. Through the window behind him, I could see the vistas of the city, all its shine and dazzle.

3

'I think I can guess why you're here,' he said. 'Our new post.'

'Yes,' I said.

He sat down, leaning forward on his desktop, resting his fingertips together. There's a bronze on his desk, a dog with its jaw hanging rather alarmingly open, an Alsatian or maybe a wolf – I'm never quite sure.

'I know it probably won't be advertised till the summer,' I said, 'but I thought it might be useful to talk about it now.'

'Absolutely,' he said.

I'd always got on well with him: it was a mentor relationship with just a hint of flirtatiousness, occasional touches on my shoulder and comments about my clothes, sometimes a decorous slow dance at unit discos. Now he smiled at me, a smile that was warm and expansive, showing his teeth.

'I wondered if you could tell me a bit about how it will be advertised,' I said.

'Of course,' he said. 'There'll be four sessions of general psychiatry, and six senior lecturer sessions for teaching and research.'

'Yes,' I said.

'There'll be plenty of opportunity for the person appointed to develop their research interests. And we'll be looking for someone who's been extensively published, and who's already achieved some recognition.'

'Yes,' I said.

'Our ideal candidate would have a special interest in depression,' he said. 'Owen Fisher's wife was a depressive herself.'

'I see,' I said, cool and still, but with a sense of mounting excitement.

He has grey eyes, somehow too light for his colouring. He fixed me with his pale benevolent gaze. 'I saw your latest paper in the *Lancet*,' he said. 'I thought it was excellent. A superb piece of work.'

4

'Thank you,' I said. I knew what he was saying: the paper had been on a study I'd done about the effectiveness of cognitive therapy in depression.

'I'd be delighted to see you working in a situation where you could really pursue that side of things,' he said.

I felt the job was mine. A hot surge of happiness washed through me.

'We're planning to advertise in the first or second week of April,' he said.

'Right. Well, I'll look out for it,' I said.

'I'll warn you when it's coming up,' he said.

In the distance behind him, there were sheets of brightness where plate-glass windows caught the light, and a plane soared high, trailing silver behind it. It seemed the loveliest thing to me then, that thin pure glittery trail.

'Thank you,' I said again.

'So: Mac OK, is he?'

'He's fine,' I said.

'I hear great things of Mac,' he said.

I saw us briefly as other people might see us: Tessa and Mac, this golden couple.

'He's really enjoying his new job,' I said.

'It's all developing so fast, of course,' said Ralph.

'I find it quite dazzling, really – I couldn't begin to do it, I don't have that kind of 3D imagination,' I said. Mac's a gastric surgeon: he operates via a screen, tying ligatures, cutting vessels, all at one remove.

'He and I must play squash again sometime,' said Ralph.

'I'll tell him,' I said. But wasn't quite sure what Mac would make of the offer. Mac tends to win these matches – he's younger than Ralph, and fit from all the rowing he does – and Ralph can get quite petulant: he's one of those men who always have to win.

'Well, Tessa, I'm so glad you came to see me,' he said, as

I rose to go. 'I'll be very interested to receive your application.'

Standing, I could see out over the city, the burning sky, the distance blue like damsons: I felt I could see for ever.

I was almost out of the door. As he came round his desk towards me I could smell his aftershave, a faint opulent scent.

'Tessa, while you're here,' he said, 'could I ask if you'd mind taking the ward round tomorrow?'

'No problem,' I said.

'The Ethics Committee has been rescheduled: I can't afford to miss it,' he said.

'No, of course not,' I said.

'Many thanks,' he said. 'We need to clear some beds – see what you can do.'

'Sure,' I said. This was his Achilles heel, I knew: a Trust audit had found that Ralph's patients stayed in longer than the patients on the other two psychiatric firms. 'Well, thanks so much for taking the time to see me.'

'Not at all,' he said. 'My pleasure.'

I walked back over the covered bridge, and the light that came through the glass fell on me and all around me.

Tim Rigby was still in the corridor, holding his head in his hands, but some of the others were coming out of the day room – they must have finished the quiz. Paula Hickey was standing by the table-tennis table, bouncing the ball with the bat. Paula was one of my favourite patients: you shouldn't have them, but of course you do. I'd always sensed a profound untutored intelligence hidden deep inside her. She'd had her first admission just after I came to work here, and I'd been in on the original diagnosis. I remembered her fear, as she'd told us haltingly about the voices in her head, well-educated voices that talked constantly about her: We're going to have to strangle her, they'd said. She was a thin pale woman, fluid as a cat, her dark hair roughly cropped – she'd hacked it all off with kitchen scissors just before we'd brought her in. But today she'd put some gel on it, so it looked weirdly stylish, in a punk sort of way: like it was meant.

Cassie Broomfield came out of the day room to join her, wearing one of the Sunday school outings dresses she likes, tartan with a trim white collar, and they began to play. Paula lunged for the ball, nicked it with the bat, it went shooting up to the ceiling. Both of them giggled.

I watched for a moment, then turned to go to the nurses' station to look in a file.

'That little girl's still crying, Dr Craig,' said Tim as I passed.

'Never mind,' I said.

Above him on the wall there were posters advertising the users' groups. The poster for Synergy, which met in the out-patient clinic, had a drawing of a turquoise coffee-cup.

'I don't know what can have happened, to make her cry like that,' he said.

'Tim, why not go to OT?' I said. 'You could do some pottery like you did before. I loved that jug you made.'

'I keep myself to myself, Dr Craig,' he said.

'But don't you think it might make you feel better, to go along and do something?' I said. 'I'm sure that Jo would be really pleased to see you.'

He ignored me. 'She's crying again. She never stops,' he said.

The journey home is by train: tube to Waterloo, then the Shepperton train. It was getting dark already as I left the hospital, purple shadow settling in the corners. The *Big Issue* seller at the entrance to the Underground had his shoulders hunched against the cold: he was wearing fingerless gloves; he blew on his fingers. As I passed him I moved my hand automatically to my bag, but I'd done up both the straps and I couldn't quite be bothered.

The train left Waterloo only five minutes late, and I managed to get a seat. I sat by the window, opposite two beautiful women in ponyskin ankle-boots who were speaking in Spanish. The man beside me was reading a slender paperback. I glanced at it over his shoulder: 'How will we know the Anti-Christ?' it said. I watched the sun go down over Clapham Junction, a round red winter sun, briefly impaled on Battersea Power Station, then sinking below the skyline: all that light and lavishness, then suddenly it was gone. It instantly seemed to get colder, even in the carriage. On the other side of the track it was veiled and smoky and blue.

My mobile rang: it was Abi.

'Where have you been, you bloody woman?'

'I've been busy,' I said. 'Really, it's been frantic.'

'Fuck that,' she said. 'It's ages since we talked.'

'I know,' I said. 'I'm sorry. I'm really sorry. I should have rung.' I suddenly felt ashamed – that I was always making excuses, putting people off, even the people I loved.

'You know how it is,' I said lamely.

But it was only a form of words – it wasn't true of Abi and me, really: we didn't know how it was for each other, not now, not anymore. Though we'd been so close since first we'd met, in the first year of our clinical training in Liverpool, our lives were poles apart.

Over the phone I could hear Lydia, her delectable five year old, singing 'The Wheels on the Bus' in a kind of tuneless shout. I pictured Abi in her red-walled kitchen, holding the phone in place with the side of her head, stirring away at an old Le Creuset pot that smelt of garlic and turmeric. Abi with her appalling language, her intricate demanding domestic life – children, guinea pigs, cooking, parish meetings – and her

8

all-encompassing warmth. I suddenly couldn't comprehend why I hadn't been round for weeks.

'Something fantastic happened today,' I said. 'I'll tell you when I see you.'

'I'm glad something nice is happening to somebody,' she said.

There was an edge to her voice.

'Abi, are you OK?'

'Sure I'm OK,' she said. 'Lydia's got some virus and is being a total pain and the cat's just puked up all over Jake's algebra and Fred's closeted with someone who's seeking salvation so he can't do a damn thing. Yeah, I'm just fine.'

'Poor love,' I said, 'I don't know how you manage.'

'Sometimes I don't,' she said.

'Look, let's meet up soon,' I said. 'I'll ring when I've got my diary in front of me.'

We said goodbye.

Outside it seemed quite dark now, the gorgeous light all faded from the sky. I rested my eyes on the dark, on the pale perfect slice-of-melon moon that was slowly rising, hugging my happiness to me.

Chapter 2

Something was out of place. A little cool draught fingered my skin, like a window was open somewhere: I had a brief scared feeling we might have been burgled. But almost immediately saw the bag, a battered old thing, the zip broken, with clothes spilling out of it, flung down on the pale cream carpet of my hallway. And then the music floating out from the living room. A piano introduction, the notes blending together, not separate lumpy things like when I play, but melding into a whole, then he started to sing.

> Sweet, stay awhile, why will you rise?
> The light you see comes from your eyes:
> The day breaks not, it is my heart,
> To think that you and I must part.

I recognized it: Elizabethan, I thought, Dowland maybe. Like Jed himself – esoteric and suggestive at the same time. He'd waited for this moment, for me to come in: he loves a bit of drama.

I went into the living room. It was all light and bright

and elegant, my cream sofas, my linen curtains, my floor of bleached stripped pine, nothing scarred or dusty or distressed in the place: and Jed sitting at my piano like some tatty dark angel in his torn denim and piercings, bent over the keyboard like he was engaged on some erotic enterprise. Jed is the only person I know who makes piano-playing look like sex. I stood and listened. His voice is a high honeyed alto, extraordinary with its troubling ambiguous pitch, and sleek as silk. I felt that mix of emotions I always feel when he turns up unannounced like this after months of absence – relief, a little irritation too, instant and powerful affection.

He'd brought me lilies: massive extravagant blooms. He's always brilliant at choosing flowers. He'd put them in one of my slender matt-white vases: they looked totally wrong and all top-heavy, as though they might topple over or break out in some way. Their scent was heavy, musty, like they were already over.

He sang three verses, finished with his wrists self-consciously raised, turned to me.

'Tess. I'm in love,' he said.

'Well, Jed,' I said, 'you usually are.'

I went to hug him. Jed is so tall and thin he sometimes seems just all beautiful bones, and the way he felt in my arms induced in me as always various terrible anxieties about his state of health. I kept them to myself.

He held me by the shoulders for a moment, looking me up and down.

'You're all tarted up,' he said. 'Eyeliner. That isn't like you.' He has a very technical understanding of makeup, which always amuses me: it seems so surprising in a man. 'So was it a special day?'

'Kind of,' I said.

'You saw someone special?'

'Kind of,' I said.

11

His eyes gleamed. 'Tell me more,' he said.

'You wouldn't be interested,' I said. 'Really.'

He looked at me quizzically, then, when I didn't say anything else: 'I brought you some flowers.'

I touched one of the petals, thought how when I was a child I'd have loved them, though now I'd probably go for something more restrained – a single white gardenia, perhaps. The petals were crimped at the edges and the stamens had a dusting of dark pollen and there were tiny hairs, like the hairs of animals, in the middle of the blooms.

'A bit over the top, aren't they?' I said.

He grinned. When he grins, his nose wrinkles and he's six and freckly again, the little boy who kept his favourite scabs in a jam jar under his bed and was always losing his plimsolls.

'You like them, though?'

'Yes,' I said. 'Of course I do. They smell amazing.'

I buried my nose in one, breathing it in, shocked by how strong and delicious it was, then saw in the mirror that I had pollen like dried blood all over my nose.

Jed flung himself down on the sofa, long limbs everywhere.

'Mac the Knife went out to get a bottle,' he said.

'Don't call him that,' I said. But didn't comment on Mac's going out. We both knew perfectly well that the bottle was a pretext, that Mac had gone out to avoid Jed – that he'd do anything to avoid spending time in Jed's company. Mac can't stand him – dismisses him as egocentric, vain, petty – all of which is true, it just isn't the whole truth about my brother. And most people forgive him for everything when he starts to sing.

I went to change, hung up my suit with the six other black trousersuits in my wardrobe, put on some jeans and a shirt. I wondered what on earth I could cook. Jed is a very strict vegetarian – lives a life of unbridled sexual excess but refuses to pollute his system with animal protein. It would have to be vegetable lasagne, I thought: not very original, but food's not really my thing.

He followed me into the kitchen, his shadow sprawling across my stainless steel fruit bowl, my pure white china. He looked all wrong, this wasn't his kind of setting. Jed belongs elsewhere – singing with one of his esoteric choirs in a chapel full of candelabra and camp ecstatic angels, or in his eccentric flat in Brixton, with its adolescent purple sheets, the moodily pornographic Mapplethorpe prints Blu-tacked to the living-room walls, and the dirty washing up heaped everywhere. Not here in this orderly kitchen, among all these gleaming things from the Conran Shop.

I poured us both a gin, started chopping onions.

'So let me guess,' I said. 'Your new lover. Blond, skinny, great dress-sense. And quite quite different from all the others?'

He had just enough self-knowledge to smile a little.

It's been like this ever since he left the drab comprehensive we both attended and went to Oxford, where he sang in the Magdalen choir. I'd visited him there sometimes, a little overawed by it all, though I'd never have admitted it: the hushed cloisters, the whispering clover lawns, the careless stylish students, all the oppressive old stone – medical school at Liverpool hadn't had quite the same glamour. And we'd eat execrable corned beef hash in the darkly panelled dining hall at Magdalen and he'd introduce me to yet another of them – always fair, thin, louche, with wonderfully elevated cheekbones: Jed's unending procession of beautiful men.

'So, Tess, what do you know about it?' he said, stung a bit by my laughter. 'When have you ever been in love?'

'Oh honestly,' I said.

'There was that guy in Liverpool, I suppose,' he said. 'Your mountaineer.'

I shrugged, chopping my onions.

'He was gorgeous,' he said.

'Mmm,' I said, non-committally.

'You were in love with him, definitely,' he said. 'I could tell. I can always tell. You had that look.'

'It was awfully long ago,' I said. The onions made my eyes water.

'Telling me,' he said. 'I mean, look at you now. All so fucking cosy. All these *things*.' He picked up my glittery new cafetière, held it at arm's length like it was some kind of alien object. 'Doesn't it sometimes make you want to scream?'

'Don't be a pain,' I said. 'I like my life.'

But he'd made me cross: and, suddenly erratic, I put the knife through my thumb instead of the onion. It didn't hurt: there was just a single drop of blood, glossy, tulip-red.

I held it out to him. 'Look what you made me do,' I said, like a child, only half teasing.

He paid no attention. 'It's a gilded cage,' he said. 'It's all very pretty, but it's still a cage.'

'Oh piss off, Jed,' I said.

I scrabbled in a drawer for an Elastoplast.

It was a relief to hear the front door slam, Mac's firm step in the hall. He came into the kitchen, still in his great coat, bringing the freshness from outside with him.

'Hi, Tess.'

He kissed me lightly on the cheek. He smelt faintly of antibacterial soap.

'I went to see Ralph,' I said to him.

'And?'

'He was really encouraging. Well, he couldn't have been nicer.'

He hugged me. 'That's wonderful, my love. Let's drink to it.'

He put the bottle down, reached for the corkscrew. Everything he does, the slightest gesture, it's clear he's a man who knows what he wants, where he's going. That was what first

14

attracted me, I think, the easy air of authority he had, and I envied it too. Sometimes I wonder if I married him because I wanted to *be* him.

He opened the bottle with a deft flick of the wrist. I watched. He has perfect hands, strong, shapely: the hands of a craftsman. Lots of women, I've noticed, like looking at his hands. In fact lots of women like Mac altogether: the precision of his profile, the smooth dark hair that falls across his forehead, and his work, of course, they really go for his work.

Jed was looking at me curiously.

'It's a job I want,' I said.

'Oh,' he said, turning away slightly, drinking his gin, immediately losing interest.

I was happy that Jed was there – in spite of the grittiness between him and Mac: his presence made the evening seem more special. I laid the table with care, placed the lilies carefully in the centre: their scent was so thick you felt you should be able to see it, blue like smoke from a censer. I lit lots of candles, their reflections catching in all the shiny things, everywhere little pale flickery flames. After all, I had something to celebrate: only a hope – but still worth celebrating.

The wine was good, an expensive Pinot Noir, dark and delicious. Mac knows about wine – he comes from the sort of background where people learn this stuff, just breathe it in as they grow up – not like Jed and me. Once when I was at university, my parents came to Liverpool and took me out to a meal at the Adelphi: and the waiter poured the wine and my father just sat there, not knowing what to do, and I had to tell him to taste it. The waiter's face had this shuttered look, one eyebrow raised a little. I'd felt a hot quick surge of rage, to see my father despised.

I drank quite a bit, and so did Jed. Mac kept to the single glass that is all he allows himself during the working week.

15

Jed talked a lot and entirely about himself: much of it was about Consensus Vocalis, the group he sings with; they sing music written before 1700 and their CDs achieve only very small sales but are critically acclaimed. Mac, I knew, was bored, screwing up his face to hide his yawn. Mac's cultural interests don't encompass this kind of thing: he reads fat glossy biographies of privileged dead people and listens to Vivaldi in theatre; and to look at he likes Dutch painters, Vermeer perhaps, those cool calm well-lit rooms with their symmetries and table-cloths. I tried to change the subject, slipping in snippets of hospital gossip I hoped he'd find intriguing: the state of play in the planned merger between our psychiatric unit and the nearby one at St Agatha's, which was causing Ralph considerable concern; a marvellously scurrilous tale that Sam had told me about a woman Mac had trained with, who'd accused a colleague of sticking his hand in her shirt, in order to put him out of the running for a promotion. But Mac sat there with an absent look, and in the end I just let Jed take over, droning on about some violent Venetian composer who'd written madrigals that were to die for.

Warm with the wine, I leant back in my chair. My house looked good tonight, I thought, the many candle-flames reflecting in the window – we didn't have any curtains, I like that kind of simplicity. A little light fell outside onto our tiny patio garden with its pithoi and pebbles and carefully chosen plants that didn't need much watering – all we could manage for now: though I'd love one day to have a proper garden with apple trees and damp scented hedges. Jed was talking about a CD they were making, a reinterpretation of some of the sacred music of Hildegard of Bingen – it was to be called 'In the clasp of His fire' – and I sat there only half listening, thought back over the day, thought, Yes, I am going where I want to go, I am getting there. It was one of those moments when life feels shiny and simple.

At about half ten Mac pushed his chair back, eyeing us with the distaste the sober always feel for the rather drunk.

'My list starts at nine tomorrow,' he said.

'OK,' I said. 'Sleep well.'

He said goodbye to Jed: he'd be gone when Jed got up in the morning.

'Does he always do that?' said Jed, after he'd gone upstairs.

'Do what?'

'Go to bed this early?'

'It's just being responsible,' I said. 'For God's sake, he's a surgeon. We can't all be forever dancing in the streets.'

It always makes me cross when Jed criticizes Mac. There's a disciplined unshowy love in the way Mac leads his life, and I respect that. He's not overtly compassionate or empathic – he can be brusque with patients, and he's rude about them sometimes behind their backs – but he makes them better.

Jed ran his finger round his glass, not looking at me, his shadow falling across the table.

'You're happy, are you, Tess?' he said.

'Yeah,' I said. 'Sure. Of course we are.'

'No, I didn't mean you and Mac – the marital unit,' he said. 'I meant *you*. Tessa.'

'Of course I'm happy,' I said. 'Can't you tell?'

'No,' he said. 'To be honest. Not really.'

I pulled a face, cross in a familiar, almost comfortable way. It's always like this – him loving to provoke and pry and needle – and me, wanting to inject some sense into him. It's the dance we do.

'You just don't get it,' I said. 'About married life. About having someone there for you: the security of that. It's a good feeling.'

'I don't know, Tess,' he said. A huge yawn, showing his rather decrepit teeth. 'It just all looks rather hard work to me, all this being there for one another.'

17

I didn't try to explain. I didn't really know how to express it, the way Mac made me feel, and I knew Jed wouldn't understand even if I could. That Mac was about safety, a quiet peaceful feeling, everything taken care of – like one of those Dutch paintings.

'I mean, I can never suss you out – what really turns you on,' said Jed.

'That is none of your bloody business,' I said.

'Probably not,' he said. 'It's interesting though, isn't it?'

I laughed a little, but thought how I wasn't sure I could answer his question, even if I'd wanted to.

'So tell me,' he said, 'what about babies and stuff? The old biological clock and all that? Is that part of the five-year plan?'

'Oh honestly,' I said. 'I don't really think about it very much.' And thought briefly of Abi, who'd done so well at medical school, who gave it all up to look after her children, and now does just the occasional family planning clinic: who paints the walls of her house with Tuscan colours, burnt sienna and ochre and a wonderful dark yellow she mixes herself, like sun on old stone, but has wet summer holidays in Wales where the high spot is the discovery of a dead sheep. 'I'm sure we'll do it sometime,' I said. 'Just not yet. When the time's right. When it fits in.'

He patted my hand. 'Fucking control freak,' he said affectionately.

'So tell me about him,' I said. 'This new man. Your lover.'

'Rufus,' said Jed. 'He's wonderful.' And he told me how blond and beautiful Rufus was, and how sinuously his pelvis rocked when he walked, and about the struggle he'd had to come out, and the extreme viciousness and narrow-mindedness of his parents, and the way Jed couldn't keep his eyes off him. I listened, a little dazzled by the exuberance of his passion, breathing in the heavy scent of the lilies he'd brought: feeling

18

in spite of myself a kind of fascination. It's like the way I feel about all those pornographic pictures in his living room – all those men who are there to be looked at, their sleek bodies, rather large cocks and shaded knowing eyes: a bit disturbing, yet you can't help looking. And I thought how very different it must be, this burn and tug of sex he felt so strongly. Me, I fancy roughly one man every ten years: Jed fancies anyone over five foot seven with fair hair and quite a few others as well – men at bus stops, men in the dentist's waiting room – he even lusts after his dentist. And every time it's like the first time.

At twelve o'clock I hugged him and went to bed.

Mac was asleep. He'd left the bedside light on: the lines on his face on the white embroidered pillow were sharp in the dim light.

I took off my shoes at the door. The floorboards were cool, smooth, under my feet: nothing to snag you.

He woke as I went in.

'Oh God, I'm sorry,' I said, overcome with penitence, suddenly embarrassed by how much I'd drunk and feeling selfish and thoughtless. 'Please try and get back to sleep.'

'Not now you've woken me,' he said. He reached out rather languorously. 'I like you in those trousers. Take them off.' He ran his hand up my thigh.

'I haven't cleaned my teeth,' I said.

And I went to the bathroom and then I slipped in beside him, and we made love in our usual way, the predictable moves, the easily achieved orgasms, his efficient clean well-practised hands following their familiar routes.

Afterwards I turned over and we lay for a bit with Mac tucked into my back. And I thought how I loved the peace of these moments after sex: how this is the great reward of married life, making love so easily, then drifting off to sleep together between your clean white sheets, no thoughts of

19

whether he really loves you or if he'll be there in the morning, no struggle.

'That bloody brother of yours,' he said sleepily into my ear. 'Why you're so patient beats me.'

'Well, he *is* my brother,' I said.

'It's the self-obsession I can't stand,' said Mac. He yawned, turned off the light.

In spite of the sex and the alcohol it took me a while to get to sleep. Jed always disturbs me a little, saying things that are better left unspoken. The music he'd played seemed to hang around in my head.

> *O stay, or else my joys must die,*
> *And perish in their infancy.*

And I lay there and thought of Liverpool for a while, and Nathan my mountaineer, and the moonlight through the tall windows in my flat that had looked over Sefton Park spilling onto his long-limbed body, and my need for him, a neediness that to be honest I'd never felt since – and how much, how very very much, it had all hurt. But most of us have that, don't we? A lost love, something betrayed: a love you had that you elevate in your memory into something that is probably pure fantasy. Obsession isn't everything. I married Mac quite coolly, without hunger, and it was a good decision: choosing the orderly room and the table spread with a cloth and lots of light. For who would really want to be like Jed – that magnetic tug of sex always, pulling you from true north, so you shiver and fall apart and find yourself reorganized into some unpredicted pattern?

Mac's warm wrist was slung across my thigh. I listened to his easy regular breathing, and slid down into sleep.

Chapter 3

There's a little bare room off Derwent Ward with a grey acrylic carpet and plastic chairs stacked up and an instrument trolley covered in plastic sheeting. An impersonal room, unlike the nurses' office which has photos and potted azaleas, or the dormitories with all the patients' things: it belongs to no-one, nobody puts their mark on it.

I waited for the others, looking through the windows which face out over the front of the hospital. It was nearly visiting time: cars were pulling in, people were buying flowers from the flower-stall in the car park, mostly narrow long-stemmed roses, pink or red like lipstick, the ones that persistent young men sell at traffic lights, that don't last very long.

Liz the house officer was first, predictably. She was conscientious and scrubbed with an Alice band and wonderfully neat round schoolgirl writing: you could always read her notes.

'I'm taking the ward round today,' I said.

'OK,' she said. She took a chair from the stack, sat down and took out her pen, which said Mogadon in silver lettering. A gift from a drug rep, or maybe she'd picked it up at the monthly

21

drug lunch, where there's always a table stacked with stuff. Most doctors, I guess, have a bit of residual disdain for drug reps, feeling the whole system to be so corrupt – all the time the hard sell, pushing their latest product – but we still like the gifts they bring. Sometimes you get brilliant things. I turned up early once and got an umbrella, yellow as buttercups, with the Prozac logo printed round the edge. Everybody was envious, but I let it stay damp and it started to smell of ditchwater and in the end I had to throw it away.

Liz chatted about Robin Hall, the newest admission, whom she'd seen that morning: she was keen to make conversation, but a little bit deferential.

Then Francine came in with the pile of files, looking ample and pink like a fruit, in a very short skirt and ebullient low-cut sweater. She's a brilliant ward sister, soothing and subtly observant. And Nicci the social worker arrived, with her air of urgent enthusiasm and her studenty tortoiseshell glasses, and Kevin the community psychiatric nurse, a pleasant man with bleached hair and an earring. And that was everyone; the medical students don't come to this one, they go to the teaching round in the lecture room on Mondays. We pulled chairs round, with an empty one for the patients.

Francine had just handed Liz the first file when there was a knock at the door.

'Yes?' I said.

It was Dominic Braisby. He came in, smiled. His charm always felt rather forced to me – but then I never liked him. It was envy probably: his father was a surgeon at Bart's, life doesn't chafe at him. He was wearing an Armani jacket, the colour of wheat and effortlessly elegant.

'OK if I join you?' he said.

It was a rhetorical question. He liked to sit in on this ward round from time to time, though he didn't have any direct clinical responsibility for the patients.

'Sure,' I said. But felt a sinking of the heart.

'I need a few more patients for my study,' he said.

'That's fine,' I said. He was, I remembered, setting up some research on a new antidepressant. 'I'm taking it this afternoon,' I said.

'Yes, Ralph told me,' he said.

He sat next to Francine, in the chair that was meant for the patients. Francine took another chair off the stack, sat down again and smiled at him, easing her skirt up her thigh.

I felt suddenly insecure. I found myself wishing I'd tied up my hair: it's harder to be authoritative with your hair hanging down.

We talked about Robin Hall. The police had found him wandering; he'd left a note: My beloved family, I've tried so hard but nothing I've done has worked out . . . There'd been burn marks on his skin where he'd stabbed a cigarette out on the back of his hand. Francine went to bring him in: he had his papers with him, all his rent arrears and statements from Social Security; he shuffled through the papers, his scarred hands never still, and said in a voice we could barely hear how everyone would be better off without him.

'He's a serious suicide risk, obviously,' I said, when he'd gone. 'I'd like him to be on continuous observations. Is that OK? D'you have the staff for that?'

'No problem,' said Francine.

'See that it goes in the notes,' I said to Liz.

She wrote it down with her Mogadon pen.

Then it was Cassie's turn. She'd put on her favourite dress for the ward round, a floral-print pinafore. She'd just had a poem about the bliss of Christmas printed in the users' newsletter: I said how much I liked it.

'Thank you, Dr Craig,' she said.

I asked what else she'd been doing.

'I went to OT this morning and we had to paint our feelings.

23

I painted myself in bed with Jesus,' she said. 'I've always been very romantic, Dr Craig.'

Francine bit her lip to hide her smile.

There was another knock at the door: Eva who works in the kitchen with the teatray. The teapot was a big transparent jug with a lid: you could see the teabags moving around inside. Francine poured: one for Cassie too. Francine had her own mug with Pikachu on, but for the rest of us there were plastic cups, and the tea hurt your fingers through the thin ribbed plastic. There were biscuits on a blue-rimmed plate – Francine handed them round.

'Only gingernuts?' said Dominic. 'In Dr Sutton's round we get custard creams.'

'You only have to ask,' said Francine, her eyes holding Dominic's just a little too long. 'You'll never get what you want unless you ask.' She crossed her leg, her skirt slid up, you could see the thicker bit at the top of her tights.

Cassie said goodbye with elaborate schoolgirl politeness. 'All right, Dr Craig, thank you, Dr Craig, all the best, Dr Craig,' and got up to go, taking her cup of tea with her, spilling a bit on the carpet as she went.

Dominic took his gingernut: Francine reached out and flicked a crumb from his sleeve. She was working so hard with him. I felt I could see the whole thing spooling out before me: Francine in love, looking almost luminescent, appearing in ever shorter skirts and little clingy tops, then Dominic moving on to some nubile nursing auxiliary, and Francine terribly hurt and holding forth to anyone who would listen about men and their inadequacies and their propensity for shagging anything with a pulse – well, that's the right-on ones . . . I felt she deserved better.

We drank our tea and worked on through the patients. Mark Ross, who had a history of manic depression, and last week had presented himself at Casualty, and said he thought he was getting ill and please could he be admitted, and now was high and talking very fast and thought he was a rock star. Colin Jennings, admitted after an overdose, whose depression seemed to be lifting a little: Dominic wanted to recruit Colin for his study, but I was reluctant: I planned to start some cognitive therapy with him. Kerry Hunter, a fragile freckled waif with hair the colour of wet sand who'd been sleeping rough and taking a perilous cocktail of street drugs – one of those poor lost kids who threaten to fall off the edge of the world. She had a bow in her hand that she'd taken from a chocolate box: she held it out to me. 'Pink for a girl,' she said.

Kevin fiddled with his earring, twisting it round and round. Nicci was drawing a many-petalled flower in the margins of her notepad.

Francine brought in Tim Rigby. He sat down, looked across at me: his eyes were full of tears.

'Do you still hear that child crying?' I said.

'She never stops,' he said.

You felt the futility of everything, just being near him.

Lethargy settled on the room like a light pale dust sifting down. Nicci suppressed a yawn, twisting up her mouth, Francine took the scissors off the instrument trolley and started to snip round the edge of the plastic sheeting, cutting a fringe, like bunting. The teabags turned and shifted in the jug. And we'd got through most of the patients and I hadn't discharged anybody.

'So,' I said, 'Paula Hickey.'

Liz took the file, went briefly through the history.

'Twenty-nine-year-old woman. There's a family history of mental illness – mother had a schizophrenic breakdown and hanged herself when Paula was two.'

I nodded.

'Paula and her brother were taken into Care. The foster mother seems to have been cruel – hit them and locked them in cupboards if they misbehaved. A pretty savage start in life.'

'Yes,' I said.

'First admission, 1995, acute schizophrenic episode. She was doing a fashion course at South Bank University.'

'Yes,' I said.

'Second admission, 1997. She got involved in a fight on the ward and broke a nurse's nose. I think you became her care manager then, Tessa?'

'Yes,' I said. This is unusual: Kevin or Nicci would normally be in charge of a patient's care. But I'd got to know Paula well and she'd so intrigued me: and it had seemed like the right thing, then, for me to co-ordinate everything.

'We admitted Paula again four weeks ago, after a phone call from Liam, her cohabitee,' Liz went on. 'She'd been threatening to cut herself with a kitchen knife. She came in voluntarily after a home visit by Tessa.'

I nodded, and thought back to that visit when I'd brought her in. Paula and Liam lived in a squalid block of flats near the hospital, the stairs smelling of urine and covered in graffiti, but inside their door it was fresh and clean and prettily blue-painted, and there were all the things that Paula had made – earrings from safety-pins and pebbles painted with birds and her strange ambiguous drawings, intricate pencil sketches of fabulous metamorphoses – snakes with the heads of women, a child turning into a flower, flowers that gaped like mouths. That day though everything seemed to have broken down with Paula, dirty clothes and the red-stained wrapping from last night's takeaway littering the floor, and Liam quite desperate, his face stretched, his eyes smudged with exhaustion, and Paula crouched in the corner, her hair spiky where she'd hacked at it, terrified by the voices in her head. They'd been up all night, said Liam, she'd wanted him to barricade the door, she'd kept saying, Can't you hear them?

Surely you can hear them? I'd knelt beside her, not looking directly at her, talked quietly for a bit. She hadn't responded, but when I'd said, Paula, we're going to hospital, I want you to come with me, she'd followed me to my car.

'So how does she seem?' I said.

'Much better,' said Liz. 'She doesn't believe that her thoughts are controlled any more. She still hears the voices sometimes but they're much less persecuting.'

'Francine?' I said.

She flicked through the nursing notes.

'She's been quite forthcoming in the patient group,' she said. 'And she's got this thing going with Cassie – it's really sweet. They're chalk and cheese, but they seem to click somehow.'

'Yes, I've seen it,' I said. I thought of the two of them playing table-tennis and giggling.

'And she's sleeping and eating well.'

'OK. Good. Well, I wonder if we should discharge her,' I said.

Dominic raised his eyebrows.

'Dr Craig,' he said. The sudden formality felt obscurely patronizing. 'I find that very surprising.'

Anger flared in me; she wasn't his patient, what did he know?

'She's not completely well, but she seems better and I'm not sure we can do any more for her in here,' I said.

Dominic frowned.

'OK – I don't know her,' he said. 'But I talked to her in the corridor yesterday and she told me how she's been operated on and the doctor connected her bladder to her uterus and she's rotting inside and no-one will tell her what's wrong. She's clearly still very deluded.'

'Look, we've been looking after Paula for several years,' I said. 'And that delusion dates back to the start of her illness.

27

It's still there even when she's functioning well: if we waited for that to go we'd have her in for ever.'

'Have you tried her on clozapine?' he said.

'Of course we've tried her on clozapine,' I said. 'We got a low blood count, so I had to stop it.'

I could hear the irritation in my voice.

'Well, obviously you know her and I don't,' he said, a little placating.

'She can be a bit of a drama queen, our Paula,' said Francine.

'How d'you mean?' said Dominic.

'Well,' said Francine, 'we all like a bit of attention.'

'Anyway, it's not like she's going to be stuck on her own in some god-awful bedsitter somewhere,' I said. 'She's got Liam, her boyfriend. Nicci, why don't you tell us a bit about the home set-up?'

Nicci looked up from her flower doodles, happy to contribute.

'He's brilliant, is Liam,' she said. 'Adores Paula, very supportive. Really, he puts up with an awful lot.'

'Does she have anyone else?' said Liz.

'No,' said Nicci. 'No contact with her siblings. Neither does Liam. They're alone in the world, kind of Babes in the Wood, it's touching. But, yeah, he gives her a lot of support.'

'OK,' I said. 'Let's see her.'

Francine brought her in.

She sat on the empty chair: her arms were tightly folded, as though to make herself seem smaller than she was. She was wearing a strappy top: it gets very hot on the ward. The skin of her shoulders was white, untouched by the sun.

I asked her how she'd been.

'Up and down,' she said.

'Have you been hearing the voices again?' I said.

She shrugged but didn't respond.

There was a little dragon tattoo on her upper arm, that I

hadn't noticed before – a sharp dark shape, between purple and red, like an injury. Tattoos are weird: I can never decide if I like them. There was a television programme I saw once – a Neolithic princess they'd dug up in Siberia. She'd been buried with all her gear and horses, and her skin was covered in tattoos that were perfectly preserved by the permafrost. It had seemed at once both lovely and repellent, the intricate patterning on the scraps of tattered skin.

'Paula,' I said, 'everyone seems to think you're getting better now. We think you're probably well enough to go home.'

She wasn't looking at me.

'I don't want to go home,' she said.

'You can't stay in for ever, Paula, you know that,' I said.

'I really don't think I'm ready, Dr Craig,' she said. Her voice was flat, level. No feeling in it, nothing.

'I'm sure you'll do just fine,' I said. 'You and I will meet up every month like we always do. And Kevin will give you your injection. And of course you can come in to Synergy whenever you want.'

I paused, she said nothing.

'Right, that's all, Paula. Thanks for coming to see us,' I said.

She didn't move, just sat there.

'OK, Paula. Thanks,' I said again.

Francine got up to usher her out.

But on her way out Paula stopped and turned back to us, standing there in the doorway, holding the heavy door open with her body. She wasn't looking at me. Francine waited for a moment, not knowing what to do.

'Dr Craig,' said Paula.

Then nothing.

'Paula, what is it?'

'I can't,' she said, her face working, like the words were hard to form – like someone who's had a stroke, who has to struggle to say the simplest things. 'I can't go home.'

'Paula, what's the problem?' I said. I knew it was a stupid question, but I wanted to get on. 'You're so much better now: we can all see that.'

She looked away from me, her face blank, unreadable.

I wavered for a moment. She looked so lost, so brittle, standing there. But I was very aware of my fondness for her, and that I had to compensate for that – to be fair to everyone. I thought of the referrals piling up, the many people who needed to come in, like the suicidal woman with two small children whose GP had rung that morning, desperate. You have to draw the line somewhere: it's safe, easy, in here – a clean bed with a blanket and someone to make you Ovaltine if you wake in the night and weep – some patients would never leave. And Ralph had specifically asked me to clear some beds.

'Paula, you'll be fine,' I said again.

She didn't move, stood there looking away from me, all the weight of the door on her thin pale shoulder.

Francine put her arm round her. 'It's time for the quiz,' she said.

Paula let herself be taken, like she had no will.

'OK, who's next?' I said, turning to Liz.

Dominic reached towards me, put a hand on my arm. I could smell the spearmint on his breath.

'Dr Craig, are you sure?' he said.

'Yes, I'm sure,' I said. Clear and decisive, swallowing down the unease that thickened like phlegm in my throat.

He made a slight gesture, opening out his fingers, letting go of something. 'It's your decision,' he said.

We went on to the next one. John Callaghan, schizophrenic, on his first admission, responding well to treatment, but he'd need to be in for a while. And finally Kate Barwell, another one to discharge. She'd been manic and hard to manage when she first came in, screaming at me down the corridor. You bitch! You stinking bitch! Then coming to say sorry, wrapping herself around me, covering my face in kisses. Now she was well, stabilized on lithium, this gentle woman, very contained and composed, re-emerging through all the chaos of illness. Briefly the sombre room felt a little festive, our faces brimming with smiles, wishing her well. She'd lost a lot of weight when she'd been manic: Nicci would try and get her a clothing grant from a charity.

So that was it, all done, all over. The others drifted off, Nicci and Liz and Kevin gossiping together, Francine chatting to Dominic and finally getting somewhere – Dominic was looking straight down her cleavage, which was spectacularly enhanced by the way she was holding the patients' files in front of her, upper arms pressed inwards.

I stood for a while looking out of the window, taking a moment just to centre myself. Outside it was getting dark, shadow pooling like stagnant water in the corners of the car park: most of the colour had gone from the roses on the flower stall, so the pale ones looked white, like ghost-flowers. Visiting was over and people were drifting off, leaving only their grapes and their reassurances, getting on with their lives. They looked so small and insignificant down there, their specificity erased by distance and the gathering dark.

I thought how stark it was: inhuman almost. No curved lines, no colour, the few trees pollarded so they looked deformed, the buildings utilitarian, the most colourful thing the grimy blue prefab that had been put up last year, block by block, like Duplo. Only the chapel, built in the thirties, seemed slightly more gracious, with its oriel windows. Sometimes it could look quite warm and welcoming: occasionally there'd be services there, and a carol concert at Christmas, and then you could see the colours in the stained glass shining out, jewel colours, red and cobalt and richly green, like forests. But this afternoon it was empty – there was no-one there, no light inside. High above the chapel, some tatty birds flew up

31

in the darkening sky, like torn-off bits of bin bag carried up on an airstream.

It must be very cold out there: if you put your hand to the glass, you could feel the chill.

Chapter 4

We grew up on the south coast, in a bungalow near the sea. It was a landscape of salt marsh and stunted pines and changeable weather that blew in from the Channel: a place of sudden squalls and surprising thin sunlight, and wet in summer, with luxuriant docks in the ditches.

Our father was a bank clerk. He was a clever man who might have been a scientist. He'd done well at school, but somehow messed up his A-levels, got distracted by a fascination with radio sets; so he'd gone into the bank, a safe job with a pension. He still read widely, knew the name of every plant. He was a passive man, afraid of many things – of his own anger, of anything remotely unconventional – somehow not having the nerve to act on the world. Our mother didn't work: she'd had rheumatic fever as a child which had left her with heart trouble. There wasn't much money. When our sheets wore out, our mother turned them sides-to-middle: we had a car, but no holidays, and there was little heating, just coal fires and the flimsy warmth from our new night storage heaters – I was never quite warm in winter. At university in Liverpool in my flat looking out over Sefton Park, I would read for hours on the floor in front of my gas fire, stretched out, moving to feel the heat all over my body – like there was some lingering coldness deep inside me that would take years of warmth to thaw right through.

My mother's grandparents had been servants, and I think it leaves its mark. There was something profound in her that was all about knowing your place: an exaggerated respect for the headmaster and the vicar, an aversion to self-indulgence, a need to placate. There's something of this in me, I suspect – I over-tip, I hate to meet my cleaner – I learnt this from my mother. They had the narrowest social life. Church on Sunday morning, more, I think, from custom than belief; and Sunday lunch with our grandmother, who lived just round the corner; and once a month they'd play bridge with another couple they knew. There was a sense always of scarcity – even in the way they loved each other. If he touched her wrist or kissed her on the cheek, she'd laugh lightly, withdraw a little. This made me uneasy, even as a very young child: like something had been revealed that shouldn't have been. Sometimes when Mac would touch me, when I was busy at the sink or filling the dishwasher, and I'd be in a rush, wanting to get it done, and I'd find myself pulling away a little: sometimes I'd think – Are we like them? Am I becoming my mother?

When I was twelve and Jed was ten, our father was invited up to head office, to be offered a managership. There was a vacancy for a manager coming up at the local branch, he convinced himself that that was the branch he'd be offered. He bought a new navy suit, he moved quite differently in it, somehow more sure, more certain, head held high. I can still see his face when he came home from the interview: white, shocked, like he was ill or bereaved. The job they'd offered had been a hundred miles away: it came with a bank house that we'd have had to live in, a house with two flights of stairs; our mother, with her angina, couldn't have managed the stairs.

34

He'd turned it down, knowing he'd never be offered another promotion.

I was angry with him: angry with both of them. Angry with a child's secret uncomprehending rage: I think because I couldn't bear his disappointment. I vowed I'd be different: that I'd succeed where he'd failed. And this perhaps is what's driven me more than anything: and why I do those things that Jed finds so amusing – invest in ISAs and read the business pages and consult those hungry young financial advisors with their soft-top cars and purring new Toshibas. There's always a fear in me that the life I had as a child is what I'll get again if I don't watch out; that this is what creeps up on you, what scrabbles around outside your door if you once let your vigilance lapse. A life of scarcity: a sides-to-middle life.

Yet our parents undoubtedly did the best they could. They encouraged us in our school work. And they scraped together the money for music lessons, with an eccentric but brilliant piano teacher, who sensed Jed's talent at once: which meant everything to Jed. He was a difficult child, drawn to trouble like a cat to cream, alarmingly impulsive, constantly upsetting his friends by needling them or blurting out their secrets, then charming his way back into their favour again. I was always bailing him out, cleaning him off, wrapping up the broken bits and putting them in the dustbin. I think it was hard for him from the beginning, that sense that he didn't fit. He told me once, during one of the drunken late-night confessional conversations we sometimes had in our twenties, that he knew he was different already at seven – compulsively drawn to the boys in the shower at school, wanting to gaze, to touch. Music was his salvation, I think: with the music he flourished, found himself. Music can be civilizing perhaps: even at Oxford, Jed's friends were quite a temperate crowd, not druggy like some of the medical students I knew, getting their highs instead from mildly perverse sex and luscious discords in Monteverdi madrigals.

Down the end of our road, you came to the sea. The beach was mostly shingle, and ugly still with defences left from the war – a rotting landing stage, lumps of concrete that lurked like animals on the sand, slippery with the rich brown weed spewed up by the waves. At low tide, there were acres of mud to wander over, and water seeped into your footprints, so on sunny days they seemed to fill up with sky. We played there for hours at a time, poking around near the old rowing boats, looking for tiny crabs the colour of rust that scuttled away from our spades: the hulls had an embroidered coat of prickly barnacles. Sometimes, after a storm, the beach would be littered with dead things – a smashed pincer, a chalky shell like a broken plaster cast. We'd poke at them with sticks, searching for something live, intrigued by some alien body that flinched at the touch of our fingers. Or we'd play on the sparse patches of dry sand, up where the sea never went except during the high spring tides. We had ambitious schemes, to make ramparts, turrets, a Colditz Castle of sand, like we'd seen on the television: but we were usually disappointed. You can't do much with dry sand: you can pick it up by the handful and clasp it as tight as you can, but still it sifts and trickles away through the cracks between your fingers.

Sometimes our parents came, and sat in deckchairs drinking tea from a thermos and eating lettuce sandwiches. There are photos they took then in the family album. There's one of me and Jed in our swim things. I'm wearing a spotted swimsuit with a little frill round the hips and holding my rubber ring. We must be facing the sun, I'm screwing up my eyes. Jed is only eight in the photograph, but he already has an elfin freckled campness – something about his gesture, the way he's standing: it always makes me smile. I like that photograph: it's a reminder that our childhood had its idyllic moments; it helps you forget the cold and the sense of limitation.

You couldn't walk very far. One way, where a little river ran into the sea, the beach disintegrated into salt marsh, clumps of marram grass threaded through with twisty ribbons of water. The other way, you came to a fence that went down into the water, and on the fence a sign that said Private, Keep Out. Beyond the fence was a private beach and a garden sloping down to the beach, and up at the top of the garden a great brick-built house. The house had wide windows with wooden shutters against the wind, greyish with a pale crusting of salt, and there was a terrace, and a long sweet slope of lawn, and rhododendron bushes and hydrangeas with flowers blue as the veins in a woman's wrist. Most of the year the house was shut up, the shuttered windows like blind eyes, but sometimes in summer, when the hydrangeas were in flower, the shutters would be put back, and children would play in the garden: you could hear their laughter when the sea was still. And once or twice we saw people on the terrace, the women in dresses the colour of flame or the sky, the men in black bow ties and opulent long jackets. And they talked and drank and moved around and the sunlight caught and dazzled in the jewels the women wore.

We made up stories, Jed and I, about the house, the terrace, the things that happened there. I don't know when the stories started, or which of us began them. We dreamed of white-painted grand pianos, of rugs made from tigers: of cool high-ceilinged hallways full of the scent of flowers, of women with bare shoulders, and ivory satin gloves that reached up to their shoulders. It was Jed, I think, who thought of the gloves: he was always very good on women's clothes. And we thought of cake and raspberries, and liquorice for breakfast.

It all petered out, of course, as I reached adolescence: it started to seem childish, this fantastic world we'd shared. Reaching thirteen, my hips starting to swell, my fantasies emerged fully formed from the pages of *Just 17*: I yearned for scented hairspray and silver platform shoes.

But I still dream of it sometimes. In the dream I'm quite undeterred by the fence, the Keep Out sign. I tuck my dress up into the legs of my knickers and walk down into the sea. The shingle sucks at my feet, the water is deep, it swirls around my waist, my wet clothes hanging heavy. And I round the furthest fence post, mud squidging between my toes, and I walk back up through the water, the little waves falling away from me, up to the secret beach and the house with its fountains and liquorice. And I step out of the water and all at once I wake: so still I never get there.

Sometime in our childhood, our grandmother went mad. She was always losing things: her glasses, people's names. One Sunday she came across before breakfast, still wearing her nightdress. She didn't knock: she stared in at the window, pressing her face up against the glass like a child. I ran to open the door. Her cheeks were blotched and silvery tears ran down them. 'Dora died in the night,' she said. 'She slept in my arms in the bed. And when I woke she was as cold as stone.' Dora was her sister, I knew: she'd died before I was born. I was suddenly afraid: I shouted for my mother. Jed came and watched from the doorway but didn't come in. Our mother sat Gran down, made her a cup of tea. 'It's all right, it's all right,' she kept saying. I knew she was frightened too.

Now, I know it was pre-senile dementia: then, it didn't seem to have a name; it was never talked about. Our parents couldn't manage her anymore. She was put in a hospital near Bath. Our mother warned us not to talk about it at school – she felt so terribly guilty. I knew quite clearly even then, as a child, that there were no grounds for her guilt: how could she possibly have coped with this scary elusive stranger, who didn't know who she was and wandered the streets in her undone dressing-gown? But our mother still felt such shame.

We went to visit her in the hospital, our mother and Jed and me. Our mother drove erratically all the way, though normally she was a very careful driver. It was a vast Victorian asylum, a looming edifice of dark red brick, with ornate Gothic towers and crenellations. Now it's most likely a luxury gated village, soothingly renamed Something Park, with a gym and a jacuzzi, a splendid place to live if you're blessed with a sceptical outlook and can't remember your dreams. There was an incinerator like a pointing finger, black smoke dirtying the paleness of the sky. 'That's where they burn the bodies,' whispered Jed, his breath warm in my ear. 'They chop them into little bits and burn them.' In the grounds, on the wide stretch of grass, a herd of women walked, wearing floral dresses that didn't fit. There was the same blank look on all their faces, as though the years in streaming over them had terribly diminished them, eroding and washing away whatever made them unique. They glided like ghosts, as though they had no substance, as though their weightless steps wouldn't crush the grass.

We parked at the front of the place, our mother went to bring our grandmother out. She was smaller than I remembered, her wrists like little twigs. She had the smell of those places hanging about her, a faint rank stench of incontinence. She talked ceaselessly, in a high anxious girlish voice; none of it made sense. All I can remember is that she told us we were trees: how very tall we'd grown, now we were trees. Jed and I sat in the back of the car, not saying anything, trying not to giggle.

We drove to a beauty spot our mother had discovered, a lake with waterfowl, and parked near the water. Our mother had brought sandwiches. Gran ate hungrily, with no awareness of limitation or satiety, her mouth wide open as she ate so you could see straight in, dropping bits of filling on her frock, but Jed and I didn't have much appetite. Then our mother sent us off with stale bread in a bag to feed the waterbirds. She'd thought of this, planned it.

The lake was quiet, still, darkly holding the shadows of the trees. There were geese, and vivid ducks with jade-green wings, and over on the other side of the water a swan, glimmering under an overhanging willow, its beak shiny and wet like the inside of an orange. We threw bread for the ducks. The swan came gliding over, sleek and certain. I started to feel scared: a swan can break your arm. It reached the bank, reared up and broke out of the water, wide wings lashing like whips. It's sharp, perfect, in my head: the terror. Jed cowered behind me, clutching at my cardigan, moaning a little. I shouted, clapped my hands, walked slowly back, fear shaking my heart, Jed clinging to me. I knew I mustn't turn my back, that I had to face it. Our mother was too far away to help. It was up to me, I knew I had to be brave.

Four weeks later, our grandmother was dead: she'd fallen from a window in the hospital. The verdict was accidental death. But my mother always believed it was suicide: she felt really that she'd killed her, by what she saw as her neglect – that if only she'd cared for her at home, she could have kept her alive. But even at the time I knew this made no sense – that our grandmother could have made such a choice, that such a distinct dark purpose could form in the snowstorm of her mind. I imagined instead some more casual childlike motive – saw her wandering off where she shouldn't, into some part of the hospital where the windows weren't barred: and reaching out of the window – to pick a leaf from a distant tree, to catch a passing blue butterfly. Reaching out too far into the light, and falling through the brightness with a brief sense of surprise.

The shadow of our mother's guilt hung over our adolescence. It troubled her, I think, to the day she died. And it shaped me, of course: might even be why I've chosen the path I have, seeking to care where she couldn't. A legacy of sorts: it happens. These things get handed on: a life goal, or a need for absolution. I see this so often in the work I do: that the things we aspire after, seek to expiate, or strive to avenge, may properly belong to our parents.

But none of this was explicit in me for a long time: when I went to university, I was thinking in terms of paediatrics or maybe general practice. I was eighteen when I went to Liverpool. I went in by the longer route, a physiology degree, then 2nd MB, then clinical. I found Liverpool extraordinary after the intimate leafy perspectives of my childhood – the bleak echoey tenements, the wasteland where children made fires, the yellow weed that grew everywhere through the pavements: you always felt that nature was about to take over again – that this city with its broken buildings, its empty lots flaring with ragged robin, had already half-reverted to the wild. People still talked about the riots of 1980 when Lodge Lane got burned down: how psychiatric admissions, especially for anxiety, soared sky-high that summer; how people arrived at work after the worst night of rioting and wept at what they'd seen. I think the decrepitude actively appealed to me then. You can cope with that at eighteen: dissolution's more tolerable then, it seems temporary. And there was a wild Irish glamour about it that I loved, all the late-night drinking clubs off Princes Road, and sometimes a careless beauty – a bit of bin bag caught in barbed wire against an extravagant sunset; a street of ordinary little houses that sloped sharply down to the Mersey, so you felt you might walk down the street and slide off into the wide washed sky. And though it looked so different from the place where I'd grown up, if you closed your eyes, sometimes it felt like home – the salt air like a cool hand on your skin, the smell of sea and river.

I did well. I was the perfect student, conscientious, never side-tracked, completely focused on my long-term goals. The other students' lives seemed rather anarchic to me, but I guess they mostly weren't brought up with sides-to-middle sheets. I took lots of notes in lectures; I regularly updated my card

41

index; I made elaborate timetables for revision, everything under control. And if I went to a party, I listed possible subjects of conversation before I went.

In the second year of my clinical training, I moved to the flat that looked over Sefton Park – a big room with a little kitchen off it, in a Victorian house with high elegant windows. You could see the filmy glittery domes of the glass houses, usually closed because of storm damage, and the empty pot-holed road that went round the park – never repaired because the councils couldn't decide whose responsibility it was – and the ragged jackdaws that lumbered across the lawns, and the rhododendrons with heavy velvet flowers.

It was a good time. I met Abi: she shared my umbrella as we rushed off to a lecture through a shower of that insidious Liverpool rain that seeps in under your collar. It took two minutes, perhaps, to establish an easy laughing intimacy: I knew at once that she'd always be part of my life. And my interest in psychiatry blossomed during the two months' psychiatric module – not long really, just a taster – that you get in the course of training. The fragility of the mind: that fascinated me. Mostly it works so exquisitely – yet mess up its biochemistry just a little, and you start talking in rhyming couplets, or think that the window-cleaner is Jesus. You need that fascination, I think. Compassion only takes you so far: you need something cooler to sustain you, some intellectual curiosity. Well, I do anyway. I read widely – Freud, Melanie Klein. It wasn't necessary – in fact it was pretty unfashionable – I just liked it.

The Nathan Goldberg thing began when I was doing psychiatry. He was the most beautiful man I'd ever met, fluid and fearless, with a moustache like Omar Sharif in Dr Zhivago. One day after a lecture on MAO inhibitors, suddenly emboldened, waving a little red flag of daring, I asked him back to coffee. I'd had several boyfriends, lost my virginity unmemorably at sixteen on my boyfriend's moquette sofa in front of Match of the Day when his parents were out; but I was still very sexually unassertive. When he said yes, I couldn't believe my luck. My flat was untidy, my bed littered with books: it didn't seem to matter. We never drank the coffee. He flung me down on the bed with an impetuousness that I found ineffably romantic. I lay against the pile of books that we hadn't bothered to clear, dimly aware with the only part of my consciousness not taken up with pleasure that the corner of David Enoch's *Uncommon Psychiatric Syndromes* was pressing into my leg. Later I found a stippled red bruise on my thigh, the shape of a strawberry.

He moved in – one of those quick studenty decisions. We painted the walls white, bought a battered piano at an auction. I loved that flat, all its surprises and hauntings – the art deco tiles we found behind some chipboard, the cache of ancient piano music buried under the floorboards and pulled out by an electrician who'd come to investigate the terrifying wiring. 'Rendez-vous', 'The Robin's Return', 'Valse Noble et Sentimentale', brittle and curly, yellow as winter leaves. I played 'The Robin's Return' to Nathan, smiling at its sugary thick harmonies, sitting on the piano stool with him behind me, his hands easing down my shoulders onto my breasts: I remember how I leant against him, feeling the warmth of his body against my back. The touch of him was so warm: for a year, three months and seven days I never felt the cold.

We made love a lot and all over the place, in a random impulsive way: behind the bushes in Otterspool Park, or in his old Ford Escort, when, suddenly excited by something I'd said, some little fantasy of whips and submission I'd shared, he'd pull over into an empty layby off the A59 and push a hand into my jeans. I loved the wildness of that, the sense of it all being so unpremeditated. With Nathan, briefly, I stopped planning, stopped needing to always have everything under control.

43

Nathan spent his holidays climbing mountains. I asked him once why he did it – the obvious question. 'You know you could die,' he said, with a rare fire in his eyes. 'The fear is part of the pleasure.' There was part of him that was always there, perhaps, among those glistening improbable peaks. I had that sense often when I was with him: that he was somehow elsewhere, beyond my reach. But his inaccessability I guess just added to his glamour: it seemed to hold out that tantalizing promise that women so often fall for – that you, uniquely, will be the one to reach him.

Loving him, I fell a little behind: no longer always top of the class, no longer so much the clever one, the girl from the comprehensive who's done so well. But it seemed OK, it was what I wanted. I felt at last that I had some kind of balance. It was like I was learning to float with life: no longer forever striving against the current of the day.

Then suddenly one Sunday, after making love in the afternoon, the books this time tipped onto the floor, the cool April light washing in from Sefton Park and a noise of jackdaws, he told me he was going. We were getting stale, he said, it was time to move on. It was terrible – the casualness of it, the way he'd made love knowing that afterwards he was going to tell me this, the way he'd put it. Time to move on – like you were some kind of motorway service station, somewhere to bed down for a bit before the next stretch of the road. And then, when I couldn't stop sobbing, he tried to explain. 'I mean, we never thought this would last for ever, did we?'

'Yes,' I said, in a moment of total abnegation, no pride, nothing. 'Yes, we did. I did.'

Later Nathan was seen around with a woman I knew slightly, an outdoor type who went circuit-training in Sefton Park, hard-bodied but with lots of mascara, from the year below us.

I came apart for a bit: unravelled. I missed lectures, went for long lonely walks, sat for hours in the Catholic cathedral,

44

letting the red light through the stained glass fall over me like balm, as though if only I sat there long enough I'd maybe start to heal. I hated Liverpool now – felt sickened by its summer smell of pollen and decay, as you might be put off the smell of someone you love no longer: the decrepitude that had once felt so real, so edgy, looked just a mess to me now. There were no more of those moments when I'd found some kind of transcendence in the gleam of wet bright pavements or barbed wire like thorns against the fabulous skies.

Then I appalled myself by failing pathology. I who had always passed everything, always been top of the class. I stood and stared at the list: my name wasn't there. For a brief deluded moment I thought there must have been a mistake – I couldn't believe it. I felt such shock: felt ill, bereaved even, as my father had seemed when he'd come back home from head office, in his new smart suit, with his aspirations over.

I went for a walk along the concrete path by the Mersey, in the blue cold evening. It was a bleak spot: someone who was a patient when I was doing psychiatry killed herself there, hung her handbag on the railing with a neatly written note to her mother and stepped down into the night. And I made my decision: I made a vow to the river. Never again. Never. Never again would I lose my sense of purpose: never would I let myself fail as my father had done. Looking into the water, hearing its whisper, smelling its smell of mud and decay and darkness, in the distance across the water the cranes pencilled in on the skyline on the Wirral, and a tug going silently out to sea. Never again. That work would always come first for me. Work is real, solid: not like the rainbows-in-the-gutter loveliness of love – which can dissipate with a word, a look, a tiny shift in how you see things. Work comes first: work is bread, work sustains me, love only subverts, picks you apart. Never again this sexual unravelling – to let my life come undone.

I went back home feeling light, clear, strong. I passed

pathology second time round, got back on track. I had a few more lovers, but kept myself a little apart. I started planning everything again: 'I'm not a spontaneous kind of person,' I might remark: in fact I think I said it to Mac, whom I met not long afterwards. Mostly I didn't think about it – the vow I made, the thing I'd sacrificed. I came to feel that's how I am, that's how I've always been. Mac and I got together in a sensible predictable way over the *boeuf en daube* at a dinner party – a deliberate introduction from Annabel Crichton, a friend of mine and a colleague of Mac's. It was easy from the start; we suited one another, with our companionable love, our undemanding affection. We were both ambitious, with goals in common: we knew what kind of life we wanted. And from the start we made love in bed, after dark, as though we were married already.

Love on the rebound: a marriage of convenience. Don't knock it: it can work amazingly well. Yet just occasionally I'd glimpse myself through Mac's eyes – this independent woman, cool, strong, who doesn't cling, who would never straighten his tie, who'd come reliably with three and a half minutes of appropriate stimulation, who'd never wrap her fingers like bandages round his wrist and say, Tell me you love me: tell me, tell me, say it. And I'd think – This woman you see – that's only part of me. Maybe I'm not clingy with you because you don't make me needy: because I don't need you. This isn't all of me: it's how I am with you. But a good marriage really, a friendly companionable marriage; a useful productive life.

Yet the sand is always softly trickling between your fingers: however tightly you grasp it, you can't hold it in.

46

Chapter 5

The Tuesday after Jed's visit was my duty day. It was a cloudy windy day, the wind blowing gaps in the cloud, letting through the lemon-juice light of winter that stings your eyes, and still cold: when I got called to casualty to see a teenage girl admitted after taking an overdose, and walked across the covered bridge that looks out across the roof of the central foyer, I saw there were still heaps of hailstones that had fallen days before, piled up in the shadowed corners where the sun never shines.

The girl had gelled hair and a Care Bears nightshirt. She was miserable but quite opaque: she'd once run away from home but couldn't say why; she had no sign of mental illness and said she didn't know why she'd taken the overdose. I saw the parents briefly. The mother was rather submissive, not meeting my eye, said everything was fine and they'd always given their daughter everything she'd wanted. The father was a bit over-protective, complaining about his daughter's boyfriend, and going into rather too much detail about what he thought they got up to together. I wondered if the father was abusing her. There was nothing definite, it was just a feeling, picking up on the tiny clues that so often are negative things – absences

or incongruities or an inability to account for something –
running away from home with no explanation, an overdose that
didn't make sense, a father who couldn't tolerate his daughter's
boyfriends. I said she could go, gave her an outpatient appointment: I knew I'd have to tread carefully with this one.

I had lunch in the canteen, chatting to Martha Oppenheimer.
She and I had briefly shared a house when I was first living in
London. Now she was working in intensive care and I didn't
often see her. She'd seemed terribly cool then, heavy boots and
no bra, got through her house year by smoking marijuana which
she grew in her window-boxes: it helped her sleep, she'd said.
Once, confessing to some dazzling erotic adventure – I think
it was oral sex in the loo on Eurostar with a rugged lorry-driver
she'd briefly been involved with – she'd shrugged a little and
said, 'Tessa, you see, the trouble is, I just find sex so easy.' I'd
been tremendously impressed. But we didn't talk about such
things anymore: now, she was happily married to a stockbroker
and living affluently in Parson's Green, and over our indifferent
lasagne we moaned about our rotas and exchanged bits of gossip
and the latest rumours about the psychiatric merger. One of
those conversations that people must be having all over the
canteen.

I had coffee in the lounge, went back on the ward. I was
just about to see a woman with puerperal psychosis who'd been
admitted that morning when my bleep went. I took the call
in the nurses' office, where Francine was eating After Eights,
a present from Cassie's mother, and studying her horoscope in
the *Daily Mail*.

'Hi, Tessa, it's Fiona Gibson from social services.'

I said hello. I knew Fiona a little. She was one of the social
workers approved to work with the mentally ill – a pleasant
woman in her fifties, looked like a university lecturer, with
quiet clothes and academic hair.

'I think you're on duty, Tessa?'

'Yes,' I said.

'It's rather a heavy one, this,' she said. 'Graham Page just rang me.'

I felt a quiver along my skin. Graham Page is one of the forensic doctors employed by the police.

'Tell me,' I said.

'They've got this woman at Richmond Road Police Station. She sounds psychotic.'

'The name?' I said. But the cold creeping through me, as though my body knew.

'Paula Hickey.'

Everything lurched.

'She's one of mine,' I said.

Francine was staring at me. I turned away.

'Oh hell, Tessa,' said Fiona. 'It's rather grim, I'm afraid.' There was something careful, wary, in her voice. 'She was brought in after an incident.'

An incident. A cold hard formal word: filling me with fear. She was taking me through it so carefully, step by step, preparing me almost as though I was a relative. I know how this is done.

'Go on,' I said.

'Tessa, I'm afraid she stabbed somebody,' she said.

Everything so clear, so sharp, around me – the whole world turned to glass, pure, perfect – infinitely fragile.

'Liam?' I said.

'A woman,' she said. 'Not anyone she knew. The woman's in intensive care. Look, Paula Hickey's obviously going to need sectioning. I haven't got the other doctor yet.'

'Right,' I said. My body was rigid from holding onto the phone. 'Ring me back when you've got the other doctor, and I'll come straight down.'

I put the phone back, very carefully. My wrist hurt like I'd strained it.

Francine had pushed her paper away. She leaned a little towards me, her face a question. 'Trouble?' she said.

I nodded. But I couldn't tell her, not yet, feeling such shame wash through me.

I went down the corridor. Cassie and Kerry were sticking up a spring collage they'd made in occupational therapy, with lots of cheerful tulips. It kept curling away from them; the drawing pins weren't strong enough to hold it. The cleaners were mopping the floor, they'd put out their yellow sign that said Danger: Slippery Floor. I walked quite slowly, the vinyl felt so perilous.

I went to the doctors' room, made coffee, pretended to read the paper.

Sam came in, hungry-looking and badly in need of a shave. He was wearing one of his crumpled lumberjack shirts.

'Hi, Tess. How's it going?'

I shrugged, muttered something.

He had his back to me, he was making coffee.

'Dominic's trying to get a group together to go to the River Café. A fortnight tomorrow, probably. The Lundbec rep's taking us. D'you know her?'

'I don't think so,' I said.

'Tarty shoes, very pushy. How about it?' he said.

'I don't know,' I said.

'I'd have thought it was just your scene,' he said. 'You're a polenta eater if ever I saw one.' He raised his mug to his lips, turned to me, stopped suddenly. 'Hell, Tess,' he said, staring at me. 'What the hell's happened?'

I put down my paper. 'Sam . . .'

But his bleep went. 'Fuck,' he said. 'It's always the same. Just as you open your mouth for that first fucking sip of coffee. How do they fucking know? We'll catch up later, OK?' He went off down the corridor.

Then I was called again. It was Fiona.

'OK, we're on,' she said. 'I've got Jamie Logan. He'll be there in ten minutes, he says. And I'm going down now.'

'I'll come straight round,' I said.

Richmond Road Police Station isn't far from the hospital. I walked there carefully through the lemon-juice light. There was a building site opposite the entrance to the Underground where an old five-storey block of shops and flats was being demolished. Half the façade was left, just the fancy Victorian brickwork, with nothing at all behind it, like a child's cardboard cut-out of a building. It looked very fragile, as though it could easily crumble into dust. Men in hard hats stood around and shouted at one another, their voices echoing in the emptiness. When I turned the corner of the street into shadow, the wind hit me full in the face.

The detective was waiting at the reception desk, chatting to the custody sergeant. He knew at once who I was. He was DS Neville, he said: he shook my hand, a firm hard shake, but I sensed his hostility.

'A bad business,' he said. 'Dr Logan and Miss Gibson are here already. I'll take you through.'

There were wire racks of leaflets: Left Home? Run Away? and the wall was covered in scuff marks as though it had been kicked. He took me through the security door and into a cluttered office, where there were filing cabinets and blue police folders and dirty coffee cups and a faint smell of Pot Noodles. Fiona and Jamie were both already there: they looked up, greeted me, but didn't smile.

I knew Jamie a little: he worked at The Pantiles Resource Centre, a different kind of setting from St Jude's – more community work, less academic. A pleasant man, I'd always thought: rather ungainly with huge hands, all knuckles, and a touch of the Western Isles in his voice that would calm the most agitated patient. I was so glad it was him, felt a disproportionate pleasure in greeting him, my eyes filling up.

'We haven't seen her yet,' said Fiona. 'I thought we'd all go in together and get it over and done with – make it less of an ordeal for her.'

'Sure,' I said.

'She's wrapped up in a blanket,' said Fiona. 'They took away most of her clothes.'

I was suddenly angry my patient was being treated like this. 'That's a bit much, isn't it?' I said. 'I mean, you could see they would take her belt and the laces from her trainers. But it's not so easy to kill yourself with a t-shirt and some jeans.'

They both looked at me like I just hadn't got it.

'Tess – her clothes are needed by forensics,' said Fiona gently.

I didn't understand for an instant: then thought of the blood. The air felt dense, like water, hard to breathe. I sat down. 'Tell me,' I said.

Her face was working. 'There was a woman standing smoking outside the Marshgate Centre. You know, that shopping centre down the road?'

I nodded.

'It was at lunchtime. She was just someone in the street – they think it wasn't anyone Paula Hickey knew, just a random stranger. Paula Hickey went and stabbed her in the back. Several people saw it.'

'Oh God,' I said.

'You know Paula Hickey?' said Jamie.

'She was my patient,' I said.

He reached rather awkwardly across the desk and put his big hand on my arm. I felt his warmth right through me. I wanted to cling to him, to bury my face in his shoulder.

'Look, I'll do most of the talking if you want,' he said.

I shook my head. 'Thanks. But I'd rather it was me. And if I don't get anywhere, you could take over.'

'OK,' he said. 'Let's go.'

52

The detective was waiting. 'D'you want me to come in with you?' he said. 'She's not given any trouble since we brought her in, I mean, she just sits there – but she's certainly out to lunch.'

'We'll be OK,' I said.

'If you're sure,' he said doubtfully. 'Just leave the door ajar, and I'll be waiting outside. You know where the panic strip is.'

They'd taken her to the interview room already. She was huddled up on the chair, wrapped in a felted grey blanket, her body turned sideways, away from us, curled in on herself like a foetus, absolutely still. She seemed spent, like a husk of herself. There were two chairs opposite her, one beside her. Jamie sat beside her. Fiona and I instinctively pulled our chairs out so we weren't sitting in line like in an interrogation.

'Paula, we need to talk,' I said. I kept my voice calm, low. 'These people are Jamie and Fiona. Jamie's another doctor and Fiona's a social worker. We need to talk together.'

Her face was white as bone, her hair all spiky where she'd cut it. I thought of how she'd been last week, chatting with Cassie at the table-tennis table, mis-hitting the ball, laughing. The deterioration in her appalled me.

'Paula, I wondered if you could tell us how things have been since you left the ward?' I said.

She said nothing, but I could feel her fear, as though it was some tangible thing that seeped out of her pores.

'Paula, I know you sometimes hear voices – we've talked about that before. Have you been hearing the voices again?' I said.

She moved slightly, turned her head away from me. The blanket slipped an inch or two off her shoulder, you could see the tattoo, the little dragon, dark on her white skin, the colour of bruises.

Fiona had some cigarettes and a lighter she always carries:

she held a cigarette out to Paula. Paula took it and Fiona lit it for her: the flame reflected briefly in Paula's eyes, the only bright thing in the room.

'Paula, I know it's hard,' I said. 'But we can't help you unless you'll talk to us.'

She turned her head away very slightly. 'Help?' she said. 'Did she say help?' She drew on the cigarette, blew out the smoke. Her hand holding the cigarette shook a little. There was a long long silence.

I felt an infantile anger burning away inside me: that she had done this terrible thing – that she had done this to *me*, when all these years I'd only been trying to help her. And then was overwhelmed with guilt, that I could think such a thing.

I nodded at Jamie. He leant forward.

'Paula, it's important that you talk to us,' he said. 'You see, we have to decide what happens next, where you should go. Tessa says you hear voices sometimes. Is that right?' he said.

'There's so much pressure,' she said, her voice flat, slow, with no emotion, her eyes dull and veiled.

'Have you been hearing voices, Paula?' he said again.

She inclined her head in the slightest nod.

'Do they tell you to do things?' he said.

'They talk about me,' she said.

'Do they tell you what to do?' he said again. Taking it all slowly, leaving her lots of silence, lots of space.

Again that inclination of the head.

'D'you feel you have to do the things they tell you?' he said.

She shrugged.

'What do they tell you, Paula?'

'Things,' she said. She drew on her cigarette. 'You're a doctor,' she said. 'Like her. I don't like her. You doctors are all the same.'

'What did the doctors do?' he said.

'The doctors messed me up,' she said. 'They did it all wrong, I can't tell you, the things they did.' She had the cigarette in front of her face, her dark eyes held the brightness of it. 'She did it too,' she said to Jamie. 'She had a hand in it. She'll say she didn't, she'll be all nice, but she did it too. She's so *nice*, Dr Tessa Craig,' she said, spitting out the words. 'But she did it too. You're all in it together,' she said.

'Tell me what they did,' he said.

'They cut me up,' she said, speaking in a voice so low we could barely catch the words. 'They cut me up and sewed me back all wrong. The things they did.'

She was shivering, though it was warm in the room. The things she was telling us made her afraid: you could taste her fear like iron in your mouth.

'Paula,' said Jamie, 'd'you ever feel that your thoughts are being controlled?'

'It's always questions,' she said. She was shaking more now, getting more agitated as we talked. 'I've heard them all before. They always ask questions.' She turned towards Fiona, not quite looking at her. 'It's the pressure I can't stand. They never leave me alone. Sometimes I wonder what I'd be if there wasn't all the pressure.'

She'd smoked to the end of the cigarette. There was an ash-tray on the table. Fiona pushed it towards her. Paula stubbed her cigarette out in the ash-tray, round and round and round, smashing it down so hard that it broke up, the bright fibres scattering, so she must have burnt her fingers: but she seemed unaware of the pain.

Jamie must have known, as I did, that we wouldn't get much further: that soon she'd turn her face to the wall, close up entirely.

'Paula,' he said then. 'We know there's been an incident. That you attacked someone. Could you tell us what happened?'

She turned away.

55

'Could you tell us what happened in the Marshgate Centre, Paula?'

She sat with her back to us, the blanket falling off her shoulders, trembling a little.

We looked at one another. Fiona nodded.

'OK, Paula, that's all: thank you for talking to us,' said Jamie. We got up, pushed our chairs back in to the table.

'Is she dead?' she said, in a small flat voice, so quietly that for a moment I thought I'd made it up.

'No, she isn't dead,' I said. 'She's in hospital: she's being cared for.' I suddenly wanted to cry. 'Paula, look, you'll be cold like this,' I said. I pulled the blanket up on her shoulders, wrapped it round her. A policeman came to take her back to the cell.

The detective led the way to the office where our things were.

'We're going wrong somewhere,' he said, allowing himself a moment of exasperated rage. 'It beats me why someone like that was out on the streets.'

We sat down among the filing cabinets and unwashed coffee cups. You could hear the street noises through the half-open window – bus brakes, ambulance sirens, a car alarm going off – the screaming of everyday things.

'OK,' said Fiona. 'Well, I don't think that one needs much discussion.'

We filled in the forms that you use to confine and treat someone under the Mental Health Act. The words swam in front of my eyes. I concentrated hard: if you make a mistake the order isn't binding, you have to do it again.

At the bottom of the page you have to give the grounds for your assessment. I wrote, 'Paula Hickey was discharged from Derwent Ward at St Jude's Hospital on 15 February. She had been admitted four weeks previously with a diagnosis of acute schizophrenia. She is currently being held at Richmond Road Police Station after stabbing a woman in the street. Mental state examination showed paranoid delusions and auditory hallucinations that she feels compelled to obey.' And I signed where it said, 'I am of the opinion that it is necessary with a view to the protection of other persons that this patient should receive treatment and it cannot be provided unless she is detained under section 3 of the Act.'

And then that was all we had to do: the police would get her a lawyer and then charge her. I didn't know where they'd take her. She'd need a bed in a regional secure unit, but she'd probably have to wait: secure beds are like gold dust. There are private hospitals with locked wards that sometimes have empty beds, but mostly they're after patients with a neat little drug habit and no history of violence. I guessed she'd be sent for a while to the hospital wing at Holloway.

Jamie came to the door of the police station with me. As we said goodbye, he put his arm lightly round me.

'It could have been any one of us, Tessa,' he said. 'Believe me. Any one of us.'

I nodded but couldn't speak.

As I walked back, I realized I was shivering: it seemed to have got much colder in the time that we'd been there. Darker too, the sun sinking, the shadows of the buildings stretching out across the street. The only sunlight came through the gap where the block of shops was being demolished and fell on the entrance to the Underground: as people went down the steps they'd be illuminated for a moment, the brightness cutting straight across their bodies, then suddenly they'd be swallowed up by the dark.

I went back up to the unit and onto Derwent Ward. Cassie Broomfield was coming down the corridor. She must have been out for a walk with one of the nurses, her face was pink with cold. She still had on her woolly hat and her gloves, she was patting her hands together in the gloves to warm them, making a soft dull sound, doing it over and over, like a little child.

'Hello, Dr Craig. D'you think it'll snow, Dr Craig?'

'Well, it's certainly cold enough,' I said.

'I think it'll snow,' she said. Then, fixing me with her eyes that were blue and clear as water, 'Are you all right, Dr Craig?'

'I'm OK, Cassie, thanks for asking. Just a bit tired,' I said.

'You don't look all right, Dr Craig, if you don't mind me saying,' she said.

I went to the room where we'd had the ward round, shut the door, rang Ralph.

'He's gone, I'm afraid, Dr Craig,' said his secretary. 'He's going to the opera. He wanted to get off early.'

I tried Will Spooner, one of the Trust managers.

A woman's voice. 'Trudy James speaking.' I knew her slightly. She was a recent appointment, glamorous in sleek dark dress-for-success suits and shoes with spindly heels. She sounded less impressive on the phone, when you couldn't see the shoes.

'I'm afraid Will Spooner isn't available,' she said. 'He's doing a presentation for the multi-agency partnership working-party.'

'Well, I need to talk to someone,' I said. 'It's Tessa Craig.'

'Oh, Dr Craig. Thank goodness.' It was as if she'd let herself breathe out, her Manchester accent suddenly coming through. 'Am I glad to speak to one of you guys. I was just trying to get hold of Professor Patterson. There's been an incident. I keep getting calls.'

'Paula Hickey?' I said.

'Are you involved then?' she said.

I told her.

'Oh,' she said. 'Oh dear.' She sounded scared. 'Well, we've got procedures of course. But I think I'd better try and talk to Will.'

'Yes,' I said. 'I guess you should.'

'OK,' she said. 'Leave it with me.'

And then I'd done everything I could. I stood for a moment looking out of the window. The clouds were massing above the roof of the chapel: tonight there would be no stars. Way down in the car park, the No Entry signs and the corroded white arrows on the tarmac gleamed in the light of the street lamps. Workmen outside the kitchens were tipping rubbish from rubbish sacks into skips: some newspaper was caught by the wind, thrown randomly around, flying high over the hospital, then flung down into the darkness under the pollarded elms.

The crying that Tim Rigby hears, it's like I can hear it too.

Chapter 6

The cleaners had been. My kitchen was immaculate, everything precise and shiny, the spotlights reflecting in the clean sharp shapes of my glass carafes and my stainless steel fruit bowls and my pure white china. There was a strong smell of the cleaning fluid they'd used, Ajax or something. Just breathing made my throat sore.

I put on the kettle, made a coffee, but it seemed to taste of the cleaning fluid, a foul antiseptic taste. I tipped it away, made another. I sat there at the table amid the gleaming surfaces, the reflections. I was very aware of the little kitchen noises, the pulse and sigh of the fridge, the thin tick of the oven clock. I sat very still, closed in on myself, my hands clasped tight round the mug. I realized I was holding my breath. As though I was walking on ice.

I heard Mac come in, stamp on the mat, put down his keys on the hall bookcase. I felt a sudden dread because I'd have to tell him.

He came into the room, his long coat moving around him, his *Evening Standard* in his pocket, brisk, rubbing his hands — he must have forgotten his gloves.

'Hi, Tess.'

He leant over to kiss me, then suddenly stopped, like he'd hit some invisible barrier, seeing my face.

'Tessa? What on earth is it?'

I swallowed. It was hard to form the words. 'I discharged this patient last week and today she knifed a woman in the street,' I said.

He pulled away abruptly, standing back from me, staring at me.

'Oh my God,' he said. 'She was one of yours? Oh my God, Tessa.'

He took the paper from his pocket, pushed it across the table towards me, warily, like it was a trap that might spring shut.

It was the front page headline, the letters screaming out at me. 'Stabbed Out Shopping'. The article was short: they hadn't got much information yet. 'The victim's condition is described as critical. Her name is not being released until relatives have been informed . . . A woman was arrested at the scene of the attack and is being held by police.'

He sat down opposite me, still in his coat, took both my hands in his. His skin was cold and smooth, like some expensive fabric.

'Tell me,' he said, head tilted, the way he looks at patients. I didn't mind: I wanted to be taken care of.

'It was Paula – you know, I've talked about her.'

His eyes widened.

'What – you mean, *your* Paula?' he said.

I flinched a little at that. I nodded.

'Paula that you're fond of? Paula that you brought in last time she was psychotic?'

'Yes,' I said.

The darkness of the garden was behind him where he sat, dense where the walls and bushes were, layer on layer of shadow. Suddenly I didn't like the dark, how unprotected, open, we were with nothing across the windows. Anyone could be outside and you wouldn't know they were there, looking in on you.

I tried to clear my throat, but my mouth felt as though it was lined with blotting paper.

'Ralph asked me to take the ward round last week,' I said. 'I thought Paula was better, she seemed so lucid – I mean, she couldn't stay in hospital for ever. I was so sure she was better – that she could easily be managed in the community . . .' And I told him how I'd discharged her, and what had happened. I didn't tell him about Dominic's warning, or that Paula had asked to stay in.

He listened patiently, questioned me gently. At the end of it, he patted my hand. 'Everyone makes mistakes,' he said. 'You know that. Julia was telling me something over coffee just this morning – this case her husband was involved with – this kid they thought had kidney failure and it was Munchausen's: the mother had pricked her finger and put blood in the urine. Poor little kid had had all the investigations before they sussed it out.'

I didn't say anything. Julia was a colleague of Mac's – one of those rare women who seemed to be making it as a surgeon: knee-length skirts and very sensible, always called me 'pet'. I knew he was trying to help – but something Julia had said about her husband over coffee didn't seem to have anything to do with me.

'It goes with the territory,' he said. And when I said nothing, 'I'll get you a whisky.'

I wasn't sure I wanted it, feared it might loosen something inside me, that I might fall apart. But I let him get on with it, make the decisions.

He brought me the glass. Even the whisky seemed to taste of Ajax – it was like my mouth, my nose, had been immersed in it. But I drank.

'It'll be all right, won't it?' I said. 'It'll all blow over?' I knew I sounded like a child, seeking for reassurances he couldn't give.

'Yes, of course,' he said. 'Of course it'll be all right.'

I was waiting for more.

'Look,' he went on, sensing my need, his voice level, reasonable. 'Nothing will happen, probably. This is probably all there'll be.' He turned the paper over, hiding the headline. 'Unless . . .' He stopped. I looked up sharply. He flushed a little. 'Well – you know – unless it doesn't . . . she doesn't . . .' His voice faded. He got up, turned to take off his coat.

'Will they back me, d'you think?' I said. 'Ralph, the Trust?'

'Have you spoken to Ralph?'

'Not yet,' I said. 'I couldn't get hold of him. What will he say? Will he support me?'

'Tess,' he said, so gentle, reasonable, 'why're you asking me? You know these people – I don't.'

'But you play squash with Ralph,' I said.

'What's that got to do with anything?' he said.

Some plates I'd handwashed that morning were in the draining rack: he got the teatowel and started to dry them vigorously, though they'd been there all day.

'I'm starving,' he said. 'I've been in theatre since nine, I didn't have time for lunch.'

'I'll see what I can find,' I said.

I went to the freezer. My body felt awkward, as though it wasn't quite properly fitted together. There was a Marks and Spencers chicken korma: I stuck it in the microwave. The ping of the timer made me flinch.

Mac put his hand on my shoulder. 'Take it easy,' he said.

I tried to eat but everything tasted wrong. I tipped on lots of salt and still couldn't get it down, but Mac ate with undiminished appetite. Somehow I minded that he was eating so lustily.

I pushed my plate away.

He finished his portion quickly. 'These ready meals don't have any calories,' he said.

'Have mine,' I said.

'Ok, I will,' he said. 'If you're sure you don't want it.'

The phone rang.

'Tessa, it's Ralph.'

I was so comforted by his voice, smooth, urbane, like an arm around me: so grateful that he was going to take over and make everything all right.

'Will Spooner called,' he said. 'About Paula Hickey. How terribly unfortunate.'

'Thanks so much for ringing,' I said.

'Well, of course I would ring,' he said. 'I haven't got long though, we're just off to see *Boris Godounov*.'

'What happens now?' I said.

'We'll talk it through properly tomorrow. Come and see me in the morning – after my outpatient clinic. And you'll need to see Will yourself of course. There has to be a management review and so on.' He sounded so relaxed about it all: I wanted to cling to him.

'Yes,' I said.

'We did do a proper risk assessment, didn't we?' he said.

'Yes,' I said.

'Good,' he said.

'Ralph,' I said, 'it's in the *Standard*.'

'Yes, I saw it,' he said. 'I'm afraid we're probably in for a bit of trouble from those people. There's always some cheesy bloke in grey plastic shoes who gets the wrong side of the story. They get their copy and they don't care. I'd string them up.'

'I know,' I said.

'I've spoken to Trevor Smethwick: he's looking after the woman who was attacked. I know him a little – we were at Peterhouse together.'

'Oh,' I said. 'Ralph – is she all right?' I hated the way my voice shook. I hoped he couldn't hear down the other end of the phone.

'Apparently the knife just missed the aorta,' he said. 'It sounds like she had a lucky escape.'

'Thank goodness,' I said.

'Look, Tessa, you'll need to get onto your defence union. I should do that first thing tomorrow.'

'Yes,' I said – a little shocked, yet it was obvious, of course. 'Yes, I suppose I should.'

'Tessa, listen, you mustn't worry too much,' he said, his voice emollient as Vaseline. 'You're a valued member of the team. You know that, don't you?'

'Yes,' I said. 'Thank you.' But remembering how he had been when I went to see him about the Fisher Memorial – how I hadn't felt like just a member of a team – how he'd seemed to single me out.

'The timing couldn't be worse, unfortunately,' he said, 'with the merger coming up. Still, these things happen.'

I said nothing.

'Obviously we'll need to keep things under review. We'll just have to pray that poor woman pulls through,' he said.

Pray. It wasn't a word I'd ever heard him use: I wondered briefly what kind of a god he believed in.

'She will, won't she, Ralph? She will pull through?' My voice so shrill it didn't sound like mine.

'Well, we can be sure she's having the best possible care,' he said. Like doctors say to relatives. 'Look, I really must go, Tessa. Clara's signalling furiously. You get that husband of yours to pour you a brandy and try not to worry. We'll talk tomorrow, all right?'

'Yes,' I said. I put down the phone.

'Was that OK?' said Mac.

'I don't know,' I said. 'He said some stuff about the merger.'

'Did he?' There are little sharp vertical lines between his eyebrows when he frowns. 'I guess he's the kind of guy who likes to watch his back.'

'What's that supposed to mean?' I said.

'Well, he's not in an easy position,' he said.

I could see my reflection in the shiny sides of the kettle – weirdly distorted, with a narrow stupid forehead and big greedy mouth. I thought back uneasily over the conversation, hearing again the quavering in my voice. I felt I'd handled it wrong. Not like the kind of person who knows they have a right to things: more like someone who's always afraid, who goes round placating people, who grew up perhaps with sides-to-middle sheets.

I went to get more whisky. The door of the wall-cupboard was open and I walked straight into it, the corner jabbing sharply into my upper arm. For a moment the pain was all I could think of. Briefly I knew exactly why people hurt themselves, carve on their arms with Stanley knives, do all these seemingly incomprehensible things: actively seeking that pain because it blots out what's happening in your head.

I poured another drink and we went through to the living room. We sat on our cream linen sofa and watched the news, which was all about the falling-apart of Kosovo. The lilies that Jed had brought were drooping a little, the petals thinner, translucent, the scent still musty and strong. After the news there was a Minette Walters dramatization that Mac had liked the look of, with an anguished blonde woman and a man with a white beard who was mad in a lyrical, telegenic kind of way and lots of gleaming cars. But because for whole chunks of time I wasn't concentrating, none of it seemed to make sense: it was like there was no motive for what people did, like their actions were meaningless and random.

In the end I went back to sit in the kitchen, just sat there and drank, reading the article again and again.

Mac came to find me before he went to bed: he was in his dressing-gown. He saw I still had the *Evening Standard* in front of me: he put it in the bin.

'Mac. What does it feel like to be stabbed?' I said.

He shook his head. 'Don't do this to yourself, Tess,' he said.

'I've heard it feels like you're being punched,' I said. My voice high, urgent, the words blurring together. 'Or being kicked incredibly hard. This terrible pressure. Like that woman said who had a knife put in her head in a train carriage: I thought the train had fallen on my head.'

'Don't,' he said. 'Just don't. This isn't getting you anywhere.'

I wanted him to hold me, as though his warmth would ground me, make me real. He moved a little away.

'Would she have known what was happening?' I said. 'Would she have been afraid? Would she have had time to be afraid, do you think? Before she felt it?'

'Stop it,' he said. 'Just stop it. Don't do this to yourself.' He started to collect up some dirty plates, put them in the dishwasher. 'You have to keep some distance: that's how we cope, you know that,' he said. He had his back to me, bending over the dishwasher. 'You mustn't think too much: you always do that, you think too much, you dwell on things.'

He was saying all these things with his back to me.

'I don't see why that's such a crime,' I said.

He heard the edge in my voice: he turned to me.

'You really ought to come to bed,' he said, gentler, more placating. And when I didn't move, he leaned towards me, resting his hands on the table between us. 'Tess, listen to me. You've got to pull yourself together. You've got to be strong, you've got to not let it get to you – so you can carry on and be of use to people.'

I knew he was really trying, really wanting to help me. That every day he had to face these things – people's fear of death,

67

and death itself, and the risk that in seeking to heal he might cause terrible harm. He coped with that, and so should I. And I would carry on, I thought, of course I would. I would show everyone that I was strong.

'Yes,' I said. 'I'm sorry – I've drunk too much. I'll be all right tomorrow. It's just such a shock.'

'Sure,' he said. 'Come to bed now.'

I followed him upstairs. And I went to the bathroom to brush my teeth and stood there in front of the mirror with the toothpaste on my toothbrush and suddenly couldn't remember how I did it: that there was a sequence I never thought about, and I wasn't sure what it was, whether I brushed the top or the bottom teeth first. That panicked me for a moment. It was as though some crucial circuit had been disconnected. I told myself it was the whisky.

Mac was already in bed, his back to me. I turned out the light, curved myself into him. He felt strong, solid, comforting, his familiar smell, the thickness of flesh on his back. I wanted to make love: wanted the warmth of it, wanted the orgasm, shaking some of this terrible tension out of me. I ran my hand down his thigh – he stirred, moved slightly away from me – I couldn't tell if he was asleep or not, then he started to snore gently. I wasn't surprised by his lack of response: I knew he wouldn't like me like this, vulnerable, needy. It wasn't what he'd married me for.

I lay there, eyes wide open, staring into the night for hours, till like when you're a child the dark seemed all broken up into pinpoints of deep colour. Pictures flitted through my mind – fragments of my life. The room looking out over Sefton Park, the washed afternoon light, and Nathan leaving me. My father coming back from London when he'd turned down the promotion, his white sick look. And Mac and our life together, our sensible life with its pleasant reliable sex and its Conran Shop fruit bowls: I saw that too, and in some strange way it was just like the other bits, just another part of the story, the present breaking away like a slab of ice from a steep winter shore and sliding off into the past. And I saw the interview room, and Paula Hickey huddled there, the blanket slipping from her shoulder, and the dragon on her arm, the colour of bruises, of storms.

Chapter 7

I walked across the car park into the hospital, my long straight
shadow stretching out in front of me. I told myself that I would
cope, that I would show I was strong. I only had to keep going
and survive the next few days.

On the ward, it wasn't nearly as bad as I'd feared. Everyone
knew, of course: but everyone was solicitous, said, Tell me
if I can do anything, and, It could have been any of us. I
thought how nice people were. Francine was full of a very
straightforward rage with Paula, which I envied: it was so
much simpler, to blame her and not yourself.

'I never did like her,' she said. 'A manipulative little madam,
if ever there was one. She always had that dangerous streak;
you never knew when it would come out.'

Sam came to find me as soon as he got in.

'Hell, Tess,' he said. 'So we're up shit creek?'

'Yes,' I said.

He grabbed my wrist.

'Why didn't you tell me yesterday?' he said.

'I tried to,' I said. 'But your bleep went.'

'Why the fuck didn't you come and find me?' he said,

appalled. 'You always think you've got to tough it out on your own. I mean, what are friends for?'

'I'm OK,' I said.

'You look dreadful,' he said.

'Thanks,' I said.

'Look, if I can do anything . . .'

'It's sweet of you,' I said. 'But I'm OK. Really.'

The wards were full of light, and there were some daffodils on Cassie's locker: I noticed them as I went down the corridor to check on Robin Hall's medication. They were fluted and frilly with tiny gilded hearts.

I went to tell her how much I liked them – to show I wasn't afraid, that I could be normal, pass the time of day, appreciate someone's flowers. She was reading on her bed, surrounded by all her postcards, the photos of the Pope, the picture of Jesus with eyes that followed wherever you went. She looked up as I approached.

'Dr Craig, that woman in the paper – was it Paula?'

'Yes,' I said. Our patients always know everything about each other: often long before we do.

'She's in big trouble now, Dr Craig,' she said, looking at me unblinking, her gaze as blue and wide as the summer sky.

'Yes, I'm afraid so,' I said.

'She'll be locked up for ever now, won't she, Dr Craig?'

'I don't know,' I said. I could smell the daffodils, their thin sharp peppery scent.

'I'm praying for her,' she said.

'Good,' I said lightly. 'I think she could do with some prayers.'

She looked straight into my eyes, that limpid childlike look.

'You shouldn't have discharged her, Dr Craig. She was safe in here,' she said. 'She wouldn't have come to any harm in here.'

71

I turned away without saying anything.

I was at the nurse's station talking to Francine about Robin Hall, who'd been up all night weeping with one of the night staff, when I saw Ralph come onto the ward. Francine saw him too, went into one of her little flirty routines, flicking her hair back, running a finger down the side of her face. Ralph came straight to me. I was surprised: he'd told me to see him after outpatients, but his clinic wouldn't have started yet, he must have decided first to make time for me. I felt a sudden warmth, a sense of being cared for.

He put his hand rather heavily on my shoulder.

'I hoped I'd find you here, Tessa,' he said. 'Could I have a word?'

'Yes, sure,' I said. Though it seemed a slightly strange way of putting it: when we'd arranged this meeting last night on the phone.

I followed him into the interview room where we'd had the Thursday ward round. Somebody must have used it overnight: the curtains were still drawn. He flicked on the light and pushed the curtains back.

'Sit down, Tessa,' he said.

The chairs had all been piled up by the cleaners. I took one off the pile and sat on it, next to the instrument trolley. No-one had replaced the plastic sheeting that Francine had snipped. Ralph stayed standing, looking out of the window for a moment, dark against the exuberant spring light, his back to me, his shadow falling across me. The silence stretched out between us and started to feel strained.

'So was it good, *Boris Godounov*?' I said.

'Heavenly,' he said emphatically. 'Very good indeed.' But didn't develop the point – though normally he loved talking about opera.

He turned towards me. He was frowning a little. The bright light seemed to leach all the colour out of his face. He didn't

72

look well, I thought: I wondered if he'd drunk a bit too much at the Coliseum, or whether he was going down with something.

'Tessa, to get straight to the point,' he said. I could see his throat moving as he swallowed. 'The woman Paula Hickey stabbed. Alysson Gates. She's called Alysson . . .' He stopped himself. 'The name is Alysson Gates.'

'Yes,' I said, thinking it was rather odd, the formal way he'd put it.

'Alysson Gates is dead,' he said.

'But you told me . . .' I said, my voice high, shrill, protesting stupidly, trying to tell him it wasn't so. 'You told me the knife missed the aorta.'

'Tessa, she's dead,' he said. A downward intonation in his voice, gentle, insistent, like it was my grief, like I was the one who'd been bereaved. 'Trevor Smethwick just rang. She never regained consciousness. She haemorrhaged into the pericardium. Alysson Gates is dead.'

The words echoed in my head – round and round, like a child's rhyme, a nursery chant, with its endless repetitions. Is dead, is dead, is dead. I felt everything shift around me – as though the room moved, clicked into focus, and the edges of things became sharper: like you could feel their sharpness, like you could cut yourself on them. A jagged pulse careered off under my eye.

'What happens now?' I said. Struggling to keep my voice level, to show I wasn't afraid.

'There'll be the management review first,' he said. 'Will Spooner wants to see you straightaway.'

'Sure,' I said.

'Then there'll be the formal internal inquiry, in a week or two.'

'Yes,' I said.

'They're never very pleasant,' he said. 'You need to be

73

prepared for that – we both do. The chairman will probably think he's Lord Chief Justice.'

'Yes,' I said.

'Have you rung your defence union?'

'No,' I said. 'Not yet.'

He frowned, suddenly agitated. 'You should have done it already, Tess,' he said. 'You've got to think of yourself. And you'll want to talk to the Trust solicitors, of course. Harper and Drew. Luke Jenkins is very good – ask for him. Do those things now. Do them before you see Will.'

'Yes,' I said, his insistence frightening me even more.

'We'll give you every support, of course,' he said.

'Thank you,' I said.

Finally he took a chair from the pile, sat down opposite me. 'Tessa,' he said, sitting back, legs crossed, yet very alert, his eyes never leaving my face, 'I need to know exactly what happened.'

I took a deep breath: I felt utterly unprepared. Phrases from the police caution came into my head, like in that thriller we'd watched on television the night before – that anything I said might be given in evidence. As though this man was my enemy. Yet this was Ralph, my mentor, who'd flirted discreetly with me at unit parties, who played squash with my husband, who'd read my latest paper in the *Lancet* and said it was superb.

'She seemed so much better. She said the voices had gone. She was quite subdued, quiet . . .'

'Did she ask to stay in hospital?' he said.

I hesitated, felt his pale eyes on me. I could sense him reading my hesitation, speculating about it.

'Well, not in so many words,' I said. 'I mean, you know Paula. She can be very demanding, she likes a bit of attention.'

'Absolutely,' he said.

His face seemed thinner, sharper, as he looked at me: I thought of the wolf on his desk.

74

'In a way she likes to be in hospital – likes the safety of it,' I said.

'Absolutely,' he said.

'She was eating and sleeping well. She was quite sociable on the ward.' There was a kind of urgency in my voice: like I was pleading or arguing my case. I tried to make my voice level, calm, but it was hard to breathe. 'Her auditory hallucinations had become much less persecuting.'

'Yes,' he said.

'I felt it was the right time to discharge her,' I said. Then wished I hadn't said 'felt': I should have used a stronger, more masculine word – considered, assessed.

'Is there anything else you want to tell me?' he said.

A silence opened up between us, like a pit: I feared I might fall in.

I shook my head.

'Right,' he said. 'Thank you, Tessa. You'd better be off to see Will. But make those phone calls first.'

'Yes,' I said.

'There'll be a press conference later. Four o'clock prob-ably. Will Spooner will take it. We're getting calls all the time. Bloody journalists sniffing around. I hate those people,' he said.

As I got up, he said, 'Look, Tess, go home if you want to, once you've had a word with Will. Go and put your feet up, take some time out.'

'Thanks,' I said. 'But I'd feel worse at home with nothing to do. I'd rather just get on.'

'That's the spirit,' he said.

I did the things I had to do. I rang the union. I rang Luke Jenkins, who said he'd help me prepare for the internal inquiry and I could ring him anytime. I went to see Will Spooner. He has red hair and pale eyelashes, and he always moves in a bit too close. He was wearing a tie with a pattern of

75

saxophones and an over-powering aftershave that hinted at male changing rooms.

'Jesus, Tessa,' he said. 'I've had fifteen calls already today.' He seemed full of adrenaline, eyes gleaming.

It was all quite informal: he was perfectly pleasant. He asked me the questions that Ralph had asked and wrote my answers down.

I couldn't face lunch. I just got on with my work, choosing the easier things I had to do, walking warily through the long thin light of the February afternoon that fell across the ward. I talked for a while to Robin, who sat shuffling his bills as though they were some kind of complicated puzzle, and if he could only get them in the right order, something might be salvaged or restored. I went to see Kerry, but she was asleep, lying on top of her bedcover, shifting in her sleep, her arms flung out in front of her, hands clasped as though she was begging or maybe pleading with someone. And all the time my sharp light pulse skittering in my wrist.

At about three o'clock the WRVS volunteers came round with their trolley: Bounty bars, soft drinks, newspapers. I bought an *Evening Standard*.

It was the lead story again. 'Murder'. And there was a photograph of the woman who'd died. I hadn't intended to read it there and then – I'd thought I'd hide it away, look at it later, where nobody could see. But the photograph drew me.

The first thing you saw was that she was beautiful. She had big dark eyes, a full mouth, a dark mass of hair. The photograph had been taken outside, against leaves in the wind – she was wearing a scarf of some delicate fabric that was caught by the wind, that swirled around her, her hair was blowing too, a strand of dark hair blowing across her face. The photograph was full of a sense of something about to happen, a smile playing round her mouth, as though in a moment she'd turn to someone and laugh and push back her hair. Like it was all alive – all that movement of leaves and laughter and the hair that blew over her mouth.

I went to the nurses' room where I'd left my coat, picked up my bag, put the paper away.

'I'm going home,' I said to Francine's back.

She turned quickly, responding to something in my voice, perhaps – and got up and reached out and put her arms around me. She'd never touched me before.

'It was all of us,' she said. 'We were all there. We all made that decision. Don't take it all on yourself, Tessa.'

'No,' I said. 'Thanks.' I clung to her for a moment, so grateful for her warmth. But knew that what she said wasn't precisely true: that it wasn't all of us.

At Waterloo my train was delayed: the driver seemed to have disappeared, they kept putting out calls over the loudspeaker urging him to come and present himself. A little knot of us stood waiting under the Departures board and the banner advertising the latest Nicholas Evans novel, listening to the announcements. The intercity from Southampton pulled in at platform 11: it had been full, a crowd of people surged off it, joined up with those who were waiting for them, friends and colleagues and relatives greeting one another, always with that air of faint surprise, for the person you said goodbye to – last year, last week, this morning – is never quite the same as the person who returns. Around me, the early commuters waiting for the Shepperton train peeled back the cellophane from their baguettes, flicked through their copies of *Cosmopolitan*, drank that thin bitter coffee that blisters your lips from crackly styrofoam cups. And then I couldn't wait any longer. Safe among strangers, under the Arrivals and Departures, I took the paper out.

The cover story was quite short, most of the page taken up with the photograph and the headline. The story continued inside. I learnt that she'd been twenty-nine, that she'd been a

PA. That she lived in South London, that she'd died as Ralph had told me following a haemorrhage, that her partner had been with her when she died. The journalist had spoken to eyewitnesses: it had all been over so quickly, no-one could intervene. Paula had just walked up and stabbed the woman from behind, then she'd dropped the knife and started to walk away, and two witnesses had grabbed her and held her till the security men came: she hadn't put up any resistance. The paper called her 'Knife Maniac Paula'. It said that she'd recently been discharged from St Jude's psychiatric unit, and that she'd been arrested and was being held in the hospital wing of Holloway.

The journalist, a woman called Charlie Cavanagh, whose name I recognized, had attempted to trace out the last moments of Alysson Gates' life. She'd been standing in the doorway of the Marshgate Centre, she'd been having a cigarette, taking a break from shopping. She'd spent her lunch hour going round the clothes shops and she'd bought herself some shoes. The journalist had talked to the person in the shoe shop who'd sold her the shoes: they were strappy red suede with three-inch heels, he'd said. I wished I hadn't known that, about those red suede shoes that never took her anywhere: I wished I hadn't known about the shoes.

In the end they found the driver and let us onto the train: there was the usual low murmur of complaint and resignation grumbling round the carriage. I sat there, looking through the windows that were white with London dirt, staring out into the brightness. The bare twigs and tendrils along the embankment were colouring up with spring, turning pink and purple. A man and a little boy sat on the seat opposite me. The boy knelt with his face pressed to the window, breathing onto it, fogging up the pane, kept asking his father for the names of things. Their lives seemed so beautiful, so desirable to me, in their ordinariness – enjoying that simplest thing, the sharing of names. I longed so much to be like them.

My house was clear, still, bars of sunlight lying across the kitchen. I sat at the table and spread the paper out. I kept flicking from one to the other, the picture, the story. Staring at Alysson's picture till I felt almost that I had known her – till the image was familiar, like the image of someone who's part of your life. And the shoes she'd bought: I couldn't stop thinking about the shoes. I tried to imagine exactly what they'd looked like: they'd surely been shoes to be looked at in, to draw the eye – she must have been used to that, for she'd have been looked at wherever she went. And I thought of how she'd made her decision, choosing them to match some outfit perhaps, planning how she'd wear them, what shade of tights and would she need some more Scotchguard and a different brush. Planning for a future that had been taken from her.

I was home so early. Mac wouldn't be back for hours. I sat in my white kitchen and thought about death. Deaths that had touched me: the first death as a doctor that had really moved me. Lots of doctors have them, I've found – a death that makes you weep. An initiation, in a way. Someone's dying that tears at you. And after that you grow the necessary layer of shell, you get a little hardened as you must. Brian O'Donovan had been a patient on the surgical ward where I did one of my house jobs – he'd been on the ward for weeks. He was twenty-three. He'd reminded me of Jed: he wore his hair very short, had narrow elegant hands. We used to chat about films, an interest I'd developed at the Bluecoat Film Society in Liverpool: we both loved *film noir*, the louche private eyes and perversely complex plots and Lauren Bacall. There was a Sunday when I'd been unrelentingly busy: I'd done the routine blood tests on the ward, then I'd been needed in casualty all day. I remember the arrest call coming and hearing that it was my ward, and running down the corridor with that terrible cold dread, not knowing

79

which patient it was but that it must be one of mine: and finding it was Brian. And that strange feeling of resuscitating someone I knew – I'd been through the procedure lots of times, but I'd never done it before with anyone I knew: and then confirming death, shining a light in his face, feeling for the carotid artery, closing his eyes. Being there with this person who'd completely gone, someone who'd become utterly unknown to me – when I'd taken his blood and chatted to him about *The Maltese Falcon* just that morning. Nothing else that happened at work had ever hurt as much: not until now.

I thought of my mother too – the nearest death had come to me – going to see her in hospital after her stroke, the broken look on her face and the stench of her breath. I'd known at once she was dying. The stroke had been in the right side of her brain, and if my father stood to her left she didn't seem to see him, which distressed him terribly till I explained it to him. Afterwards we'd gone to the pub, Mac and Jed and my father and me, and there'd been some sentimental song on the jukebox, and Mac had bought us all brandy, and I'd cried a little for what was about to happen, and I'd thought how they were all ending now – all the entangled stories of her life, the narratives that made her who she was, all the things she'd longed for – thinking of how she'd sought to make a good life for her family, and of the music lessons she'd struggled to afford for Jed and me. And I'd drunk my brandy from its big round glass, and my outbreath in the glass had seemed to smell of her, as though I'd breathed her in.

I sat there, just seeing, smelling these things, these broken-up bits of my life – the stench of my mother's breath, closing Brian's eyes. These fragments that were all I had to try and make sense of this thing. And looking at the picture, thinking about the strappy red suede shoes: all that I knew of Alysson. Holding myself a little apart, rather stiff and still, not letting myself feel.

Eventually Mac came home.

'You're early,' he said. 'I thought I'd be first tonight.'

'I came home this afternoon.'

He came and put his arm round me, looking down at the paper over my shoulder.

'Oh,' he said. I knew he was registering her loveliness, biting back the urge to comment on it.

'She's dead,' I said superfluously.

'Hell,' he said.

'Mac.' I grabbed his arm, clung to him, seeking to hold him there. 'Mac, what will happen to me?'

'Tessa, we've been into all this,' he said, gently peeling my fingers from his arm.

'She wasn't dead then,' I said.

He held my hand between his. 'Look, it'll all blow over,' he said. 'People will understand – I mean, it's not your fault really. Everyone knows these decisions are difficult.'

I hated that 'really'.

I wanted something he wasn't giving me – some total reassurance, something unequivocal. I knew it was childish – but if he didn't give it to me, who would?

'What if one of the inquiries finds me negligent?'

'Of course they won't,' he said.

'The Fisher Memorial – will it affect that?'

'I don't suppose it'll affect anything,' said Mac. He sat down beside me. 'Let's face it though,' he said. 'It's bloody bad luck she was such a looker.'

I hated that expression, hated him. I didn't say anything.

He didn't notice. He was still looking at the paper.

'I mean, the story'll run and run if they can print that picture,' he said.

'For God's sake,' I said.

He turned to me, suddenly penitent.

'I'm sorry, my love,' he said. 'I'm sorry. I shouldn't have put it like that. It's just that it isn't easy for me either.'

'No,' I said. 'I know.'

He was sweet to me all evening – gentle, comforting. He poured me a drink, cooked dinner, did what had to be done, seeking to make it up to me for his crassness, while I sat there uselessly at the table, my hands clasped tight in front of me. Almost as though I was trying to hold my life between my hands, this prosperous useful life we'd made together.

In the end I rang Abi. She knew at once what I had to tell her: she'd seen the story in the paper and wondered immediately whether I'd been involved.

'You poor poor love,' she said. 'Come round. Come round at once.'

I said I wouldn't, I didn't think I could drive, I'd come on Saturday.

I could hear squabbling in the background and someone playing 'Yesterday' on the flute, struggling with it, playing it quite lumpily, then picking up speed when they came to an easier bit, the bright sound singing out. I could picture it all, her warm red walls, her kitchen full of children, her life that seemed more than ever remote from mine.

Chapter 8

At lunchtime next day, Sam found me writing up some notes in Francine's office.

'I'm taking you to the canteen,' he said.

'I'm really not hungry,' I said.

'Do as you're told,' he said.

So I went to lunch with him, and from the first mouthful of cod and chips I realized I was famished, that I hadn't eaten properly for days.

Sam just let me eat, didn't ask me anything, entertained me with tales of the woman he was currently pursuing, Maria Lopez, a rather exotic Chilean anaesthetist. I knew her a little: she wore prim velvet hairbands and expensive conservative shoes and was full of magic. Once she'd got me to pull a hair out of my head and she'd borrowed someone's wedding ring and suspended the hair from the ring and swung it over a glass of water and announced I'd have two children, a boy and a girl. Which, in some secret place, had pleased me.

Sam complained it was costing him. He talks about money a lot: his father had a cornershop, and worked nights in a pet food factory to fund Sam's education.

'Still, you've got to do all that stuff, you know, Tess. I've learned that, you've got to plan the whole duck-shoot. Flowers, booze, the works. These women who go on about being treated as equals – it's a load of bollocks,' he said.

He scraped the last bit of fish from his plate, put his cutlery down. He still looked hungry, though: he usually looks hungry. Women are always wanting to nurture him, to straighten his tie and cook him fattening casseroles: it drives him crazy. This might have explained the lure of Maria Lopez: I suspected that kind of thing really wasn't her scene.

'Tess, are you OK?' he said then.

'No,' I said. 'Not really.'

He looked at me quite seriously for a moment. 'You're the one they ask for,' he said. I could only just hear him above the clatter and talk that surged around us. 'You're the one they believe in. Don't you ever forget.'

'You're sweet to me,' I said.

'I'm not being sweet,' he said. 'It's true. You know it is.'

I felt embarrassed but touched.

'We make decisions like you made every day of the week,' he said. 'Discharging people who'd rather stay in, who aren't exactly well. If we didn't the whole bloody system would collapse.'

'Yes,' I said.

Sitting there with Sam, surrounded by all the ordinariness, the bright plastic, the packets of tartare sauce, the smells of chips and vinegar, I let myself be soothed.

I went to get some pudding, rhubarb crumble with custard, the bland glossy childhood custard you only get in canteens: I needed nursery food. I got back to our table, was just on my first mouthful when I looked up and saw Will Spooner in the queue for fish and chips. I quickly looked away again, not wanting to catch his eye.

'Uh-oh,' said Sam.

Will had seen me there, had left the line and was coming in my direction, weaving his way between people and their trays with exaggerated care. I had a dragging feeling in my chest.

'D'you mind if I . . . ?' Indicating the empty seat beside us.

His tie had peonies on it and he was wearing that pungent aftershave. I didn't fancy the crumble quite so much anymore.

'Give the girl a break, can't you?' said Sam. 'She's only just started her pudding.'

Will Spooner ignored him. He was resting on his elbows, leaning across the table towards me, getting a little too close.

'Alysson Gates,' he said.

'Yes,' I said.

And thought how weird this was – the way I responded to her name, almost as though it was mine.

'Brace yourself, Tessa,' he said. 'It gets worse.'

I put my spoon down. What the hell did he mean? I thought. The worst had already happened.

There was a sound of shattering as someone broke a glass: then a brief silence and a slow building of noise as people picked up the dropped stitches of their conversations.

'A bit of a downer, this,' he said, 'to put it mildly.' He spoke into the quiet: I was worried that everyone would hear. 'Alysson Gates' boyfriend. Intelligent, articulate, a total fucking nightmare.'

The crumble seemed to stick to the roof of my mouth, I swallowed hard.

'Job?' said Sam for me.

'Works at the university, lectures on their social policy course: welfare rights, we think. Sounds rather principled – does some sessions at a neighbourhood advice centre, you know the kind of thing, a community project, very idealistic.'

Will waited for my response, but I didn't say anything.

'There's more,' he said. 'There's this woman he knows who's

a journalist: Charlie Cavanagh. She wrote the piece that was in the paper last night. It seems they go back a long way, and he's a bit of a campaigner and she's publicized some of his issues. Sorry to spoil your day, Tessa. I thought you ought to know.'

And he went off to get his fish and chips, leaving the smell of his aftershave hanging around behind him.

It was a thick misty evening, the air heavy with wet; when I got home my hair and my gloves were soaked. I took off my coat, flicked through the mail. Several offers of credit: a Racing Green catalogue; and a little notice, quite undesigned, just word-processed and delivered. 'A few years ago the end of the cold war between the USSR and the west was welcomed by all. Unfortunately the breakup of the USSR has led to great hardship for the population of Lithuania. High unemployment and food shortages mean that there are many people including children who need your help!' They asked for unwanted clothes or household items to be left outside your door on Saturday morning, but I never keep stuff I don't need – I had nothing to give.

I went into the kitchen to pour a drink. Almost immediately the phone rang. It was Abi.

'Turn on your television,' she said. 'Beeb 1. Do it now.'

A newscaster with blonde expensive hair and a middle-aged man in a suit were discussing mental health provision. The man had a worn serious face, a very direct gaze. I assumed he must be some expert commentator, a spokesman for one of the self-help organizations perhaps – he was very authoritative and articulate – but someone who was new to the job, perhaps, and still a little too emphatic, a little intense: such things are always exaggerated on television. And then the newscaster said, 'Mr Connelly, in the wake of your loss, could you tell us your

86

feelings about the hospital that discharged the woman who is now being held in connection with this terrible incident?' and I realized this must be the man Will had told me about – Alysson's partner.

'We have to question the whole policy on which this unit is being run,' he said.

His voice was level, his hands quite still as he spoke, but his eyes were somehow too bright.

'And in particular,' he said, 'there must of course be grave doubts about the doctor who made the decision to discharge this woman – about her experience and fitness to make that decision. If, as I've been informed, she was young and inexperienced, we have to ask if it was right that she was given so much responsibility. We have to look at the whole decision-making machinery – and most particularly at her role in that.'

I realized I was shivering, as though someone had come in from the night and touched me with a bare hand, bringing the cold right up against my body. And I thought – What does he know? Does he know all about me? Does he know where I live? I had a brief wild fear that he could actually see me through the screen: a crazy sense of his presence, that he was there in the house with me. That he knew everything that had happened, this stranger with the burning eyes: knew even the things I hadn't told anyone.

The newscaster looked a little worried, as though she needed to keep him under control, not sure what he might say next. 'Well, obviously, we're just speculating here, aren't we?' she said carefully. 'Presumably this will all come out at the inquiry.'

'The fact remains,' he said, 'that someone discharged this woman: and that person must be brought to account. In the past, doctors have rarely or never been made culpable for the grave errors of judgment they sometimes make. I believe that's changing: I'm determined that it should change. The doctor concerned has to be made to take full responsibility for what she did.'

'So what demands will you be making of the Department of Health?' she said. 'There will of course be an independent inquiry – that's statutory. What else will you be asking for?'

'I'll be calling above all for the inquiry to be held in public,' he said. 'There must be no secrecy. The decision-making process that led to Alysson's murder must be open to public scrutiny.'

'Thank you so much for talking to me, Mr Connelly,' she said.

He nodded briefly.

The camera lingered on his still face for a moment. You could see the frown cut into his forehead, and the long taut lines of the veins in his neck. The shadows under his eyes were black, as though he'd been beaten up. For a moment, forgetting myself, I saw these things only, the outward signs of his unguessable grief.

The newscaster was back at her desk.

'That was Ben Connelly,' she said, 'Alysson Gates' partner, talking to me earlier this afternoon.'

She kept her face composed and serious for a moment, before going on to the next item. A twenty-four-hour tube strike was being threatened: I sat in front of the screen, not taking it in, still seeing his face.

But for the closing credits they went back to the lead story. They showed the picture of Alysson that had been in the paper, then a shot of the doorway of the Marshgate Centre that had presumably been shown earlier in the programme. With the news of Alysson's death that morning, people had started to leave flowers: roses in cellophane, freesias, some primroses chosen perhaps by a child, the colours so rich – carnival colours, gaudy in the dark day. They were still quite fresh, as if their stems were drenched in water, the petals vivid, perfect, although they'd fade so soon. All these flowers brought by strangers, bright against the stone.

Chapter 9

In the days that followed, there were two parts of me – a sensible part that just got on with it, tried to be normal – the aspect of me that people acknowledged when they said, as they frequently did, how well I seemed to be coping, a part that was controlled and bright and brittle and determined; and deep inside, a wilder part, full of fear, that only Mac knew about, and even he didn't know all of it. A part that was coming undone.

The story ran for several days in the *Evening Standard*, though relegated now to the inside pages. Charlie Cavanagh wrote a profile of Ben Connelly: she'd gone to see him, she wrote, in the 'rather shabby cluttered office in St John's Street where he runs advice sessions for the local tenants' association . . .' She wrote as though she didn't know him, though from what Will Spooner had said she knew him very well. She portrayed him as a kind of urban hero, fighting for justice for the disadvantaged. And she found out my name, inevitably, and used it in the paper, in a lengthy and impassioned article about the arrogance of doctors and the inadequacies of community care. She didn't exactly say it was all my fault, but certainly hinted at it. I hated her. The mere sight of her mugshot – the sharp hair smooth and shiny as glass, the supremely confident smile – would induce helpless rage in me. But at least she never tried to talk to me. Other journalists did: one of them said she was a single parent and her little boy had leukaemia and she might lose her job if I wouldn't give her her story. We left the answer machine on all the time.

There was another news item I almost missed – I only spotted it when I spread an old paper out on the floor to wrap up some vegetable peelings. It was quite a small item, about a drop-in centre called the Hollies that catered for a handful of people with psychiatric problems. It was in a residential street near where Ben Connelly lived, and local people were trying to get it closed. Their spokesman was the deputy head of a local comprehensive: a thoughtful, conscientious-looking man, photographed with his wife and their three young children. 'In the light of recent events,' he said, 'we feel our children must not be exposed to this kind of risk.' He meant Alysson, of course, though this was never explicitly stated. And there were quotes from mothers whose children went to school down the road that ran along the back of the building. They said how frightened they were for their children, how they felt they couldn't let them walk there on their own while the Hollies remained open. Their local MP was supporting them, and the article was very sympathetic to their views.

I felt the cold spread through me as I read. I knew what places like that mean to the people who use them, and to their families. It seemed there was no end to it: the waves just went on spreading, darkly rippling out from what I had done.

Inevitably it all affected the way I worked. I was extremely cautious in the decisions I made, wary of letting people out on weekend leave, admitting people who could probably have coped just fine at home. When Cassie was late returning from a day out with her mother, I started to panic. I went off to have a coffee, trying to get a grip. And then she was back, all smiles, in a neat new coat with a little velvet collar, and her mother, anxious, apologetic, hands fluttering like trapped birds, explaining that they'd been to Chessington World of Adventures, and Cassie had so enjoyed herself, and then they'd gone on to Cassie's sister's to see her wedding dress, and they hadn't noticed the time.

'Was it a nice dress?' I said to Cassie.

'It was very nice, thank you, Dr Craig,' she said politely. 'But when I'm married, my dress will be embroidered with all the stars in the sky.'

I gave her a hug which she didn't really like, I was so glad to have her back, and found myself uttering a little prayer of thanks to some inchoate god or other – though I'm not really someone who prays.

I felt such fear. I'd jump at the slightest thing – someone coughing beside me, my hair falling over my face. Waves of anxiety would overwhelm me – my pulse tumbling, my heart pounding – my whole body signalling that something terrible was about to happen: then I'd realize that it already had.

I was going home one night, stuck at Wimbledon because the Shepperton train was held up by a points failure at Vauxhall, waiting there with a crowd of other passengers, all of us wearing the winter uniforms of the city, long heavy coats or boots with thick ridged soles or combat trousers, as though dressed for inhospitable terrain – when a young man in a Reebok anorak who'd been sitting next to me got to his feet and offered me a card. His voice was very gentle. Can I give you this? I took it, glanced briefly at it: there were details of the services at a local Pentecostal church. I felt sorry for him: it must be embarrassing handing these things around, it was perhaps something he had to do as proof of his devotion. It was quiet on the platform, just the rattly tick of the clock, a woman talking brightly into a mobile, the distant roar of traffic you try to convince yourself is the sound of a train. The young man walked up and down, handing out the cards. Most people didn't take them. Then he went and stood at the very edge of the platform, standing behind the yellow line, much too close to the track. He faced us, started to preach. My brothers, my sisters, you shall know the truth, and the truth shall make you free. Rising up on his toes, his voice loud now, impassioned. You are here to know the truth – that Jesus Christ came into the world to save sinners. That God so loved the world that he gave his only son. Pigeons clattered on the wooden canopy above us, and the sky behind the preacher was the colour of grapes, dark and very soft with a deep purplish bloom. And when he'd used up all the Scripture he knew, he started repeating things. You are not *late*, he kept saying, my brothers, my sisters: you are here to know the truth, the train is not *late*, the truth shall set you free. His gestures increasingly forceful, arms flailing, fists punching the air, his voice becoming a shout, fighting against the screech of brakes as a train drew in at the opposite platform. Greater love has no man, my brothers, my sisters, than that a man should lay down his life for his friend. The incoming passengers stared as they walked past, the rest of us just stood there, read our paperbacks and our evening papers, studied our fingernails, looked away from him down the line, where the gilded thin thread of the track spooled off into darkness. The other train pulled out, and his voice rose still higher, screaming out his ragged sermon of random Biblical phrases, standing there on the very edge of the platform. Our train at last came hurtling into the station, and I was so afraid: for him, for me, for all of us. Afraid he was going to lay down his life in front of the Shepperton train.

I was haunted in those days. Images would come to me, vivid as flashbacks. I'd see Paula, huddled up in the interview room at the police station, shivering in the heat, with terrible fear in her eyes: the knowledge of what she had done, filtered through who knew what delusional system, what web of bizarre belief — but that knowledge still there, burning away at her. Or I'd see Alysson, the image of her largely imagined and yet so real to me, standing outside the Marshgate Centre: I'd see the white cloud of her smoky breathing and the dark cloud of her hair, and in a carrier bag in her hand, the bright extravagant shoes that she never wore. The image as I held it there in my mind, appalled, would be always tinged with red, like the smear you get across a bloodshot eye. And I'd see her lover too, his shadowed implacable face staring at me as he'd stared out from the television, like he could see right into me.

The images that pursued me were always worst at night. It took me ages to get to sleep, and then I'd often wake again at three or half past three and lie awake for hours. Once I had a vivid dream of the man, Alysson's partner. The setting was vague, I think it took place in the hospital canteen where I'd first been told about him, somewhere banal and full of cheerful plastic. It wasn't a dream in which anything much happened. He just sat there and looked at me, he was very precisely delineated, with none of the uncertainty about who this person is that you often have in dreams, when identities fuse and dissipate: and he seemed very big in the dream. And I half woke, so I was aware of myself in the bedroom, aware of my surroundings, of Mac's hushed breathing, and stared into the dark: yet wasn't really quite awake, like in those dreams of violence where you're being pursued, and then you feel you've woken, but you're still half in the dream — and you lie there full of fear, believing the predator to be in the bedroom beside you. And I went on seeing him in my mind, stared into the night, seeing him so clearly, his corroded face, the lines cut into his face round his eyes and his mouth that you knew were so recent, that spoke of what he'd been through. Strange to remember so vividly someone so briefly seen. I felt it so powerfully then, the absolute pity of it, what he'd

94

had to suffer: sitting by her bed as she died; going home without her.

I sat up, gasping for breath, turned on the light.

Mac shifted, opened his eyes.

'For God's sake, Tessa,' he said, the words unformed, only half opening his mouth. 'What is it now?'

'It's OK,' I said, 'I had a nightmare.' I made myself breathe deeply.

A police helicopter was hunting around overhead.

'I'm sorry,' I said. 'I'll be fine now. It was just a dream. Go back to sleep.'

Mac did what he could. The next night he gave me a sleeping pill, a big green shiny thing that was hard to swallow, a sample a drug company rep had given him with a lot of promotional material: they were pushing it to help people sleep after operations. I obediently took it, and was knocked out for the night, slept a sleep like white noise, dreamless and unhaunted: and woke with my head full of sand.

Chapter 10

Abi brushed the earth from her hands and hugged me tenderly. She was in wellingtons, she smelt of the garden.

We went through her hall to the back. The vicarage is draughty and a bit decrepit. The lovely old black and white tiles on the hall floor are coming loose, they rattle under your feet, and there are sepia stains on the walls where the damp gets in, but everywhere you go there are photographs of her children.

I followed her into the garden.

'We're cleaning out the pond,' she said. 'It's all a bit pornographic.'

The pond had been drained: Jake and Simon and Lydia were scooping a rich black gunge of slime and weed into rubbish bags. Lydia came running up when she saw me.

'We found some frogs that were mating. Come and see,' she said. She grabbed my hand: she was warm through the damp wool of her mitten.

The frogs they'd rescued from the pond were in a washing up bowl.

'Look,' said Lydia. 'That is *sick*.'

We watched, both of us, in awed fascination. The mating frogs were stuck together as though they were glued, brown as mud, with eyes like marble and strange impassive faces.

It was a cold still day, the air smelling of spring. I drew it into my lungs, enjoying the fresh thin scent: it was the first time in days I'd really breathed. The lawn was all mud, churned up where the children had been kicking a football around, but bulbs were coming up everywhere, sharp little spears of green, and there were pools of snowdrops like spilt milk under the pear tree. Abi's good at gardening: everything she touches grows.

She put a new liner in the pond, weighted it down with stones, turned on the hose to fill it up again. The frogs were tipped back, fermenting like yeast in the clean water. We went into the house.

Abi's kitchen smells of spices, and her curtains have a pattern of fat bright hens, and her red ragrolled walls are covered in Lydia's drawings of women with lots of hair accessories and complicated footwear. She'd lit a log fire: firelight glinted everywhere, on the bars of the hamster's cage, the shiny jars of pasta, the metal rack where some ginger flapjacks the children had cooked were cooling. I curled up on the sofa that sits in front of the fire and warmed my hands. Sometimes when I've been lazing on Abi's battered sofa, in her busy kitchen that's so full of things, my own taste seems austere – as though all my simplicity and clarity and matt white crockery, which are meant to seem so minimalist and classy, are actually about some kind of denial or limitation. And just occasionally I'll yearn for a life like Abi's – the simple demands, cleaning out small rodents and sticking on Elastoplasts. We talk about it sometimes, the way it's all worked out – how you couldn't have predicted it – because Abi fits the medical mould so much better than me: and to see us both at medical school in Liverpool you might have said she'd be the high-flyer. But then she met Fred, got accidentally pregnant with Jake, and was knocked out by the

97

passion she felt for her baby. Once I'd asked her why she'd made this choice – what it was about mothering. She'd looked at me with her level gaze and shrugged a little. 'No-one else ever loves you so much,' she'd said.

Now she grinned as though she knew exactly what I was thinking.

'Don't go getting all soppy, Tess,' she said. 'There is a downside to this life of mine, you know. You feel something squishy under your foot, and there's this bit of old pasta stuck to your sock, and you think, This isn't what I planned.'

The children were flinging off their anoraks, rinsing the mud off their hands. She gave them drinks and flapjacks.

'You lot can just clear off and mutilate somebody in cyberspace,' she said. 'I want to talk to Tess.'

There was an open bottle of Beaujolais on the grate. She poured two glasses. She was wearing one of Fred's old jumpers with holes in the elbows. This is her style now: she wears hippyish long skirts and no shoes in the house and Fred's cast-off Guernsey jumpers. And she's putting on weight: she minds this. But I love it in her, I think it suits her – the way she's so solid and grounded. Like I love the level measured look she has, weighing everything up, and the dark loose careless coil of her hair. Her fingernails had earth in them.

'Anyway,' she said, 'you know you couldn't stand my life. And sometimes I'd really like to be you. I mean, there's the money – let's face it, I do envy that: going abroad and all the slinky jackets.'

'I know. Well, I like it too,' I said.

She stood in front of the fire in her socks, warming herself, sipping her wine. There was a friendly smell of warm corduroy.

'And having an impact – I envy you that too. Being a parent governor of the Orchards Primary School isn't quite the same, is it? Sometimes I'd love to be part of the public world again. Making things happen.'

I shuddered.

'Oh hell,' she said. 'That wasn't stunningly tactful, was it?' She sat beside me on the sofa. 'Tell me,' she said.

'Abi, I'm so frightened,' I said.

She put her hand on mine. 'But what could happen?' she said. 'I mean, there's no threat to your job or anything is there? You're scarcely going to be found negligent for what you did. I mean, how could you be? You didn't do anything wrong. You acted in good faith. And Ralph will support you, won't he?'

'Yes.'

'Well then.'

'That guy's really gunning for me,' I said. 'I mean, you saw him.'

'Grief takes people like that,' she said. 'It's like the poor bastard in casualty who socks you in the eye when you tell him his wife's died. It's what people do – they take a blind swipe at the nearest person.'

'He's clever,' I said.

'Come on, Tessa,' she said, 'what can he do to you? You've got to get this into your thick head: *you* didn't kill that poor woman.'

'No,' I said. 'But sometimes that's how it feels.'

She was saying all the right things: yet none of it seemed really to touch me. I'd wanted to go through it all with her, spell it out – say the things I hadn't said to anyone. But now I was here, I found I couldn't do it – she seemed so clear and definite, it was all so simple to her.

'You were just unlucky,' she said. 'The trouble is, it's the ultimate urban nightmare. Some psycho who comes and knifes you in the street. It's all our fears really. The stranger, the underclass. All those things.'

'Yes,' I said.

The fire crackled and sighed, glowing caverns opening up as the logs shifted and settled.

'Is Mac being nice?' she said.

'He tries,' I said.

'That means no,' she said.

'It's hard for him,' I said. 'I hear myself just going on and on – I hate it.'

'Well, he *is* a surgeon,' she said. 'Empathy isn't their unique selling point. I guess that's not what Mac was put on this earth for: to be empathic.'

'I should have married a vicar,' I said. 'Fred must be brilliant at that emotional stuff.'

'Fred?' Her thick eyebrows shot up, creasing her forehead. 'In your dreams,' she said. 'Quite honestly, our worst patch ever was when he went on a counselling course. He was forever reflecting things back and telling me how I was feeling: it drove me mad . . . "You must be feeling very frustrated."' She sounded just like him, his growling voice, his Anglican intonation. '"You must be feeling very angry." Too right.'

I laughed and she grimaced, briefly penitent. 'I'm being horrid, aren't I? I do think he's good really: it's just that it doesn't work when it's your partner. His parishioners adore him. People are always coming to see him and pouring out their hearts.'

And I thought I should do that too: I should pour out my heart. Fred could help me through. I could go into his study, perhaps, and sit on one of his tatty leather armchairs in front of the shelves that are stuffed with earnest demanding books by Tom Wright and Don Cupitt, and I could confess and be absolved, the guilt all sluiced away.

She read my thought. 'I'll give him a shout,' she said. 'He'd hate to miss you.'

He came, his usual pleasant self, in a cheerful red pullover that was too tight over his stomach, with his fading beard, his slightly sticking-out ears.

'Hi, Tessa.' He hugged me, his beard briefly stippling my face. 'Look, if I can do anything . . .'

'Thanks,' I said. 'That's sweet of you.' But there wasn't anything he could do: it had been a mad idea, my brief romantic fantasy of absolution. I felt embarrassed by my hopes of him, knew exactly how it would be if I followed him into his study – how we'd shift in our chairs and flush a little and not know what to say. Somehow in my need I'd built him up into someone he wasn't and couldn't ever be. I saw him for what he was: well-intentioned, intelligent, not especially saintly; always rushing around doing good, leaving Abi with the washing.

We sat and talked for a while, Fred with some familiar plaint about the country being run by Millbank spin-doctors. Then he went to finish his sermon.

Abi cut up vegetables for supper, slicing some carrots she'd just pulled from the garden. She chatted about her children. Jake's glue ear had cleared up since she'd taken him off milk. Simon's school had had an Ofsted inspection, and their maths teacher, who was brilliant and much beloved, had told Simon's class that during the inspection they must all put their hands up every time he asked a question – their right hand if they knew the answer and their left hand if they didn't.

Lydia came stamping in, looking cross: she was sick of Diddy Kong Racing, the boys kept winning, she said. She had things to show me: a big new scab on her knee, a drawing of her hamster, a book of fairytales she'd been given for Christmas. I admired the scab and the drawing and she snuggled up beside me on the sofa and opened the story book. We looked through it together, just flicking through at first, looking at the pictures, Hansel and Gretel lost in the forest, Bluebeard's wife in her moment of fabulous trespass, as she opens the illicit door and finds the many dead wives, their white and elegant bones. Each page was bordered with tiny pictures in gold and terracotta and ochre and blue, gentling the grim edges of the stories. We looked at the detail of the pictures, loving this multiplicity of things, a gilded lizard, a sun with yellow rays like braided hair, nectarines heaped up in a sky-blue bowl.

Lydia smelt of soap and earth and her hair was silky and fine, still baby hair, and kept slipping in front of her face: she twisted it between her fingers and pulled it behind her ears. The firelight moved across her face: there were little warm flames in the middle of her eyes. I read her Hansel and Gretel, and Rumpelstiltskin, and the Russian tale about the girl sent into the forest to fetch a needle and thread from Baba Yaga the witch.

'I used to be scared of the witch,' said Lydia.

'I'm not surprised,' I said. 'I'm scared myself.'

And truly she was fearsome, with gappy iron teeth in a black mouth like a cave and eyes with no pupils, absolutely vacant, twin vortices to suck you in: and her hut of bones on its scaley chicken legs that danced in the tangled forest.

I read it to her, and thought how savage it was: the step-mother who seeks to rid herself of the child, the witch who schemes to eat her; the child herself, going into the forest, going there all alone to face the thing she fears. I turned the page, and there was a big illustration, the witch filling the page, and Lydia hid her eyes. I moved on quickly towards the magical ending: the child escaped with all her gifts and helpers, the cat did her weaving, the comb became a forest of spindly trees, and Lydia parted her fingers a little and looked.

'That's what I used to do,' she said. 'When I was little.'

I left at seven. Abi urged me to stay, but I said I had to get home.

'You've been lovely,' I said.

She looked at me like she was trying to read me.

'I wish I could help,' she said.

'I guess it's just a matter of time,' I said.

'He can't do anything,' she said. 'That guy. Her partner.'

Both of us knew that wasn't true.

She put her arms around me. 'Don't be afraid,' she said.

I went home, sat on my cream sofa amid the gleaming empty spaces of my house – so bare, like some kind of deprivation, after Abi's cluttered kitchen with its fat red hens and carrots.

'Nice time?' said Mac, when he got back from his afternoon of rowing.

'Of course,' I said. I told him the story about the Ofsted inspection.

'Abi sorted you out?' he said.

I nodded because it was easier than trying to explain.

Chapter 11

On Tuesday there was to be a drinks party at Mac's hospital, to celebrate the opening of a new coronary unit. I got home a little early, it wasn't time to get ready. I poured myself a drink, turned on the television. I caught the end of the national news: then London Tonight.

The newsreader looked solemn: her voice was serious, slow. 'Today,' she said, 'was the funeral of Alysson Gates, the young woman killed in a random attack outside the Marshgate Centre.' I saw it pass in front of me on the screen: the city churchyard under a grey metal sky, the grass still frosted although it was afternoon, everything held, stilled by the cold, and the slow black line of mourners and the coffin with its heaps and heaps of flowers. The bell tolled and the mourners wound their way through the whitened churchyard, and my body started to shudder, so strongly I spilt my drink. I reached for the remote. Yet heard the bell still tolling in my head, knew I would hear it always.

I went upstairs, had a shower, put on makeup – just to keep busy, trying not to think. I looked in my wardrobe for a dress but almost nothing was clean: I hadn't been to the dry-cleaners for ages. The only thing I could find was a red linen dress, sleeveless, floor-length, flaring to the hem, that I'd bought for our summer holiday. It wasn't quite right for winter and a bit too formal perhaps, but I put it on, and felt quite pleased with my choice. There was something about the colour that made me feel stronger: it was an unafraid sort of dress. You could still see the bruise on my upper arm, where I'd walked into the door of the kitchen unit. It had a clear yellow aureole, as though it had been daubed with iodine.

I was ready when Mac came home.

'Oh,' he said. He seemed at a loss to see me all dressed up.

'It's that party,' I said.

He frowned. 'I was assuming I'd have to put in an appearance, of course,' he said. 'But I didn't think for a moment you'd want to come.'

'It's been on the calendar for months,' I said. 'I mean, we talked about it, surely – when you first got the invite.'

'Yeah, well – that was then,' he said. 'It didn't occur to me you'd want to come now. While all this is going on.'

I was shaken. 'Look – I just want to be normal.' I almost shouted. 'Surely that's good. Isn't that what you want?'

'That's not what I meant,' he said. 'It's about how you're *seen*. I'd have thought you'd want to keep a low profile till all this has died down.'

'I'm going to come,' I said.

He shrugged. 'It's up to you, I guess,' he said. 'But if you must come, don't you at least think you should wear something a bit less – well – noticeable?'

'I thought you liked this dress,' I said. 'You liked it when I bought it. You liked it in the summer.'

'That's not the point,' he said wearily. And then, turning away, 'Oh, for God's sake, have it your own way.'

He went to shower, came down looking sleek in his suit.

We went by car: Mac's hospital is on this side of town. He

drove fast, in a fierce silent concentrated way. I could tell he was still cross. I felt it was utterly unreasonable, but I didn't have the energy to justify myself. My confidence started to seep away: I couldn't understand why I'd been so keen to come. I knew exactly how it would be: medical parties are always dull. It had been different, of course, when we were students. Like when we'd just qualified, and there'd been a drunken triumphant dinner in someone's flat: I'd asked Jed along, because I hadn't had a boyfriend at the time, and I remember it as a moment of glorious certainty, of knowing you'd got there, feeling for once that I could ease up a little, just float with the current: and I drank too much Slivovitz, smoked a rather suspect joint, and, to Jed's lasting delight, on the way home fell backwards over a fence. But it changes as you get older: well, it has to, I guess. Tonight there'd be sliced beef and pasta salad and conversation about prep schools.

The party was in the bar. We hung our coats on the rail, went in. The room was full already. Party noise broke over us: vivid high voices, gushes of laughter. I felt exhausted before we'd even begun. Most of the women had that casually expensive London look, designer t-shirts and restrained gold jewellery. The lights were too bright for a party, hurting my eyes after the darkness outside, shining into every corner, with now and then a flash from a camera: a photographer in leather trousers was doing the rounds – someone from the local paper presumably.

We drank rosé, ate some bits of focaccia with roast vegetables on top, chatted to one of Mac's colleagues. It was hard to manage the roast vegetable thing and the wine together, the bread crumbled when I bit it, half of it fell to the floor. I could hear myself breaking clumsily into the conversation, laughing a little too loudly, my voice like glass, shiny and brittle. I loathed this shrill emphatic person I seemed to have become.

Mac moved off and I looked round, wondering who to talk

to. There were people here that I recognized, that I'd worked with or knew through Mac. I thought about these people and the things I knew about them. Claudia Thomas, a discreetly sexy haematologist who skated round the hospital on white rollerblades – and, the last time I talked to her, had been going out with an actor whose surname she couldn't remember, suggesting a life of dazzling debauchery. Hugh Granville, a self-effacing obstetrician, who'd got onto the national news when a woman on a plane on which he was a passenger went prematurely into labour: he'd delivered twins, one of them breech, at 35,000 feet. Tony and Kim Watson, married GPs, who had an exquisite minimalist flat, all elegant echoing spaces and perfectly placed black pebbles, and who spent their holidays sky-diving or trekking in Nepal and picking up obscure infections, as though they felt impelled to inject some risk, some disorder, into their pristine lives. And over by the drinks table, I could see Kevin Bywater, a flamboyant colleague of Mac's, who as a student had claimed to have learned the positioning of the internal organs by drawing them with great exactitude on the naked body of his then girlfriend, a paediatric nurse with lavish breasts. The stories we hear and repeat about each another: the bits of biography clinging like burrs in the mind. And what would people think when they looked at me? I wondered. Oh, there's Tessa Craig – well, you know who *she* is: she's the psychiatrist who discharged the schizophrenic who killed that lovely young woman, Alysson Gates.

The little groups in which these people were embedded seemed suddenly excluding: I didn't know how to break in. Like when you're a teenager, I thought, and you're so sure you're different, that you've got some kind of stigma, and you can't believe that anyone would want to talk to you. I pushed the thought away.

I was about to make myself go and talk to Claudia when I noticed Brendan O'Toole heading in my direction. Brendan's a gynaecologist: he's in Mac's rowing club, he's a muscly bear of a man with wide square shoulders and understanding eyes.

'Tess, that is a spectacular dress,' he said.

'Thanks,' I said.

He put a finger on my arm, just below my bruise: his skin was very warm. I felt a shiver of arousal which alarmed me rather: we'd often had Brendan to dinner and I liked him a lot but I'd never felt the least attraction to him. It was like my nervous system was firing off at random – a spurt of rage, a few tears, perhaps a flicker of sex – none of it making sense.

He circled my bruise with his finger. 'Mac been beating you up again, has he?'

I laughed. The photographer in leather trousers was standing next to us. She turned to face us, raised her camera. The flash sealed the laughter in my throat. I heard my quick intake of breath, like someone had hit me: instantly felt foolish.

Brendan let his hand rest a moment on my arm.

The photographer asked for our names. Brendan told her. She wrote them down, moved on.

'So, Tess, are you OK?' he said then, all serious again.

'Kind of,' I said.

'I was so sorry to hear about your troubles,' he said.

'Well,' I said.

'Ralph's standing by you?'

'Yes.'

'Good for him. I'm glad to hear it. I did my psychiatry module with him during my clinical,' he said. 'To be honest, I always had him down as a slippery git.'

'He's been good to me, really,' I said.

'Well, I expect you bring out the best in him,' he said, with a pleasantly lecherous smile.

'Goodness knows,' I said.

He looked at me in a quizzical way. 'Everyone has something, Tessa,' he said. 'You know that, don't you?'

I nodded.

'When I was a house officer,' he said, 'this woman came in with abdominal pain. Young woman, twenty-six, two kids. All the rest of my team were in theatre, and I knew she was getting very unwell, and I took a blood gas – I'd never done it before, I mean, it's a bloody tricky procedure – and I went and analysed the gases and they were very abnormal – so I took it to my team in theatre, I said, This woman's really ill. They were right in the thick of it, they said, You must have missed, go and try again. And I knew I'd done it right, but I didn't insist, I went and did it again, and it was exactly the same. She was actually dying – she had pancreatitis.' His face had a veiled look. 'She was so young, she had these two little kids,' he said.

'Maybe she couldn't have been saved,' I said.

His eyes were on me, full and bright. 'That's what you tell yourself,' he said. 'But nothing since has ever been so bad.'

'No,' I said.

'You're not alone,' he said. 'It's just that when most of us make a mistake, it doesn't get into the press.'

'Thanks,' I said. 'For telling me.'

He was staring into his glass.

'You know, Tess,' he went on slowly, 'there are times I think we make trouble for ourselves because we're all so fucking self-centred: we put ourselves right there in the middle, we think we did it. But sometimes things have their own momentum,' he said.

'I don't know,' I said.

'Maybe in the end things happen as they must,' he said. 'And all this making sense of it – working out what we did to make it happen: maybe that's all illusion.'

'Maybe,' I said.

I only partly understood, and I wanted him to say more, but some woman in huge platform boots and a tiny skirt made of netting came and hauled him off.

I looked around for Mac. He was over the other side of the room, talking to a woman I recognized vaguely – a psychologist, called, I thought, Jane Pickering. She was pretty in an orderly, conventional way – the sort of thing he likes – immaculate shiny white-blonde hair, a curvy little suit. Now and then she'd run her tongue over her lips, which were glossed so they looked wet: it seemed quite blatant to me, even from that distance. Women adore surgeons: it's the power thing; and they have such clever hands. Mac was animated, leaning in towards her, waving his hands around: I could tell he was being charming, his eyes never leaving her face, listening with total attention, as he had when he'd flirted with me over Annabel's *boeuf en daube*. I felt I ought to mind but somehow I didn't, as though the part of me that should have minded was numb, anaesthetized. I watched, and thought how he was very good-looking really, his well-honed body, his well-cut suit, his manner, alert, assured. Yet he had to be the other side of the room before I could see it now.

I stood there, feeling invisible amid the glittery laughing people, stood and sipped my wine and wondered how it would be if Mac had an affair. Would he start to smell of some feminine scent, sultry but ephemeral – so I'd wonder for a moment, then think I'd dreamed it up? Would he make love with more urgency, want to try something new, come more quickly because he was thinking of her? Would there perhaps be a remoteness about him, expressions passing like cloud shadows over his face, and I'd ask what he was thinking, and he'd start and say, Oh, nothing? Would there be revelations, ominous little clues, a short blonde hair on his shoulder, the thin bright wire of an earring in the carpet in his car? And if I found out about it, would I mind? I seemed to be able to consider all this with absolute equanimity: that scared me.

I imagined myself talking to someone about my lack of concern, justifying it, arguing that it was all about being mature. That this, you see, is a highly contemporary marriage, without angst or possessiveness. Mac and me, we just get on with our lives, we trust one another. Yet I didn't know if that was true: if we did. I wondered if it was something rather less precious than trust, more like the absence of something.

I knew I couldn't just stand there, that I ought to talk to people. I made myself go to the buffet, took a handful of peanuts. The salt stung the raw places on my hands, where I'd torn the bits of skin at the sides of my nails.

A woman in an embroidered Monsoon dress came up to me and introduced herself. She was married to a dermatologist, she said. I turned to her gratefully, told her I was Mac's wife. She started on about how stay-at-home mothers are seriously undervalued, and how lovely it is to make your own playdoh and meet your child from school: I didn't have to say much.

Eventually there was a pause.

'You've got children?' she said.

I shook my head.

'And where do you work?' she said.

'I'm a psychiatrist,' I said.

'I wouldn't like your job,' she said with fervour. 'I wouldn't do that for anything. Did you read about that dreadful case – that poor girl who got stabbed?'

I made some non-committal noise, moved my hand rather suddenly, spilt wine over my arm. I tried to wipe it off with my other hand. She didn't seem to notice.

'A terrible thing,' she said. 'Terrible. How could they have let that woman out when she was obviously crazy?'

I murmured something.

She paid no attention. 'Sometimes I wonder whether there was something to be said for the old asylums,' she said. She was pleased with herself, like she'd only just thought of this, like it was a fresh and new observation. 'Maybe we were in too

111

much of a rush to get rid of those places. You know, there are clearly people who need them . . .'

I held tight to my glass.

'Maybe,' I said. 'Well, please excuse me.'

I went to the loo, stood in front of the mirror, pointlessly combing my hair. There was a smell of mingled scents that women had sprayed on. The red wine had lined my lips, staining the little cracks that you get in cold weather, so I looked excessively lipsticked, almost vampirish. There was a wall of glass between me and everyone else. I needed to go.

I went to get Mac. He'd moved on from the psychologist in the sexy suit, he was chatting to one of the other consultants.

He looked at me warily, as though scared I might burst into tears or fling off my clothes or something.

'I wouldn't mind going,' I said. 'If that's OK with you.'

'Sure, let's go,' he said rapidly.

I went to get my coat.

Other people were leaving too, spilling out into the night, their colour and glitter taken away the minute they stepped through the door, their faces sickly in the light of the street lamps in the car park. I shivered, the lining of my coat felt chilly against my bare arms: my linen frock was far too thin for winter.

Our headlights raked the cold streets as we drove home. A police helicopter moved around overhead, sounding too low in the sky. I was drunk and cold and tired: worn out with the effort of pretending to be normal.

The next day in the *Evening Standard*, there was an account of Alysson Gates' funeral service. It was the lead story on an inside page. The picture was like I'd seen on the television – the city churchyard, the winding dark line of mourners, the bleakness, the coffin piled with flowers. And halfway down the page was a picture of me at the party. The photographer with the leather trousers must have realized who I was and sold the photograph on. I was laughing, I looked drunk, my eyes half-closed, my mouth wide open so you could see my teeth, the strap slipping off my shoulder. The caption didn't say much: it didn't need to. 'Doctor Who Released Knife Maniac Paula.' And underneath, in smaller print: 'Dr Tessa Craig, the psychiatrist who discharged Paula Hickey into the community, pictured at a medical party on the day that Alysson Gates is finally laid to rest.'

Chapter 12

I rang home and left a message on our answerphone. Hi, it's me. Mac, look, I've got caught up here, I'm having to work late; I should be back around seven, something like that. My voice brisk, matter-of-fact, as though it was a day like any other, an ordinary work problem.

I sat on the train to Wimbledon, looking down on the rooftops, the tenements, the windows with dirty net curtains, the hidden lives of Vauxhall and Clapham, and the cemetery at Earlsfield, bleak in the thin afternoon light: in the distance the colours of the flowers on the graves faded to grey. I had never in my life been so afraid.

At Wimbledon I changed, got on the blue and yellow train that goes south. It's crowded in the rush hour, you see it on the news sometimes, people pushed up against one another, jostling for seats: but that afternoon there was hardly anyone travelling that way, and the cold stations we passed through were empty except for the pigeons. The embankments were covered with brambles: you could see people's back gardens, their sheds and heaps of compost, the back ends of things, a football pitch with worn grass in front of the goal-posts. I sat there in the silent carriage, feeling unreal. And arrived and stepped down onto the platform, in this place where I'd never been. Only a girl with a buggy and a tired slow man got out as well as me. The platform was high above the houses on either side, looking down into the winter gardens.

Thinking back to that moment, I find it hard to recall what was going through my mind: some notion perhaps that I might be able to salvage something, to put my case, restore the balance of life. But this is pure supposition: I really can't remember, it's all been blotted out by what happened afterwards; it's hard to put myself back there and make any sense of it all. Yet the things I saw around me are all there in my memory, as clear almost as if I was standing there now: the feathery shapes of the bare trees, the colours of the gardens, brown and russet and sepia, warm like the hides of animals, the tangled banks that sloped down to the gardens and that at midsummer, I guessed, would be brimming over with flowers; the precise quality of the light, filmy, blueish, already into evening. The train struck fabulous sparks from the track as it pulled away into the blue distance.

There was an underpass with white tiles, all bare and echoey like a space in a dream, no posters stuck up, not even any graffiti. Some of the ceiling tiles were coming away. I went out through the empty ticket hall. There was a wide pillar in the middle with a hole where the ticket office presumably once had been, but there was nothing there now.

In the road I had to stop and get out my *A to Z*: it was ages since I'd needed a map for anything. I worked out that I had to go down Gulliver Street and turn left into St John's Street. Gulliver Street was tatty, run-down: there were tall houses divided into flats, a few shops, some boarded up, on the corner a bargain shop with mops and tins of cat food jumbled up in the window. A grey Sierra had crashed and gone up on the pavement: the front tyres were flat, the bonnet crunched in, a crumpled notice that said Police Aware was stuck behind one of the wipers. Way over to the left, a vast high-rise estate loomed over the street: the pale concrete bulk of it was stained and streaked with damp. I passed a street market, now being cleared away: discarded fruit was rotting in the gutters. There was a smell of burning: it made me think of Liverpool.

I walked all down St John's Street but I couldn't see anything that looked right, just dreary terraced houses with tiny front gardens with little crumbling walls. Two ragged cherry trees leaned out across the pavement, a few dark wrinkled fruit still clinging to the branches. On the corner there was a ponderous brick-built Victorian church with a church hall beside it, and a hoarding that said, 'God: the best Christmas presence'. I stood on the corner, looking in my *A to Z*, wondering if there was another bit of St John's Street somewhere else. A couple of people passed me but no-one offered to help. You could give up now, said a voice inside me, soothing, persuasive. You've tried, you've done your best. What more could anyone do? Just go home, forget you ever came . . . But I walked back up the street.

When I passed the church hall again, the door had been opened and there were sounds of children. I went in.

It was some kind of playgroup. The boys were mostly tearing around on plastic vehicles, the girls standing at tables in aprons making things. There was a table for paints, and a table for dough where some girls were making snakes and puddings, and cutting shapes with knives. One of them held up the dough, stretching it out between her hands, pulling her hands apart, so the dough started to thin and the light shone through it. There were four or five adult helpers, in baggy tops and leggings. They'd tried to brighten up the place: there were pictures on the walls, ABCs and counting posters, seven earwigs, eight caterpillars. The smells of orange squash, paint, damp sand, took me briefly back to childhood.

A little girl with Down's came up to me: she had a sweet smile, a translucent line of snot from her nose to her lip. She waggled a glove puppet with hair like a doll in front of my face. One of the women got up, came over, looking at me curiously. I was suddenly crazily afraid that she'd know at once who I was and kick me out or even call the police. But she only asked if she could help.

'I think there's an advice centre somewhere in this street,' I said. 'I can't find it.'

'Oh,' she said, looking even more puzzled, taking in my confident jacket, my sleekly expensive shoes, wondering perhaps why someone as obviously affluent as me should want this. 'It's out the back. Flo' – she bent to the little girl – 'Flo, can you take the lady to see Ben?'

Flo was pleased with this commission. She put her free hand in mine, held me fiercely, as though to make quite sure I wouldn't run off. She led me out of a door at the back of the hall, into a maze of corridors. The air was thick and hot and the place was so dark it felt as though it was underground, and you'd had to climb down many steps to get there. Water pipes along the ceiling hissed and pulsed like live things. We passed the doors to the children's toilets and a kitchen littered with used plastic cups and spilled juice. Right down the end there was a door with a handwritten notice that said Welfare Advice, propped a little ajar. Flo pointed triumphantly to the door, then turned and lumbered off, giggling. I pushed the door open.

He was standing behind the desk, shuffling papers. He had his coat on. When he looked up and saw me, he went quite still. He stared: his face was white.

'I'm Tessa Craig,' I said.

'I know who you are,' he said.

He was bigger than I'd expected. Quite a lot taller than me,

117

and rather heavy. His size surprised me – he wasn't like he'd looked on television, more like the way I'd dreamed him. He was wearing this heavy black coat, and a scarf round his neck like Dr Who wore when we were children, made of many colours. I wondered who had knitted it for him.

'I wanted to talk to you,' I said.

He didn't respond. I felt suddenly dizzy, like when you've given blood.

'Can I sit down?' I said, and I turned to the only chair which wasn't piled with stuff: the whole room was cluttered, files and bits of paper everywhere, though my sense of these things was blurred, as though only he was in focus.

'I'm just going,' he said abruptly. 'I'm seeing somebody, I'm late already as it is.'

There was something slightly unkempt about him, he needed a haircut, a shave. And he was a difficult man, I thought: not just now and with me, but probably always difficult. Someone who wouldn't make concessions. Not letting me sit, not taking off his coat.

'I'll only keep you a moment,' I said.

'I don't understand why you're here at all,' he said.

'I wanted to talk about the paper – that photograph of me,' I said. 'To tell you I'm not like that – not like it made me seem.'

'No?' he said, his voice very cold. 'So what are you like?'

I didn't know what to say. I breathed in, tried again.

'I guess I thought that we could talk – perhaps kind of understand one another,' I said.

'You thought wrong,' he said. He had this way of looking at me: hostile, but puzzled too, as though he found me different from the woman he'd imagined. 'How could we possibly do that? You and me? Kind of understand one another?' There was an edge of contempt to his voice.

'Well, perhaps we could come to see each other's point

of view,' I said. Then wished I hadn't said that: it sounded so facile.

'I can see absolutely no point in talking,' he said. 'The therapy business is full of people like you.' His voice rising suddenly, harsh and animated, as though this at least he could safely get angry about. 'People who think they can change things by talking about them – make things come right. Undo what's been done. It's total bullshit, all of it.'

'I don't think that,' I said. 'I'm not that kind of therapist. I'm not hopeful like that.' Surprised by myself, seeing that this was true: thinking briefly of the hopefulness I'd had when I started out, and how I'd lost that somewhere. And then thought how stupid I sounded, making these rather self-pitying statements about myself. I felt frivolous – my clothes, my hair, and everything I said – as though I was somehow belittling Alysson's death by my very presence there.

'You want to ask me to lay off a bit – is that it?' he said. 'You're afraid. You know a public inquiry would implicate you. You don't want to be in the papers. You've come to ask me to be nice, to be reasonable.'

'No,' I said. 'No.' Then, feeling that his directness required something truer of me, 'Well, of course I would feel those things. You know that. But that's not why I've come.'

I'd imagined it would be better once I'd got here, that perhaps my fear of him would start to go; and yet I just felt more and more afraid.

'I was told to clear some beds,' I said.

Behind him on the wall, there were notices about local community groups – Meet up with friends old and new at Club 50/99! – and advice sheets about Incapacity Benefit. I tried to focus on the notices, but I still felt his stare, like a tangible thing, like something that touched me.

'Paula Hickey was a patient I was quite involved with,' I said. 'I'd known her for a while – I thought I understood her.'

119

'You shouldn't have discharged her,' he said. 'Nothing, nothing can excuse what you did.'

'We were under a lot of pressure,' I said.

'Of course you were,' he said. 'And you were underfunded and it's all a question of resources and Paula Hickey was a disaster waiting to happen.' His throat moved as he swallowed. He pushed his hair back from his face as though it angered him, and I saw that his nails were bitten to the quick. 'Alysson was someone I loved,' he said. 'None of that means anything to me.'

He looked away from me then, but not before I saw a shadow pass over his face: and I saw how stricken he was and felt I had no right to see it, that he'd let me see something in him I shouldn't have seen.

There was the sound of a toilet flushing, footsteps in the corridor, children chattering. The sound seemed to release him: he looked back to me. 'Tell me,' he said, that hard serious stare, looking right into me. 'Is this something you've had to do yet? D'you know how it is, what it's like, to lose somebody close to you? Is it something you've had to do?'

'No,' I said. 'Not really. But, of course, you know, as a doctor . . .'

'I don't mean as a bloody doctor,' he said. 'I mean you, as yourself. As Tessa.' There was something so raw about his use of my Christian name, as though he'd cut me with it. 'Is it something you've had to do for yourself? To feel how it is to lose someone who's that close to you – who's part of your life?'

'My mother,' I said. My face was burning. 'My mother died three years ago.'

He shook his head abruptly. I'd tried to give him all I had to offer and he'd thrown it back in my face.

'No,' he said. 'Someone who's part of you now. Someone young: who shouldn't have died.'

I shook my head. 'But I can imagine . . .'

'No, you can't,' he said. 'How the fuck can you possibly imagine?' He leaned across the desk towards me: for a moment I wondered if he was going to attack me. 'You can't have the faintest fucking idea what it's like for me. That's absolutely apparent to me – that you don't know what you're talking about.'

'Please,' I said. I couldn't breathe. The room seemed to be filling up with water. 'Just let me say I'm sorry. About what happened – what I did. That I made a terrible mistake and I'm so sorry.' I swallowed. 'About Alysson.' Needing to say her name, like a charm – to say it out loud, take away some of its power. 'Let me say that at least. That's what I came to say.'

'Forgiveness isn't like that,' he said. 'You can't just turn it on like that because someone says sorry. Because it would be nice or big or something.'

'I'm not asking for forgiveness,' I said. 'Of course I'm not. I didn't mean . . .'

He interrupted me. 'It's done,' he said. 'Nothing can change it.'

He started to button his coat. The gesture was final, rejecting. I knew it was time to go, to bring this to an end, but the air felt so heavy, pressing down on me, I couldn't move.

He came round to my side of the desk, doing it for me.

I picked up my bag. 'I shouldn't have come,' I said. 'It was a stupid thing to do. I just keep getting things wrong.' Not really talking to him: just saying it because it was true. 'Everything I do. It all kind of falls apart.' Jesus, what a confession, I thought. Why did I say that? And felt tears of self-pity welling up in me because I'd come all this way and tried to say I was sorry and he'd refused to hear. I swallowed them down. I knew I couldn't bear to let this man see my tears, my weakness: that would be the worst thing – that exposure.

He reached past me, put out a hand to pull the door open.

He was very close to me: I could smell the warm wool of his greatcoat, the indefinable smell of his skin. And as he reached out I thought for an instant that he was going to hit me or maybe touch my face, I didn't know which.

'Thank you for seeing me,' I said.

He shrugged, stepped aside to let me pass.

I went off down the corridor in the dark. Someone was playing 'Moon River' on the out-of-tune piano in the church hall. One of the children was joining in, banging away at the bottom of the keyboard with huge clumpy discords, but the yearning in the music still came through. There was daylight ahead of me, a side-door onto the street. I went out that way, I couldn't face the women in the hall, couldn't face anyone. I felt shaken right through: it was as though the thing itself, the news of the death, was still absolutely fresh and new, as though it had just happened, as though I'd just been told.

I didn't have long to wait for the train. The branches of the silver birches on the embankment looked white, like something undressed, as they reached up to the street lamps: the entangled bramble-stems were purple in the evening. I shared the carriage with two women talking in a language that I didn't understand.

I was back long before seven – Mac wasn't even home. The answer machine was flashing but it was only the message I'd left. I listened to the sound of my voice – how brisk, emotionless, I sounded – and wondered what on earth I'd been expecting when I'd predicted that I'd be back so late. I found myself wishing we'd talked longer, kept thinking of things I could have said. It was as though I'd been cheated: that something that should have happened hadn't happened.

Mac came home and I behaved as though everything was just the same as usual. It wasn't so difficult. Back in my orderly house, everything clean and in its place and gleaming, my conversation with Ben Connelly already felt unreal, like something I'd made up. We ate penne, watched some TV drama about complicated relationships in a police station, went to bed early.

But that night I dreamed about him. He was with the children in the church hall, at the table with the dough. He was leading the group, showing them how to make something. The children gathered round watching. He is good at this, I thought in the dream, as the dough in his hands took shape, its proportions and texture magically transmuted, holding its shape like pitta bread yet pliable still like dough – as one thing in a dream may seem to become another yet still retain something of its original form. He held the dough out like I'd seen the little girl do, stretching it, pulling it till the light shone through, and I saw it was a kind of puppet he was making, the sort you put your hand in, like the puppet Flo had waved in front of my face. And the puppet grew hair and eyes and a mouth, and I saw in the dream that the dark woolly hair and the face were just like mine: and the children watched wide-eyed as the puppet that was me seemed to come alive, his hand easing into it, stretching it where it was tight around his wrist, moulding it to the shape of his hand, making it move.

Chapter 13

'We are here today,' said the coroner, 'to establish when, where and how Alysson Gates met her death, and to confirm her personal details.'

She was a warm courteous woman, with quiet formal clothes and a brooch on her lapel and a gentle smile.

'This case,' she went on, 'as we will all be aware, has attracted a great deal of media attention. I would stress that we are here today simply to establish facts – the facts of how Ms Gates came by her death. Any other issue is beyond the jurisdiction of this court.'

The courtroom was up at the top of a high building, with Artexed walls and comfortable chairs upholstered in tweed and pushed too close together. The place was crowded, full of journalists, but I'd managed to get a seat at the back, at the end of a row. I could see down over the red and black tiled rooftops of Fulham and out towards the river. There was grimy double-glazing at the windows, and the room was hushed, you were cut off from all the noise and busyness of the street, the lorries beeping as they backed into a catering depot, the wind that tugged at the branches of the trees: you could only see the roofs and the slow clouds, the single living thing in that whole wide cityscape a brown pigeon flapping emptily through the spaces between the buildings.

The coroner asked Alysson's relatives to come to the front of the court. Ben Connelly got up from his seat several rows in front of me. He was wearing a dark suit like when he'd been on television, he was frowning, composed, intent. I saw him and felt afraid. He seemed absolutely a stranger – someone with whom I had no connection, except for this terrible event that had wrenched our lives together – he didn't seem at all like someone I'd spoken to, and to whom I'd revealed a little of myself. I regretted it so much: I couldn't imagine what had possessed me to do it. And seeing him there I thought how Mac had tried to dissuade me from coming here today, and how I'd insisted, how I'd said I needed to hear it all, to know what Paula had done: yet now I wondered if this too was something I might regret.

A man and a woman stood up with Ben Connelly and together they moved to the front of the room. I knew they must be Alysson's parents: they looked a little like her. The woman was wearing a neat suit, bought specially perhaps because she'd be in the public eye. She had regular features, well-cut hair, you could tell she'd still be pretty when she smiled. Everything about her seemed tidy and controlled – the suit with its brass buttons, the blouse with a bow at the collar, her appearance suggesting a whole way of life that was safe and predictable – a garden with a lawn and rosebeds, a house that smelt of polish, with the parish magazine on the hall table and family photographs in silver frames. She sat down at the end of the row that was reserved for relatives and I could see her quite clearly when she turned a little. She sat with her hands in her lap: and I saw she was wringing her hands, that gesture you only ever see in the profoundly depressed or the bereaved, the hands wrapping

125

around one another, never still, like someone wringing water out of cloth.

Alysson's father was sworn in and confirmed Alysson's age and address and then sat down beside the mother again. Sometimes he put his hand on her arm, but she didn't seem to notice.

The coroner first called one of the security staff from the Marshgate Centre: he'd been one of the earliest on the scene, he'd held Paula until the police arrived. He told how Paula had stabbed Alysson from behind, with a single thrust of the blade, then she'd dropped the knife on the floor and walked slowly away. The murder weapon had been bought from Debenham's household department that morning, he said. Then DS Neville was called, and the consultant who'd treated Alysson in the intensive care unit, and the pathologist who'd conducted the postmortem. The pathologist was plainly used to all this, he turned towards Ben Connelly and Alysson's parents, talked very directly to them, explaining the chain of events that had led to Alysson's death, how the stabbing had led to the haemorrhage that had killed her. When he paused for a drink, the sound of the water being poured into a glass was picked up by the microphone, the intimate sound unnerving in that solemn public space.

It ended much as you'd predict: the coroner brought in a verdict of unlawful killing and thanked Alysson's relatives for attending.

'There is one issue which has dominated public discussion of this very tragic case,' she said then, 'and that is the degree of culpability of the medical staff who made the decision to discharge from hospital the woman who has now been charged with this offence. As I said at the start of this inquest, this issue is beyond the jurisdiction of my court. But I do wish to put it on record that I share the great concerns of those who feel that serious mistakes may have been made in the care of this woman and that it is imperative that these concerns be fully addressed by the inquiry into these events, which I understand will soon be convened.' And she turned off her tape recorder and left the court.

People got up, shuffled a bit, talked in little groups, but quietly, like in church.

Alysson's parents and Ben were already on their way out: I waited for a while for the court to empty, all Alysson's relatives to go.

But when I did get down to the doorway, I saw that Ben Connelly was standing on the pavement, talking to a group of reporters. I moved back into the shadow, hoped I hadn't been seen.

'The public have a right to know all the circumstances that led to Alysson's death,' he was saying. His voice was quiet and level, but as he spoke his hand cut the air like a blade. 'The very last thing we need is yet another secret inquiry behind closed doors. Doctors have been able to evade all responsibility for the consequences of their errors of judgment for far too long.'

I stood there very still, and heard the thud of my heart.

'Tell us, Ben, do you have plans to sue the St Jude's Trust?' said one of the journalists, a blonde woman in a pinstripe trouser suit. I recognized her from the mugshot in the column that she writes, knew she must be Charlie Cavanagh.

'It's certainly a course of action I'm investigating,' he said.

'Thank you, Ben,' she said. And there was something about her use of his Christian name and the way she held his eyes that seemed to hint at some past intimacy between them. I remembered what Will Spooner had said – that they went back a long way.

'Can you tell us your feelings about Dr Craig who discharged Paula Hickey?' shouted somebody from the back of the group.

A lorry roared past the court and Ben paused for a moment.

I slipped out of the building at the back of a knot of people. Nobody seemed to see.

I'd planned to go straight back to work. But I thought of how it would be – people saying it wasn't my fault; Cassie's wide eyes on me. Something in me shrank from that.

I walked quickly away from the court, turned into King's Road, found one of those French cafés where the coffee's usually reasonably strong. I went in. It was a pleasant place, the walls washed with paint the colour of clementines, with newspapers to read and black and white photos of Paris that showed the falling of leaves from the plane trees on the banks of the Seine and people kissing on bridges.

I went to a table in the corner, sat with my back to the wall so I could see the street. Around me women with shopping bags were eating cakes and chatting or reading newspapers. I felt surprisingly calm among all these people who didn't know me, who just carried on with their lives, eating their *pains aux raisins* and talking about their children. The waitress brought my coffee. It was too hot to drink, I took tiny sips of the froth, the chocolate powder scattered on top a sudden sweetness on my tongue.

The door opened. I looked up, saw someone coming in. Alysson's mother.

I put my head down quickly, some instinct making me sit quite still like a hunted animal. I so hoped she hadn't seen me: then realized it was me she'd come for. Even with my head down I could feel her slow purposeful approach between the tables, could hear the thin click of her smart court shoes on the floor.

She stood by my table.

'Dr Tessa Craig.'

128

I looked up, nodded. 'Mrs Gates, please sit down. We can talk.'

She said nothing.

'Let me get you a coffee,' I said, and turned as though to catch the waiter's eye, trying to make it normal, a social occasion.

She just stood there, her shadow falling across me.

'You did this,' she said at last, her voice splintering like glass. 'You did this to my daughter.'

I could smell alcohol on her breath, I realized she'd been drinking, although it was still morning: it seemed shocking, in this sweet-faced immaculate woman.

'You let that woman go. You could have stopped her. You killed my daughter.' The voice wrenched out of her, full of pain.

I had no words: there was nothing I could say. I knew I should be trying to calm her down, using all my skill, expressing sympathy, placating her. I couldn't do it, the facile words stuck in my throat.

She leant forward across the table. Her hands were clenched into fists, the veins like knotted blue cord. I thought she might hit me. People at the other tables, the women with their cakes and newspapers, turned and stared uneasily. Over her shoulder I could see her husband standing miserably in the doorway, embarrassed, fragile, his eyes watery, his forehead creased in a frown, just standing there not knowing what to do.

'Do you deny it?' she said. 'You can't deny it, can you?' In the foundation on her face there were shiny streaks of tears.

I saw that the manageress had come out. She stood some distance from the table, not sure what to do, hoping perhaps it would all go away.

I swallowed hard. It seemed so discourteous to stay sitting, but I was afraid that if I stood she'd lash out.

'Mrs Gates,' I said, 'we're all so very distressed that this has happened. Please sit down, we can talk about it.'

My words sounded obscene to me, in the face of this woman's distress, that seemed like something you could smell, as though it oozed from her pores. But I wasn't sure she'd even heard what I'd said. She turned to the people at the next table, who shuffled a little, flushing, embarrassed.

'She killed my daughter, my beautiful Alysson,' she said. Her voice was far too loud for a public place. 'This woman did it. My Alysson is dead. My beautiful daughter is dead. This is Dr Craig. I want you to look at her. She's a murderer.'

The women at the next table glanced at me and stared down into their coffee.

She turned back to me and paused, suddenly uncertain: then took a step towards me, as though some resolve had hardened in her.

'But let me tell you this,' she said. 'You won't get away with it, Dr Tessa Craig. You think you've got away with it, but we're not going to let you.' She spat out the words as though they were pith in her mouth. 'Believe me, Dr Tessa Craig, we're going to destroy you for this. You'll never work again.'

The door slammed back as Ben Connelly came in, came rapidly towards us. I felt really afraid then, physically afraid: I thought he was going to join in with her, to abuse me too, to smash his fist in my face. I cursed myself that I'd been to see him, that I'd made myself so vulnerable: that he knew how afraid and weak I was.

He came to the table, didn't look at me. He put his arm round the woman's shoulder, speaking to her as though I wasn't there.

'Diane,' he said. 'Leave her alone, Diane. This isn't the way.'

He stood there with his arm around her, stroking her shoulder, repeating her name, as you might soothe a child. 'Come with me,' he said. And when she just stood there, as though she couldn't see or hear him, 'Diane, come on.'

He turned her away from me, pointed her towards the door, gentle but insistent. 'Ron needs you. Look, he's waiting.'

Her husband, hearing, moved a little towards her.

'Go to Ron,' he said.

She started to walk between the tables – one foot carefully in front of the other, like someone walking on a wire stretched out across a void. She was crying quietly, making no attempt to wipe the tears from her face.

He made to follow her, but as he went, without saying anything, without even looking at me, he touched my shoulder. Tense and scared as I was, I felt acutely that brief surprising imprint of his fingers.

My mouth went completely dry. I bit my tongue to make myself salivate, ran my tongue over my lips, the bittersweet taste of chocolate powder on my mouth. Then they were gone – the manageress hastening to hold the door open for them, the women in the café turning back to their cakes, talking a little too brightly.

I waited till they'd completely disappeared down the street, then I paid for my coffee and left it undrunk and went.

Chapter 14

The internal inquiry was convened. There were three of them on the panel – Tony Black, one of the Trust managers, and Jean Henderson, a senior social worker, and Jack Dunwoody, a psychiatric consultant at St Agatha's.

I was due to appear before them on the Tuesday afternoon. I had lunch that day with Sam: I found it hard to eat.

'Don't let them rile you, Tess,' he said. 'They always want to blame somebody – even if it's the poor bloody nursing auxiliary who left the door open when the patient ran off.'

Sam knew about these things: he'd had to appear before an inquiry two years before, when one of his patients had got hold of some shoelaces and hanged herself in the shower-room on the ward. I remembered him coming out of the inquiry and going into the doctors' room and throwing cushions against the wall.

'It goes to people's heads,' he said. 'It's a kangaroo court. They'll think they're judge and jury rolled into one. And watch out for that Jean Henderson. Social workers love the power trip. Mostly they'd like to be doctors themselves: they love to get doctors on the carpet.'

They sat there in their most sober suits, behind an imposing table littered with papers. They asked me the obvious stuff – my previous involvement with Paula, and how I'd made the decision to discharge her, and the plans I'd made to support her in the community.

'Looking back,' said Jack Dunwoody then, 'do you have any concerns about the decision you made?'

'Obviously with the benefit of hindsight, it was a tragically wrong decision,' I said. 'But I consider that I made the best judgment I could with the information available to me.'

It sounded so rational – this considered decision I'd made in the clear light of day. And what I said was true as far as it went: and yet it left out so much – my guilty awareness of my fondness for Paula, my irritation with Dominic and the patronizing way he'd put his hand on my arm, the job I'd so terribly wanted. I felt that I was lying.

Jean Henderson, the senior social worker, leaned towards me. She didn't seem at all the destructive and embittered woman that Sam had warned me against; she had silver dolphin earrings and warm brown eyes. She smiled a little as she spoke.

'Dr Craig, I'm getting the impression that you had quite a close relationship with Paula Hickey.' She had a soothing sibilant voice from years of calming desperate people. 'Is that true?' she said.

'Yes,' I said. 'I've known her a long time.'

'Perhaps an unusually close relationship?'

'No – not unusually close,' I said.

'But surely,' she said, 'it wouldn't be normal practice for a specialist registrar to be a patient's care manager?'

'It seemed the right way to handle it at the time,' I said.

'Dr Craig, would you agree that your over-involvement with this patient perhaps clouded your judgment?'

'I would question whether I was over-involved,' I said,

clinging to the sound of Sam's voice in my mind, determined not to be riled. 'Paula Hickey was a patient I was interested in and had known for a long time. My relationship with her was entirely professionally appropriate.'

I hated Jean Henderson: for her smile and her sibilant voice and her little glittery earrings; for the fact that there was such truth in what she said.

I asked when they would report. They told me the inquiry would take about two weeks, and the report would come out a week or so after that.

The weather was bright, cold: daffodil-yellow days, with a wind like a knife. Tim Rigby was very afraid when he heard the wind rising outside the hospital: he hid his head in his hands, blocking up his ears, terrified that the wind was going to get inside him. We admitted an ex-Trade Union regional organizer, Ed Boyce, who'd been depressed for years. He described himself as 'old old Labour' and was rather aggressive – Just let me finish, will you, doctor? The male doctors kept remarking how he was really rather likeable – it was, I suspected, a way of coping with all his aggression and competitiveness. The pollarded ash trees in the hospital grounds were coming into leaf, and the bud on Cassie's amaryllis fattened and opened out, an opulent flame-red flower, its brightness like a trumpet note in the stillness of the ward: everyone admired it.

I longed to ask Ralph about the Fisher Memorial – whether what had happened had put me out of the running – but didn't dare, fearing what he might say. Ralph was in a foul mood anyway, roundly abusing a medical student who was two minutes late, irritated with Francine when she forgot to bring a file to his ward round: revealing how fragile he was under that urbane air. There were rumours and counter-rumours about the merger, and he never let slip a chance to make some deprecating comment about how they did things at St Agatha's. It didn't seem an auspicious time to approach him.

I'm sure everyone at work thought I was coping fine – except perhaps Sam, who understood me best, who'd sometimes look at me in a tender worried way but didn't know what to say: and I didn't know how to start a conversation about myself – I was never very good at getting help.

Instead I drank too much. There was a nearly full bottle of Bushmills left over from Christmas. I finished it in four evenings and went and bought another. What I was doing didn't quite qualify as problem drinking: but it was moving fast in that direction. I'd never before drunk every night: certainly never started drinking the moment I came in. I'd cope OK at work, then come home in the train and yearn for my drink, the way it blotted out what was happening in my head. I'd drink steadily through the evening and carry on long after Mac had gone upstairs. It was partly because I dreaded going to bed. It always took me ages to get to sleep, and when I did finally drift off, I'd dream strange deathly dreams – of a house with the windows all concreted up, like sightless eyes; of a woman dressed only in jewelled bangles and buried under a mountain of sand; dreams of predators and intruders which would plummet me into wakefulness, blood shaking my heart.

At eleven o'clock the heating would go off and the house would get very cold, and I wouldn't want to put it on again because the clunking in the pipes might wake Mac, so I'd get the duvet from the spare room, a flowery thing that had been a wedding present from Mac's parents, and I'd curl up on the sofa with the duvet pulled up to my neck, and watch those weird programmes you get on late-night television, documentaries about transvestite prostitutes in Amsterdam and people who have sex on Clapham Common, and I'd finally crawl into bed at about half one. Mac would be asleep always: I'd try not to wake him, but sometimes he'd stir, perhaps reach out a hand, touch the nearest part of me, murmur something, and then his breathing would slow and he'd sink back down into sleep. And so we never made love. I didn't think about this much, certainly didn't worry about it. I saw it as a temporary thing, just a brief intermission in a happy married life. I had a sense then of my marriage as something that was always there, like the place where you live – something that could wait – that I could easily return to or rediscover, when life felt easier. As, if you're sick, you may let your house get cobwebby and dusty, with piles of newspaper in the corners, then wake one day restored and clean it up, and it's as vivid and gleaming as ever it was. Desire, I guess, had gone long ago, sidled away as it does: or perhaps it had never quite been there, really, for Mac and me. To me then, that kind of sexual yearning was something quite remote, only vaguely remembered – that need to know, to possess, the other person, to become in some sense part of them, lost in that labyrinth of longing: it was something I hadn't felt in years – quite honestly, not since Nathan Goldberg – and I didn't notice its lack. So the fact that for a while we didn't make love seemed without significance: a byproduct of my disordered sleep.

Yet something shifted then. I can see that quite clearly now. It's frightening, how this can happen, and how quickly. The little spaces opening up between us, the new coolness, the almost imperceptible movement of air.

One day in the week following the inquest – I don't know quite when because it didn't seem significant at the time – I came in from work and he was on the phone so I didn't go to kiss him, I poured my drink and sat at the kitchen table and then he put down the phone and I didn't go to him and he didn't come to me, we just talked about the day, it all seemed perfectly natural: and after that we never kissed when one of us came in. Then there was an invitation to dinner with Julia, his colleague at the hospital, and her paediatrician husband, and I couldn't quite face it, said I didn't want to go. D'you mind if I go? he said. No, no, that's fine, I said, and so he went without me. These the little stones – pale, unmarked, innocuous if seen in isolation – that yet trace out a path.

I started to hide things from him, things I was doing that I knew might seem a bit bizarre. On Saturday when I was out shopping, I went quite deliberately down to the basement of John Lewis, to the household department. I lingered there for a while in the kitchenware section, among all the bright coloured plastic, the lemon squeezers and colanders and apron and teatowel sets. There was a tall display of kitchen knives, their blades all sheathed in perspex. I stood and looked at them: the filleting knives and salmon slicers and meat cleavers, with names like Laser and Forever Sharp, and the Sabatier knives like some I had at home that I used to cut up meat, and I thought of Paula looking at such a display and wondered how she'd made her choice, what had been going through her troubled mind. Had she picked one entirely at random or had there been some kind of crazy logic to it – some terrible meaning that only she could see in the shape of the blade or the name? I lingered there too long, and an assistant came up, said, 'Can I help you, madam?' 'No,' I said, 'No, I'm fine, thanks,' a bit embarrassed. And I bought a garlic press I didn't want – so that she wouldn't think there was anything odd about me.

I didn't tell Mac this: it was part of a need I had that he couldn't comprehend: a need to immerse myself in it. I think that was what he found most troubling about me. He felt I'm sure that the way was not through, but past – to put it behind you and get on and not to think about it: which would have been his way. Yet if I knew anything I knew this, at least: that I could not find a way to carry on, by evading what had happened. I could not.

On Monday Mac came home after me. I was sitting at the kitchen table with my first drink of the evening. He was still wearing his coat, it swung out behind him as he moved

137

towards me. I thought he was going to kiss me, like he'd once have done.

'This has got to stop,' he said.

He moved before I could stop him, picked up the bottle of Bushmills, twisted off the top, tipped it into the sink. The whiskey smell washed through the room, thick, suddenly sickening.

'Shit, Mac,' I said, trying to swallow my rage. 'You don't have to treat me like an alcoholic. I'm only trying to cope.'

'This isn't the way to cope,' he said. He dropped the empty bottle in the bin.

I knew with a small cool sane part of me that he was just trying to look after me: and perhaps there was something in me that wanted this – wanted somebody to take control.

'OK, I know I'm drinking too much,' I said. 'But I'm trying to survive.'

'I can't bear to see you let yourself go downhill like this,' he said. 'Can't bear it.'

'It's only for the moment,' I said.

'You're deluding yourself, Tessa,' he said. 'That's what alcoholics do – they delude themselves. Well, you're meant to know this stuff.'

'Of course I'm not an alcoholic,' I said. 'That's ludicrous. It's just to see me through.'

'Oh Tessa, give it a break,' he said, his voice on the edge of a shout, harsh with exasperation. 'I simply don't understand you. There must be other ways. You're a psychiatrist, for God's sake. You ought to be able to get a grip.'

He often said things like that. You can handle this, surely, with all that therapy you do. You must have some insight. You must have ways of thinking about this.

This stung me. Did I have any insight that helped? I wondered. Did I have a way of thinking about it? I knew what happens when people grieve, and I thought I knew how to help them – to understand the stages of grief, not to be too scared of the things you feel – the panic attacks, the obsession. I knew about guilt, and about the unconscious mind, the way it can catch you out or undermine you. I had all the books on my shelves, the Penguin volumes of Freud in orange and green and purple. But I wasn't clear that any of this knowledge was any use to me now.

I went to visit Freud's house in Maresfield Gardens once. It was just before I met Mac, one dripping February day when there was nothing to do in London: my guide to London's lesser-known museums had said it was worth a visit. The pavements were silent, the branches dark with wet, the lawns sodden, a solitary blackbird singing out of season. There were just a few of us looking round – an elderly man, a couple of psychoanalytic-looking women in sombre expensive clothes, a hippyish young woman wearing a patchwork waistcoat and feeding a malted milk biscuit to her child.

Freud only lived there for a year – he had advanced cancer already when he came to London from Vienna in 1939, fleeing the Nazis. Yet the house had a powerful atmosphere: perhaps it was the smell of it, a smell of the past, of very old people's houses, nostalgic but not unpleasant, a mixture of polish and musty books and the warmth of central heating on old fabric. There were heavy cabinets painted with stylized flowers, and printed notices with quotes from *The Interpretation of Dreams*, and many sepia photographs of Freud.

In the study, the heart of the place, the curtains were drawn, velvet faded curtains the colour of rust, and the other visitors spoke in lowered voices. All his archaeological finds were there – Buddhas and Chinese horses and tiny angels – and the consulting couch, of course, which was brought from Berggasse 19 in Vienna, and on which his patients would lie while Freud sat out of sight in a velvet tub armchair. The couch was a lovely thing, covered in a rug that was woven of rich colours, ochre and crimson and cobalt, like the intricate beautiful borders in Lydia's fairytale book.

There was a little shop in the conservatory at the back, where discreet piano music was playing, and you could see out into the wide quiet garden, brown and grey except for the few frayed roses that clung to the rosebushes in the circular flower-bed. I lingered by the shelves of books, and wondered if I should buy something erudite and improving, then chose some silver earrings I never wore. And left – weighed down by a sad-ness I didn't understand. Something touched me, in that place where he'd been, surrounded by his possessions, as it never had when I'd first read some of his essays in the library at Liverpool, relishing the glamour of a lost era. I'd had a naive fantasy about the Vienna he'd lived in, a heady mixture of dreams and sex and chocolate, decadent and exciting, the claustrophobic con-sulting rooms and the patients with their buttoned-up blouses and almost unspeakable imaginings: and there was a memory too of a story by Schnitzler I'd read, about dances where the women were naked except for their veils; and a glimpse on some school trip of an opulent Viennese café smelling of sachertorte. Yet that February afternoon, in the place where he'd briefly lived, I felt nothing of that glamour: just felt oppressed by the bleakness of what he'd said. For underlying the extravagant theory there is a terrible teaching: that the rea-soned speech of the present is all but drowned out by the raging of the past. That we cannot escape our history – what has been done to us, what we have done. That none of it can be evaded.

The woman and the child left a little before me. I saw them walking down the street as the heavy door closed behind me and I made my way back to the alleyway that leads to Finchley Road, the two of them moving slowly away along the shiny dark pavement, the child still eating his biscuit and dropping pale crumbs in the puddles, leaving a trail like a fairytale child in a wood, cast out, but hoping to find a way home.

Chapter 15

The door was ajar. He was sitting at his desk, hunched over, writing. He looked up as I went in.

This time I didn't try to sit.

'I wanted to thank you,' I said. 'For what you did after the inquest.'

He stared at me as though he didn't know what I was talking about. I felt a brief anxiety that I'd made the whole thing up – Alysson's mother, his hand touching my shoulder – that it had just been some troubled dream of mine.

'You know, in the café,' I said.

He frowned. 'It shouldn't have happened,' he said.

'Thank you,' I said again. 'For helping me.' And, when he said nothing, 'I would have rung you. But it's more difficult, ringing: I don't really like phones, things can come out wrong, it's harder to say what you mean.' I was gabbling on like a nervous teenager. I'd worked it all out beforehand, exactly what I'd say: this wasn't how I'd planned it.

'So,' he said, his eyes still on my face, searching in me for something, 'you've come all this way to say that?'

'It's my research afternoon – I left early. I just felt I owed it to you, that's all.' I turned to go, determined that this time I'd go in my own time.

I pulled the door open.

'Tessa.'

I turned. He was putting the top on his pen.

'There's a pub round the corner,' he said.

There was a crazy pulse beating away at my temple. I nodded, but he wasn't looking at me.

'We could go there perhaps.'

'OK,' I said. Like it was nothing to me.

'It's a long way to come: I'll buy you a drink,' he said.

'OK,' I said.

'I usually close around this time anyway.'

He piled some papers together, making very little impression on the disorder on his desk, and switched on his answer machine. He moved slowly, heavily – as though he was very tired or somehow resigned. He got up and took his coat down from the peg. As he shook it out, pulling it over his shoulders, I smelt again a faint warm smell of wool.

We went out through the church hall. The women who ran the playgroup were packing up, one or two last children being collected. The hall looked cheerfully chaotic – scraps of paper everywhere, spilt orange juice on the floor, the eight earwigs poster hanging by a single blob of Blu-tack. The women waved at Ben.

Outside it seemed already colder than when I'd come, the sky pink and shining behind the tower of the church, the shadows around the buildings thickening towards evening. There was a sweet unwholesome smell of rotting melons from the market. I only had my jacket on: the cold crept in between my clothes and my skin.

It was a big Victorian pub painted an alarming shade of green, advertising a Big Screen and Quiz Night on Tuesdays. In the doorway he hesitated – it was the only time I'd seen him uncertain.

'I guess this isn't the kind of thing you're used to.'

'It'll be fine. Really,' I said.

It was nearly empty. A couple of women playing darts, a solitary man in a frayed jacket standing at the bar, slowly sipping his beer and looking round unsmiling, the barmaid wiping some glasses in a desultory way. There was lots of rather oppressive dark varnished wood, and on the walls there were etchings of men with guns, and glass cases with stuffed fish in them, and the lampshades on the wall-lights had long red silky fringes. A fleshy Alsatian sprawled on the floor in front of the bar, chewing a plastic bone. There were smells of cigarettes and toasted sandwiches.

He bought beer for both of us. We sat side by side at a wooden settle which was tucked in too close to the table. The space was far too small, my arm brushed his sleeve when I drank. I was very aware of that warm wool smell of his coat.

He put his hand towards mine: for a moment I thought he was going to touch me – my skin prickled. He was pointing at my ring.

'Your husband – is he a doctor too?'

'Yes.'

'A psychiatrist?'

'No. He's a surgeon – a gastro-enterologist,' I said.

'Called?'

'Mac,' I said. Reluctantly, as though I was giving something away.

'Does he know you came to see me?'

'No,' I said. 'He doesn't know.'

I took a quick gulp of beer, then saw to my embarrassment I'd drunk from his glass.

He waved my apology aside.

'And Ralph Patterson? Did you tell him?'

'No,' I said.

He nodded, as though this confirmed something for him.

'I was in a rush when you came to see me before,' he said. 'It was a shock, to be honest, you turning up like that.'

'I thought if I rang you'd refuse to see me,' I said.

'That conversation that we didn't have when you were here before,' he said. 'Perhaps we could have it now. The things you came to say.'

I nodded.

'Could you answer some of my questions?' he said.

'Yes,' I said. After all, I thought, this wasn't secret: it would all come out at the trial.

'Paula Hickey,' he said. 'Tell me some more about her.'

I looked down into my glass.

'She was a patient I was quite close to,' I said. 'Most of us have patients that we're closer to than others – you shouldn't, but you do. People you feel you can help . . .' My voice faded.

'Just tell me,' he said.

So I told him about Paula's history, about her three admissions to the unit: about her delusions about her body.

'Sometimes she functions, sometimes she doesn't. But the drugs only contain the illness – she's never completely well. Sometimes she might seem to be, but if you question her a little, the delusions are still there.'

'Yes,' he said.

'She had a savage start in life, a sadistic foster mother, maybe if it hadn't been so awful she wouldn't have got ill: there's no knowing.'

He nodded.

'I thought I was good with her,' I said. I felt his eyes on my face. I had a sudden dangerous compulsion to be completely open. 'I thought I understood her. Twice when she was very ill I went to see if she needed sectioning, and I was the one who could always calm her down and get her to come into hospital without getting too heavy. There was just something that clicked. She trusted me.'

I couldn't do this any more.

'I'm sorry,' I said.

I hid my face in my hands.

He waited for a moment. I rubbed my face, turned away from him, trying to ground myself in the ordinary things, the hunting pictures, the lights that chased around the fruit machine.

'Go on,' he said. 'Please.'

'She makes things,' I said. 'Jewellery sometimes – earrings out of safety-pins. I thought I could see something special in her – all the talent she had, all wasted. Well, I guess that's not relevant. It touched me though.'

'And she's been violent before?' he said, his eyes never leaving me. 'You knew she was violent?'

I wondered what they would say – Mac, Ralph – if they knew what I was doing. But I pushed the thought away: it seemed to belong to a different place, a different way of being. An orderly place where everything made sense. Not this scruffy pub with this man in his dark overcoat who sat so close to me.

'She punched a male nurse who was restraining her – she'd got into a fight on the ward,' I said. 'Several years ago. When she came into hospital this time, her boyfriend told us she'd taken a knife and she'd threatened him, then she'd tried to cut herself. She's hurt herself before – once she drank some Paraquat – but the knife thing was new.'

We sat silently for a moment.

'Thank you,' he said then. 'For telling me.'

Someone behind the bar put on a tape: the pub flooded with sudden sound, tinny and harsh, it wasn't a very good sound system. Ben flinched. I felt how raw and strained he was: how every sensation was magnified, overwhelming.

'This is ghastly,' he said. 'We can't talk with this going on.'

'No,' I said.

145

'Perhaps we could go somewhere?' he said. 'Somewhere we could talk?'

'OK,' I said.

'There's a path I know by the river,' he said. 'There's a market there on Sundays, but it's usually quite quiet. That would be better, wouldn't it? What do you think?'

'Sure,' I said. That fast light pulse again, skittering in my temple.

We got up, left our beer, went towards the door. Halfway there he stopped, suddenly, awkwardly, like he'd changed his mind.

'Won't you be cold, though?' he said, looking me up and down in my thin jacket. 'You haven't got a coat. You'll be cold.'

'I'll be all right.'

The street lights were on now and the street was full of noise, it was just before the rush hour really got going. His car was parked by the church.

He drove carefully: it seemed to confirm the impression I'd had of him when first we'd met – that the passion and rage in him were all to do with the grief, not usually part of him. The sky was a deeper pink now, dazzling, the skyline of gas holders and chimneys and the roofs of buildings, sharp and precise as though cut from black paper. People in the street walked hurriedly, breathing on their fingers, hunched against the cold.

It wasn't far. There was a car park, almost empty, a few skips. The market, as he'd said, was closed, but there were some permanent stalls, roofed in, and a few Christmas lights strung from roof to roof to advertise the place. He took me past the market stalls to a footbridge over the river. The main bridge where the road crossed the river was a few yards off to our right: the rush-hour traffic roared across it. We walked over the footbridge, turned away from the road, followed a gravel path along the riverbank. There was a rich smell under the trees, of sodden leaves and water. Big willows leaned into the river, their branches hanging down like unkempt crinkled hair. The sound of the traffic faded behind us.

'It's very quiet,' I said stupidly.

'I come here sometimes when I'm trying to think,' he said.

There was a noticeboard by the path with historical information. I stopped and looked at it, but sap from the tree above had dropped and congealed on the glass, and the words were covered over and couldn't be read.

'There was an abbey here in the Middle Ages,' he said. 'They weren't allowed to just knock it down so they buried it under the road.'

The path followed the river. There were matted bushes – nettles, and bramble bushes with last year's unpicked blackberries, dark and dried out as though a fire had passed over them. On the other side of this strip of waste land where we walked, there was the back of an industrial estate: the lights were still on in some of the warehouses. You could hear the river against the railway sleepers set into the banks, a lapping sound like the slap of an open palm, and the crackling of powerlines, and the soft rushing of the motors that drove the ventilators in the warehouses. The river ran quickly here, with its random cargo of plastic bags and sandwich wrappers and tyres. Kentucky Fried Chicken boxes and sheets of paper were white against the water, like the fallen petals of some obscure pale flower.

'The river's full of rubbish,' I said, searching for something to say.

'I like it here,' he said. Defensively, as though he didn't like me criticizing the place. 'I've seen burnet moths in the summer.'

We walked for a while without speaking. There were street lamps here and there, orange light spilling briefly across us,

147

and the deadnettle flowers were luminous in the gloom. It felt very hidden, although the rush-hour traffic wasn't so far away: one of those places round the backs of things which nobody tends or cuts down, where foxes dig and surprising flowers flourish.

'I went to see her,' he said.

I was confused for a moment – then realized he was still in the conversation we'd had in the pub.

'Paula Hickey?'

'Yes.'

'You went to see Paula? In the secure unit?'

'Yes,' he said. 'Her doctor sat in with us. I told him before-hand what I was going to say.'

'Why did you go?' I said.

'It's not as though we're enemies exactly.' He turned to me. 'I don't want you to think I blame Paula. I know she wasn't responsible for what she did.'

'No.'

But if he doesn't blame Paula, I thought, then the murderer is me.

'How was she?' I said.

'A bit better apparently,' he said. 'Better than when . . . better than she was. We talked for about ten minutes – she was getting agitated towards the end.'

'Oh,' I said. I wondered what course their conversation could possibly have taken.

'Liam has got her a solicitor,' he said. 'After the trial, she's probably going to sue the Trust. To claim that they had a duty of care towards her and they failed in their duty.'

'Will you do that too?' I said.

'I can't,' he said. 'The Trust didn't have any duty of care towards Alysson. I don't know yet what I'll do.'

It was almost dark: the moon was rising over the warehouses. There were gardens now on the other side of the river: where people hadn't drawn their curtains, the light from their houses shone out over muddy trampled lawns. The pale blue paint on a child's swing stood out in the dusk, as though it was fluorescent, the swing seat tied up on top so it wouldn't get wet. Our shadows crossed and blended as we walked.

'I sat by Alysson's bed for that whole day before she died,' he said. 'Drinking coffee from those awful styrofoam cups – watching the monitors, watching her face.'

I think I made some kind of noise.

'It's the hope that kills you,' he said. 'It's the worst thing. If you didn't have any hope it wouldn't be so hard.'

'Is that why you brought me here?' I said. 'To tell me that? Don't you think I can picture it for myself?'

He didn't say anything and we walked on for a while, the moon hanging there like a yellow fruit above us, my shadow disappearing into his.

'I'm sorry,' he said then. He sounded tired. He put his hand on my arm: the fabric of my jacket was so thin, I could feel his hand precisely, every finger, as though he had touched my bare skin. 'I shouldn't have said that,' he said. 'There's something in me that wants to tell you these things. Something compulsive. I don't know if it's wanting to hurt you – or just wanting you to know what it's like so you'll understand.'

'Maybe those two things aren't so very different,' I said.

He didn't respond. There was no sound but the river, and the hushed sigh of the ventilators, our footsteps crunching, our breath. It came to me that this was a dangerous place: not a place I'd dream of walking after dark on my own. If you got into trouble, if someone approached you and you were worried or scared, you'd have to call out to the houses over the water, and they seemed so far away, you could shout but no-one could reach you, you'd be cut off from help by the dark quiet surge of the river.

He read my thought.

149

'D'you want to go back now?' he said. 'We could if you like.'

'No,' I said. 'I don't mind.'

'You're too cold,' he said. 'You're shivering. We should go back. We shouldn't go any further.'

'I'm all right,' I said. But it was true. My teeth were chattering.

'Have this,' he said.

He slipped off his coat and put it round my shoulders. It was warm but very heavy: it slowed me down.

'What are you thinking?' he said. He stopped walking and I stopped too. 'I can't tell what you're thinking. I can't see you properly with all that hair.' And he pushed the hair off the sides of my face with both hands, held it back quite firmly, and bent down and kissed me. Quite tentatively at first, his lips just brushing mine, then definitely, deeply, like a man who has his answer, who knows his mind. We kissed for a long time, and I was very afraid, afraid because of the sexual charge of it, feeling him all around and in me – his coat, his arms, his mouth warm against mine, the pressure of his tongue inside my mouth – afraid because of what might happen when we stopped. I just went on kissing him and felt my whole being unravelling. Whatever had held me together these past four weeks had finally come undone.

When we pulled away from one another I found that I was crying, like I hadn't cried since it happened, since Alysson died.

He had that embarrassed look that men always have when you cry. He put out his hand and tried to wipe the tears away. His warm hand all over my face.

'I've made you cry,' he said.

'No,' I said. 'It's not you.'

I could feel my nose running. I hunted out a crumpled tissue from somewhere in my jacket.

'I'm sorry,' I said. 'I think I'd better go home.'

'Yes,' he said. 'Yes, of course. Of course you must.'

We turned, walked back silently under the powerlines and the yellow moon, between the bramble bushes with their dark scorched fruit. We were walking downstream now, so the river seemed to flow faster, the spectral flowers of rubbish moving rapidly past. It didn't take long to get back, though I felt we'd walked so far.

'I'll drop you at the station,' he said, when we got to the car park. 'Or would you like me to take you further?'

'No, that's fine,' I said.

We sat silently in the car. When we got to the station, I got out and took off his coat and folded it and put it on the seat. I was so cold without it, I felt I would die from the cold.

He didn't touch me, just leant across the passenger seat towards me.

'I want you to come and see me again,' he said.

'I don't know,' I said. 'I don't know whether I should.'

He didn't smile when we said goodbye. It was one of the many strange things about it all – that we kissed long before we saw each other smile.

Waiting on the platform, going back to Wimbledon on the slow train, worrying if people could see I'd been crying, if everything that had happened was written in my face, I tried to make sense of it. And I couldn't – just thought of his touch, his kiss, his hands on my face, and couldn't make sense of any of it at all. So I tried to tell myself that a kiss is not irrevocable: that it could all be undone.

Chapter 16

But the next week I went there again.

The door was shut and I could hear voices, Ben's voice, soothing, persistent, and a woman's voice, high-pitched, with a break in it as though she'd been crying or was about to cry. I wondered what it was like for him, having to cope with other people's troubles when in the grip of such distress himself.

I knocked: he came to the door. I could see the woman behind him, her bleached hair, frayed face, and the tiredness round her eyes. She had a cigarette in her hand, the air was thick and smeared with smoke. A toddler on her lap was sucking at the feet of a bedraggled Barbie.

'I've got someone with me,' he said.

'I'm sorry,' I said.

'Don't go,' he said.

'I'll wait in the hall,' I said.

I went out and sat at the edge of the hall just under the clock, feeling superfluous there in my work clothes amid the busy vivid children, expecting them all to stare. But no-one bothered about me except Flora – who came up grinning, and rested her head in my lap. I tickled her with the handpuppet and read her *Where The Wild Things Are* and the women looked over and smiled, and all the time I felt afraid, my body poised for flight.

I was gathering up my things to go, when he came to the doorway and called me.

I followed him back to the office. We stood there in the whiteness of the smoke looking at one another.

'I live round the corner,' he said.

I nodded very slightly, watching his mouth, his face.

'We could go there if you like,' he said. 'Would you like that?'

'OK,' I said. Casually. Maybe I even shrugged a little, as though it didn't really matter.

We walked, not saying anything: past the pub, down a side street of Edwardian terraces, most of them shabby, with lumps of pebbledash coming off or rusting cars outside, but a few with cream linen curtains and palms in blue glazed pots in the windows. A woman in a black veil walked in front of us: we had to step out into the road to pass her. It was cold, with a chill rain, and the thin banal light of early afternoon, a time without enchantment. We were awkward together, bumping into each other as we turned into his street, nothing seemed to flow. I couldn't work out his mood – whether he was nervous or even angry – didn't know if he wanted to be here with me at all.

His was one of the houses with pale curtains and a palm. There was a box hedge and the dustbins were out in front of the house. He unlocked the door and ushered me in, his hand on my elbow for a moment.

The hall was bare – no carpet, a dado rail, the walls stripped to the plaster. There was a Victorian hallstand, a mirror in an elaborate gilt frame, and lozenges of stained glass above the door: squares of light the colour of claret fell on the floor.

'It needs decorating of course. We never got round to decorating this bit,' he said.

153

He pushed the door shut behind him. A tile that had come unstuck rattled under my foot as I turned to him. We stood there and looked at one another for a moment, his eyes dilated and dark in the dimness of the hall, a square of stained light falling on his shoulder. Then he reached out a hand and took the clip out of my hair, I felt my hair spilling down onto my shoulders, felt the weight of it as it fell. I heard myself gasp. He put the clip down on the hall table, his eyes never leaving mine, and kissed me, pushing me back against the wall so the dado rail cut into my back, pressing himself into me, so I could feel all the hard outlines of him against me – the hardness of his face, his hands, his penis, as though he was imprinting himself on me, as though forcing the shape of me to change, to mould to him. He kissed me till I had to turn my mouth away, and I felt my heart pounding against his chest, the sensation magnified because of the way he pressed against me.

He took me upstairs, led me into one of the back bedrooms – a small room with a wardrobe along one wall and a mattress laid out on the floor.

'This is the spare room,' he said, as though he could read my thought. 'We never slept in here.'

'It's cold,' I said, shuddering a little, hugging my arms around me.

'I could put on the heating,' he said. 'But it wouldn't warm up in time.'

There was an old-fashioned one-bar electric fire. He plugged it in: it smelt of scorched dust as it heated up. There was a stylish but crooked blind of wooden slats: he pulled it down, cursing a bit when it wouldn't come straight, the bleached light filtering in between the slats. I was glad he did that, though the room wasn't overlooked.

We made love as though we had no choice, undoing one another's clothes with a kind of desperation. He flung my clothes down on the floor, not looking where they fell, and

I worried briefly that something might land on the fire, that the whole place would burn. My own fingers were slow, still cold, defeated by his belt, so he did it himself. The thin white afternoon light fell on him through the slats; his pale skin glimmered. There was purple veining on his penis and the insides of his arms: I wanted to look and look at him, but felt shy, felt that I had no right. He kept his shirt half-on, and I hated that, it made the whole thing seem still more temporary – something done in haste, with as little concession as possible. But I couldn't ask him to take it off, I couldn't say anything that first time: we made love wordlessly, quick and secret as thieves. It was as though we felt our words might give us away: as though if we spoke we would realize who we were.

He pulled me down onto the mattress, tipping over side-ways: it was a long way to fall, I noticed I'd hurt my ankle, then stopped noticing, aware only of the shocking softness of certain parts of his skin, of the taste of salt on him, of the moving of his hard thoughtful hands over and into me, everything in me opening up to him. He moved down me, used his mouth on me as though he liked to do it, hungrily, as though he was hungry for my response, so I came twice in rapid succession with an ease and a crying-out intensity that almost shamed me, and he'd have gone on, he only stopped because I told him to, feeling I'd be completely undone if I carried on. When he turned me over and pushed inside me, wanting to come without seeing my face perhaps, the electric fire smell hit me, scorched, a little dangerous, I felt the glare of it over my face like a kind of violence, had to close my eyes.

We lay together for a while, my head on his shoulder, still saying nothing. But he got up far too soon and started to put on his clothes. I turned away on my side, I wished there was a sheet to cover me. A sudden sadness washed through me, an overwhelming thing – desolation, almost. I watched him, trying to read him – his hurried movements, his bowed head,

155

his silence – and I feared he felt it too. It was as though by making love we'd been seeking to heal something, and of course it hadn't happened, and the hollowness of that fantasy we'd had had been exposed: so now it was all even worse than before.

He buttoned up his shirt. I knew in a moment he'd turn to me and say something and try to make it all ordinary again. I was so afraid he was going to say he was sorry – that it had been an aberration, that we both knew it – and of course we must both pretend it had never happened. I feared that so much: I felt if he said that I wouldn't be able to bear it.

He stood in the doorway looking down at me, doing up his belt.

'It's so bloody cold in this house,' he said. 'We could have some coffee. Would you like coffee?'

'Yes,' I said. 'Yes, I would.'

I had a huge sense of reprieve. Coffee, talking together: these are the things that ordinary lovers do.

He went downstairs. I could hear him clattering in the kitchen, the sharp sounds of washing up, the kettle going on.

I got up, put on my clothes. They felt weirdly uncomfortable, as though my skin was newly sensitive, like something had been peeled away, the sharp wool cuffs of my smart jacket grazing my wrists when I raised my hands to shake my hair out from under my collar.

I went downstairs. You had to go through the back room to get to the kitchen. It was a pleasant room, bookshelves, a stripped floor, two red IKEA sofas: simple, slightly hippyish taste. Yet it felt neglected, sad, the horror of what had happened hanging about here, where she had lived, where Ben now grieved for her. It was dusty, not tidied – it seemed he'd done nothing since Alysson died, just left it. There were several unwashed coffee cups, stained inside – they must have had black coffee in them.

I lingered in front of his bookshelves for a moment – just like a perfectly normal adulteress, who looks for clues to the man she loves, signs of his taste. There were lots of novels. Nothing technical – his work books he presumably kept elsewhere. I ran my eyes over the titles, wondering which ones he'd liked, which he'd tried and given up: did he read thrillers to get him to sleep, had he too been defeated by *The Satanic Verses*, still pristine in its jacket, in spite of his best intentions? But I couldn't ask, because any of them might have been hers. And thought how strange it was – these places where I couldn't step. I could let him see my neediness and hunger for him, and how my face contorted when I came – yet couldn't possibly say, This copy of *Cold Mountain*, is it yours or hers?

I needed badly to pee. He showed me to the downstairs bathroom. I went in, shut the door. There was the usual clutter – dental floss and mouthwash – and a bottle of antidepressants – Dothiapin – unopened: prescribed for him perhaps when Alysson died. And then I saw with a thumping heart that the shelf above the basin was covered with her things – her bottle of L'Air du Temps, her body lotion, makeup – the pretty containers all thickly furred with dust like an animal's pelt: and a hairbrush matted with long dark curly hairs. Tears spilled from my eyes and I scrubbed at my face with a bit of loo paper, but the tears just went on coming, I was scared they'd never stop.

I washed my face, but I was still crying when I went back into the kitchen. He saw but didn't say anything. He gave me my coffee. I clutched it to me, welcoming the warmth of the mug on my hands.

It was a long thin kitchen like Victorian terraces often have, built out into the yard, with a small pine table and a Georgia O'Keefe calendar and old kitchen units that didn't fit together properly. On the floor in the corner there was a paint tray with a roller: the paint had dried on it, it had never been washed out,

157

as though someone had been interrupted right in the middle of decorating. I went to the window, looked out.

'Oh,' I said. 'Oh. That's so beautiful.'

It was a small yard – no bigger than mine. It was only overlooked from one side, and surrounded by high walls of London brick in soft warm complicated colours, and lovingly tended, full of plants, full of promise, of things about to happen.

He unlocked the door.

'We could go out if you like,' he said.

It was raining still: the rain spattered the surface of my coffee.

There was a little flower-bed, with straggly plants in it, dormant for the moment, with tiny dried leaves – herbs, perhaps, and lavender. Old fruit trees grew up the walls, shaped into fans and espaliers, reaching out with extraordinary grace, the smooth tendrils at the ends of their branches pink and shiny like skin. Pot plants had been put down all anyhow, some of the pots blue or sea-green like in Mediterranean back yards, the plants lovely even now in February because of the intricate shapes of the bare twigs, the varied subtle colours of the bark, but you could tell that by April or May, it would all be a lavish green tangle and full of flowers. There was a smell of hyacinths.

'I love this,' I said. 'I love walled gardens. They make you feel so safe.' Then thought how strange this was – to say this here, to feel for a moment safe.

'It was good already when we bought it,' he said. 'The fig and the pear were here already – well, obviously. But I like growing things.'

There were drifts of dead leaves, pink and purple and brown, crumbling to a soft damp dust under our feet. Ben looked at the heaps of leaves as though suddenly noticing them, suddenly seeing the place with my eyes.

'I haven't swept it for a while,' he said.

'No,' I said. 'Well, you wouldn't have.'

We stood and drank our coffee. It was less oppressive here, out in the freshness, away from the sadness of the house, the traces of her.

'There are lots more plants to bring out later,' he said. 'The tender ones. I keep them in one of the bedrooms till the frost stops. I'll show you what's here.'

He took me round his yard and showed me the plants: told me their names – Latinate and formal, some of them, but sounding intimate, the way he said them, like the names of women he'd loved. He showed me the camellia and the agapanthus and the pear, which was called Doyenne du Comice, and the little mulberry tree that, he said, only produced a couple of fruit, so ephemeral, so delicious, just a slick of sugar and dark like wine, then gone. I didn't have to worry whether these were hers or his: I knew they were his from the way he touched them. I liked watching his hands, the turn of his wrists, and the whiteness of his wrists and their lilac veining, and the way he pushed up the sleeves of his shirt and dug his fingers in, pulling away a weed or two from the soil in the pots, lightly touching the edges of the leaves or moving them apart to show me the tiny buds, bitter green, secret, swelling, and the hyacinths with their strong clear columns of flowers blue as water that were opening under the pear tree, with their powdery clingy scent, that's a little claustrophobic, yet so sweet.

'They're so lovely,' I said. 'I don't have any plants. Well, just two scrappy fir trees. It's the nurturing they need: really, I'm hopeless at it.'

'Well, that's not very surprising, it's what you do all day,' he said. 'I don't suppose you've much energy for it when you get home.'

I stood there, the rain falling into my coffee.

'I've tried,' I said, 'but I always forget to water them. Quite

159

honestly, I don't think I'm any good at looking after things, they always die on me.' I stopped, appalled.

He said nothing.

I turned away. 'I think I'd better go,' I said.

'You haven't finished your coffee,' he said.

If he'd touched me I'd have stayed for a while, tried to make it all right, but he didn't.

I shook my head. I thought I might cry again.

'Well,' I said. 'You know, I really think I should go.'

I put my coffee cup in the sink, went into the hall. I found my handbag, took out my comb, and started combing my hair, looking in the mirror with its opulent gilt frame. The glass was flawed perhaps: I looked weird in it – as though I'd been taken apart and put back together again and the pieces didn't quite fit together properly. He'd followed me, he stood watching me, a little apart, leaning against the wall.

I felt such a need to say something – knowing I somehow had to find my way back to the normal world, the street, the hospital, my life with Mac. I felt I had to talk about it, to spell it all out, to ask the questions that might bring all this back into relationship with the world out there. How can we do this – when I'm married and Alysson is dead and you have every right to hate me? How can we?

But I said nothing.

I took my clasp from the hall table where he'd put it and started to gather up my hair. He watched me in the mirror. Seeing the way he watched me, I felt a sudden sharp longing to make love again, to feel his weight on me, pressing into me, to lose myself, to feel him deep inside me, not to have to make sense of everything.

I pulled the hair up off my neck, put in the clasp, exposing my skin. He moved forward a little, put out his hand, ran one finger slowly down the back of my neck, his finger tracing out the curve of every bone, sliding his finger down as far

160

as he could inside the back of my jacket, so the front of
the collar caught against my throat. I could smell the earth
on his hands.

'Ring me,' he said.

'Yes,' I said.

On the edge of the street it was colder, wetter than in his
yard: the wind was keen there. My clothes felt light, thin on
me, the cold coming in.

Chapter 17

I didn't ring, I don't know why. It wasn't just a fear of being overheard. I think I needed to keep him separate: not to bring his voice, his presence, into my house, my work. But I always knew what I was going to do.

It was windy all week. When I tried to open the kitchen door, it pushed back against me, as if someone was there behind it, and last year's leaves blew in and littered my tiles. I swept them up and they crumbled into a dust that was dull and pale as moths' wings.

A woman came to my house one evening. She had a child and gold teeth: she was wearing a grubby flowery frock and a headscarf and blue ankle-socks. She thrust a postcard at me, a misspelt message in biro, in block letters. I glanced at it, could only pick out Albania. The child held out her hand for money: the woman pushed back her headscarf, touched her oily dark hair. 'Shamp?' she said, 'Shamp?' I found her an unopened bottle of Pantene Pro-V and gave the child some change. The next day they came back and I didn't know what to do. So I shook my head and they went away again, grumbling. I felt troubled, dirty, like I'd injured someone.

On Saturday we went to dinner at Brendan's. His flat is comfortable but very male, with an elaborate sound system and downlighters. He had a new woman, called Ginny. She was nervous and intense, in a trendy grey sweater. She wrote, she said, for a women's magazine. She told us, over Brendan's excellent *soupe de poissons*, how fed up she was with her new editor. Ginny wrote an advice column where she interviewed people at length about their problems, and this editor wouldn't let her ever mention the past, or people's childhoods. Show people as they are here and now, she'd been told. None of that Freudian stuff. I mused on this, sipping my *soupe de poissons*. What life would be like if it was just here and now. Every day fresh and new, the past wiped away, no absent others crowding in between you and those you love, no ghosts, no revenants. Mac didn't say anything, but I knew he'd be sympathetic to the magazine editor.

We moved on to the guinea fowl: Brendan and Ginny talked about how they'd met, at a fortieth birthday party given by a mutual friend, pleasantly drunk and playing a game of Sardines – where somebody hides and everybody has to find them and join them, all squashed up together behind the shower curtain. We had a conversation about interesting subsets of lovers: those like Brendan and Ginny who discover a profound sexual attraction during party games; those who meet when working on opposite sides in a political campaign. Ginny had a friend who'd confessed she'd been moved to commit adultery by a poem by Miroslav Holub, full of the fear of death, that she'd seen on a District Line tube train.

I slept better. Something, it seemed, had eased: that tension that had had me waking at three in the morning with my teeth clenched together. But my dreams were still troubled. Once I dreamt of being on a crowded road somewhere in the country with many refugees in sandals and blue headscarves, and Mac was there, and Ben, and Ben reached out to touch my mouth with his hand, the tenderness of that touch undoing me even in the dream, and I couldn't move away yet was terrified in the dream that everyone would know. And I dreamt of random sexual encounters with specific men I knew – though rarely Ben: and sometimes I had dreams that shocked me, dreams of violence, of a nameless man who came up to me from behind and took off my clothes and blindfolded me: and the dreams were all shot through with the scent of hyacinths. I had never before smelt anything so clearly in my dreams.

On Friday, my research afternoon, I didn't go to the library. I took the tube to Wimbledon, then the blue and yellow overground train, got out at the empty station where the convolvulus was opening up on the fence, its flowers like cups of china, and went down the road to the advice centre. It was a hot clear day, the sky blue and dazzling. I did it all without thinking, some faculty completely suspended, not letting my mind rest or linger on anything.

I went through the church hall, where the children were making pictures with glue and kidney beans and the women nodded at me as though I was expected and Flora rushed up and gave me a big disorganized hug. And I went into the corridor at the back, my heart noisy as a teenager's.

He was on his own, writing something. We didn't smile.

'I could close now,' he said.

'Should you do that? I mean, what if someone needs you?' I said, worrying that this was wrong and irresponsible and my fault. In the midst of all the other wrong-doing.

'I don't see why not,' he said. 'I'll leave a note on the door. I'll come back later. I've got lots of paperwork to do – I can do it as easily then as now.'

We walked quickly round to his house, talking about the weather. We went upstairs to the spare room and he pulled down the blind and kissed me and undid the buttons of my cardigan, easing each button carefully out of its hole, dragging cool fingers down my stomach till I thought I'd unravel completely. We fell over onto the mattress and took off all our clothes and made love: wordlessly, again, but this time slowly, easily. I felt it all with such vividness, his slow and elaborate investigation of my body, his warm slide into me, the way his breathing quickened. Everything beyond those walls was cancelled out, as though it had ceased to exist. On top of him, looking down at him, feeling him deep inside me, I saw how the bars of light and shade where the sun shone through the slatted blind fell across us, across my thighs, across his body, his face – joining us, these dark lines like brands – and I watched him come, crying out but saying nothing, his face twisted up, closing his eyes.

As I lay wrapped round him, I saw that the room was different – it had been dusted, things had been put away, it no longer had that neglected look, the sheets smelt cleanly of Alysson's soap powder: something had changed in him.

He got up far too soon for me, like he had before, and pulled on his clothes and went down to the kitchen.

He was leaning against the sink when I joined him, waiting for the kettle. Some climbing plant that had draped itself round the window-frame was coming into leaf, a delicate fretwork of tiny heart-shaped leaves.

'How long have you got?' he said.

'I'm not in a rush,' I said.

'We could go out,' he said. 'We could go off somewhere perhaps.'

'I'd like that,' I said.

'I don't stay in much,' he said. 'Not since it happened. Half the time I can't stand being here. I'd go mad if I stayed in.'

We drove to Wimbledon, parked at the edge of the common, where there was a hot smell of new tarmac: some workmen were resurfacing the path. At the weekends it would be busy here, but today there was hardly anyone around. He

165

took me through some wrought iron gates, into a little formal place called Cannizaro Park: I hadn't known it was there. It was neat, pretty, like a child's drawing, with a glittery fountain and, everywhere, white flowers – wall-flowers with their velvety cinnamon smell, and tulips like cupped hands, and a haze of tiny edging plants whose names I didn't know. There was a big old house that now seemed to be a hotel or conference centre. A woman in a dark jacket looked out from a first-floor window, her hands on the sill, unsmiling, very still, her gaze resting lightly on us for a moment, the cool incurious stare of a stranger: the room behind her was all in shadow, black as a room at night against the brightness outside.

The wind was very warm. I pushed up the sleeves of my cardigan, feeling the air moving over my skin.

'You want to just soak it up,' I said. 'Like in Scandinavia, when the sun first comes out in the spring, and people just go out and do nothing, just sit in it.'

'Yes,' he said. But he didn't take off his jacket.

We walked down a silky sweep of lawn, the sappy smell of crushed grass all around us. There was a pond, its banks brimming with bluebells, where mothers with toddlers were throwing bread to the ducks: the water held the blue of the sky and the bluebells, held them very still, like something precious. We passed purple azaleas, ultra-violet bright, their smell when I buried my nose in them musty, unwholesome. At the bottom of the slope there was a rougher place, some grass between two little brooks with soft margins of marsh, next to the golf course. The giant rhubarb was just coming out, its leaves scrunched-up and crinkly, and there were arums, unnaturally yellow, as though dipped in some chemical. A casual blue butterfly hovered above the stream.

We didn't talk much. There were things I could have told him, yearned to tell him: of the wrongness of what we were doing, and of my longing for it – the warring of these things in me. The words were there on the tip of my tongue, but somehow couldn't be said.

In the roots of a tree we found a weird fungus, poisonous-looking, with frilly purple tissue-paper flowers. Ben knew its name.

'Look,' he said, 'the leaves are white: it's got no chlorophyll, because it's a parasite, it just feeds off the tree.'

'You know a lot of things,' I said, mocking him a little.

When we bent together to look at it, I could smell his skin.

We took a muddy track past some allotments, where men in white vests dug laconically but nothing much was growing yet. You could hear the sound of spades, smell the rich serious scent of broken earth. We came out onto the common, walked through the harsh grass and the shaggy polleny dandelions, across anthills where you could easily turn your ankle: to one side, the road round the common, and the big expensive houses with steps up to the front doors and ruched curtains at the windows. They seemed to speak of a life of impossible glamour, of great French windows opening onto terraces, of women with gold at their throats and wrists, whose long skirts whispered silkily in the grass. And I told him about the house on the beach where I'd played with Jed, the stories we'd told, the things we'd dreamed of. That was easy, that I could talk about. Far-off things.

'I didn't know you had a brother,' he said. 'That wasn't how I imagined it somehow.'

'How did you imagine it?' I said.

'I thought you'd be an only child. There's something so solitary about you,' he said.

This surprised me, and yet I could see it was true. I wondered what else he knew about me – things perhaps that I scarcely knew myself.

The path led through an oakwood on the way back to the

car. The trees had no leaves yet: the colours of the wood, the russets and browns of the bark, the tired matt purple of the brambles, the faded smokiness of last year's leaves – these seemed all wrong against the summery brilliance of the sky. It was absolutely still except for the many birds, the shimmer of their singing, the rustle and clap of their wings amid the bare branches. When I closed my eyes when he kissed me – a little uneasy at first, worried we might be seen, then just giving in, for a moment simply not caring, wanting him to possess me again, to push his hands between my clothes and my skin – I could still see the colour and movement against my lids, the dazzle of the sky, the flickering of wings.

Chapter 18

This became our pattern. All loves, I guess, have their conventions, their rules. Even this most illicit love, which I sometimes pretended wasn't even happening, telling myself it was just some baroque fantasy, an invention of my over-heated imagination – this too had some kind of organization. Even when we're at our most fevered and anarchic, we keep some things the same.

I went there every Friday, on the afternoon I was meant to spend in the library. I just turned up at his office, I never rang. To ring felt far too risky – I might be overheard, or maybe it was more complicated than that, maybe I couldn't bear to bring together these different worlds I inhabited – Ben as my lover intruding into the everyday world of the hospital where he was the opponent, the enemy: where people speculated on what he might be planning and waited nervously for his next move. So, unannounced but expected, I'd take the train to Wimbledon, then the branch line south, and get out at the echoey station, where things were starting to change, plants scrambling over the fencing, the banks spilling over with a foam of bramble flowers – all the fattening, the reaching up, the opening out, of spring – and I'd go down the road past the sooty church where there was a new hoarding: God's love is not Lent. It is given and lasts for ever: and I'd come to his office, always afraid – this too was part of the pattern – and we'd walk round to his house and make love, not speaking, with a kind of compulsiveness that made the pleasure, though so intense, almost secondary. Afterwards we'd drink coffee in his yard where the hyacinths were over now, but some white narcissi were nodding in a pot, their petals thin and milky, with their rainy freshwater scent, and the twisted old fig tree was coming into leaf. Then, even if it was raining or cold, we'd drive off and walk for an hour or two in one of those places he knew.

It suited me, this pattern. The house oppressed me always. It was all so full of her still, as the walls of warehouses where spices have been stored will hold those smells for years, the very fabric of the place impregnated with the opulence of cinnamon and ginger. I could breathe more easily elsewhere, away from that sense of her – her footprints in the dust and the fingerprints of her taste and the sheets smelling of the soap powder she'd chosen and the long dark hairs in the hairbrush in the bathroom. But in him I sensed a need that was much more intense than mine – an imperative to keep moving.

He was by nature, I learned, a physically active man: who played lots of squash, who didn't find stillness soothing, whose worst fear, like many men's, was of some injury or mutilation that would leave him paralysed. And he'd always walked, he said – to work out ideas, plan his lectures, get to grips with some complex benefits issue – but with Alysson's death he'd become still more driven, always moving on. It's an animal thing, that anxious restlessness of grieving, a drive that's found in all creatures that mate for life, the desolate search that's frustrated over and over: like the snow goose when his mate dies, flying across many acres, looking for her. I saw that restlessness in the way he'd drum his fingers as he'd wait for

170

the kettle to boil, in the twitch under his eyebrow that he'd try to brush away, in the way he'd pace if we were drinking coffee in the yard – walking up and down, pausing to lightly touch a leaf, to pull up a weed from a pot, then pacing again. It was perhaps why I never felt really at peace with my head on his shoulder: even briefly satiated after sex. He'd lie there because he knew I needed that, wanting to be held, not to part too quickly. But it was an effort for him: he'd shift, get up too soon, hastily pull on his clothes. I learnt not to hate this. Sometimes I wondered if even the most cerebral part of his response to her death – that energy that had been directed at first at me, the urge to litigate, to right this wrong – was also in its way an expression of that animal urge that drove him. Trying to find her.

I liked the going out, all the places he knew. He took me to secret places in the heart of the city: an overgrown churchyard with fat glossy kingcups and a stone marking a plague pit; a path past hills of waste and rubbish, grassed over, where we heard the thin sweet singing of a skylark although it was still so early in the year; a railway cutting where mallow and willowherb grew. Unpromising places with unexpected gifts. Once we saw a fox, somehow dissolute, with its melancholy face, leaping off a wall, nimble like water. Once on Wimbledon Common we saw four gold parakeets that must have ecaped from somewhere, perching high in an oak tree, tiny, bright, precise, as if they were carved from metal: the skin of my throat got stretched and sore from staring up at them. And we went again on the walk by the river where the abbey was buried – the place where we'd first kissed.

We were earlier than we'd been that time and the market was still open, though there weren't many people about. There were clothes stalls smelling richly of leather, and flower stalls, and New Age stalls selling dream-catchers with pale feathers and

171

tiny Feng Shui dragons the colour of blood to enhance your prosperity.

'Those are so pretty,' I said idly, passing the flower stall, pointing out some sprays of little purple flowers in cellophane. They were Peruvian lilies, he said. He bought me some, like proper lovers do. I was so touched, I kissed his cheek.

'But how can I take them home?' I said.

'It's not that difficult, surely,' he said, a little impatient with my feebleness. 'Say you bought them for yourself.'

So I did, when Mac asked – when he said how they were kind of nice, but why the hell had I bought them when that wasn't at all like me – to buy flowers.

'I'm trying to be positive,' I said.

'Well, that's good,' said Mac. 'At least you seem to have got over that depression. Really you're looking tons better now.'

'I'm feeling better,' I said. Not meeting his eye.

I couldn't bear to throw them away – even when they were nearly over – the leaves yellow and tatty, the petals washed out and pale as though soaked for too long in water, the stamens the colour of dirt: but the shape of the flowers still intact, still pretty; the flowers outlasting the leaves. Then binned them hurriedly, suddenly scared that they might give me away, these delicate dying flowers.

As we walked in the hidden places he'd found, the bedraggled lost gardens of Mitcham or Morden, he started to open up to me a little. It didn't happen always. There'd be times when he'd be silent, hard to reach, when I'd make a few attempts at conversation and he'd be monosyllabic and unapproachable, and we'd walk for ages without saying anything, till the silence itself became a heavy thing, pushing down on us, pushing us further apart. But sometimes he'd relax and tell me about himself and this was important to me: I needed to make this into a proper relationship, a relationship with other kinds of connection, so it wasn't just about this astonishing sex we had.

172

Yet our talking was often fraught – full of places to skirt round with care, places you could fall into. There were many things we couldn't say or were scared to talk about – my life with Mac, my work, his life with Alysson – and this too was part of the patterning of our love: the many forbidden things. Mostly we talked about our distant pasts, our childhoods, where we came from: never where we were going to.

His father had been a Methodist minister in the West Midlands, his childhood spent in gloomy inner city manses, the annual treat a fortnight in a Methodist boarding-house in Worthing, with crab paste sandwiches on the blowy beach. His parents were both now dead: his father had been a patriarch in his own home, his congregation always coming first; his mother a gentle complaining woman from Roscommon who had migraines and did a lot of darning. He had one sister, older than him, now a special needs teacher. It had been a childhood without culture – no music or art, few books that were read for pleasure – he made occasional errors in pronunciation, as people do who've been educated beyond their class and read more widely than they've talked: I know I do this too. For his parents, the aesthetic had been an indulgence, an irrelevance. The children wore hand-me-downs, furniture was chosen for its usefulness, and if the garden got out of hand, his father hired a flame-thrower. So I understood the flowers in his yard, the useless beautiful things that clambered all over his walls, trailing their long elegant fingers everywhere, the agapanthus, the smell of hyacinth: and the absolute lure of a woman as extravagantly lovely as Alysson had been.

His father's religion had dominated his childhood. It had been a religion of right action, with none of the glamour or mystery of Catholicism – a religion that valued principled conduct and trade union loyalty, and substituted Ribena for consecrated wine. In adult life, he'd rejected it all in a total way that's quite unusual today, in our New Age culture that speaks so lightly of spirit.

'I went to John Wesley's chapel once,' he said. 'In Bristol. Where all this Methodism of my father's came from. It's a room with some chairs in. There's nothing there. Nothing. It's the most banal place. It's a lie,' he said. 'The whole thing's a lie.'

So there were no shreds left of that childhood belief to give him a little comfort, a little tentative hope, when Alysson died.

Yet his upbringing had left clear marks on him: he had a Puritan streak – a denial of the self, a lack of care for himself. Once, when he talked about his childhood, the chilly manses, the utilitarian food, I said, 'That's like the way you live now – not looking after yourself.' Thinking of the sparseness of his lifestyle, the endless cups of black instant coffee and the peanut butter sandwiches. 'Well, it's got worse,' he said. And I guessed that with Alysson's death he'd become still more driven, more careless of himself. There was a kind of Puritanism, too, behind that refusal to make concessions that I'd sensed in him in that moment when first we'd met. He told me once that he'd refused to speak to his sister for months after she'd decided to send her son to a private school. The story made me shudder. He was well-suited to the role of avenger. Like his father with the flame-thrower he'd torch anyone in his way.

I loved it when he talked about himself: I was hungry to know all I could, to understand him. But there were many silent times, when I couldn't find any words to fill in the space between us, times when he felt like a stranger, and I'd wonder why we were there together at all.

There was a day, walking again on the path by the river, a day of shimmering brightness and the sun warm on your skin, when he seemed so closed in on himself, all my attempts at conversation faltering: as though the river was flowing between us, slow and bright and unbridgeable. In the end

I couldn't bear it, said stupidly, 'What's wrong?' Though so obviously everything was.

'This woman came to see me,' he said.

'Oh,' I said. It wasn't what I'd expected. Some problem from the everyday world of his work: not something that belonged to this secret life we shared and these untended places where we walked together.

'Who was she?' I said.

'She's called Angie Lewis,' he said.

'What did she want?' I said, expecting a detailed exposition of a problem with her benefit she wanted him to disentangle.

He didn't say anything for a while. We walked on through the dazzling light and the smell of the river and the cries of the gulls.

'She's got a son,' he said then.

'Oh,' I said.

'Clive. He's called Clive. She even brought some photographs. Photos of him as a little boy dressed for Cubs and stuff. Talk about laying it on thick.' His face was twisted up: he was struggling with something. 'He's schizophrenic,' he said.

'Yes,' I said.

'She told me — there's this drop-in centre, the Hollies, that people in the street are trying to get closed down,' he said.

'I saw about it,' I said. 'I saw it in the paper.'

I felt my heart thud, had this sick feeling like when I'd read about it — the campaign that had been triggered by the murder of Alysson.

'Clive goes there,' he said. 'He goes there every day. He walks round there and sits in the kitchen and drinks lots of cups of drinking chocolate, and sometimes he does a bit of macramé. He's getting good at macramé, she said.'

'Yes,' I said.

Our footsteps crunched in the gravel. I saw how it was all changing around us: the blackberry bushes were putting

175

out new shoots, and on the nettle beds there was a sheen of celandines.

'She said it doesn't look much, but it matters to him: it's his world, she said. She and some other relatives and users are trying to keep the place open. But she said they couldn't even get their viewpoint in the paper – that nobody wants to know.

'"Maybe a word from you," she said to me. "To put the other side." She said people would listen to me after all I've been through. That if I'd put in a word, support her, it would be a news story, and people would sit up and take notice. Just a word, she said. People would listen.'

I didn't say anything. The shadows of birds passed over us.

'How can I?' he said.

There was rage in his voice, something uncontrolled. I'd never before seen him really express the anger that I knew was in him. And I feared he was angry with me as well as her: for I like her had come to him asking for something so hard for him to give.

'Who's to say there isn't another Paula Hickey at the Hollies?' he said. 'Someone who could do some other terrible thing? Jesus, I understand those views that people have in that street. I understand them completely.'

He chopped at the tall grasses we passed with the side of his hand. It was a fierce, thoughtless gesture. It came into my mind that he could hit me, in this mood: could lash out, almost without seeing me.

'How can I possibly give her what she wants? People expect so much,' he said. 'Too much. People expect you to be fucking perfect.'

It was dusk, blue like lavender, when I went home on the train – past the factories and the walls with their graffiti of wide-open mouths and names that couldn't be read, and the gardens with white plastic chairs tipped up so they wouldn't get wet. The seat opposite me had been slashed and sewn up. I sat looking out through the window or watching the other passengers – a tough-looking man in heavy boots with some frail pink roses wrapped in tissue paper, a woman with her shopping in a Disney Shop bag on her lap and a look of despair, her head flung down, dandruffy hair everywhere – and I thought about him, what I knew about him, the anger in him and his father with the flame-thrower, and for a while I felt afraid: thinking of everything I risked in coming to see him, and all the things he knew about me, and how if he chose he could use all that against me. But then, staring out through the dirty window at the vast graveyard in Earlsfield where the velvet darkness fell softly over the stones, a phrase of music from nowhere alighted like a bird in my mind, Jed singing, Sweet, stay awhile: and I could feel Ben's touch, his finger on the back of my neck, moving down so the front of my collar caught against my throat. I sat there without thought, just feeling the sensation of it, his cool unequivocal fingers, and hearing the music singing in my mind.

Chapter 19

In the second week of April, we heard that Paula was fit to plead. It was anybody's guess when the trial would be – but maybe June or July.

I felt a little stronger, though sometimes I still over-reacted to things. I was watching the television with Mac, and the phone rang and I went to answer it – it was no longer necessary to leave the answer machine on all the time because the press had lost interest in me – and it was a young woman, seventeen perhaps, her voice suggesting private school and horse-riding. 'Harry, I was wondering about lunch on Thursday,' she said, all in a rush – as if she'd prepared what she was going to say and she was so nervous about saying it she hadn't registered it wasn't Harry at all who'd answered the phone. I gently told her she had the wrong number, sensed her shame as though she was there with me. When I put down the phone, I wept for her – stupidly, secretly, into a piece of kitchen towel.

The internal inquiry reported. The report only had a limited circulation and I had to ask to see it. It was fairly short and not directly critical of me – though the panel did recommend that doctors should never take on the role of care manager for patients in the community. I felt briefly relieved, though the stage of the process I most dreaded was yet to come. After the trial, there would be a formal inquiry which would sit for weeks, and its conclusions would be widely publicized.

The murder was no longer the big story on the unit: people stopped talking about it, got on with other things. The current gossip was mostly about Dominic and Francine. There'd been a disco for unit staff organized by the nurses: I didn't go, but I heard they'd spent all evening welded together on the dance floor, and the next day Francine had a dreamy satiated look and yawned a lot. After the ward round I saw them chatting in the corridor, Francine with her hand resting in the hollow of his back, her thumb tucked into the waistband of his sharply cut taupe trousers. Not the way a nurse touches a lecturer unless they're having sex. Sam wanted to open a book and take bets on how long it would last, but I told him off.

There were new patients, new crises, to preoccupy us. Rosie Cooper, in particular, who'd been admitted at the end of March, and was a one-woman crisis. She was flamboyantly manic, and sometimes very difficult to manage because she fell into dreadful rages. Yet she brightened the ward, in a way, with her exuberance and the fecundity of her thinking and the anarchic things she did. She took a shine to a withdrawn male patient, Martin Gould, who'd played first violin in a prestigious string quartet before he became depressed: he'd sunk with terrible rapidity and we'd admitted him from a dilapidated bed and breakfast hotel. When there was classical music on the television in the day room, he sat and listened, intent, his fine long fingers fluttering, and you could picture him playing Bartok in his opulent dinner jacket. He told Francine one morning he'd had a terrible dream that Rosie Cooper had come into the dormitory and stretched out on top of him and tried to stuff a melon into his mouth. The dream had quite shaken him, he said. No-one had the nerve to tell him it hadn't been a dream.

Cassie was still on the ward, and I was still trying to work out how to help her, whether there was any way to shift her delusions. I'd decided to try her on clozapine, which often helps, but there are risks, especially at first, and it has to be scrupulously monitored. It didn't seem to be effective with her, and in the end we had to take her off it and put her back on her old medication and discharge her. When she left she gave me a present wrapped in sparkly paper. I unwrapped it carefully on her bed: it was a china shepherdess with a frilly skirt. It must have cost her a lot. I was touched. I've noticed this peculiar rule about patients who give you presents: they're never the people you'd predict, the ones you've really helped. The people you've made a difference for don't even bother to thank you: they go and get on with their lives without a backward look. The ones who give you things are the ones who move you – the ones you agonize over and lie awake and worry about but who, in the end, can't be reached by anything you try. People like Cassie – who now sat primly watching me with eyes of unsullied blue, like a clear sky over Brighton on a December day.

'That's lovely,' I said. My impulse was to give her a kiss but I knew she wouldn't like it. 'Thank you.'

'It made me think of you,' she said. 'I'll pray for you, Dr Craig.'

I carried the china shepherdess carefully home, put it on the mantelpiece next to my long thin black-stained beechwood candlestick.

'Do we have to have that thing on the mantelpiece?' said Mac.

'Yes,' I said. 'It was a present.'

The corner of his mouth puckered up. 'We'll just have to hope that people think it's ironic,' he said.

Jed rang. He was solicitous, asked me lots of questions about how I was coping. I talked more openly than I'd talked to anyone, grateful for his interest – though I knew it was slightly salacious. I suspected he found it exciting to have a sister who was caught up in something so sensational: but that was Jed.

Most of his news was about Consensus Vocalis, his singing group. They had a concert planned for July, in a church in the City: it was to be Elizabethan music – madrigals and motets – and he really hoped I'd come. And they'd finished recording 'In the Clasp of His Fire', their Hildegard of Bingen CD: it would be released in the autumn. He had a solo, which he sang to me, a hymn to the Virgin, at once both pure and sensuous. Over the phone I was very aware of the strangeness of his voice and the contradiction in it, the reedy male strength and the silkiness. He translated a stanza for me: Hail, hail to you, because the heat of the sun has exuded from you, like the aroma of balm.

And then, without missing a beat, he told me he'd just been to the London Lighthouse: someone he knew had been admitted, in the last stages of illness, dementing and losing his sight.

'I'm so sorry,' I said.

I recognized the man's name, a musician from Oxford: I remembered an opera he'd staged, when he was the golden boy, a setting of some Jacobean melodrama; Jed had been the executioner, gleefully sinister in a vast black cloak.

'How's Rufus?' I said then – expecting him to say, Rufus who? or, Tess, that was *so* last season. But it wasn't like that at all. To my surprise, he went into great detail. Rufus was very well really – yes, absolutely fine. He'd had a bit of a triumph at work, acquired some cutting-edge video installation. I was still vague about what Rufus did, but a gallery seemed to come into it. And they'd had a great weekend, said Jed: they'd been to Sissinghurst, to look at the white garden – Rufus was passionate about gardens, apparently. Sissinghurst didn't sound like Jed's kind of thing at all – too monochrome and subtle, all those grey leaves – but he was rapturous about it. He'd always preferred extravagant flowers – peonies, perhaps, voluptuously red, or plants with musky decadent scents, like the lilies he'd brought me. Rufus was evidently modifying Jed's taste: perhaps this was true love at last. I put the concert date in my diary.

My thoughts, my dreams, were all of Ben: he was there when I woke and when I drifted off to sleep, in any moment when the demands of the day didn't preoccupy me; my mind returning to the spare room, and the bars of light through the blinds that fell across our bodies, and the things we did there. As though, in the terrible complexity of what had happened, only this was simple. There was a hallucinatory intensity to these imaginings, and strange reversals sometimes, so I was him in the fantasy – him making love to me – or both of us, maybe, shifting from one to the other, leaving me unsure where I ended and he began. This fascinated me: as though these fantasies of mine were more like dreams than waking thoughts, as though I was half asleep or entranced when I thought these things. For in dreams you can be both subject and object, and therapists who work with dreams will teach that every part of the dream is part of you: you are the person racing onto the platform a little too late with your clothes undone, and you too are the train that pulls away. And in some sexual vision of submission and control, you may be both the cool intransigent man who binds and inflicts pain, and the woman whose body is stretched out and marked and shamed. Though in the waking world we none of us hesitate, we know which role is ours.

Yet when I was home with Mac, it seemed much the same as ever. Doing the ordinary things: sitting round in the evening watching a slick thriller about unusually horrible people in a pleasant minimalist penthouse; cooking something Italian; having people to dinner – Brendan and the nervy girl in the grey sweater, Julia and her husband, who was an impassioned paediatrician whose mission in life seemed to be to take children away from their parents, or chatting about the day with Mac over a glass of Rioja. Mac with some cleverness had instituted an evening glass of wine which we had together in an attempt to control my drinking, to make sure it wasn't something I did secretly. But it wasn't a problem now, I didn't feel that craving for oblivion in the same way anymore. Or maybe I had found my oblivion elsewhere.

I felt us pulling further apart. Was he aware of it too? Did he notice that we didn't kiss, that we'd be irritated by things that once we wouldn't have noticed: an apple core left on the kitchen table, the television turned up too loud – that somehow there was always some eminently sensible reason not to make love? I don't know. In most ways, and certainly to anyone outside looking in, like Julia and her paediatrician, we probably still seemed the golden couple. There were two separate worlds I inhabited, and I believed that I could keep them apart. Though I did sometimes worry that Mac might see through me. Once, when I was, as so often, thinking of Ben, briefly lost in some imagining, Mac startled me by saying, 'What's the matter, Tess? You look unhappy.'

'Nothing,' I said, shrugged, smiled at him, got up to make coffee.

'You were frowning,' he said.

It surprised me, because the thought itself had been so pleasurable, that I had looked troubled.

Occasionally I thought, How terrible if he found out – how he'd be so hurt by the knowledge. But I didn't think this often.

I think my guilt was all about Alysson. As though she could still be hurt by my actions. There was something else too in my feeling about her – a feverish curiosity about Ben's relationship with her, and her loveliness and how she had surely fascinated him and what their love life had been like. In my mind –

183

because it was so utterly unknown to me – because he never talked about it, couldn't talk about it, and I, of course, couldn't ask him – it became the ultimate affair, ecstatic, perfect. There are jealousies we have no right to feel.

One day when I was out shopping I found myself at the cosmetic counter in John Lewis, lingering in front of the display of L'Air du Temps, the perfume I'd seen in the bathroom at Ben's house: lurking there like a thief. There was a delicate glass bottle with pale scent inside, the stopper shaped like wings. The label said Tester. I reached out a hand, sprayed it all over my wrist: it had a light sweet smell of mingled flowers. The woman behind the counter had a red shiny mouth and the kind of mask-like foundation you only ever see on department-store assistants, and lots of little fair hairs on her face, from excessive exfoliation perhaps. She was very keen to sell it to me, she said it was a lovely fragrance, and just my style, because I was obviously a very feminine person who would have a natural affinity with the floral fragrance family, and she promised me a free lipstick and a makeup bag with a daisy on if I bought even the smallest size – it was their spring promotion – and I really did need a good moisturizer too, just look at all that dry skin round my mouth, she really did feel I needed help with that.

Walking away, I felt ashamed: suddenly hated the scent, which changed as it dried on my skin, the floweriness fading, so it became musty and oppressive, like a scent an old woman might wear, its synthetic undertones making me nauseous. I went to the cloakroom and washed my wrist with soap and water. But even the soap didn't get rid of the smell. I had a mad fear that this scent, Alysson's scent, had somehow impregnated my body, that I'd have to wait for the slow peeling-off of my skin, flake by flake, to rid myself of it.

*   *   *

One cold evening in April I went to see Abi. We sat in her kitchen: there was a prayer meeting, she said, in the front room, people from the parish praying for Kosovo. It felt rather sacrilegious, sitting drinking gin and complaining about things, while people were praying the other side of the wall.

Abi looked tired. She'd organized some parents to decorate the classrooms at Simon's school: the paint had been peeling where the damp was getting in, but there hadn't been any money to pay for decorators. It had been good fun, she said. They'd painted Simon's classroom pink: she'd read about some experiment in the States in which violent offenders were put in a room that was painted bubble-gum pink and were as a consequence much better behaved. 'Who knows, it might work. Even on Simon's class,' she said. She grinned, yet she seemed brittle, in spite of her joking, with smudges of shadow round her eyes. She was seeing almost nothing of Fred: dry rot had been found in the roof timbers at the church, and he'd started a Raising the Roof appeal which was taking all his energy.

'I admire you so much, you know,' I said. 'The way you just get on with it.'

She shrugged. 'Well, what else can you do?' she said.

She was wearing a long skirt that looked like it was made from a blanket, and woolly socks, and she'd lit a fire, even though it was April. We sat close to the fire but the cold came down the chimney, blowing smoke into the room.

'One blessing, at least,' she said. 'Our hamster's finally snuffed it. Believe me, that is the very last rodent we have. Rodents are the pits. Lots of cleaning out, and a very low cuddle-factor.'

Abi has a brisk approach to the deaths of animals. Once they had a rabbit die just before Bonfire Night and she'd buried it, not quite deep enough, in the rough patch at the bottom of the garden where they always had the bonfire. At the firework party, she said, there'd been curious remarks about the delicious smell of roast meat permeating the garden.

I asked her how the children had coped.

'Lydia cried a little,' she said. 'But the novelty wears off. Like when we had goldfish. The first dead fish got the full funeral service, the second got the flower petal treatment, the third went in the bin.'

I laughed; she poured more gin.

'You're looking better, anyway,' she said.

'Well, I am a bit,' I said. The oily blue scent of the gin went up my nose, made me sneeze.

'Not just a bit,' she said. 'I didn't mean just a bit. *Tons* better. You don't have that dreadful hunted look anymore.'

The fire shuffled a little, the coals settling.

'Was it that bad?' I said.

She frowned, looked into her glass. 'I was so worried about you,' she said. 'I didn't know what to do.'

'Well,' I said. 'You were sweet to me. You always are.'

I felt guilty and duplicitous. As though I was doing wrong by not telling her about Ben – as though in keeping my secret I'd placed a barrier between us, or witch-like woven a circle around myself, a circle that couldn't be seen, so no-one could come near.

'What happens now?' she said.

'Nothing for a bit,' I said. 'Nothing till the trial.'

'So there's been no more from that guy – you know, her partner?'

'No,' I said. 'Nothing more.'

I hated to talk about him as though he was a stranger: it made our love less real. I swilled the scented gin round my mouth, and wondered if this is why the urge to tell is so strong, and people give away their secrets so liberally and lightly – even when it can only lead to trouble. To tell your secret is to make it real.

The door swung back and Lydia crashed into the room. She was wearing stripy pyjamas, her face flushed and soft, as though she'd been suddenly woken from sleep. She looked at me without smiling.

'Hammy's died,' she said. Her eyes were dilated from the dark, the pupils a deep elusive colour.

'Your Mum told me,' I said. 'Are you sad?'

'I made him a grave,' she said. 'I'll show you.' She took my hand, pulled me to the door.

'Put something on your feet,' said Abi.

Lydia found some wellingtons belonging to one of the boys. They were far too big for her, they creased at the ankle. She waddled across the floor, giggling, fascinated by her huge green feet.

We went into the garden. There were roses along the fence, great buttery flowers with honey-coloured stamens, and the arum lilies were out, their tense pure flowers the shape of a hand half-opening, and smooth as vellum. A strong cold wind blew, petals falling everywhere.

She took me to the place where she'd buried him. There was a bit of tile she'd written on in gold ink: Hammy the Hamster. A loved pet and hard work for Mum. She'd scattered some sprigs of rosemary on the ground.

'I feel so sorry for them all,' she said. 'All the dead people and all the dead animals.'

She took me round the back of the raspberry canes to see where she'd planted some sunflowers, walking carefully, ponderously, in the big green boots.

Chapter 20

I opened the door. He wasn't there. A young woman was sitting on his desk, her back to me, swinging her legs as though she owned the place. Short hair, black and shiny as liquorice, held back with butterfly clips, clumpy raffia sandals that made her jean-clad legs look like thin sticks, lots of silver bangles.

I nearly went straight out again, but she heard me and turned. I saw that she was very young and gorgeously pretty, her skin very dark but with the luminous quality you only ever see in girls on the cusp of womanhood. Her presence there in the secret world I shared with Ben unnerved me.

'Hi.' She slipped off the desk.

'I'm Tessa,' I said uncertainly.

'I thought you were,' she said. She held out her hand for me to shake, a little self-consciously. She had the fragile self-assurance of the very young. 'I'm Nita.'

'Hello,' I said.

'I don't know where he is,' she said. 'I've only just come. He's probably gone to the post.' A clear open stare, curious, taking me in.

'Right,' I said.

The door banged back as Ben came in. He turned from me to her, looked amused.

'Tessa,' he said. 'So you've met Nita? You've introduced yourselves?' He went to her, put his arm round her, enjoying my uncertainty. It was the first time I'd seen him really smile. 'My daughter,' he said.

'Oh,' I said. The surprise in my voice only made him grin more. I was shocked: it was the realization of how little I knew him; that there were whole swathes of his life that I knew almost nothing about. I didn't know how old he was or who he'd loved before Alysson or whether he'd ever been married: hadn't even known he had a child. And what was so strange was that I'd never asked, scarcely even thought about these things.

'Dad, don't be gross.' She slipped out from under his arm.

'So why are you here exactly?' he said to her.

'We've got an Academic Mentoring day. We go to see our form tutors and they tell us to try harder, then we get the day off. I'm meeting Tiffany later – we're going to shop till we drop.'

'And?' he said.

'Well, Dad, I don't really have much money,' she said.

'That's a surprise,' he said.

'There are these trainers – all the other girls have them. I feel I'm not achieving my full potential at school 'cos I keep thinking about them. Really, Dad. My self-esteem is suffering,' she said.

'Hmm,' he said.

'I'll pay you back,' she said. 'I promise. I'm getting a Saturday job in BHS as soon as I'm sixteen.'

'And what does your mother think of that?'

'She'll come round,' said Nita.

He got out his wallet, gave her the money.

She kissed him lightly on the cheek.

'I'll get you some lunch,' he said. 'You'll need some lunch if you're shopping all afternoon.'

'I'm OK,' she said.

'No,' he said. 'That's the bargain – I give you the cash – you eat with me and Tessa.'

She looked at me slightly helplessly, as though wanting to enlist my support, then shrugged. 'OK,' she said.

'Prawn and mayonnaise?' he said. 'You like that, don't you?'

'It doesn't really matter,' she said.

'Tessa?' he said.

'The same for me,' I said. Not hungry, but aware that something else was going on here.

He went. Nita sat on the desk again, kicking off her sandals and wriggling her toes. A scent of tangerines seemed to hang around her, some product she used perhaps.

'You're a doctor, aren't you?' she said.

'Yes,' I said.

'Dad's told me about you. You know, that you're friends.' She was embarrassed.

'Oh,' I said.

'You don't mind, do you? I guess he knew I was sure to meet you sooner or later.'

Did I mind? I thought – thinking how our love affair was so secret, so illicit – and yet he'd told this gossipy daughter of his. I could see how it would happen: that you would tell Nita things.

'No,' I said. 'Of course I don't mind.'

'I'd like to be a doctor,' she said. 'That's my ambition really. Trouble is, biology really freaks me out. We've got these dreadful biology books, they smell like those green beans you get for school dinners.'

'I didn't like biology either,' I said. 'Well, not till A-level.'

'We've just finished this module,' she said. 'Humans as

190

Organisms. We had to learn about different kinds of enzymes, polypeptides and stuff. I got an A for that.'

'Well done,' I said.

'And then we did the heart,' she said. 'That was difficult: I never really understood the heart. I kept thinking I'd got it, and then I forgot it again.'

'Well, the heart's quite complicated,' I said.

'What I'd really like – I'd like to be a surgeon.' She laughed at herself a little. 'Like ER. Saving lives and stuff.'

I smiled. 'Well, it isn't always like that, of course,' I said. 'You know, saving lives. It isn't always like that.' Then, realizing what I'd said, I felt a sudden shadow fall between us.

Nita looked sharply across at me, then went boldly on. 'It was terrible about Alysson,' she said, walking bravely into the dark place. 'I still don't believe it really, I just can't get my head round it. Like – she's here one day – and the next day she's gone. Just like that. I kept thinking, I can't believe it, I can't believe this is happening.' She waited for a moment, looking at me. She had her father's eyes, that clear intelligent gaze, without concessions. 'It must have been terrible for you too,' she said.

I loved her for that. 'Yes,' I said. 'Yes, it was. Well, it still is.'

She got up, walking round barefoot, touching things as though they were hers, seeming to study the notices on the walls, the welfare rights advice sheets, and the details of the next meeting of the Sickle Cell and Thalassaemia Group. When she reached out, her bracelets made a thin metallic music.

'It's freaky,' she said. Her voice was quiet, veiled. 'You look a bit like her. That hair all down your back. Alysson's was like that.' Tracing out the border of a poster with her finger.

She heard my sharp inbreath. She turned to me, moved rapidly on.

'Look,' she said. She held out her arm, pushed up the sleeve of her t-shirt. She had a Celtic armband tattoo around her upper arm. 'D'you like it?' she said.

'It's very pretty,' I said.

'It's not real,' she said. 'Just one of those stick-on things. A transfer. I don't know if I'd dare to have it done for real.'

'Well, being tattooed is really painful, I think,' I said. 'And of course it's very hard to undo.'

'Would you have it done?' she said.

I shook my head.

'Me neither – well, probably not. I don't know if I could hurt myself like that.'

Ben came back with the sandwiches, and we sat and ate. Nita didn't eat much: she pulled out bits of filling, ate the prawns, first licking off the mayonnaise with a flickering tongue like a cat, then put the bread back in its bag and dropped it in the bin. Ben didn't say anything, took the prawns from his own sandwich and handed them to her, casually, as though he hoped she wouldn't notice what he was doing.

'Really, that's masses, I'm full,' she said. 'It's not that long since I had breakfast. Really.'

'Oh yeah?' said Ben. 'Two Polos probably.'

'No,' she said. Then, ruefully, 'Well, Softmints actually. And it was nearly half a packet. I mean, they've got calories, haven't they?'

He shook his head. 'I wish you'd look after yourself,' he said.

'Dad, you get so stressed,' she said. She got up. 'Thanks for this,' and she patted the money in her bag and waved at me and went.

'So,' I said, as we walked to his house through the dull warm afternoon, 'd'you have lots of children you haven't told me about?'

He smiled, shook his head.

'Just Nita,' he said.

I waited.

'Kamlesh and I got married very young,' he said. 'When Nita was two, Kam started a business studies course and went off with this turgid accountant. We're still friends – well, we weren't for a long time. When people claim they had an amicable split I think they're always lying.'

'Yes,' I said.

'But we're friends now. Nita comes round a lot and that really matters to me.'

He made it sound very matter-of-fact.

'I know almost nothing about you,' I said.

'I've told you a lot about myself,' he said.

I shook my head. 'You know what I mean: I don't know about you now – your adult life,' I said.

'Well, what do you want to know?' he said.

My mind was full of things to ask, but he closed the door behind us and pulled me to him so I felt all the length of his body against me. And I forgot my questions, just wanting the simplicity of this, to be filled up and taken over and not to have to understand: needing to be silent, not to ask anything that might encroach on my pleasure in him – my obsession with these patternings of bones, skin, pulses: wanting to be reduced to these things, everything else forgotten or erased, feeling his hard warm hands across my breasts, my stomach, his fingers opening me, and the way I responded to him, my body changed, clamorous and shaky, transmuted by his touch. As though with his touch I entered some different element: like the woman in the fairytale, who marries a turtle and enters his kingdom under the sea, who lives oblivious under that great weight of water, everything she'd loved before abandoned, and on his death returns to her home to find that many years have passed and her mirror holds the image of an old old woman.

*   *   *

193

We went through the elaborate gates into Cannizaro Park. The flower borders were full of summer bedding, blue lobelias, geraniums bright as blood. There was hardly anyone around, just a few mothers pushing buggies with frilly canopies. It all seemed jaded, too much used, with ice-cream wrappers floating in the fountain. We went round the back of the house and down the slope of lawn, where the grass was dying, turned coarse and blond by the sun, like hair that's been cheaply bleached. With the grass so worn, you were very aware of the long hard flank of the land.

'Nita's gorgeous. You must be proud of her,' I said.

'Yes,' he said. 'Yes, I am.' He walked on a little. 'And scared for her too.'

'Her eating, you mean,' I said.

'Well, you saw,' he said. 'They're all like that at Nita's school. And half of them are forever puking up.'

'Does she?' I said.

'No, I don't think so. But sometimes she doesn't seem to eat enough to sustain life,' he said.

We came to the little pond where there'd been bluebells in spring. The pond had been fenced in: there'd been an accident maybe, or children had ridden their bicycles into the water. The surface of the water was dark, holding the shapes of the trees and the purple of the sky that spoke of storms, and you couldn't tell how deep it was. A woman – a nanny perhaps – was showing a toddler the ducks. The toddler shook the fence: the ducks flurried off, breaking up the pictures on the surface of the water.

As we passed the woman turned. I saw that she wasn't a nanny: she was older than most nannies are, and she didn't have that unfinished look of a life with few commitments; there was something definite about her, as though she knew her mind. Blonde hair scraped back, combat trousers, no makeup. She reminded me of someone: I didn't know who. She stared at

194

me, nodded slightly. 'Hi,' she said, like a question: not quite smiling, puzzled. I half-smiled back, with that uneasiness you have when you feel you ought to know someone. Before I could return her greeting she turned rapidly back to the child, who was shaking the fence so vigorously it looked like he might break it.

I didn't think much more of it: presumed she must be a relative of a patient. You see so many people.

'Being a teenager can be awful. Especially for a girl,' I said. 'But lots of girls have weird attitudes to food, and most of them are fine, just get on with their lives. And there's something about Nita: I don't know – something that seems sensible, kind of healthy.'

'God, I hope you're right,' he said. 'Since Alysson, it preys on my mind even more.'

'Yes,' I said, with the quickening of the pulse I'd always feel – still do – at the mention of Alysson's name. My body gearing up for flight from some terrible thing. Sometimes our emotions have no sense of time – cannot distinguish between the past and the future, between what is about to take place and what is already irrevocable.

'You know that anything can happen,' he said. 'You can't tell yourself it will all be OK.'

'No,' I said.

We walked past the azaleas. The flowers that had glowed purple in the spring were now papery and dry.

'What can I do?' he said.

'I don't think you can do anything,' I said. 'Just tell her she's lovely often: well, I'm sure you do. There aren't any short cuts.'

'She's starting to go out with boys,' he said. 'That's what I really dread: when things go wrong, how she'll cope with that. It's hard for anyone. But when you're just fifteen . . .'

'I know,' I said.

195

'Everyone gets hurt: it's built in,' he said. 'I just so fear for her.'

'Of course,' I said.

'There's this boy she likes especially: Hassein,' he said. 'His parents are quite strict, they don't approve of him going out with her. It can only end in trouble.'

We walked between the muddy streams. There were smells of earth and leaves and the rain that was to come, and an elusive flower scent like the scent left on a pavement where a perfumed woman has walked. The wild rhubarb was taller than us now, looming like something out of an old science fiction film, and moths flitted over the water, like broken-off bits of darkness.

'Nita said my hair's a bit like Alysson's,' I said. Keeping my voice light, level – as though this was just a casual fact of only passing interest.

For a long time he didn't say anything. My heart thudded so loud I wondered if he could hear.

'Yes,' he said then, slowly, puzzling something out. 'In a way it was. It is.' He struggled for the right tense. 'But only from the back. Your face is entirely different – you know that, you've seen the photograph.' He turned to me, put his hand on my arm. 'I mean, in most ways you're utterly different. But you're the same height and your hair's the same length – hers was kind of wavy like yours. If you were approaching from the back – if you just glanced, didn't look properly – you could almost imagine you were Alysson.'

Or that Alysson was me, I thought – seeing her standing there in the doorway of the Marshgate Centre: the white swirl of her cigarette smoke and her long black hair hanging down.

He saw my distress, but didn't understand. 'OK, I noticed your hair,' he said. 'I've always liked hair like that.' Struggling to be honest, precise. 'But attraction's like that, isn't it?' he said. 'It's the little specific things that make you notice somebody.

Particular signals that draw you. Is that so terrible?'

'No,' I said. 'No. Don't you see? I was thinking of Paula.'

He was silent.

'Maybe Paula was angry with me,' I said. 'Was that why she chose Alysson? Perhaps it wasn't random. Perhaps she thought she was me – or chose her because she was like me – or saw her and felt the anger she'd felt with me.'

He stopped, turned sharply to me. He grasped my arm just above the wrist: his fingers hurt.

'What anger?' he said. 'Was Paula angry with you?'

'Maybe,' I said, backtracking a little.

'Why?'

I couldn't tell him. I was too afraid, feared what he might do, feared his withdrawing from me. 'Well, patients do often get angry with us – with doctors,' I said. 'When we can't make them well.'

We passed the wood where he'd kissed me the very first time we'd come here. It was dark and hidden now, thickly curtained with leaves. If you went in there now, it would swallow you up: you could do anything you wanted and not fear you might be seen. The way he didn't say anything frightened me.

'I think we should maybe go back now,' I said.

'OK,' he said. 'We can cut through down the road.'

We got back to the car, got silently in. I wanted to scream out, Say something, speak to me. But I just sat quietly.

And then he said, 'Tess, what good can it possibly do to think about all this? How can we ever know what was going through Paula's mind?'

'I'm sorry,' I said.

'Even if we could know, it wouldn't make any difference,' he said.

'No,' I said.

He didn't say anything else as we drove back, and I felt I'd broken some tentative peace we'd achieved, that had been

197

shored up by our silences and omissions, and maybe couldn't easily be restored.

I lay awake for hours that night, and struggled with the troubling thing I'd learnt – that you might think I was Alysson. I stared into the darkness, seeking to make sense of it, what it had meant for Paula, what it might mean for Ben: till the storm that had been threatening finally broke, and I heard the beginnings of rain like many people walking outside my window.

There's a doctor somewhere in the States who treats people with phantom limbs. It was in the *BMJ*. The pain of an amputated limb can be terrible: it's an illusion, of course – you feel the pain in a limb that no longer exists – yet the pain can be so appalling as to deprive you of any normal life, for the memory held by the nerves is of the moment of catastrophe – the ten-ton truck searing across your hand. This doctor had made a box that was walled with mirrors, and you slid your good limb in and saw it reflected – and as you moved your arm the other arm moved in the mirror, so your eyes would tell your brain you had two good limbs. And sometimes, for patients who'd been in agony for years, the pain would instantly go – at least until the patient closed his eyes: the nervous system learning something new – that there was a healthy arm that could move, that wasn't damaged – which for some patients with practice might blot out the pain for ever: cancelling out one illusion with another. And maybe, I thought, I for him was the hand in the mirror, filling in for a while his incompleteness: the illusion that started to heal him, where part of him had been ripped away.

Chapter 21

May. The ceanothus that smells of honey was in flower, its tiny blue petals falling, lining the cracks in the pavement so it looked like someone had drawn there with blue indelible pencil.

I went to an art exhibition. It was a moment of pure self-indulgence, a brief escape – someone I'd met at a party two years before had written to say there was an exhibition of paintings he'd done on a tour of India. They were happy paintings in blue and gold and scarlet, with sketched-in shapes of Indian hills and trees; you could sink down into them for a while, lose yourself in those red and blue valleys and forests. One I liked especially: it was called *Night*, a picture of jungle, full of shadow, so you had to look for a while to make out the fabulous shapes of the trees.

There was no-one else looking round when I went, and the owner of the gallery made me a cup of Earl Grey and told me stories. There was a man, he said, who'd come to the gallery and been amazed by a painting he saw there and said, I dreamed of that painting before I saw it: and of course he'd wanted to buy it, but when he brought his wife to see it she didn't like it at all, so he never got to own the painting of which he'd dreamed.

There was a new batch of medical students on the unit. When I went into the lecture room for Ralph's teaching round on Monday, they were all ready and waiting, eager and attentive, their chairs pulled into rows: the hard-working girls in conscientious skirts, the public-school men with hefty sporting shoulders, a pretty girl in pedal-pushers, a man in a leather jacket who sat at the back and probably had secret ambitions to become a script-writer.

Francine came in, wearing a polka-dot t-shirt and summery strappy sandals, and sat down next to Dominic. She leant on the arm of her chair, her body tilted towards him: their love affair was evidently still on. Though not, perhaps, for long: Sam had said he'd seen Dominic in the bar round the corner from the hospital, having a conversation of quite excessive intensity with a sultry physiotherapist.

Ralph is popular with students, in spite of his patrician air: he likes teaching, has all the right attributes – authority, charisma, an ear for a story. He sprawled, very relaxed, a bit too big for his chair, long legs stretched out in front of him: the students all sat upright in their seats.

'Let me tell you about some people I've known,' he said. 'A high-ranking detective who could only sleep with his teddy bear in bed with him. A happily married teacher who copied down graffiti from toilet walls and wrote them out in a special notebook in beautiful copperplate handwriting, recording the type of ink and the colour and the location in the toilet. Were these people psychotic?'

The students tentatively shook their heads.

'No, that is eccentricity,' said Ralph. 'Eccentricity is not psychosis.'

Through the glass behind him you could see the sky, tattered white flags of cloud streaming in front of the wind, the sun appearing now and then through the cloud and spilling in through the window. Everything looked dusty in that light, even our clothes, our faces.

'In southern Italy,' said Ralph, 'people quite often have visions of the Virgin. Peasants in rural communities.' He always likes to bring Italy into his teaching: he has a villa in Liguria. 'They see her sitting in a tree, or she pops up beside them when they're at their devotions. Are these people psychotic?'

The students looked uncertain.

'Probably not,' said Ralph. 'You see, you always have to look at the context. Such a vision in a pious peasant community may simply be an expression of profound religious feeling.'

The girls in sensible skirts made some notes on their clipboards.

At the teaching round only one patient is seen: today it was to be Kerry. Liz did the presentation, talked about Kerry's auditory hallucinations and her belief that her thoughts were being controlled: talked too about how hard she was to manage – she sometimes threatened people, and once she'd thrown an ash-tray in the day room.

Francine brought Kerry in: she sat huddled up on her chair, her hands clasped in her lap. Rosie Cooper had done her hair for her, put in some rainbow hairwraps: she looked beguilingly pretty.

Ralph asked how she was.

'I'm better, thank you, doctor,' she said, in a thin bright voice.

'So what's better now than it was before?'

'It's hard to say, doctor.'

'Why is it hard to say?'

'I still think too much, doctor.'

The students shifted a little: the ghost of a smile passed over someone's face.

'D'you still feel that the television is talking about you?' he said.

'Well, there have been references,' she said. She looked away: her hands were gripped together so tightly the veins stood up on the backs of them; her voice was quiet, veiled.

Ralph invited the students to question her, but none of them did.

When Francine had taken her back to the day room, the man in the leather jacket raised his hand.

'Professor Patterson,' he said, 'surely Miss Hunter should be cared for in a secure unit?'

'Because?' said Ralph, pretending to be puzzled.

'Because she might be dangerous to others.'

'Maybe we should talk about dangerousness,' said Ralph. 'Who would like to tell me which is the most dangerous condition in psychiatry?'

It was one of his set pieces.

'Schizophrenia,' said the girl in the pedal-pushers.

Ralph shook his head. 'Now, people with schizophrenia *are* very occasionally dangerous,' he said. 'Indeed, we've had a most unfortunate incident involving a patient who was discharged from this unit. Of which you will undoubtedly be aware.'

One or two of the students smiled complicitly.

'But this is exceptional,' he said. 'Only a tiny proportion of murders are committed by people with psychiatric illnesses. And the proportion has stayed constant in spite of care in the community. The enormous amount of press coverage these cases receive gives a somewhat distorted impression.'

I kept my face composed, but felt my heartbeat quicken.

'No,' he said, 'schizophrenia is not the most dangerous condition in psychiatry – though the suicide rate is very high indeed. The most dangerous psychiatric condition is jealousy: pathological jealousy.'

There was a faint intake of breath: the students looked

202

surprised. This wasn't an alien thing, like the belief that your thoughts are being controlled by the television newscaster. Jealousy we can understand, perhaps a little too well: we all have it within us, the seed of the poison tree.

'In cases of pathological jealousy, murder is always a very real risk,' he said. He talked about some cases he'd worked with, and the whole issue of risk assessment and the pro forma we use when a patient is admitted.

I admired the way he'd brought Paula into his teaching, the way he'd faced it so directly: I thought that took courage. It was like saying – This happened, it was devastating, but we can talk about it and look it in the eye.

Afterwards, as the students went, he came across to me.

'Tessa, could I have a word?'

'Sure,' I said.

'Sit down again for a moment,' he said.

The chairs had been left at odd angles: I pulled one up and sat.

He waited till the room was clear.

'So Paula Hickey's fit to stand trial,' he said.

'Yes,' I said. 'I heard.'

'I thought it might be an idea to have a word with you. About the Fisher Memorial,' he said.

I nodded.

'I'm aware we've talked about this before, of course,' he said. He was flushed and avoided my eye. 'I just – now, how should I put this? – wanted to advise caution.'

'Oh,' I said.

He put his hand on my shoulder. I could smell his aftershave. I tensed against his touch.

'Tess, you know I believe you to have tremendous potential. Don't you? You know I think that.'

I nodded slightly because it was expected. I could feel my lower lip trembling.

'It's an issue of timing, really,' he said. 'What's happened has of course been most unfortunate.' He walked towards the window. 'The Fisher Memorial will be a very high-profile job, after all.' He stood there looking out, in front of him the sky, the ragged streaming clouds, his body blotting out the light.

'Perhaps a sideways move for now,' he said. 'A little consolidation. That would be my advice. It's a pity in a way you can't move out of London. Somewhere quiet for a bit. You know, the provinces. That would be ideal.'

'I'll start looking elsewhere then,' I said, trying so hard to be calm and controlled, but something in my tone made him turn towards me, frowning.

'This is all highly illicit, of course,' he said, his voice hushed, urgent. 'This is absolutely just between ourselves.'

There was a question in his voice, requiring something of me.

'Of course,' I said.

'I just wouldn't want you to put yourself through all that. The unnecessary grief. When it can only lead to disappointment,' he said.

I got up to go: there seemed nothing more to say.

'Tessa,' he said then. 'Dominic did tell me – in strictest confidence of course – that he tried to dissuade you from discharging Paula Hickey.'

I bit my lower lip.

'We disagreed, yes,' I said. 'But his judgment wasn't based on any knowledge of her. It was a shot in the dark. OK, so I got it wrong. But I started from what I knew. She was my patient.'

I felt his pale eyes on me as I went.

When Mac got in, I told him what Ralph had said and burst into furious tears.

He stared at me. 'But, Tessa,' he said, in that gentle reason-able tone, the one he uses with his patients, 'you must have realized . . .'

'Of course I did,' I said. 'Of course I realized. It's just having it made explicit. Hearing him say the words. Can't you see that?'

'No,' he said. 'I don't see what difference that makes, to be honest.'

'He was so bloody patronizing,' I said.

'Look,' said Mac, 'he was taking a risk, saying those things. Like he said, he just wanted to save you the grief. You could see that as quite caring, in a way.'

'That's not how it feels,' I said.

That night I dreamt again of the beach where I'd played with Jed, and in the dream I walked down into the sea and round the fence that went out into the water, striving to walk back up the shingle slope, up to the private beach and the terrace and the fountains: and the water was black and thick with mud, like when the seabed's stirred by a storm, and the undertow tugged at my thighs, drenching the skirt of my frock that was tucked into my knickers, swirling round me dark as oil, pulling me back and dragging me out to sea.

Chapter 22

The sky got softer, heavier: you could feel the wetness in the air. Then it started to rain, the water ripping the blossom from the branches, so the pavement under the cherry trees in St John's Street was littered with sodden petals, thick as a poultice, the puddles choked up with them. I didn't have my umbrella and I was soaked when I got there. He hugged me, then held me a little away from him, looking at me, running his hands across me where my clothes clung.

'Your hair smells of the rain,' he said. 'I like that.'

We went to his house. He put on the heating. There was a faint scorched smell: he obviously hadn't had it on for a while. I took off my wet clothes and spread them out on the radiator on the landing.

After we'd made love, when he went downstairs, I got up, went to the fitted cupboard that lined one wall of the room: unthinking, still a bit blurred and stupid with sex, looking for something of his that I could put on while my clothes were drying, a bathrobe perhaps.

There was a flimsy key to turn. The door was stiff, I tugged. It shook a little, one of those chipboard things, not very well made. I pulled it open: the wardrobe was full of her clothes. I was transfixed: I felt I'd trespassed, or violated something – but I couldn't look away. There were sensuous things – velvet, devore, inviting you to touch – and things that caught the light. They were mostly in dark subtle colours like turmeric or nutmeg, but right at the end of the rail there was a dress in silk as red as flame – the colour of my linen summer dress, the red that dark-haired women often choose, women with her colouring and mine. I rubbed the silk gently between my fingers, and it was as though a scent came from it, elusive and quickly fading as the scent of coriander when you crush the seeds to release the smell. The fabric was so delicate I feared it might dissolve, like cloth from tombs, and fall apart and sift down into dust. Tenderness filled me, as I stood there touching her dress that was soft as skin, and the sadness of it all overwhelmed me, and my jealousy dissolved – not completely and not for ever – but just for that moment it simply melted away. She was no longer a woman I'd never known, about whom I had complicated illicit feelings: but someone who seemed real, separate. I thought how she'd lived and breathed and longed for things, and stood in front of the mirror in changing rooms in the more expensive high street stores, tucking her hair behind her ears: Should it be this – or this? The red, or the aubergine? Is the waistband a bit too tight? And will he like me in it? Things we all feel: things I had felt.

'Tessa.'

I turned quickly. He was standing in the doorway watching me.

'Don't,' he said. 'Don't do that.' His voice was hard and sharp. 'Don't go in there.'

I knew he'd seen me touching her dress. I felt shamed.

'I'm sorry,' I said.

I tried to close the door, but the key wouldn't turn and it swung wide open again.

'I thought there might be something I could borrow,' I said. 'I didn't know those things were there.'

He went to shut the door, turned the key to secure it, turned to me. I saw he was angry with himself.

'I must get rid of them,' he said, as though I'd accused him of something. 'I just can't do it yet.'

'No,' I said, carefully. 'Well, of course not. Not yet.'

We stood there for a moment, neither of us knowing what to do next. His face was heavy and tired and there was a web of faint new lines at the corners of his eyes.

'There are some shoes in there,' he said.

'Yes,' I said.

'She bought them the day she died,' he said. 'She'd gone out in her lunch hour and bought a pair of shoes.'

'Yes,' I said.

'They gave them to me at the hospital, when they gave me her stuff. There wasn't much, her clothes all had blood on. But the shoes were new, untouched.'

'I read about it in the paper,' I said.

'I didn't know what to do with them. I didn't want them – I felt I had to take them: it would have seemed so rejecting not to take them.'

'I can imagine,' I said.

'I thought for a moment, maybe I should take them back to the shop or something: the kind of stupid thing you think. You don't know how to behave really. I mean – who would wear them now? I asked this doctor, What should I do with these? She just said, Take them and stick them in the bottom of the wardrobe. Don't make yourself do anything. Just keep them there. And one day you'll look in the wardrobe and you'll think, What are those things doing there? and you'll give them to that Romanian charity that collects outside Tesco's.'

'She was good, I think, that doctor,' I said.

'She was OK,' he said.

He got up, walked over to the window, stood there resting his hands on the sill. The rain was still falling.

'She said to me, It can take a long time. Books on grief say, It takes two years to start to recover. But most people tell me at least three, so be prepared for that. Somewhere along the way, I think you'll find you give away her shoes.'

He went to his bedroom, came back with an old dressing-gown.

'You could wear this till your clothes are dry,' he said.

We sat in the stillness of the kitchen, with our mugs of instant coffee. The rain was pouring down more heavily: the leaves of the jasmine that grew around the window trembled with the force of it. Through the glass you could see the colours in the yard, but the shapes of things were blurred by the rain, the colours dissolving into one another, as though a child had painted them on wet paper. There wasn't much flowering yet: the pear tree just starting to blossom, a solitary pink camellia.

'I like the camellia,' I said.

'The flowers will lose their petals in this storm,' he said.

I sat and sipped my coffee, and felt strongly the awkwardness and sense of disjunction I often felt when I was close to him, except when we made love. It was as if we had to touch to be connected – then it all flowed, we were caught up in the current of it, carried along, it was easy. Around us the house creaked and shifted, the old boards moving because the heating was on.

'It doesn't seem like summer,' I said.

'It's far too hot in here though,' he said. He opened the window.

The wet air smelt of smoke and earth and flowers, and you could hear the slap of the rain in the puddles that were forming in the yard. The sky was many-coloured like a pearl, and the surface of my coffee held the reflection of the window and the subtle light from the sky, the lines of the frames bowing as the liquid moved as though under some intolerable pressure. I could still feel the texture of silk on the tips of my fingers, like skin on skin.

'D'you dream of her?' I said, looking into my cup at the shifting patterns held there, not looking at him.

He was silent and I was scared – thinking I'd ventured somewhere forbidden. But then I looked up, and saw he was silent because he was thinking: wanting to be accurate, precise.

'Sometimes,' he said. 'They're usually perfectly ordinary dreams, banal almost: she's alive and sitting here at the table drinking some wine after coming in from work, and I think I've made a mistake – I think how stupid I've been – to think she was dead when she was alive all the time.'

The dressing-gown had big baggy cuffs that were rather frayed: when I put my hand on his, the cuff dipped in the coffee.

'And I go towards her,' he said, 'and she moves a little away, just beyond the reach of my fingers however much I stretch out, just glides away from me.'

Chapter 23

Jed's concert was in an eighteenth-century church in the city. I'd suggested to Mac that he might like to come, but without much expectation that he would. Once he'd have come just to please me, unless he had some other more pressing engagement, as I might have gone to watch him rowing, but now he shook his head and said he'd rather read.

The church was very ornate, full of angels and glitter, with gilt candlesticks everywhere, like an elaborate birthday party, and obese pink cherubs all over the ceiling – a well-fed and abundant vision of holiness – but behind the altar there was a murky painting in need of cleaning, in a quite different mood to the rest of the place: it seemed to be the Day of Judgment, with grovelling figures in the foreground, and a looming avenging angel with a corroded face and vast dark wings.

The place was full already when I got there: I had to sit at the back. I was glad for Jed that so many people had come. It was a hot evening: my thighs stuck to the pew. The women in the audience were mostly wearing sleeveless dresses: the men wiped their foreheads with their handkerchiefs. Many of them were middle-aged or older: some had brought music scores with them. You could hear enticing ripples of sound from the vestry where the singers were warming up.

And then they came in, the men in dinner jackets, the women in long black dresses. There were faces I recognized from other concerts, mostly people whom Jed had known at Oxford: now they live for these events, taking unexciting day jobs that leave time for rehearsals. There was a striking woman dressed in high-necked linen, with red hair piled up: her face was too unconventional to be pretty – the mouth too wide, the cheekbones sticking out – but still the kind of face you can't help staring at. She's called Fenella something, she was at Magdalen with Jed, and I've always disliked her. There was a formal dinner Jed invited me to, with lots of port and venison, and afterwards we'd gone back to his panelled room that looked out over the Cherwell. It had been chilly although it was June, and we'd shivered in our flimsy formal clothes, and I'd gone off down the corridor to try and scrounge some matches to light his fire. I knocked at several doors but nobody was in, then I came to one that was open, voices and soft laughter leaking out of the room. I knocked, someone said Yes. The room smelt of lilac and French cigarettes. There were two men and two women, and they didn't seem to notice me, they didn't even turn: as though my presence required no acknowledgement, no concession from them, nothing. The woman called Fenella was lying on the bed, entangled with one of the men, and the other two seemed to be acting out something, the man with a glass of wine, standing over the woman, who knelt with her hands clasped together. She had a velvet dress, and heavy low breasts that seemed to spill out of the dress, and a tan acquired on some expensive coast, her skin as warm as honey. This is my blood, which is given for you, said the man. He held the glass to her lips, tipped it too acutely, filling her mouth before she could swallow it down, so the wine ran out of her mouth and down her chin. Fenella and the man wrapped round her laughed.

It had disturbed me, though I'd felt it shouldn't: I was surely too worldly, my Anglican upbringing far too vague and dilute, to be upset by a minor blasphemy. But really I hated them for it, and envied them too. They seemed in that moment so privileged and oblivious, with a gloss and certainty that I could never have. I stood there for a moment, hearing Fenella's laughter, and through the open window the sounds of the city, its clocks and hollow bells, and the clatter of the swans as they took off from the river. Then I turned quickly, went back down the corridor, borrowed the matches from some raucous and straightforward young men who said again and again how much they liked my dress.

The conductor raised his hand, people in the audience shifted a little: a silence fell, the choir started to sing. They sang a Tallis mass, then a hushed prayer by John Shepherd. They sang with absolute clarity, the women's voices thin, dazzlingly high, sexless as choirboys, so you could pick out each thread in the mesh of sound. I leant back, breathed out, felt the tension ease out of me. Nothing is so sure as a phrase of music, smoothing off the jagged edges of things.

The first half was all church music. There was a short interval, then madrigals. Jed came to the front to sing two lute songs – the first the song he'd played on my piano on that frosty evening in February.

> *The day breaks not, it is my heart,*
> *To think that you and I must part.*

I thought back to the orderliness of my life then, my crisp clean house, my crisp clean purposes. There was a little collective sigh when he'd finished: he always enchants an audience.

They ended with more madrigals. The audience stood to applaud, I was so pleased for Jed. Afterwards, the women in sleeveless dresses and the men with their scores lingered and talked together.

There was a wine bar round the corner, where Jed had told me to meet him. It was a pleasant place, with blond pine and big brown leather armchairs. I bought a gin, found a table in the corner and sat and happily sipped, the music lingering in my mind. Members of the choir drifted in, looking slightly exalted in their conspicuous clothes, and were greeted by their friends. Fenella was there already, over by the bar, and I saw that her black linen dress was slit virtually to the thigh. As she talked she kept lightly brushing the groin of the man beside her with the back of her hand.

Jed saw me and came over. He had a young man with him.

'Tess, I want you to meet Rufus.'

He was a complete surprise – linen jacket, stripey club tie. Neat and conservative and a little shy. Someone who led a sensible organized life: who visited his dentist regularly and had a lot of insurance policies. Not Jed's type at all, I'd have said.

We shook hands.

'He was wonderful, wasn't he?' said Rufus.

'Yes, he was,' I said.

'Rufus comes to all my concerts,' said Jed proudly.

They put down their drinks and sat opposite me. They seemed very much in love, touching a lot, holding each other's gaze.

'We wanted to tell you.' Jed put his hand on Rufus' arm. 'I'm moving in with Rufus.'

There was something rather traditional about the way he said it, suggesting an old-style engagement, with a ruby ring and announcements in *The Times*. They smiled at one another.

'Well, great,' I said. 'That's great.'

I could see this was what he wanted – some kind of family

recognition, a blessing for what he was about to do, the way any couple might feel. I felt touched.

We chatted for a while about the music, then Rufus had to go. He was going to an exhibition of photograms and X-rays at the Groucho Club, he said. He gave me his card; it was elegantly embossed, an address in Chelsea.

Jed turned a little, his eyes following Rufus – who was weaving his way through the crowd with lots of apologies.

'Isn't he wonderful?' he said.

'He seems very nice,' I said.

'And he looks really well, doesn't he? Don't you think he looks well tonight?'

'Yes,' I said. 'Well – why wouldn't he?'

He looked at me, a clear level stare.

'Rufus is positive,' he said.

'No,' I said. Too loud. The people at the next table turned. I grasped Jed's wrist. 'No.'

'Just calm down, Tess,' he said. He peeled my fingers from his wrist.

'Jed – you mustn't think it's all over – that it's all treatable.'

'Tessa. For God's sake, listen to me.'

'No,' I said. 'No. *You* listen to *me*.' My voice harsh, urgent. 'The new therapies help, but it isn't that straightforward. It's talked about as though it's all in the past – but it's still a killer. You have to know that.'

He looked at me coolly. 'Why d'you imagine you know more about it than me?' he said. 'Just because you're a doctor? Does that give you some kind of God-given insight? How many of your friends have died?'

I felt chastened. 'I'm sorry,' I said. I thought of the things he'd told me about sometimes – the friend who was going blind in the London Lighthouse, the succession of funerals. 'Why didn't you tell me?'

'That's pretty damn obvious, isn't it?' he said.

215

There was a tense silence between us.

'And you?' I said. 'What about you?'

'I was fine,' he said. 'When I last took the test. In October.' He was casual, laconic; but his forehead had a light sheen of sweat. I remembered the lake, the swan: the little boy, his face glossy with snot and tears, who'd clutched at the hem of my fair-isle cardigan; his high sharp cries and the clap of the wings of the swan. 'And are you careful . . .'

He interrupted me, exasperated. 'For God's sake, Tess. Yes, we're careful. We're careful enough.'

'Jed,' I said. 'Think again. Please. It can't be worth this. There are other relationships surely . . .'

'What do you know about it?' said Jed. 'You've never really loved anyone.'

'Oh,' I said, angry now. 'That's not fair.'

'It's true,' he said. 'You've never dared. You'd never take the risk. You'd rather hide away in that smug marriage of yours with all your bloody cafetières and your pepper grinders. You don't fucking know what love is.'

The music sang on in my head.

'I do,' I said. 'I do know what love is. For God's sake, I'm having an affair.'

A few short words.

He was quite unfazed: he seemed rather pleased, smiled.

'So – man or woman?'

'Honestly,' I said. 'A man, of course.'

'Who?' he said. 'Anyone I know?'

I shook my head.

'Called?'

I said nothing.

'But I don't know him anyway, you said.'

'Ben,' I said. Not thinking.

He stared at me. 'Not *the* Ben?'

I didn't say anything.

'Jesus, it is, isn't it?'

I nodded very slightly. I hadn't realized how closely he'd followed the story.

'The guy who works at the university? Ben Connelly?'

I nodded again.

He was briefly speechless. His whole demeanour towards me had changed. He made a low whistling sound, looked at me with something like respect.

'Well, Tess, you do play your cards close to your chest. Ben Connelly. Jesus,' he said again. 'And it's the Real Thing? Truly Madly Deeply?'

I nodded. Something in me liked the extravagance of this, confessing my love so openly.

'Well. And what does Mac the Knife make of all this?'

'Don't call him that,' I said. 'And he doesn't know. Of course he doesn't.'

'So when are you leaving?' he said.

'I am not leaving,' I said. 'We have a good marriage.'

He pulled a face. 'Oh yeah. And you're cheerfully shagging somebody else?' He shook his head. 'Ben Connelly. I can't get over this . . . You say you love him?'

'Yes.'

'Well then.'

'Jed, grow up,' I said. 'It's not like that. It's more complicated than that. Relationships are complicated. There are different kinds of loving.'

He shrugged, shook his head. 'Tessa, you're just not making any kind of sense.'

I didn't respond: I didn't want a row.

The singers were starting to drift off, perhaps to drink till late in Soho, or to eat pan-fried goat's cheese at some stylish restaurant, all metal and glass and blue neon. I got him to tell me about Rufus, bit back my urge to give him lots of advice and warnings: heard about Rufus's treatment, and Linzi his doctor who was so brilliant, and Jed's attempts to feed him healthily on soya milk and tofu and make him keep up his weight. I realized that Jed was moving in to nurse him and care for him and make sure he took his thirty-two pills a day. I'd thought it was an engagement with a ruby ring: but I saw it was more than that, an altogether sterner contract. If I managed for a moment to put aside my fear for Jed, that moved me.

Chapter 24

One Tuesday at the end of June, we saw the candidates for the Fisher Memorial being shown round the unit. There were four of them, including Dominic: two women, another man, all in their sharpest suits, the women with discreet matt lipstick and conservative shoes. Smiling, talking brightly, affecting to be nonchalant and composed – but hungry.

I tried not to see, but my envy was like poison. I imagined I could taste it in my mouth, like bile.

I went to the doctors' room to make a coffee. Sam was reading the *Sun*: he looked up quizzically, as though he were trying to read me. I spooned the coffee into the cup, trying to breathe deeply, to get a grip, and I knocked the spoon against the rim. Granules scattered everywhere.

'Fuck.' I wanted to hurl the cup across the room.

Sam came straight over and put his arm around me.

'I'm not enjoying today,' I said.

'Of course you're bloody not,' he said. 'That should be your job, for Chrissake.'

I hadn't told Sam that Ralph had warned me off, I'd kept my promise: but Sam knew why I hadn't applied.

'And what a load of wankers they look,' he said. 'I mean, are these really the cream of our profession? You've seen that blonde woman with the fat ankles? I trained with her. Definitely special needs . . .'

He sat me down, cleared up the mess and made my coffee for me.

'It's a bloody injustice,' he said. 'You having to take the rap for this, for making a decision that anyone might make. The wide boys, the ones who really do damage, they get to practise for years, and nobody stops them.'

We drank our coffee and he told me a story about an obstetrics consultant he'd known when he was doing paediatrics, who was called Graham Whittaker, and who should have been stopped, because he had really bad hands. 'One day when I was in theatre,' said Sam, 'he had to do a Caesarean, and as he went in, he just stopped and cauterized everything that bled. I mean, what's it meant to be – knife to skin to baby in three minutes or something? But he just went in so very very slowly. He did it all perfectly and forgot about the baby. Nobody said anything, that was what was so terrible, Tess. The anaesthetist was pacing, kept looking pointedly at his watch. But Whittaker was the fucking consultant and nobody said a thing.'

'And the baby?' I said.

'Not too good,' he said grimly. 'It had had far too much gas. It was as if he thought he was doing a normal operation, like he'd forgotten that there was a baby there. Somebody like that can carry on for years, and someone as good as you gets penalized for doing something that anyone might have done. It's so unjust,' he said.

I was touched by his sweet unswerving loyalty. Yet it did nothing to still my sense of the unfairness of it all. I thought of my father coming back from London, in his new navy suit with his face ill and white and his future fallen apart.

Next day, we heard that Dominic had been appointed. Nobody was surprised.

In time the feeling faded a little, and I learnt to live with it, as you learn to live with a bruise or graze that's taking ages to heal, mostly unaware of it or managing to forget it, but always flinching if anything comes too close.

It was a gorgeous summer. There were vases of roses on the patients' lockers, not the thin tight-budded ones that are sold all year at the roadside, but proper roses, pink and white and yellow, their rich scent lingering everywhere, thick petals dripping down onto the lockers as the flowers eased apart. And in Ben's yard, there were the tender exotic plants he'd brought from the back bedroom – a lemon tree, a creamy hibiscus with Burgundy red at its centre. The lilies were almost out, you could see their pinkness through the green of the bud, like when you hold your hand to the light and you see the blood through the skin.

I still met him at the advice centre – still turned up unannounced, never rang. I never questioned these rules. Sometimes he had people with him: I saw them as they left. A woman in a sari patterned with the planets, wearing many jewels, weeping. A hunched old man, his clothes and face shabby and worn and grey, who greeted me courteously. A man with lots of tattoos and all his belongings in a Kwik Save carrier, just out of prison perhaps. And always, the women with babies in buggies and children who tugged at their hands: women in young clothes, pastel t-shirts and jeans and leather-look jackets, with old faces, written on by poverty.

One day I was in the corridor, waiting for him and dreaming, in that moment before we touched, when he still seemed so far from me – when a shuffle close behind me startled me out of my thought. I spun round.

'Don't worry, love, it's only me.' A nicotine-stained voice, a hand on my arm. She was standing between me and the door to the street, with the light behind her: I couldn't see her clearly.

'I'm Angie, love,' she said.

I took in the cheap tight perm, the anonymous catalogue clothes – sweatshirt, leggings, trainers. The yellow afternoon light from the street put gilt around her hair. I was confused by the way she seemed to think I'd know her, and the brightness behind her that made me blink.

'Angie Lewis, love,' she said.

'Yes,' I said.

I remembered the woman Ben had told me about, who'd seemed to so upset him.

'I made you jump,' she said.

'Don't worry,' I said. 'Everything makes me jump.'

We could hear the laughter of children, and the ragged cheerful sound of the piano.

'You must be a friend of his, then, love,' she said.

'Yes,' I said.

'He needs his friends,' she said.

She looked at me in a level way, and I felt a warmth go through me – a distinct physical feeling, like moving into the sun. I didn't know where it came from or why I felt it.

The music from the playgroup came to an end. In the sudden silence we could hear voices from Ben's room, and a baby crying then stopping, as though a dummy had been put in its mouth.

'Look, I'll go,' she said. 'As you're here. He won't want me to keep him now you're here. I'll come back another time.'

'No, of course not,' I said. 'You mustn't go. You must see him. I'll go and buy myself a paper – really, I can wait. You see him.'

'Well, if you're sure,' she said.

'I'm sure.'

'Thanks then, love,' she said.

Later, as we drank our coffee in the yard that smelt of lemon flowers, I wondered if I'd been wrong. He paced while I sat on the step: he had that shuttered look, everything closed up in him.

'That woman came again,' he said.

'Yes, I saw her,' I said. 'She seemed pleasant.'

He shrugged.

I wanted to say more, to say I'd felt there was something unusual, something good, about her. But I knew that was something he wouldn't want to hear.

On the mulberry tree, the first fruit were forming, hard and tiny and green. I love mulberries, everything about them, their delectable sharp-sweetness, the way they stain your skin. I wondered whether I'd be there to taste them when they ripened.

'What did she want?' I said.

'The same thing,' he said. 'She's always very polite – she just keeps on coming. Just talks about Clive and his bloody cups of drinking chocolate and how much the Hollies matters to him.'

He sat down heavily on the step beside me. When he put up his hand to rub his face it threw a cool dark shadow across me.

'There are people,' he said slowly, 'who do amazing things after someone they love has been killed. You know, start self-help groups and campaign for things, and somehow get beyond it. All that stuff. They say, I want some good to come out of this terrible thing – and they make it happen. What I don't get is, how the fuck you do that.'

'Maybe she doesn't realize what she's asking,' I said.

'I don't know,' he said. 'I just wish she'd leave me alone.'

Chapter 25

He took me to Morden cemetery; there were wildflower meadows he wanted to show me, he said.

'Honestly,' I said, 'isn't that too depressing?'

'You'll see,' he said.

We parked at the gate, walked in under the pointed entrance arch and down a long slow driveway between Lombardy poplars, then he took me off to the side, away from the ugly chapels, where between the ranks of gravestones there were great swathes of grass left uncut. The long grass was jewelled with flowers like the painted borders of a medieval Book of Hours: yellow potentilla, vetch with intricate flowers like tiny gilded sweet-peas, purple thistles and ragged ox-eye daisies, and everywhere through the flowers the high grasses growing, up to your waist in places, their feathery seed-heads blurring together like pale delicate smoke.

'How do they make it happen – all these flowers?' I said.

'You have to get the nitrogen out of the soil,' he said. 'You get just grass to start with. No flowers. You have to keep cutting the grass till there's hardly any goodness left in the soil – that's when you get the greatest variety of plants.'

It was a vast place and very quiet, hardly anyone around – just a few people with trowels and plastic bags tending the graves, and in the distance an ice-cream van playing a nursery rhyme and the sound of a loudspeaker from a recreation ground somewhere. The noise of the wind in the poplars along the edge of the meadow was like waves tugging on shingle.

I thought of Angie, thought of the shuttered look in his face when he'd talked about her.

'D'you still feel angry with me sometimes?' I said.

He didn't reply.

The wind was very warm. I felt the feather-touch of the grasses against my bare legs.

'I wonder about that sometimes,' I said. 'I mean, it wouldn't be surprising if you did.'

He looked at me, reached out and pushed the hair from my face. I could smell the salty summer smell of his skin.

He stopped as we walked, crouched down.

'Look,' he said.

He had a flower cupped between two fingers, bending its head very gently towards me.

'It's a kind of orchid,' he said. 'It's the only place in London where they grow.'

It was a complicated ugly flower – not friendly, orchids aren't really: like an open mouth. I smelt it, but it had no scent.

'I don't know whether I like it or not,' I said.

We walked on around the edge of the meadow. A dazzling bird flew across our path, green as grass, a woodpecker perhaps, its flight straight and clear. The sadness of the place, the wind moving the pale grasses, the white and gold carpets of flowers, made me want to hide in him, to wrap him all around me, to press my mouth into his.

'Sometimes I feel I must have made it more difficult for you,' I said.

He shook his head a little, but I didn't know what he was saying no to.

The wind made the grasses ripple in the distance, like a great expanse of shining water.

'Well, I know I must have,' I said. 'More difficult, more complicated.'

I waited: hearing just the sound the wind made in the poplars.

He walked on a little.

'When Alysson first died,' he said then, 'everything was so vivid, so alive. Every blade of grass – all so clear and bright. It's the adrenaline, I suppose. I didn't sleep, I didn't eat, I couldn't sit still. I felt I could take on the world. I had a clear complete desire – revenge, I suppose. There is,' he said, 'something very basic about vengeance. It's a strong thing: strong as hunger. Part of me knew it was wrong, even then, I think. That it was just destructive – that it would achieve nothing – that it wouldn't bring her back. That it would just drag other people down. But it gave me a kind of power . . .' He had his head down. He sounded so tired.

'And I took that away from you,' I said.

He didn't say anything, and we walked on through the grasses and the summer scents of flowers.

I was collecting my bag from the back room where I'd left it when we heard the scrape of a key in the door, a thud as the door was flung open, footsteps in the hall. I froze, with a sudden fearful apprehension of ghosts or presences, a mad expectation that it was Alysson, that she was standing there in the hall like someone rising from the sea, with the past and death and all the things that had happened streaming from her like water.

He was watching me. He put his hand on my arm.

'It must be Nita,' he said.

226

It was Nita. She came through, stood in the doorway. She hesitated, seeing me there, as though her father's house suddenly wasn't quite hers. She was wearing a very short skirt and huge platform trainers with glittery laces and perspex bubbles in the sides of the soles.

'Sorry,' she said. She flushed a little. She looked from Ben to me. 'I forgot my technology project.'

'It's good to see you,' said Ben. He put an arm lightly round her shoulder. 'Are these the famous trainers?'

'Yes.' She stuck out a foot.

'They're really nice,' he said.

'Actually, Dad, I don't care what you think. You don't know about this stuff. I want to know what Tessa thinks. Tessa's got style,' she said.

I was absurdly flattered.

'I think they're brilliant,' I said.

She did a dance for us, her feet thudding a drumbeat out on the boards. She had a crazy angular grace, all bony wrists and ankles.

'I'll make you a coffee,' said Ben.

'Sorry, Dad, can't stay,' she said. 'I'm seeing Tiffany – we're going bowling.'

She went to pick up her technology folder, which was tucked down the side of the book case. One side was transparent plastic – you could see the cover of her project, elaborate sketches of clocks and watches, immaculately drawn. She waved it vaguely at me.

'We had to design a clock for the millennium. It took me weeks,' she said. 'We had to do all these drawings with fine-line pen, so it looks really professional. It has to be perfect, or she slaughters you.'

'I think it looks wonderful,' I said.

I was just off to catch my train: I suggested we went together. She seemed pleased.

227

Ben took us in his car. At the station he didn't kiss me, just touched my arm, because Nita was there.

She sat beside me on the train and chatted about her school: about history, which was invariably about the Weimar Republic, and got so boring you wanted to eat your hair; about their year head, who was very in your face, and rumoured to be planning an assembly about the Fallopian tubes. 'If ever she does it, I'm going off sick,' said Nita. And she told me about Hassein.

'He's well fit,' she said. 'We have a real laugh.'

'That sounds good,' I said.

'We've been going out for six and a half weeks,' she said. 'I didn't think he was ever going to ask me. I used to go and hang around by the drinks machine, and I bought all these new tops and stuff. Boys can be *very* slow. You have to give them a little push.'

'I think that's right,' I said.

'The thing is,' she said, 'I don't know if I'm in love with him exactly. I think I might be, though. But I don't know how you can really really be sure.'

There was such openness about her. It made me afraid for her, as though she were somehow unprotected: like the magician's assistant, who does a twirl in her sequins, then steps down into the basket through which the magician will thrust the quivering bright blades.

I asked if she was still thinking she might do medicine.

She shrugged. 'Dunno,' she said. 'Maybe. Or I might do media studies. Media studies sounds good – you get to write about soaps and stuff. Hassein's going to do media studies.'

'Nita,' I said, with a sternness that was at least half serious, 'you shouldn't let that influence you – some boy you like. However much you like him.'

'Oh yeah?' she said, looking at me knowingly, fixing her big dark eyes on me – Ben's eyes. And we both laughed.

228

She got a packet of love hearts out of her pocket and waved them questioningly at me. I took one. It said 'Page Me', but it tasted of childhood.

'Is my Dad in love with you?' she said, chewing thoughtfully.

It was the other side of her openness: expecting equal candour of other people. I felt acutely embarrassed.

'Goodness,' I said.

'Sorry, naff question,' she said. 'I shouldn't have asked.'

The love heart crumbled in my mouth, tasting scented and sweet, but with a fizzy sherbet sharpness too, like violets might taste if you could eat them.

The train was on an embankment, level with the bedroom windows of the houses we passed: where there weren't any net curtains, you could see straight in – someone with his shirt off, up a ladder, a dressing table cluttered with little bottles, vests drying in a spare room on a makeshift washing line. Things that strangers were never meant to see.

She was turned away from me. I hoped she was going to confide in me, tell me some secret: about Hassein, perhaps, or her problems with eating.

The window misted up with the warmth of her breathing. She drew on it with her finger; I couldn't tell if she was drawing a picture, like a child might do – a cat, a house with an apple tree – or making random patterns.

'I didn't like Alysson all that much,' she said, her voice quiet, thickened by the love heart she was chewing, so I only just heard her above the sound of the train. 'She and Dad didn't get on really, you know.' Turned away from me, drawing on the window.

'Oh,' I said. I didn't know what to say. My heart was suddenly wild, and I could taste the flowery chalkiness in my mouth, the taste that was both sharp and sweet, everything shifting a little.

'She didn't like him doing the work he did. She thought he ought to make more money. Alysson liked nice things,' she said.

'Well,' I said, keeping my voice measured, bland, 'people often feel like that. You know, these things are important, I suppose.'

The train was slowing, the rhythm easing down. We were nearly at her stop.

'I bet he hasn't told you that,' she said. 'My Dad.'

I shrugged, made some vague face. Greedy to hear more and hating myself so much for it.

'I mean, it's not very nice, is it? When somebody's dead. Saying things like that. She was very pretty, but she wasn't always a very nice person,' she said.

The train was drawing to a halt. She tucked her technology folder under her arm.

'Still, nobody's perfect, I guess,' she said. 'It's just all so terribly sad. I still can't believe that she's dead.'

She got up.

'See you,' she said, and moved away before I could respond, stepping blithely off the train in her bouncy platform trainers, the sequiny laces glittering in the light.

Chapter 26

The trial was held at the Old Bailey, in the first week of July. Paula's defence had wanted to plead guilty to manslaughter, but the prosecution hadn't accepted her plea and she was being tried for murder. Mac and I watched the trial on the evening news. They showed sketches of Paula in the dock, not a very good likeness, the lines on her face drawn in with dark pastel crayon, so that she looked much older than she was.

I was called on the third day of the trial for the start of the afternoon session. I'd left lots of time: I walked there slowly from St Paul's tube station, through the sound of pile drivers on a vast construction site and the roar of traffic noise. The sky was grey and a fierce warm wind whipped around the high buildings in Newgate Street. On the pavement outside the court, tourists with backpacks and *A to Z*s in their hands looked at the lists of cases displayed on noticeboards, and brisk men and women with black over-stuffed briefcases crowded in through the door.

I didn't have long to wait. An usher with a deep solarium suntan and discreet gold earrings took me into the court. I felt surprisingly calm, my mind still, almost empty, but my body didn't seem to be fitted together quite right: it was as though I had to make a deliberate effort of will to walk to the witness box.

The room was hushed and still and rather opulent, with a carpet and soft tip-up seats the colour of moss. There was something about the place that was a bit like being underwater: the green colour and the thick still air and the sense of being somehow enclosed, apart. I looked briefly to the back of the court, saw Paula in the dock, with her anorak on, a warder beside her noting something on a clipboard. Paula wasn't looking at me, her head was bowed a little, but I could see the whiteness of her face. The public gallery was high up behind me, I couldn't see the people I knew would be there – Ben, Alysson's father, Alysson's mother who had shouted at me in the café. And Liam I knew would be there too, wearing perhaps an ill-fitting suit that he'd borrowed from someone, with a stretched look in his face. All these people to whom I was so powerfully connected, whose lives I had changed.

I was sworn in. The defence barrister stood. She was an attractive woman in her forties, with wisps of bleached hair slipping out from her wig.

'Dr Craig, could you tell us how you first became professionally involved with Paula Hickey?'

I told her about Paula's first admission.

Opposite me, the jurors sat with concentrated expressions, elbows resting on the arms of their comfortable chairs. A woman in a tracksuit top had a carton of orange juice that she'd placed on the bench in front of her: now and then she sipped from it.

The barrister took me through the history of Paula's illness, her symptoms, her relapses.

'What is Paula's diagnosis?'

'Her diagnosis is schizophrenia,' I said.

I tried to focus on the barrister, on her reasonable face, her

232

level voice, the little wisps of blonde hair, but Paula's face floated on the edge of my vision, white and still, like someone drowned.

'And how was her illness managed in the community?'

'A community psychiatric nurse would visit every week and give her an injection of depixol,' I said.

This was easy, I knew how I would answer, I'd been through it all with Paula's solicitor. But the palms of my hands that I clasped together in front of me were wet.

'Has Paula Hickey ever been violent?' she said.

'Yes,' I said. 'There was an incident two years ago, during a previous admission, when she was involved in a fight on the ward.'

'And is it correct that at that time she was being compulsorily treated under the Mental Health Act?'

'That's correct,' I said.

'So this violent behaviour was judged at the time to be directly attributable to her mental illness?'

'Yes,' I said.

'Thank you. No further questions.'

The prosecution barrister stood, a tall man, bony and imposing, with a jutting jaw that seemed too big for his face. He smiled at me slightly.

'Dr Craig, we have heard how you have been involved professionally with Paula Hickey for three years. Is that correct?'

'Yes,' I said.

'And on 15 February you and your team of mental health professionals reviewed Paula Hickey's condition at the weekly ward round?'

'Yes,' I said.

'Can you tell me who else was present on that occasion?'

I told him.

'And these are all professionals with extensive experience with mental health patients?'

233

'Yes,' I said.

I knew where he was leading. Yet I sensed in a way that his heart wasn't in it: that this was a kind of ritual we had to go through – but that the outcome of it all was never really in doubt.

'And on 15 February, with your three years' involvement with Paula Hickey, you and your team together came to the decision that she should be discharged into the community. Is that correct?'

'Yes,' I said. 'There had been a distinct improvement in Paula Hickey's condition during the week preceding 15 February. But there is always a risk. This is an illness that may be controlled with medication, but unfortunately is unlikely to go away entirely.'

He leant forward a little, moved his hands around as he talked, his fingers splayed: his signet ring glinted.

'Nonetheless, in your judgment and in the judgment of your fellow mental health professionals, Paula Hickey was on the afternoon of 15 February well enough to be discharged into the community – well enough to be considered responsible for her own actions,' he said.

The defence barrister objected, but the judge overrode her objection.

'That was our decision at that point,' I said.

'No further questions, your Honour,' said the barrister.

'Thank you, Dr Craig,' said the judge. 'You are free to stay in court, or to go about your business.'

I went. I didn't want to stay around – I didn't want a repeat of what had happened after the inquest.

I had the day off. I went home.

I sat in the kitchen and made a coffee. But I was too restless to sit there, couldn't stay in. I left my coffee undrunk, picked up my jacket and went out and started walking, not knowing where I'd go, just needing to keep moving. It was something I'd never done before, walking these streets for the sake of it. It passed through my mind that this was something I'd learnt from Ben – to keep moving, when something cannot be borne.

It was a windy grey day, smelling of car exhaust and roses. I went down a street of sprawling Edwardian red-brick houses with little front gardens. There were lots of messy purple flowers in the borders, and sometimes pale hollyhocks, fleshy and listless, so heavy they leant out of the gardens where they weren't fenced and sprawled across the pavement: the flowers brushed me as I passed, like fat white hands.

I came to the railway station, where a man with a high-pressure hose was cleaning graffiti off the walls. A *Big Issue* seller was standing at the back of the station, though there weren't any people about: I gave him all my change. I walked on through the quiet streets, aware of things I'd never normally notice, a spider white as bone on a blue petunia, a pigeon flying over me and a single small grey feather falling. Someone had spilt yellow paint on the pavement and there were yellow footprints everywhere. I wasn't thinking really. I just walked and walked. Sometimes I saw Paula, her drowned face, or the face of Alysson's mother, or Alysson.

I felt tired and hot and thirsty. I went into a cornershop to get a drink. A man with a dirty rucksack and lots of packages tied to his belt with string was standing in front of the counter. He had a long beard, his clothes and hands were filthy, his face was flushed and purple with broken veins. He was looking at a copy of the *Financial Times* – he'd spread the front page out on the counter, on top of the boxes of chocolate bars and copies of *Elle*, using up lots of space. The headline was about Kosovo.

The woman by the till caught my eye: she had a rather helpless look, as though she didn't know quite how to manage this or how to get him to leave.

He turned to me.

'What's this darlin'?' He pointed to the headline, his hands were lined with old dirt, like in an etching, every crease drawn in. I could smell the staleness of his clothes, the thick alcohol smell of his breath.

'It's about the war,' I said.

'Does it mean they've backed down?'

'Yes, that's what it means,' I said, soothing, moving into professional mode, calming and slow. He was drunk and I sensed he was probably quite disinhibited, that he could do anything.

'So the war's over?' he said.

'Yes, it's over,' I said. 'The bombing's over.'

This seemed to please him.

'We've bombed the shit?' he said.

'Yes,' I said again, 'it's all over.'

I bought my can of Coke – reaching carefully in front of him with my money, feeling he would be easily alarmed, might readily interpret the simplest gesture as an attack. The woman behind the counter gave me a slight complicit look, raising her eyebrows.

He was still there when I left, staring at the *Financial Times* on the counter, shaking his head, smiling a little, his voice fat with satisfaction.

'We bombed the shit,' he said.

It was late when I got back, nearly six. I was very tired, but in a way I welcomed the tiredness. At least now I could sit still.

I poured some wine, settled myself on the sofa in front of the television. I sipped my wine and watched the news.

The trial was the second item. The jury had only been out for twenty minutes. Paula had been found guilty of manslaughter and ordered to be detained indefinitely under section 37 and section 41 of the Mental Health Act. There was a brief account of the proceedings, another sketch of Paula from a different angle, and film of Ben leaving the court, though he didn't give any comment.

I watched to the end of the news, and then it was *London Tonight*, which was leading on the trial: the newsreader said they were going live to the press conference which had just begun.

Ralph and Will Spooner and a lawyer for the Trust were sitting at a table in a room crowded with eager journalists. Ralph's suit had a slight check: the screen couldn't cope with it, the pattern shifted and shimmered, broke up into rainbow colours.

Ralph read from a piece of paper in front of him.

'We wish,' he said, 'to reiterate the very deep regret we feel about this tragic incident, and to extend our deepest condolences to the family and loved ones of Ms Alysson Gates.' He read with considerable gravitas: his patrician bearing seemed exaggerated and somehow old-fashioned on television. 'As you will all be aware,' he went on, 'the Secretary of State has today ordered a full inquiry into the events surrounding this case: we will of course pay very careful heed to the recommendations of that inquiry.'

'Are there any questions?' said the Trust lawyer.

A journalist in the front row jumped to his feet. 'It's widely known that there were anxieties about the length of inpatient stay in the psychiatric unit at St Jude's,' he said. 'Did this have any impact on the decision to discharge Paula Hickey?'

'Absolutely not,' said Ralph. 'And the inquiry will of course consider all the circumstances surrounding Miss Hickey's discharge.' The careful answer was delivered in measured tones, but I knew he was uneasy: his face was flushed, his eyes a bit too bright.

Charlie Cavanagh stood. The Trust lawyer nodded at her.

'Professor Patterson.' There was a slight sarcastic edge to her voice. 'Are you really trying to tell us that you have complete confidence in the decision-making process that led to this terrible murder?'

He didn't answer for a moment. I couldn't understand his hesitation.

She stood there, hard, bright, sleek, her blonde hair gleaming like metal. She had him in her sights.

'Professor Patterson, you haven't answered my question,' she said.

'Look, Ms Cavanagh,' he said. His face was glossy with sweat in the harsh lights, the broken-up colours in the check of his suit shifting and dancing on the screen. 'At the time I had every confidence in the – admittedly not hugely experienced – doctor who took the ward round at which the decision to discharge Paula Hickey was made.' He cleared his throat. 'In retrospect, clearly that confidence was misplaced.'

I felt it deep in my stomach, as though I had been kicked. My glass fell from my hand, red wine falling all over my white rug.

Ralph turned to the Trust lawyer. The lawyer nodded.

'No more questions,' he said.

Chapter 27

We went to Crete for the last two weeks of August, to a village on the south coast, inaccessible, built on the slopes of a narrow ravine leading down to the sea. Crete had been Mac's idea: it was where we'd been for the first holiday we'd had together. I can see now he was seeking, perhaps not quite consciously, to restore or recover something.

That part of Crete is ugly in places, with muddled towns of half-finished concrete buildings near the coast, and the Messara Plain littered with rags of torn plastic. But inland you come to the mountains, heaped up, smelling of dittany, turning pink and gold and lavender towards evening, and the emptiness shimmers with heat and the noise of grasshoppers, as though the earth and stones are live things.

We'd booked late, and there hadn't been much choice of accommodation. Our room had a balcony looking straight down the main street to the sea, and it was incredibly hot and noisy, the nights febrile, with Hondas buzzing past our window, and music and talk that never seemed to stop. Once we were woken by a shrill girl's voice, an English voice: Stop it, you're hurting me, extraordinarily clear and loud right across the village. Mac got out of bed, still half-asleep, moved by some inchoate impulse to go and help her: then we heard a foreign voice shouting in English, intervening, another woman's voice: Fuck off. Fuck off: and we went back to sleep.

The only quiet time was the early morning, when we'd sit on the balcony. Mac would always be up first; he woke so early, I wondered if he was unhappy. But I couldn't ask him: I guess I was scared of what might be opened up between us if I did. He'd be reading a fat biography he'd brought, I'd join him, I'd just sit and sip thin instant coffee and listen to the silence. You could hear a door closing or someone sneezing the other side of the village. There'd be birdsong before the grasshoppers started, and sometimes there'd be a wind that came from nowhere, suddenly roaring down the mountain like an animal, blowing my hair, turning the pages of Mac's book, rushing down into the stillness of the morning: and then it would be gone.

The beach was crowded. There were lots of couples from Italy and Greece, the women fluid and dark, at ease in the heat. I'd join with Mac in admiring them: some luminous woman, perhaps, who caught his eye, her head down, her long hair flung up and forward over her face, pouring water from a mineral water bottle through her hair to rinse out the salt, her breasts hanging full and heavy, the water shining on her. She's so perfect, so lovely, I'd say, as women do – protecting ourselves, our generosity a shield against the ferociousness of this competition.

I spent hours swimming a long way out from the shore, passing into a half-hypnotic state, rocked by the water, my mind scoured by the light. I didn't think much, or certainly not in that problem-solving purposeful way I'm used to: didn't think about work, about my future, about what Ralph had said and where that left me; it was easy, some-how, to push that aside for now, as though it belonged to another world. If I thought at all, it was about Ben, my

240

mind floating around, skimming through my memories and images of him.

And sometimes, as I swam, out there in the glimmer and clarity of the sea, so far away from him that he seemed almost a fantasy, I'd feel for a moment or two that I could be free of him. Would that be a good thing, the right thing? Could I let him go? Could I tell him it was over? Politely, lovingly even: thanking him for everything he'd given me – but saying that of course the circumstances of our meeting were so very strange: and I was, after all, married. Believing that if I ended it now, I would be safe for ever: safe from discovery. All I had to do was decide: I could do that from one moment to another. Now. Or now. I used to test this out with the utmost care and tentativeness – as you might put your hand to a candle-flame – or as you might touch something you've taken out of the oven to see if it's still too hot to hold: quick deft fingertip touches.

It was amazingly hot. We fell into a gentle routine, slowed down, acknowledging the supremacy of the heat. We'd go to the beach quite early. Then towards mid-day we'd wander back through the village, past the tourist shops. Sometimes I bought things – a sarong, a baseball cap to keep the glare off my face, a fruit bowl. The bowl was blue with a pattern of birds, rather coarse and flawed, but there was something about the colour of it, like holding onto a bit of that light, that sky. We'd pick up food for lunch: huge nectarines, bread from the village bakery that always had a warm sharp edge of cinnamon – they obviously didn't wash out the baking trays properly. And we'd go back to our apartment and eat the bread and the nectarines and stay there till three or four when it was bearable to go outside again.

Mac would sit and read on the balcony, and I'd doze – I was perpetually tired because I couldn't sleep at night. I'd lie there on the hard starched sheet, and the wind would take the striped curtain that hung from a pole over the door onto the balcony, so the fabric leapt and swirled, streaked with a white bar of sunlight; and in that state between sleep and waking, dipping in and out of sleep, I'd have dreams of extraordinary vividness, rich with images from my past – as though this time away had made a space into which all these half-forgotten things came crowding back – fragments of sensation, places I'd been, lovers I'd had, the smell and feel of their skin and the tones in their voices. Once I woke from one of these half-sleeps to see Mac standing in the open doorway onto the balcony, the white light lying along his arms, watching me. He came and took off my clothes and we made love, and I enjoyed it – more than for a long time.

'Your body feels different,' he said. 'You're taut and toned. It's good. I like it.'

In the evening, we ate at a taverna on the beach. The food wasn't great, but the place was quiet, away from the noise of the village, and there were vines heavy with grapes sagging from the trellis overhead, and lanky long-necked cats skittering around, and bats skimming the dark, and a woman singing in Greek over the loudspeaker, her voice low and breathy, making everything easy. A paraffin lamp burned in the middle of the table, its blue flame guttering in the wind; and the place smelt of the sea and the paraffin lamp. It wasn't always easy to find things to talk about, but the silence felt comfortable, companionable. I wondered if we could somehow take this easiness home with us, make everything all right between us again.

One evening as we finished our meal, he put his hand out and rested it on mine.

'Are you feeling any better?' he said.

'Mmm,' I said. 'Much. Much better.'

'We needed a holiday,' he said.

We sat there in a friendly silence. Mac looked good, I

thought: his skin darkening, his well-balanced features sharply delineated in the light from the lamp, his face less set, more mobile, the tiny blue flame reflecting in his eyes. The corners of the paper tablecloth flapped and cracked in the wind.

'Tess, d'you ever feel it's time to think about that baby?' he said.

'Goodness,' I said. And was surprised by a certain immediate pleasure in the thought. But then the doubts, as always, came crowding in. 'But why bring it up now? When I'm in the middle of all this? It doesn't seem like quite the right time to me.'

'Well, you know what they say,' he said. 'There's never a right time.'

I shrugged. 'I guess not,' I said. 'But I've always felt you'd want to be really prepared: you know, have everything in place.'

'Well, you would think that,' he said. 'I just thought it might be one approach. Have a baby, take time out.'

'Oh,' I said. 'Oh. You mean as a strategy for coping? A way of staying out of sight for a while? That's a lousy way to embark on parenthood, surely.'

'There's no need to get upset,' he said. 'But perhaps you do need to look at it all in a more radical way.'

'Meaning what exactly?'

'Just that,' he said. 'Think a bit more laterally.'

And he stroked my hand and the free raki came and we both got rather drunk and I told myself he was only trying to help.

The next day there was a fire on the mountain above the village. We'd got up early to go to a different beach, drove back towards our village around lunchtime, saw the smoke from miles off. The fire was eating its way down the cleft in the mountain towards the houses: swirls of yellow-grey smoke, dense, shutting off the sunlight, and the red fierce streak of flame. Tourists were standing out in the road, watching, silent, some taking photographs. The smoke was already so thick you

243

couldn't see to the other side of the village. Now and then, as the smoke billowed and parted, you could make out the fire engines moving about on the hillside: they seemed tiny against the immensity of the fire. White scraps fluttered high up where the smoke thinned, catching the light: you couldn't tell if they were birds or burnt things.

We went onto the balcony at the back of the apartment, looking up at the fire, not knowing whether panic was called for: the moment before disaster, the moment when you have a choice, can seem like any other.

'I know they have fires here all the time in summer,' I said. 'But not quite like this, surely.'

Mac stood looking at it for a moment, frowning. 'It's pretty close,' he said.

We drove off again, spent the afternoon exploring the ruins of a Minoan city, and came back at nine o'clock, when it was already dark, to see what was happening. The firemen were still busy, collecting up the rubbish that had blown all over the place and might be feeding the fire. The thin bright lines of burning had spread out everywhere, so the mountain seemed like some slouching animal caught in a net of flame. But it hadn't come any closer to the village. And when we woke the next morning it had retreated, moving back up over the mountain. Ash was still falling, though, catching in spiderwebs, piling up in the corners like tiny bits of wire or hair clippings, turning to mud when we walked on it with wet feet, so the tiled floor where we'd stepped after having a shower was covered with dark footprints, and our toothbrushes tasted of smoke.

The second Sunday we drove inland, just wandering round in the countryside, through the heat and the smells of herbs and the light you could drink in like water. There were villages with olive trees and pomegranates and blue beehives set on a hillside, and you could hear the tuneless singing of priests through the open doors and open towers of their churches.

244

We drove for miles, feeling lost and far from anywhere, and liking that feeling.

At siesta time we came to a village in the mountains. The taverna was closed, no-one about, all the shutters down. We parked on the main street, walked down a lane that led through an olive grove, the trees thick with age, twisted, their limbs propped up, black plastic bin bags spread on the ground around them to catch the falling fruit.

In the middle of the grove there was a chapel, the door held shut with wire.

'There are twelfth-century frescoes in here,' I said. I'd read the guide book. I untwisted the wire.

Mac, I knew, wouldn't want to come in. He went to take photographs of the view to the side of the chapel, where the hill dropped steeply away.

Inside, it was dim and scruffy, the walls streaked green with damp and algae. There was a rood screen with a gap to see the altar through: the shelf on the screen was covered with newspaper, and there were icons, three on each side, madonna and child, all the same style, modern and over-sweet with curly eyelashes, like one of Cassie's postcards; and there was a jam jar with dead flowers in it, and through the screen a pitted stone slab of an altar messy with bird shit. Though it looked old and abandoned, the oil lamp hanging in front of the altar was lit: somebody must come here. There was no glass in any of the windows. The wind came up the valley and blew through everything, warm and loud and surprising, like the breath of a lover, making the place seem alive.

The frescoes were all over the walls and ceiling, their texture faded and wrinkled, like old skin: no-one had bothered about them. At first you couldn't make out the pictures at all – but if you didn't try, just stood there and let your eyes rest lightly on the forms and didn't struggle, they came into focus and you could see what they were – the stern saints with their gaunt

245

bodies, their gaze that seemed so sad – I guess the sadness came from the conventions of the painting, the many lines, the small unsmiling mouths, the dark intentness of the faces. There were several bishops in gilded robes and mitres, and John the Baptist, and in the corner two women. I could recall enough from church as a child to know it was the Visitation – pregnant Mary being blessed by Elizabeth. The women leant in towards one another, heads almost touching, sharing their secret.

There was a bowl for votive candles, filled with sand. I lit one with a cigarette lighter that had been left there and stuck it in the sand. The flame streamed out in the wind, and the movement of air on my skin was warm like the touch of a hand. I thought I might say a prayer, in the rare belief that what I asked for might be given: it was the kind of place where you feel such things are possible. Yet at the same time I felt there was no need to ask for anything: that it was all happening as it was meant to happen; that it all happens as it must, in its appointed time, and we just move through it all, or it moves through us. That there was nothing to regret or strive for. I knew such peace there, for a moment, in that old chapel with the decaying frescoes and the littering of bird shit on the rough altar and the wind blowing up the valley: it was extraordinary. I tried to tell Ben about it once, but you can't really convey such things to another person, however much you love them: I worried it sounded stupid, wished I hadn't tried to explain. But just thinking about it stills me even now.

I don't know how long I stayed. But when I left the candle I'd lit was still burning in spite of the wind.

The last night we went to our taverna on the beach again. I felt nostalgia for our holiday already, even before it had ended: for this easiness between us. Mac's skin was really dark now, all the little lines of strain around his eyes and mouth erased, behind him the stitching of stars in the velvet sky.

'Tess, we need to talk,' he said.

246

'That sounds a bit formal,' I said.

'I haven't pressed it,' he said. 'I knew you wanted to get away for a bit. But I do think we need to talk about your future. It's got to be faced, and I want us to face it together.'

I touched his hand. 'Do we have to talk about it now?' I said. 'Can't it wait till we get home?'

He shook his head. 'The fact is,' he said, 'you're not going to be so employable after this, especially after what Ralph said. I mean, that happened, you can't avoid it. That's a fact, Tessa, that's how it is.'

Someone put music on, the woman singing in Greek again, her voice husky with breath.

'Well,' I said coldly, 'what do you suggest I do about it?'

'Perhaps you could take some time out. A sabbatical. People have short memories. I'm sure it could be arranged.'

It all came out a little too readily, as if he'd been planning to say it for ages. The terrible suspicion that Mac and Ralph had talked together about me filled me with fury.

'No,' I said. 'No. I don't want to run away. Nothing's ever achieved by running away.'

'OK, OK, it was just a thought,' he said. 'There are other options, of course.'

'Such as?' I said.

He was looking away from me, mopping his plate with his bread, wiping it round and round.

'There's someone who could come and talk to you – a woman I know who's a rep for Wellcome.'

'I don't believe this,' I said.

He wasn't deterred. 'Susanna Westcotes. She started out as a doctor, she wanted to spend more time with her family. I'm sure she'd talk to you.'

'Why are you so sure? Have you asked her?' I said.

'She's someone I know quite well,' he said again.

247

'You had no right to talk to her about me,' I said. I could hear the anger in my voice, like splintered glass.

'Tessa, I really think you should consider it,' he said, looking straight at me now, cool and clear. 'I mean, it doesn't have anything like the stigma it did when we were training. Some of these guys are really bright. Well, you must find that too.' He took the carafe, filled up my glass, as though it was all like it had been before, as though nothing had been broken. 'And the money's good, of course,' he said. 'Very good. Much better than what you're on now. Susanna drives a BMW Cabriolet.'

'Shut up,' I said. 'Just shut up.' I was appalled by this vision: that I should become a salesperson for a drug company, hosting lunches and putting on slide shows, taking doctors off for weekends in Paris to push the latest dubious drug. The antithesis of everything I'd worked for and wanted to be. 'I can't believe you're saying these things,' I said.

It felt like something soft and heavy was pressing on my chest, making it hard to breathe.

'Tessa,' he said, so reasonable, refusing to respond to my anger, 'you've got to start from where you are: you can't just behave as though it didn't happen.'

You could sense rather than see the bats that flew around us, the elusive jittery rhythm of their flight. Tiny flames tinged with the yellow of sulphur floated in Mac's eyes.

'Did you bring me here to tell me this?' I said. I felt so hurt: and it passed through my mind that I could hurt him too – that I had a weapon, a knife I could plunge in him. But it would cut me too.

When I unpacked, when we got back to London, the holiday just a faint blue glimmer in the margins of my mind, everything still smelt of smoke, as though we'd been right there in the heart of the conflagration, and a white dust of powdery ash sifted down out of our clothes.

Chapter 28

London seemed dark after Crete, like someone had turned out the lights, and it was hot and the streets were full of ants and mothers shouting at their children, and the railway embankments as I travelled to see Ben were littered with ragged plants – Russian vine escaped from someone's garden, with a smattering of blossom like spilt paint, and buddleia, the flowers brown and crooked like arthritic fingers. The window of the carriage was white with dirt. I sat and stared out of the smeared window at the untidy flowers and thought how it would be, how he'd undress me slowly and say how much he liked my darkened summer skin. I was hungry to see him.

But it didn't happen like that. It felt wrong from the beginning – as though everything had shifted in some subtle but irredeemable way while I'd been gone, and he wasn't quite the person I'd left behind. He didn't look right – I saw this straightaway: he looked worn, older, with smudges of shadow under his cheekbones, as though many months had elapsed since last I'd seen him.

'Was it nice?' he said.

'Yes, it was good, it was fine,' I said. 'Well, it's a lovely place.' But I couldn't say more, didn't say, I've been longing for you so much, I thought about you all the time: I felt suddenly unsure.

We went to his house, up to the bedroom, took off our clothes. He held me, started to make love to me: and though each separate touch was as sweet as ever, his fingers opening me, his hard warm mouth on me – there was something disjointed about it, as though we'd lost the flow of it, and somehow forgotten how to be together. I had a bitter sense of his absence, that he didn't really see me at all – even in this entangled intimacy, his salt in my mouth, his fingers pulling back my hair: that even when he entered me, his face contorted, part of him was elsewhere – lost in a shadowed place, a place of ghosts, and I couldn't follow him there. The silence of our love-making was suddenly intolerable to me: I wanted him to talk to me, to tell me what he liked to do to me, to call me by my name.

He got up and dressed hurriedly, as though he wanted to leave all this behind. I sensed, or feared, a kind of self-disgust in him. I wondered if it had always been like this, with him lost somewhere, and because of my blind hunger for him I simply hadn't noticed. He went downstairs without speaking, and I got up and started to pull on my clothes and felt a flicker of rage – that he expected all this of me, all this risk, all this loving, yet kept himself separate, reluctantly ceding only a fraction of himself. Yet what on earth had I been searching for – in this illicit spare-room love with this troubled raging man? Misery washed through me, I was drenched in it, heavy and water-logged, I could scarcely move. But I just went on – pulling up my zip, buckling my sandals, putting a comb through the messiness of my hair: taking the little steps.

I went downstairs. The house looked neglected, like when I'd first come here, dust furring everything, a faint rotten smell in the kitchen from a bin that should have been emptied. Alysson's

Georgia O'Keefe calendar still showed its July picture, a single apple in a glossy black bowl.

He'd made my coffee. I took it from him, not saying anything. We went into the yard.

The sun had come out: it was a beautiful afternoon, the light like honey. The plants had a tired end-of-summer look: the leaves darkening, the flowers almost over. The figs were swelling, the ornate leaves of the fig-tree dry and fragile: you could see how they'd soon crumble into dust. The roses were dying on the wall – they hadn't been dead-headed, they wouldn't flower again. Some of the papery flowers had fallen off the plants, lying in pale heaps among the drifts of leaves that he hadn't swept up, the petals without their colour, as though they'd been soaked in water or faded by the brightness of the light. There were some late lilies flowering in a pot: bees moved around in the open throats of the flowers.

I sat on the brick step and looked down into my coffee. I couldn't drink.

'Sometimes,' I said, 'when we make love, I feel you don't really see me.'

He was sitting at my side, I couldn't see his face properly. He didn't say anything. One of his neighbours was listening to GLR on a radio down the street, a love song that I knew from years ago.

'Sometimes I feel it's not really me you're making love to,' I said.

He wouldn't reach out, wouldn't rescue me. There was a rage in my head, the fire burning down towards the village, destroying everything.

'When we make love – is it me you see? Or is it her?' I said. 'That's what I feel sometimes – that's what I felt today – that it isn't me at all.'

His silence felt cruel, like an abandonment.

I got up.

251

'I'm going,' I said, unnecessarily, and turned towards the kitchen.

Is this how it ends? I thought. In this yard littered with dead flowers, the taste of him in my mouth, the love song over the wall, this rage in my head? Something screamed out in protest inside me, but I went on, went into the kitchen to put my coffee cup down.

He got up quickly, stepped in front of me, barred my way.

'No,' he said, his face working. 'You mustn't go.'

'That's up to me,' I said.

'It wasn't like you think,' he said. 'Alysson and me – it wasn't like you think.'

'Oh no?' I said.

'You must listen to me,' he said.

'Maybe I don't want to,' I said.

I moved to go past him.

He put his hands on my shoulders, roughly, jolting me. Hot coffee spilt on my wrist. I swore, for a moment I couldn't think of anything but the pain.

He took the cup from me, steered me to the cold tap, held my hand under the water. It made the whole thing messy and muddled – when I'd intended to just walk out, clear, decisive – but there was nothing I could do, my hand hurt too much. We stood there, him holding my forearm to keep the back of my hand in the stream of water.

'It's so easy, so tempting, to lie,' he said, speaking almost into my ear as he held me there, his voice loud, harsh. 'Because she's dead. It makes it easier: to pretend it was all great. But I'm not going to do that anymore. It's not right: not fair to you. Not truthful.'

'But she was so beautiful,' I said. I couldn't manage this conversation standing there child-like with my wrist under the tap. I took my wrist away and dried it on a piece of kitchen towel, though it still hurt. He turned off the tap.

'She was so lovely to look at,' I said, 'she was so attractive.'

'Yes,' he said. 'She was all those things. It was good to start with, wonderful: I adored her. You mind me telling you this, don't you?'

'Yes,' I said. But I needed to hear.

He sat down heavily at the table, but he didn't go on.

'So what happened?' I said.

'It was all falling apart,' he said. 'Not dramatically. I don't know why: I don't know what went wrong.' His hands were clasped together on the table, the knuckles white. 'But I started noticing . . . We'd be out with friends and I'd say something she didn't like, and she'd give her friends this meaningful look, her eyebrows raised a little. When you know you're despised, it's the death of a relationship. You know it's dying then.'

'Yes,' I said.

'It was one of those irreconcilable things. She wanted me to be different. It was just her fantasy of what she wanted me to be.'

'What did she want you to be?' I said.

'A lot of our rows were about money,' he said. 'She didn't like me doing the work I did. It was a long time before I realized: people present themselves in a certain way, to please you, to fit some image. I think she always thought I'd change in the end – that it was just a phase. She used to talk about the money I'd earn if I did a different kind of work.'

The jasmine at his window had half-covered the pane with its fretwork of narrow leaves: the light fell into the kitchen through the leaves, so their still small shadows patterned the table-top, patterned his hands as he held them tight together.

'In the end we were always rowing,' he said. 'I think we both knew it was only a matter of time. But it's hard to leave: you're used to one another.'

253

'Yes,' I said.

'When you row about everything, it's almost like you're creating the rows in order to have an excuse to leave – to say, Well, things are this bad, it's time to split. Because you have to have a reason – a story you can tell about what went wrong. So you tell yourself – it's because of the rows. But you've made the rows happen. It's really because she raises her eyebrows at her friend when you start to talk about things that matter to you.'

'Yes,' I said.

'We had a dreadful argument the morning . . . the morning . . .' His voice faded. He shook his head a little. 'A pointless row about cereal, about who should have bought some more. I started it. I shouted at her – things I'm ashamed of, that I shouldn't have said. You trace it all back: if I hadn't done this, then that wouldn't have happened.' He talked fast, his words abrasive, rough, but I could hear the tears in them. 'If we hadn't had that row she wouldn't have been there, outside the Marshgate Centre. When I heard she'd been attacked, I felt like I'd done it,' he said.

I let him tell it, bit back the compulsive words of comfort. No, of course you didn't, of course it wasn't you. The things we long to say: the things they'd said to me.

He turned to me then. 'She was smoking when she was stabbed,' he said. He stared at me, his eyes burning, as though he was angry with me, yet I knew he didn't see me. 'She'd stopped outside the Marshgate Centre to smoke. She'd bought the shoes and some cigarettes and she was smoking. But Alysson didn't smoke. She gave up smoking two years ago. When it was good. I hate smoking – she wanted to please me. It was a struggle for her – she went to a hypnotherapist. It became a joke between us – Look what I'm willing to do for you. Then we had that row and she went and bought those cigarettes.' His tears started falling then, and he wiped them away with a brisk repeated gesture of his hand, as though he was angry with them, but they fell too fast. 'I think she was saying something to me – with her red shoes and her packet of cigarettes. Shoes are for walking – walking out, going away. I think it was over – that she'd decided it was over.' He turned to look at me through his tears, as though he'd suddenly remembered my presence there. 'What do you think? You understand these things, don't you? Do you think that?'

'It could be,' I said. 'I don't know. It could be.'

'The last thing she said to me: that it was over. If we hadn't had that row, perhaps it wouldn't have happened like it did – she wouldn't have been standing there with her back to Paula Hickey.'

He sobbed then, bent over, his head in his hands, making the ugly gasping sounds that you make when the tears come from the core of you. I didn't go to hold him, though I longed to – I couldn't bear the sound of his sobbing, wanted so much to stop him. But I knew he had to go through this for himself – that I'd only get in the way. I sat there seeing Alysson, seeing the picture of her, the hair blowing across her mouth, all the detail quite clear, as though the photograph was just there in front of me. Alysson with her loveliness and her long dark hair and the brave extravagant shoes that never took her anywhere.

There was a long slow time that passed while he sobbed, acres and acres of time, in the still afternoon kitchen with the gold light through the jasmine leaves falling on us.

Then a time came when the sound of his crying slowed, and I was aware again of other things, the soft thud of an insect against the window, the sleepy far-off sound of a slow train pulling into a station, the voices of children. And he started to breathe more normally and wiped his face with his hand.

'So you see,' he said, in a quiet voice, 'I'm guilty too.'

I got up and went to him then. I put my arm round him, standing beside him: he rested his head against me. I could feel how his body still shook, could feel the wetness of his face against my hand. The hot sunlight through the open door hurt the scald on my skin, but I didn't move.

We stayed like that for a long time, wrapped up in the stillness, till it felt like a physical thing, like something that held us there, entranced: till you felt it could only be broken by something significant. I knew it was up to me.

I tried to swallow, but my mouth was dry.

'I'm more responsible than I've said. More guilty,' I said. 'I've never told you this: I should have done – it frightens me.' I felt him tense, but he didn't move. 'When I discharged Paula, it was more than just a mistake. It wasn't exactly a judgment I made on a purely clinical basis. You know – which shall I do – this or this? What does the clinical evidence suggest? It wasn't quite like that. It was something I did for all the wrong reasons.'

I was afraid, but I went on. 'There was a promotion I wanted,' I said. I told him about being asked to do the ward round and wanting to please Ralph and clear some beds, and about Dominic warning me against discharging Paula, and about Paula wanting to stay in. 'It was greed,' I said. 'Because I wanted to please Ralph because I wanted that job. It was greed overriding my judgment. And something in me knew I shouldn't do it, and still I did it.'

He listened in silence, his head resting against me. When I'd finished he turned to face me. He shook his head a little.

'Is that so terrible?' he said. 'To want to move up, to use your talent. Is that so bad?'

I said nothing.

'You're good at what you do,' he said.

'I don't feel that anymore,' I said.

'Ambition isn't a crime,' he said. 'Anyone might have done the same.'

It was as though there was a tiny shift, like something

glimpsed on the very edge of sight: a glimmering of a sense of possibility. Anyone might have done the same.

'Your hand,' he said. He stood and took my hand and looked at it, the shadows of the jasmine leaves falling on us. 'The skin's still red,' he said. 'Is it all right?'

'I'll be OK,' I said. 'It's not hurting so much now.'

He kissed the palm of my hand, where it wasn't hurt.

'I love your hands,' he said.

He never said he loved me, only that he loved parts of me. But I didn't mind. I liked him loving my hands. There's no pretence in my hands, nothing attractive about them – the bitten nails, the chewed skin at the side of the nails. Him saying that made me feel loved right through.

He kissed my arm, peeled up the sleeve of my t-shirt, kissed my shoulder.

'You taste of the sun,' he said.

He put his arms round me and we held one another for a long time, his wet face against mine, his body still and gentle in my arms.

Chapter 29

On Tuesday we'd been invited to dinner at Abi's. I had my therapy session with Colin Jennings on Tuesdays, so I knew I'd be late: Mac would go on without me.

The session with Colin seemed to go well. My work with him had felt stuck for weeks: but today we talked about the sudden death of his mother when he was seven and out fishing with his brother; how he'd learnt that if you risk being happy, some terrible thing may happen. They fascinate me, these moments of discovery, seeing what has shaped us: it's a kind of archaeology, digging up bits of the past, a shard of pot, a twisted blackened bracelet.

At the end of the session, Colin jumped up and moved smartly to the door.

'You're always in such a rush to go,' I said, amused.

He stood there, his hand on the door handle, looking at me warily.

'Well, it's been good today,' he said.

'And you want to leave it there: you're scared I might say the wrong thing and spoil it?' I said, seeing the fear in him, his sense of how rapidly everything can be changed, from one breath to the next: how we can hurt or heal.

He nodded and went.

I took a taxi from the station. I was still wearing my work clothes.

Abi came to the door, heavy and brown and smiling, in a dress in ice-cream colours, raspberry and pistachio: she looked like something you could eat. I hugged her.

'Sorry about this,' I said, indicating the suit, the shoes. 'I'm afraid I look like a stockbroker.'

'You look wonderful,' she said.

She took me through to the back. I could hear children laughing in the garden.

They'd made up a long table on the patio – old doors on trestles, covered with table-cloths. There were three other couples, none of whom I'd met before. Mac was down the far end of the table. I waved at him but he seemed oblivious, talking animatedly to the woman next to him. I wasn't sure he'd noticed me. I was glad he was enjoying himself: sometimes he finds Abi and Fred's friends a bit too earnest for his liking, with their impassioned discussions about sanctions against Iraq and the ethics of demonstrating against the World Trade Organization.

In Abi's garden the leaves were already yellowing. But there were roses still, scented and generous, those Elizabeth of Glamis roses that always make me think of childhood. Swallows circled in the sky, cutting the air into fragments with their thin bright wings, and the lawn was full of children, jumping on the trampoline and swarming everywhere: Abi always welcomes children to her parties.

There was a place set for me. But before I could sit, Lydia came rushing up and grabbed me. She led me to the bottom of the garden and round the back of the raspberry canes. Four huge sunflowers grew there, so top-heavy they'd had to be staked, hanging their huge shaggy heads, tawny like lions.

259

'Wow,' I said.

'I planted them,' she said.

'Yes, I remember,' I said.

Their pollen smelt warm and musty. A bee rattled around in one of the flowers.

'They were just little seeds,' she said. 'As little as that.' She held up her finger and thumb to show me. 'Itsy bitsy. Littler than Smarties. With a stripe on.'

'And now they're bigger than both of us,' I said.

She stood on tiptoe, tipped her head back, trying to reach one to sniff.

'Mummy put in the sticks,' she said. 'And Daddy did a sermon on them.'

I smiled. 'They're beautiful,' I said.

'Daddy says they follow the sun,' she said.

'Yes,' I said. 'They do.'

'Why?' she said. 'Why do they do that?'

'I'm not really sure,' I said. 'Perhaps they know what's good for them.'

But my answer maybe wasn't technical enough for her, and she drifted off, back to the climbing frame.

I sat down at the table. I glanced in Mac's direction, but he still wasn't looking at me, he was talking to Fred now, getting very animated about the virtues of some particular model of computer. I was next to Rachel and Nick. Rachel was, I learned, an accountant from Pitlochry: she worked in a prestigious office in Berkeley Square. She had a low resonant voice with a beguiling accent: I liked listening to her.

Fred filled my glass. I kicked off my shoes, rolled up the sleeves of my shirt. I drank with relish, feeling the tension of the day ease out of my body. There were black olives to nibble, glistening, deliciously sour: I ate far more than my share.

People talked about their holidays – about over-priced food and hours spent being delayed in airports eating tuna baguettes and perfect beaches discovered a little too late. Kay and Trevor had been to the Seychelles. Abi and Fred had had a damp fortnight in Pembrokeshire. Rachel and Nick had been to Corsica, where they'd seen grim, beautiful towns high up in the mountains, perilous fairytale fortresses, where the houses rose sheer like cliffs and had no front doors and people had blocked their windows with straw and scarcely gone out for years, for fear of the vendetta. Rachel had read a book about the vendetta: it fascinated her. It must have been terrible, she said, an entire society organized round revenge, as though only that mattered.

I thought of some of the things that Ben had told me: how after Alysson's death his rage had made him strong; how simple it had seemed.

Abi and Fred brought out the food: salad and salmon and bread straight from the oven. The children came up to the table and grazed like little goats on sausages and bread sticks. I realized I was famished and ate with a relish I hadn't felt for ages: the tastes and scents seemed fresh and acute, as though my palette had been cleaned. It was as if the closeness of that moment I'd shared with Ben had changed me, and I could start to let go.

Only the palest colours glowed in the garden now, the fragile glimmering pinks of the tobacco flowers, the moth white of the children's t-shirts and socks as they flitted around. The wind got up as the sun set, making the ends of the tablecloth curl like beckoning hands. Abi lit candles in glasses on the table: the flames shook in the wind, streaming out like feathers on somebody's breath.

I helped Abi clear the table and followed her into the kitchen. The light inside seemed too bright and banal.

'This was a lovely idea,' I said.

'I wanted to make the most of what's left of the summer,' she said, heaping dirty plates in the sink. 'I can't bear it when the days start drawing in.'

261

'So was it really OK, Pembrokeshire?' I said. 'Not too many dead farm animals?'

She shrugged. 'It was fine,' she said. 'Apart from some grim scenes in St David's in a hailstorm when Lydia had to be bought off with an unappealing inflatable alien. I can tell you had a good time: you look wonderful. You always go so bloody brown: it's just not fair.' She ran a finger down my arm. 'You look much better,' she said. 'Seriously. Are things a bit better with Mac?'

'Kind of,' I said. 'Though we did have this scene over dinner one night. He had a bright idea I should go and be a drug rep.'

She stared at me, shocked. 'Fuck that,' she said. 'I hope you told him where to get off.'

There were big bowls of strawberries, heaped up, glossy with sugar, with a thick red syrup in the bottom of the bowl. Their scent filled my mouth with water.

'They smell of summer,' I said.

'They're our own,' said Abi. 'The last of the year.'

We took the strawberries out to the garden. Fred poured brandy for those of us who weren't driving.

It was almost completely dark now, the sky a deep lavish blue, and the wind was cold. I put my jacket back on, did up all the buttons, but I didn't want to go in, none of us did, we wanted to stay out there with the dancing candles and the smells of flowers. Abi brought a pile of woollen things, worn old jumpers and shawls. She put a shawl on my shoulders: she has the gentlest touch.

The conversation changed as night fell. Wrapped in Abi's shawls, opening another bottle of brandy, we moved on from estate agents and holiday destinations and private tutoring, and talked about other things. Kay had had dreams in which she'd known what was going to happen; Nick had read a book that said that time is circular; Fred wondered whether the soul can leave the body in sleep. The shadows at the edges of the terrace were soft and dark as nutmeg.

Then someone asked Rachel to sing. She shook her head, but in the tentative manner of someone who intends eventually to concede.

'Sing one of those crofter's songs you sang last year,' said Abi. 'Please. We'd love that.'

Rachel straightened her back, resting her elbows on the table, her hands loosely clasped in front of her. She breathed and started to sing. All the hairs stood up on the back of my neck. Her voice was astonishing, rich, almost too deep for a woman. She sang in Gaelic, yet you knew what it was about, that it was a song of exile, because of the dark silk thread of sadness stitched into the song. Her throat and chest moved as she sang and the candle flame shook in her warm outbreath. Most of the children went on bouncing, oblivious – but Lydia crept up from the lawn and wrapped herself round Abi, listening.

I looked across at Mac, wanting to share the way the music made me feel. I saw his eyes were on me, but he turned his head away. He looked sad, I thought, almost like someone in mourning: it was an expression I'd rarely seen on his face, as though the song had touched him terribly. His eyes were full and bright in the flickering of the candles. At the time I thought it to be some trick of the light, but they seemed to be full of tears.

The singing ended, a little sigh went up. Lydia went back to the trampoline, and we ate the last of the summer strawberries with our fingers, dragging them round in the bottom of the bowl to soak up the sweet juice.

The party broke up around eleven, when Rachel's daughter fell asleep in her lap. We kissed Abi and Fred and got in the car.

'I'm frozen,' I said. I turned the heating on full, felt a blast

263

of air, still only lukewarm, up my skirt, in my face. 'That was a good evening, wasn't it?'

He didn't say anything: just drove off rather fast.

I felt mellow with the evening and sat quietly, contented for a while.

'We must have them back soon,' I said. 'Abi and Fred. They haven't been round for ages.'

I glanced at him. He was staring ahead at the road, his profile when I turned to him sharp and dark against the lighted shop-fronts as we passed, like something etched in metal. He didn't respond.

I put my hand on his arm.

'Mac, what's the matter?' I said. 'Did you have a tough day?'

I felt how his arm stiffened. I took my hand away.

'I went to journal club at lunchtime,' he said then.

I yawned luxuriously. I felt so sleepy – like I could just go to sleep there in the car, in the sensuous warmth of the heating up my skirt, and sleep for hours.

'So – was it interesting?' I said.

'Fine,' he said. A pause. 'Jane Pickering was there,' he said.

Something in his tone of voice made me suddenly alert, my pulse careering off, though I didn't know why.

'Oh,' I said. 'The psychologist? The blonde one?' I remembered the woman in the curvy suit who'd flirted with him at the hospital party.

'She said she saw you in Cannizaro Park,' he said. 'She was out with her child and she saw you there.'

I could see the scene in my mind, quite clearly, as though I was there – the fence round the water, the toddler alarming the ducks, and the woman's hair pulled back and her puzzled stare. There was a noise in my head like the noise of burning.

He cleared his throat. 'It was in the summer, she said.'

Simple words, set down in front of me like little cold stones, marking a new path.

264

'She said you were with that lecturer who was in the paper. That was how she put it: that lecturer who was in the paper, the one who was going to sue the St Jude's Trust.' A brief silence. 'I assume she must have meant Ben Connelly. Tell me, d'you think that was a reasonable assumption?'

I said nothing.

'Well, do you? The lecturer who was going to sue the Trust.'

'I know who you mean,' I said.

'She told me she was surprised.'

I didn't say anything.

'I told her she must have made a mistake,' he said. 'That it must have been some other woman. She was very insistent. She saw you at the party, she said how attractive you are, she wouldn't have forgotten. Your wife's so striking, with all that hair down her back, she said. She said that no-one could mistake you for anyone else. And you were with him.'

My mind was churning around, seeking for an answer, a solution.

'You were talking very animatedly, she said.'

I said nothing.

'Tessa, what the fuck is going on?'

I took a deep breath.

'I did go to see him,' I said. 'I wanted to say sorry for what happened. It seems idiotic, I suppose. I just wanted to explain somehow.'

'Jesus,' he said. 'Jesus.' His face was hard, set, he drove with exaggerated care, stopping elaborately at every junction, pulling away very deliberately. I was afraid.

'I know it seems odd, that we were in the park,' I said. 'He wanted to go out, he thought it would be easier to talk.' I felt so tired suddenly. I rubbed my face in my hands but my fingers smelt of strawberries, and the over-sweet scent of them made me sick. 'You know how upset I've been,' I said lamely.

265

'You can say that again,' he said.

'I had a mad idea that it would help. That I owed it to him, in a way. That I could make him understand.'

'And did he?'

'Did he what?'

'Understand. Did Ben Connelly understand?'

'Well,' I said, 'it sometimes helps to talk to someone face to face.'

'Oh yeah?'

'Mac, that's all. That's all there is.'

'What d'you mean – that's all there is? Isn't that quite enough?' he said.

'Well – I don't know what you might think,' I said. 'I know I've been stupid. But then I haven't been quite myself, I suppose.'

I didn't know if he believed me: perhaps he did, for now. But if he did accept what I said, this was, I knew, just a temporary reprieve. Believing for a while what he wanted to believe.

'Why the fuck didn't you tell me?' he said. 'Jane must have thought me a bloody idiot.'

'You'd have thought it was a weird thing to do,' I said. 'You'd have thought I was mad.'

'Too right,' he said.

His hands were clenched so tight on the steering wheel I could see the bones through the skin, his knuckles pale in the darkness of the car.

'He'll use you, Tessa. Jesus, can't you see that? He'll use you.' I could hear the harshness of his breathing. 'You're crazy, Tess. I mean, I know you've been a bit . . . unbalanced. But this. Jesus.'

We drove the rest of the way in silence.

We got home, got out of the car. The wind was stronger, cold fingers edging inside my collar and up the sleeves of my coat.

I went inside, turned on the lights: and was startled by a

sudden wave of nausea. I rushed to the downstairs loo, my stomach heaving, but only brought up a little bile. Too much brandy, too much emotion, I thought. I washed my face. There was a taste of metal in my mouth.

We got straight into bed, turned away from one another, the distance opening up between us.

I thought I'd be awake for hours, all these things churning around in my head. Yet I sank quickly, deeply, into sleep, and dreamt irrelevantly of sunflowers, of wading ecstatically through fields and fields of sunflowers, the flowers as high as my shoulders and huge and soft and polleny, not yellow in my dream, but orangey-red, like the juice of blood oranges.

I woke, needing to pee, in the middle of the night. And as I stood there washing my hands in the sink, staring at my face which seemed in the mirror soft and smudged with sleep, it was as though that sleep, the depth of it, had swept something from my mind – wiped it clean, as you wipe weeks of weather and grime from a window, and suddenly I could see. And what I saw with sudden devastating clarity was that I, with all the things I knew, and all these letters after my name, had somehow managed to overlook the most basic physiological fact: the lateness of my period.

Chapter 30

On the way into work next morning, I stopped at the chemist at Waterloo and bought a pregnancy test and hid it away at the bottom of my bag.

It was a bad morning on Derwent Ward: everyone seemed irritable. We'd just admitted a difficult new woman, an angry anorexic called Julia Cobden, and I wondered if that was the reason: a single difficult patient can shape the whole mood of a ward. Her endocrine system was messed up because she was so malnourished, and she had all this hair on her arms, thick and long as the body hair of a man: it made me think of those girls in fairytales who cover themselves in cloaks of fur or feathers to escape the sexual importunings of their fathers.

I sat beside her, asked how she was feeling.

'I just don't understand that question,' she said, her cold eyes on me. 'I'm sorry, I just don't see that it has any meaning.'

Even Francine was in a foul mood. I heard her telling Mark Ross quite sternly to pull himself together: which wasn't like her at all, she had extraordinary patience. Later I overheard her making an impassioned speech to Jo the OT – how all men are shits, how men have a sexual thought every six and a half seconds, so what can you expect; how most of them can't even *spell* commitment. So I guessed it was all over, as Sam had been predicting, and Dominic had moved on to the sultry little physio.

I didn't feel able to talk to her in the way that she probably needed, so I bought her a Mars Bar from the snack machine.

'Comfort food,' I said. 'Doctor's orders.'

'Oh Tess,' she said, and hugged me.

At lunchtime I went to the doctors' loo in the outpatient clinic and got out the pregnancy test and peed on the end of the stick. I sat there watching the second hand that seemed to drag itself round the face of my watch, taking myself yet again through the calculation that obsessed me, always coming to the same conclusion. That if there was a baby, then it was Ben's: it must have been conceived at the end of July, when Mac and I weren't even having sex.

The test was a formality really: I was pretty certain, yet my hands still trembled as I watched the colour come through. And for an instant, knowing I was pregnant, I felt a brief surprising thing, a little sherbet fizz of unpredicted pleasure.

In the afternoon I did a home visit with Nicci the social worker. A new referral, Bett Palmer, who lived with her violent adult son: her GP thought she was seriously depressed. The house was utterly neglected, the curtains drawn, the dining room table laid for afternoon tea for two, with flowery china and expensive silver, dust lying thickly on it like a soft grey veil; it must have been there for weeks. There were bowls of strawberries and cream, all covered with a velvety bloom of mould. I tried to hide my retching behind my hand. Bett Palmer sat quite still in her armchair, her face glazed over, responding in low monosyllables to our questions. We admitted her.

I left a little early, walked quickly down to the tube. It was a beautiful afternoon, seagulls rising high in the light and a lick of salt to the air, but I scarcely noticed these things. I was seized by a desperate impatience. There was a woman ahead of me in the queue who needed a season ticket and didn't speak much English: I wanted to grab her, to push her out of the way. And I got quite disproportionately cross with the slow careful gestures of the man who gave me my ticket, and the selfish young woman in front of me on the escalator, who'd parked her suitcase out so far I had to wait behind her. She'd surely seen I was rushing, but she didn't care. She turned to rest her back against the rail, spreading her arms out sideways. She was wearing a sleeveless top, not warm enough for the weather, and I saw she was a cutter, the scars as thin and straight as if they were drawn with red biro, neatly arranged at every half inch from her elbow to her wrist. She spread her arms out sideways, flaunting her scars.

St John's Street looked tatty in the brightness of the light, and bits of paper and rotten fruit were scattered over the pavements. I went in through the side door. There was the usual sound of children: laughter, someone crying, someone playing 'Yellow Submarine'. There's such emptiness to children's voices in the afternoon. His door was shut. I knocked: no answer. I tried to open it, but it was locked.

I went round to the house. It had a shut blind look, no windows open. His car wasn't there – but maybe he'd have parked it round the corner. I stood with my finger on the bell for a moment: I tried to imagine what he'd say when I told him, but I couldn't. I rang, but no-one came. I rang again and again, heard the echo of the sound in the hollow of the house, my hopefulness seeping away with every ring of the bell.

I turned. But just as I was about to go, I heard a rustle behind the door and the sound of a turning key. The door opened and it was Nita.

She stared at me, not smiling.

'He isn't in,' she said.

'Oh,' I said. 'Well, never mind.'

270

'I wasn't going to answer the door. But then I saw it was you,' she said.

Her sweater looked too baggy on her: I wondered if she'd lost more weight.

'Nita? Are you OK?' I said.

'I'm fine,' she said. 'Really.'

Behind her the undecorated hall, the dado rail that he'd pressed me against, that first time we'd made love. It seemed prosaic now – shabby where the plaster was exposed, dark against the light outside and the street with autumn's gold gloss on it.

'He ought to be back by now,' she said. 'He knew I was coming round.'

'Well,' I said, 'I guess he got held up.'

She looked at me as though she was weighing me up, wondering whether to tell me something.

'He's gone to see that woman he knows,' she said.

'Oh,' I said. 'Who's that?'

'You know,' she said. 'That Charlie person.' She saw the doubt in my face, misread it perhaps, thinking I didn't know who she meant. 'The woman who writes all those pieces in the paper. Yeah? The one he used to take out to dinner after my Mum left him. The one with the trouser suits.'

'Yes, I know,' I said. I shivered, as though there'd been a change in the weather. 'I don't think I'll wait then,' I said.

'He said he'd be back by now,' she said again. 'I don't know why he's being so long.' There was something fragile about her face: her features looked unformed, as though they might at any moment dissolve. 'I don't know what can have happened.'

'I'm sure he's fine,' I said. 'You know what the rush hour's like.'

'Why don't you come in?' she said. 'I could make you a coffee.'

271

'Thanks,' I said. 'But I won't. I guess I ought to get back. I'm meant to be somewhere else really.'

When she moved a little, so the light fell on her, I saw that she'd been crying: there were smoky mascara smudges around her eyes.

'Nita – what's the matter?' I said.

'I'm fine,' she said again.

'Has something happened?'

She shrugged. There was a scrunched-up tissue stuck up the sleeve of her sweater. She pulled it out and blew her nose.

'Hassein,' she said, through the tissue.

'Yes?' I said. 'What's happened?'

'Well, it's not Hassein really, it's his Mum and Dad. His Dad's a shit,' she said.

I nodded, waited.

'They've said he mustn't see me,' she said.

'Oh Nita,' I said.

'I think he'd still like to see me. Really. Wouldn't he?' she said. 'You think that, don't you? If only they'd let him?'

'Of course he would,' I said. 'Of course he'd want to see you.'

She raised her thin arms, pushing her hair from her eyes, and I heard the tentative music of her bracelets. I wondered if I should stay with her at least till Ben came. But I had such a fear of seeing him: I knew I wasn't strong enough, not after what she'd told me.

I stood there for a moment, not quite able to leave her. A bee moved around us, intrusive in the silence, and the shadows of the houses reached out across the street.

'Nita, I'd better go,' I said.

She shrugged a little. 'Sure,' she said. 'D'you want me to give him a message?'

'Not particularly,' I said.

'I'll just say you were here, then, shall I?'

I nodded.

'Just say that,' I said.

She watched me as I went: I could feel how her eyes held onto me, as though she half-expected I'd change my mind. Then she closed the door: I heard the slight sharp click of it from halfway down the street, like the breaking of a bone.

I passed the ragged cherry-trees and the market with its smell of over-ripe fruit. I realised I was famished. I stopped at a cornershop in Gulliver Street. There were prostitutes' cards in the window. 'Mature Busty Blonde, Friendly and Unhurried: 6 mins walk from here'. 'Cindy's £45 Inclusive Video Shower Open Very Late'. All handwritten, in coloured felt tip, the writing like the writing of children, very rounded and clear. They seemed bleak and sad: like sex, like sexual love.

I bought three packets of peanuts. The Sikh man at the till was reading a booklet of St John's Gospel: he scarcely raised his eyes from the page as he handed me my change. I walked on down to the station. Once I am on the train, I told myself, once I am safe, sitting there in the carriage; then I will let myself think. Not till that moment.

I didn't have long to wait. The train was almost empty. The window pane was dirty: there was a silver haze on it that you could scarcely see through when the train moved into the sun. I felt as though the dirt was on me and inside me. I wanted to wash my hands, my face, to scour myself out, clean everything. I sat looking out through the dirty window, and felt so very strongly the ugliness of it all, the rubbish, the dry dead buddleia on the embankment, the banks of the cuttings choked up with last year's leaves. I wondered what I'd ever found beautiful in London, in these cityscapes of factories and football pitches, the overgrown littered embankments and the razor-wire on the walls, the remnants and back ends and left-over bits of things, and all of it graffiti'd to destruction, everything written over with incomprehensible words.

I felt sick: the physical properties of things nauseated me, the texture of the seats against my skin, and the thick warm smell of them that you wouldn't normally notice. I stuffed the peanuts into my mouth to try and quell the nausea. And for a while, even then, I pushed away the knowledge of what had happened. It took all my strength, like holding a swinging door shut against a storm. And then I just let go, let it howl all round me. What this meant about our love affair, and what he might do to me. I'd told him all about the decision to discharge Paula and how I'd made it, and he had taken these things I had given him, and gone to see this woman – a woman he apparently knew so well, who'd written all those articles about me. And I thought what she could write about me now.

Suddenly I saw Ben quite differently – not the tenderness, that had so beguiled me, but the hardness and single-mindedness – like his father with the flame-thrower, torching anything that stood in his way. What I'd thought had been a kind of loving, born out of our shared obsession, had really been a perverse act of vengeance. And I made my decision – like all those years before on the grey banks of the Mersey: that I would cast a cold hard eye on things and give up my delusions. I would end this relationship – or recognize that it was already ended. I would live in a different way and see things as they are.

But then there was the baby, and I didn't know how that fitted in with anything. And it came to me in a kind of feverish rush that I'd pass the baby off as Mac's, not tell him yet, be vague about my dates, hope he wouldn't think about it too scrupulously. Perhaps I myself would come to believe that the baby was his. Maybe he didn't really suspect me anyway: maybe he'd accepted what I'd said. Often people will believe what it suits them to believe.

The train turned, the side where I was sitting moving out of the sun, so everything that had been bright when I'd travelled down was soft with shadow, and the far-off streets were blue as hyacinth flowers.

Chapter 31

Mac's things were in the hall. He must have got back early.

I went through to the kitchen. He was sitting at the table. His head was down like someone intent on what they're reading, but there wasn't anything there for him to read. He'd taken off his tie and flung it on the floor. He must have had a tough day – he looked like he used to look as a house officer, when he'd been up all night, his face lean, stretched. The gorgeous slanting sunlight flooded in through the window, light lying over the table and the blue bowl from Crete that I'd put there and filled with fruit.

'Hi,' I said.

He didn't say anything.

I went to make coffee.

'I did a home visit today,' I said. 'This really sad house.' I was going to tell him about Bett Palmer and the mouldy strawberries.

He looked up, and the words were sealed in my throat.

'I rang Jed,' he said.

Everything went still.

'Why would you want to ring Jed?' My voice small, shaky,

the words like little pebbles in a pond, instantly swallowed up.

'He told me everything,' he said. Very brisk, matter-of-fact. 'About you and Connelly. He didn't want to, but I got it out of him.'

'Jed loves to make trouble,' I said faintly, in a faltering attempt to push this away, stop it from happening.

'He told me you'd been having an affair,' he said. 'You and Connelly. That man we've all been seeking to protect you from. You and . . . that man.' As though he couldn't bring himself to say Ben's name again.

I couldn't say anything.

'I didn't believe it to start with,' he said, his voice like ice, cold and hard and on the edge of breaking. 'Even though that's what I'd rung to find out. I couldn't believe you could be that naive: to let someone take advantage of you like that. But Jed was telling the truth,' he said. 'Wasn't he?'

I was very frightened. I stood there close to the door, not knowing what he'd do.

'It's over,' I said. 'Mac, I promise. It happened: it shouldn't have happened, but it did. But it's over. I'm so sorry.'

He looked up at me: and my fear for myself was blotted out by the pain I saw in his face. I was suddenly amazed, that in everything I'd done I'd never really confronted this, never thought it through – how much I could hurt him.

'He's been using you,' he said. 'You see that, don't you? That it wasn't about whatever he said it was about? That whatever he said to you was just utter bullshit?'

'Yes,' I said. I felt shamed.

'How much does he know? How much have you told him?' he said.

'Well, not that much,' I said.

He sensed my hesitation.

'Tessa, how much?'

277

'We did talk about it a bit,' I said. 'About Paula Hickey.'

'Jesus,' he said, more quietly, shaking his head. 'Jesus.'

He was silent for a while. I didn't know what would happen when the silence ended.

A car alarm screeched in the street. Mac moved a little, cleared his throat.

'You've not been yourself, of course,' he said, stitching the words carefully together. 'It's been a terrible strain for you – the Paula Hickey thing. You've been a little crazy perhaps.'

'Yes,' I said, so keen to help him. 'Yes. I've been kind of crazy.'

'These things happen, I guess,' he said. 'People do something quite out of character. It's like they've been taken over.' It was as though he was talking to himself.

'Yes,' I said. 'It was a bit like that – like being taken over.'

'It was just an aberration,' he said.

'Yes,' I said. 'Just an aberration.'

'I know it's been hard for you,' he said, reaching out so cautiously across the space between us. 'And sometimes I haven't known how to help. It's not my scene really. Sometimes perhaps I try to find solutions, when you just want to talk. I always want to tell you what to do. I'm not much good at just sitting there and listening.'

'Well,' I said, 'it has been hard. For you too. I know that. For both of us.'

'If something goes wrong for me, I need to go off and hide away for a bit – not talk about it all the time,' he said. 'I don't think all this dwelling on things really helps people. But maybe that's just me: or maybe that's a male thing. That's what they say, isn't it? That it's what men do.'

'Maybe,' I said. I was touched by the way he was reaching out to me.

'I can see it, in a way,' he said. 'I can see how you might

behave quite out of character. After the shock of it all. Something dreadful happens – and you do a crazy thing.'

'Yes,' I said.

It was such a relief to have somebody in control. I sat down, let go a little, hearing the quiet of the kitchen, the gentle sigh of the fridge, knowing a moment of tentative peace, here in the eye of the storm.

'Listen,' he said then. 'This is what we must do. We'll make a new start. A new beginning.'

'Oh,' I said. I was amazed by his generosity, and how he was willing to undo what had happened and wipe it all away: like the man at the station with his high-pressure hose, cleaning off the messy extravagant words that were written on the wall.

'We'll take some time off,' he said. 'We could go away again – for a long weekend. We could go to Bruges, make time to talk. There's this really nice hotel – Julia went there. We could talk properly this time.'

'Yes,' I said.

I saw how it would be – the two of us drinking our cups of cappucino by a drifting green canal that held the reflections of hanging baskets of flowers, sitting there calmly, never raising our voices – making sense of everything.

'And we need really to make some decisions about your career,' he said. 'Whether perhaps what you're doing isn't quite right for you – I mean, there's no shame in that; you've got to be realistic – about what you can and can't handle.'

I thought, yes, maybe what I'm doing isn't right for me – when I'm so easily undone. Maybe I'm not tough enough after all. It seemed obvious, simple.

'I'll see that woman,' I said. 'The drug rep. The woman with the Cabriolet.'

'I think it might be good: it might clarify it, anyway,' he said.

I wondered why I'd reacted as I had, when he'd suggested

this in the taverna in Crete, and I'd been so furious, when he was only trying to help me. I sat and looked at him and thought how good he was: his restrained, puzzled caring for me. How in a moment of oblivion I'd sought out this different thing – this spare-room love with the scorched smell of the burning dust on the fire and the blind pulled down against the harshness of the light. Yet here I had a whole beautiful house, and ceramic vases and white embroidered bedsheets, and the sort of uncomplicated loving that doesn't promise the moon or make you forget who you are. Like the paintings he's fond of, the Flemish interiors, calm and content and orderly.

'I know we can work it out,' he said. 'Even after everything . . . that's happened.' He didn't say – After what you did: I thought that was so generous. 'I know we can,' he said. 'Maybe it'll force us to take stock, make some plans, decide where we're going. Maybe that's no bad thing.'

He put out his hand and rested it tentatively on mine: his skin felt cool, like some smooth fabric.

'And we could have a child,' he said. 'It's time really. If we're going to do it we need to get on with it.'

I didn't say anything.

'You'd like that really, wouldn't you?' he said. 'I've wondered whether deep down that's something you've really wanted all along – it's just that you haven't quite been able to say so.'

I moved my hand out from under his, turned away a little, a taste of ash in my mouth. I felt so ashamed I could barely speak.

'Mac, I'm pregnant,' I said.

We both sat there, quite still.

'How far on?' he said, after a while. Clinical, almost. Needing to check out the facts – though I guess he knew already, from my tone of voice, and the way I sat, turned from him.

'About seven weeks,' I said. I didn't hesitate, I knew I had to tell him.

280

He nodded. He didn't need to calculate what this meant.

'Mac, I'm so so sorry,' I said.

He sat there for a long time. The fridge breathed quietly like an animal.

'You'll have to get rid of it,' he said then, very gently. 'For us to carry on.' His voice level, the words set down carefully between us, as though they were breakable. 'You see that, don't you?'

'Yes,' I said. 'Of course.'

There was a thin pain in the back of my head, like something being driven into me.

'Go to Graham Caulder,' he said. 'He'll see you straightaway. I'll ring him first thing tomorrow.'

'Yes,' I said. 'Of course.' My voice was high, bright, rapid.

I needed to change, to clean my teeth, to wash my hands and face. I got up.

He looked up at me, holding me with his eyes.

'Tess,' he said, 'did you really believe yourself to be loved? Did you believe that?'

'I suppose so,' I said.

'When he was obviously just using you all the time.' He shook his head. 'Poor Tess.'

I turned back to him. There was a brief flickering on the edge of my awareness, a little bat's wing of something that wouldn't be stilled.

'I thought we understood one another,' I said, my voice small, uncertain. 'We both in our different ways had an obsession with what had happened. It seemed we could help one another with it. That was what it was about.'

He stared at me as though I was talking a language he didn't understand.

I thought of all the times when I'd needed him, wanted him to listen – when he'd withdrawn a little, held himself back from me. 'You didn't, couldn't give me what I needed,'

I said. 'Of course I shouldn't have looked to someone else – not like that, not like I did. But maybe it's not so surprising – that I felt that need.'

'For Chrissake, I tried,' he said. 'Don't you think it's been hard for me too? You're a foreign country to me sometimes, Tess. Your way isn't my way.'

'I'm not justifying myself,' I said. 'I'm not saying it was OK. If I seem to be doing that, I'm sorry, that would be inexcusable. I'm just trying to show you why I was drawn to him. I thought we were kind of good for one another.' It sounded preposterous, but I said it anyway. 'Maybe that was a bit crazy, and dreadfully hurtful to you, but that was how it was: I thought we could help one another get through.'

My voice was lost in the clatter as he got up, pushing his chair away so it fell to the floor.

'You're so fucking naive – it takes my breath away,' he said. His voice was changed, harsh, loud. 'People *use* one another, Tess. That's how it is, that's what the world is like. People are selfish. All of us: we're all selfish. It's a fucking jungle. You've got to look out for yourself.'

He started to pace up and down, turning abruptly, walking too fast for the space, like a caged creature.

'I'll tell you another thing,' he said. 'Having to go through a terrible thing doesn't make you any nicer. Having some grisly illness, having your girlfriend knifed in the street. People don't go through the fire and come out all honed and refined. That's just a filthy great lie. They come out bloody burnt.' He spun to face me. 'Surely you see that.'

'I don't know,' I said. 'I want to wash my face.'

I went upstairs to the bathroom. I cleaned my teeth and wiped off my makeup and scrubbed my face with soap.

There was a sound of breaking, then rapid footsteps, the front door opening, banging shut.

I went downstairs, though I knew what I'd find. I pushed

282

the kitchen door open: there was a little resistance, a sound of scraping. He'd thrown the bowl I'd brought back from Crete against the wall. There were shards of pottery everywhere, oranges still moving on the floor. I saw then what it had cost him to talk to me as he had. Not to get up and hit me.

I started to sweep up. I realized I was crying, but I just got on with it. Most of the oranges were still intact, but I threw them away – the bruising brought out their scent and it nauseated me. I swept up the bits of pottery and put them in the bin – there were far too many breaks, there was no way the bowl could be stuck back together again. I worked slowly, carefully: shards of pottery can be sharp, can cut you like glass. The little broken coloured bits made me sad: the bowl had been so lovely – blue like the sky, with its ring of birds. A sense of my own immeasurable destructiveness overwhelmed me, everything shattered around me, the floor crunching with broken bits beneath my feet.

Chapter 32

Mac told me he'd fixed the abortion for Friday. They wanted me to get there for half past ten, he said. After that we didn't talk about it.

On Thursday night I hardly slept. It was such a windy night and full of noise: the bangings of side-gates that hadn't been properly fastened, the wailing of car alarms set off by the wind. There was a milk bottle rolling around in the road, so that even half-asleep I kept steeling myself against the breaking of glass, which never came. I kept meaning to go and deal with it, but didn't have the energy, or kept dozing off before I could get up – so it went on through my dreams and my half-wakefulness – the threat of breaking and the sound of the storm.

In the end I got up, went to the kitchen, made a coffee. It was still only six thirty. I sat sipping as light slid into the sky, till it was a pale wash of many colours, like an opal. Little purple clouds scudded in front of the wind; a ragged web across the outside of the window shivered and glittered. I couldn't sit still, had that nervous restlessness you get when you've scarcely slept.

Then a resolve formed in me, sudden and complete, and I

found myself going back upstairs and dressing, very quietly. I was quick, careful, I didn't wake Mac. I left him a note on the kitchen table: I couldn't sleep, I've gone out for a while. Love, T. I'd go by car, I thought, to be sure I made it to the clinic in time: it seemed safer not to rely on public transport for something so crucial. I was fairly sure of the way, though I'd never driven it before, but I took my *A to Z*.

Outside the sun was up properly now, and the streets were clear and golden and full of long sharp shadows. But the wind had an edge that made you think of winter, in spite of the febrile gorgeousness of the light. I drove there slowly though the heavy traffic. Phrases echoed in my head. I wanted to tell you how angry you've made me feel, how betrayed, about how you've used me . . . Little sharp fragments splintering off from the solid rage inside me. But I couldn't picture it somehow, me standing there in front of him, telling him these things. I just drove on through the glare of the morning and the press of the traffic, towards something I couldn't see.

I parked, rang the bell. He opened the door instantly, he must have been in the hall. His briefcase was in his hand. It was surprising, somehow, to see him standing there, just the same as ever. He had a brisk incomplete morning look, rubbing the sleep from his eyes. There was a smell of coffee.

'Tessa?' he said. He seemed so pleased to see me.

'I need to talk,' I said.

He made a slight apologetic gesture. 'I have to go to college in a minute,' he said. 'I'm lecturing this morning. I'll be free from about twelve – we could meet somewhere perhaps?'

I shook my head.

'We have to talk now,' I said.

I pushed past him, into the house, and tripped stupidly on the doorstep, grabbing the door-jamb to steady myself, as though with pregnancy my body had reverted to all the awkwardness of adolescence.

285

He moved to let me through.

'But shouldn't you be at work too?' he said.

'No,' I said. 'I'm not going in today.'

The hall was dim after the brightness outside. I could see myself in the mirror, my face fierce and white, my hair tangled and hanging down.

He put his briefcase on the hall stand. 'Just for a minute then,' he said. 'Come and sit down.' He pushed open the door of the living room.

'No,' I said. I didn't want to go through. I had a fear that if I went further in I might soften, be drawn in, concede something I hadn't intended.

I cleared my throat. 'I wanted to tell you – I wanted to say – that I'm so angry. About what you did.' My voice not strong, like I'd planned, but wavering.

As I started to speak, he reached towards me, moving his hand through the clear red light that spilled from the panes of glass above the door. Then suddenly he stopped, as if his hand had met some invisible wall I'd built about me. A shadow passed over his face.

'Tessa, what the fuck is this?'

I tried again. 'When you find that things aren't how you thought they were, you feel so used,' I said.

He stared at me. 'I don't know what you're on about,' he said.

'Of course you do,' I said. 'For Chrissake. Of course you know.'

'You're talking in riddles,' he said.

He was angry now, his eyes cold, hard, the pupils contracted.

'Nita told me . . .' I swallowed. 'Nita told me you went to see that woman. Charlie Cavanagh.'

He looked at me blankly. 'What the fuck does that have to do with anything?' he said.

'If you can't see that . . .'

I felt so tired: the pregnancy seemed to press on me, as though the baby already had some kind of substance, weighing me down. I wanted to hide away, to be anywhere but here, in this shabby unfinished hall, with the red light falling on us, and all these things to say that I somehow had to wrench out of myself.

I shook my head, tried again.

'It's over,' I said. 'It has to be. I'd have thought that was completely obvious.'

He stood there looking at me. In some disconnected part of myself that hadn't quite caught up, I wanted to put out my hand and move it across his face and feel his cool skin, his mouth, against my hand: and the things I needed to tell him somehow couldn't be reached. He stared at me, waiting for me to speak. The silence between us panicked me, as though it might rise like water and close above our heads.

And in that silence, the things that Mac had said kept repeating themselves in my head. The sensible words: explaining me to myself. I'd run out of words of my own: they'd do as well as any.

'I've been a bit crazy,' I said. 'I haven't been myself. I don't know what came over me.' I could hear how my voice faded and faltered. 'We should never have let this happen. We should never have let ourselves get into this.'

I hated the way he looked at me, his frown, his narrow eyes. His fists were clenched. I was very aware of his size and his physical power, that there was no physical inhibition between us at all, after all the intimacy we'd had.

'I got swept away,' I said. 'Obsessed. It happens.'

I could see myself in the mirror: I was trying to be so strong and clear and determined, but the woman in the mirror seemed on the edge of tears.

287

I charged on. 'You forget who you are for a while, get swept away. People do. People get swept away.'

His face flushed, but he said nothing.

'Ben – what I'm saying – I mustn't see you again.'

He shrugged, turned away a little.

'If that's what you want,' he said.

There was a metallic taste in my mouth, like after having a tooth out, when your mouth fills up with blood.

'There's something else,' I said. 'There's something you need to know.' The thin pain boring into the back of my skull. 'I've just found out. It seems that we – that I . . .' The words seemed to block up my throat like solid things.

'Tessa, what are you trying to say?'

I swallowed.

There was a clatter outside, then the key turning.

'*Shit*,' he said. 'Not now.'

The door banged open behind us.

He spun round. Nita stood there, her school bag over her shoulder, her technology folder under her arm. She was wearing her oldest trainers, and there were stains on her sweatshirt. She had a dulled tired look, as though all the light had gone out in her.

She faltered when she saw me, didn't say anything. I felt a surge of rage with her for erupting like this into our conversation with all her wilful adolescent self-centredness. There were all these things I had to say to him: and now I couldn't say them. I couldn't bear it.

Ben must have felt this too: he turned on her.

'For God's sake, Nita. What the fuck are you doing here?' It was as if all the exasperation he felt with me was loaded onto her.

I'd never known him be angry with her before. She flinched, a distinct little movement. But she stared at him defiantly.

'Well, sorry for existing,' she said.

'Nita,' he said, a little more conciliatory. 'Why aren't you in college?'

'College sucks,' she said.

She let her bag, her folder, drop onto the floor. I saw that her technology drawings – the perfect intricate drawings of watches and clocks – were crumpled and creased with little rips in the edges, as though someone had screwed them up and binned them, then they'd maybe been rescued and straightened out again.

'I've had it with college,' she said.

'I can't talk now,' he said, like he'd said to me. 'I have to be in that lecture hall.'

'OK,' she said, shrugging. 'OK. Fine. Go off and do your thing. I just want to stay here for a bit today. That's not so much to ask, is it?'

'Stay here?' he said. 'Why?'

She shrugged. 'To think about things,' she said.

She rubbed her face in her hands: her bracelets glinted red in the stained light.

'What things?' he said.

They were talking as though I wasn't there. I thought of what the day held for me and felt my eyes fill up.

But he just waited for her.

She shrugged. 'You know, where I'm going and stuff.'

'Where you're going is back to college to get your GCSEs,' he said.

'Yeah well,' she said. 'Where does any of that ever get you, exactly?' Her voice was quiet now: we could only just hear her above the noise through the open door, the clatter and rush of morning sounds in the street, a car starting up and people on the pavement. 'The world is full of shit,' she said. 'Sometimes I feel I've just about had enough.'

'Nita, I could do without all this right now,' he said, 'Look,

289

stay here and make yourself a coffee, if you must, but promise me you'll go in later.'

'Yeah yeah,' she said. 'Whatever.'

'And I want you to give college a ring and say you've been held up. Make some excuse.'

She shrugged. 'OK,' she said. 'But I don't suppose anyone will give a fuck.'

'I'll ring your Mum,' he said.

'No, Dad. Please.' Her voice was suddenly high, urgent. She stepped forward, grasped his wrist. 'Don't ring her. Not now. We had a bit of a row. Me and Mum. Please. Just give me a break, OK?'

He shook his head a little, but it was as though when she'd touched him he'd given up. 'Make sure you phone in, at least,' he said.

She nodded.

'Have you had breakfast?' he said.

'Nope,' she said.

'There are some pop tarts,' he said. 'I'll find them for you. But then I really must go.'

He was about to go into the kitchen. I turned to the door.

'I'm going too,' I said. 'There's somewhere I have to be. I have to be there for ten thirty.' And went and left them there, hearing Ben's voice following me, troubled suddenly, not angry anymore.

'Tessa?'

Like a thin string thrown out after me, a line to reel me in. But I went on.

And drove off through the bright morning, the purposeful rush-hour traffic, the wind blowing everywhere, the first of winter's yellow leaves falling. The sky that had been opalescent was blotted all over with cloud. And at first, driving off, I actually felt that, rushing away as I had, I must have left something behind. My handbag perhaps – my jacket? But

290

they were there on the passenger seat beside me. It was a very strong and specific feeling, a feeling of such incompleteness. As though I'd lost or forgotten something, that something that was mine remained there, in the house with the slatted blind and the tangle of green in the yard and all the light the colour of claret falling in the hallway.

Chapter 33

I drove too fast, though I didn't need to hurry. We hadn't talked for long, it was still only twenty to nine: I had plenty of time to get to the clinic. But I wanted to be there now, to get it done: wanted to get beyond it, to have everything sorted out, to find myself in some new unimaginable place where I could be normal again.

The rush-hour traffic was thinning now: it was that moment when there's a change in the ownership of the street, the roads and pavements taken over by mothers and children. I drove through acres of dispiriting thirties semis. They all looked much alike, though here and there people had tried to put their own stamp on them: there were coach lamps, and new porches full of plants, and bits of mock Tudor timbering. Cars that people were working on were parked on concrete in front of the houses, rags of late roses blew on garden fences. They were the kind of streets that teenagers long to escape from, feeling they embody all that is oppressive and banal.

I realized I was crying, my vision misted up. I had to keep rubbing my eyes so I could see.

I came to the end of the semis, went round a one-way system

past a Petsmart covered in steel cladding. I had to concentrate hard, to change lanes with care: my driving today was quite erratic, I knew. I wondered if it was an effect of pregnancy hormones, and the thought passed through me before I could stop it: I'll have to be careful for a while, not take on too much, put the baby first. As though something in me hadn't caught up with what I was going to do.

I passed a huge Homebase, a horrible yellow church, a waste transfer station, a carpet warehouse advertising a sale. I didn't recognize any of this at all. I wondered if I'd taken a wrong turning. I needed to stop but there was nowhere. I darted across lanes: somebody hooted – probably at me.

I pulled off hastily into a side road. Caldecote Road, it said. I got out my *A to Z*. I had to look up Caldecote Road in the index – it wasn't on the page where I was meant to be; and when I did find the right page, Caldecote Road reached over the central binding and didn't align properly. And then I saw that I was miles out of my way. I was appalled. A sense of London's vastness overwhelmed me, a nightmare feeling – that you could drive and drive for ever and never find yourself again, that fear of being far from home, where all the people are strangers and anything can happen: like in dreams when you're sucked into some quixotic transport system, some huge network of nightmare roads that carries you on and on under an extravagant jade-green sky, drawing you far away from the place where you should be. I cursed myself, that I had been so stupid, when I had an appointment so crucial – my chance to restore some order to my world – and somehow I'd driven off in exactly the opposite direction. I couldn't believe it.

I sat quite still, trying to quiet my breathing. The wind that blew in through my half-open window chilled my wet face, and the little screwdriver pain in the back of my head sharpened, bored into me. I forced myself to take some deep breaths, focus, work it out slowly, step by step. I could see what I had to do – turn left, turn right, find my way onto the dual carriageway that should eventually take me back in the right direction. I drove on, breathing deeply.

You had to go slowly, the road was all parked up and there were speed bumps. I passed more semis, a dreary recreation ground littered with seagulls like white blown bits of paper, a junior school. The latecomers were straggling up to the school gate, some of them in fancy dress: the girls as Little Miss Muffet or fairytale princesses in party frocks, the boys as Superman or robots. They're always doing this at Lydia's school – having to dress as a book character or something – Abi moans about it, there's all this ghastly gender stereotyping, she says, and anyway she hates sewing. On the pavement coming towards me there was a woman with a baby in a buggy and a girl of six or seven. The girl was dressed as a shepherdess from a nursery rhyme: she was wearing a shiny frock in a strong bright kingfisher blue, looped up in front to show her underskirt. She looked just like the ornament Cassie had given me, and in my heightened emotional state this seemed somehow significant, almost as though she'd walked out of some dream of mine. She had a walking stick for a crook, and a hat she'd trimmed herself: it was a plain little straw boater, but she'd put a lot of work into it, all these bits of ribbon and heaps of paper flowers. The girl was slow, stopping to talk to a cat, the woman was trying to hurry her along. The woman had the frayed look, the smudged eyes, narrowed mouth, of those who parent in poor conditions – for whom feeding and clothing the children and keeping the house together take every ounce of cunning and resilience they have. The girl still dawdled, poking in a puddle with her crook: her mother told her off.

And then as I watched a gust of wind took the hat from her head and blew it into the road, across the front of my car and into the path of a lorry that was coming the other way. The little girl screamed; I could hear her through my half-open window. And then, quick as a heartbeat, she darted in front of my car. I stamped on the brake. She didn't pause, charged on, absolutely oblivious, seeing only the one thing, the thing she'd lost, diving straight in front of the lorry. There was a wail of brakes and the lorry came to a halt, just missed her. I could see the driver swearing and flinging up his hands. The mother called out, ran after her. The girl picked up the hat from the kerb where it had come to rest, looked round, uncertain, as though she didn't know how she'd got there, looked down at the hat and cried because the brim was broken and muddy. The lorry driver shook his head at her. I was vaguely aware of hooting behind me, a sense of traffic piling up and irritated drivers. And then the woman grabbed the child and pulled her back to the opposite pavement, and the lorry drove off.

I'd stopped so sharply I'd stalled. As I started up again, I saw how the woman took the child's face in her hands; you could see she was telling her off. And then she took the hat and tried to smooth out the crumples in the brim. It wasn't as nice as it had been before, but it would do. The girl was still crying but quietly now. The woman put the hat back on the girl's head, scolding still, but her hands were gentle, and they walked on to school.

I drove off very carefully, my heart kicking away, adrenaline surging through me. I kept seeing the shiny kingfisher streak of her darting out in front of me, as though it was still happening. I felt such fear, because it had been so close, because I could have killed her: yet mixed up with the fear there was a strange and powerful tenderness towards this impulsive little stranger, almost as though I was cradling her there between my hands. And it was so obvious suddenly, and I knew what I must do. I would just get on with it – with this baby of mine, whose appalling timing marked the end of my marriage, but who still required a welcome – and with my work too, which was blighted but still possible, in some setting, somewhere. The things that Mac had suggested and that I'd taken on board so eagerly – having the abortion, becoming a drug rep: these were just deluded attempts to make it all crisp and neat and unsullied, to undo something that couldn't be undone. What I had to do was just to keep going and muddle through, with this life that was now so different from what I'd planned: and to save whatever I could.

But I didn't rest long in that clarity. Just a few yards, just a street or two. It was like a fog was lifting all around me and I could see much further than before, and what I saw was Nita – her blank face, her technology project that looked as though it had been crumpled up then straightened out again. I saw what I hadn't taken in because I'd been so wrapped up in myself and my anger with Ben. The image came to me with the kind of certainty you learn to recognize: the intuitive knowledge I'd always relied on till recently, till Paula, when it had so devastatingly deserted me. And I heard Nita speaking in my head: The world is full of shit. Sometimes I feel I've just about had enough. I don't suppose anyone will give a fuck.

I pressed down on the accelerator, driving with absolute urgency. Tracing my way back, past the Homebase, the warehouse, the thirties semis, my *A to Z* open on the seat beside me, because I couldn't afford to get lost again. Driving roughly across the speed bumps: jumping a red light. Taking risks, but not too many risks, because above all I had to get there. Gripped by the fear that I had made another terrible mistake: and now I was too late.

At Ben's house, I parked roughly, grabbed my bag but didn't pause to lock the car. I saw the curtains had been drawn in the big front bedroom – Ben and Alysson's bedroom, that I'd never been in. I banged at the door. Nothing. I opened the letterbox, shouted for her through it, waited a moment. But all I could hear was the hollowness of the house: a tap dripping somewhere, a creak.

The side gate was open. I went through, into the yard. All the back windows were shut. I stood there just for a moment among the plants, the lilies with their heavy pollen, and the mulberry tree and the fig, where I'd sat so often with Ben through those scented strange afternoons of the life that was now over, drinking coffee, talking. It was very quiet, very peaceful: I doubted for a moment, wondered if I had the nerve to disturb that peace, to do what I had to do. A voice smooth as oil murmured in my head. You're exaggerating, it said to me, you're panicking unnecessarily: you're a little hysterical maybe – a little unhinged by everything that's happened – Alysson's murder, your marriage falling apart – always fearing the worst after Alysson. It'll all be all right, there's nothing to worry about. But I recognized the thought for the old enemy it was, like when I'd discharged Paula. Everything's just fine, the emollient voice went on, bland, persuasive. I didn't listen.

There was an empty terracotta flowerpot on the wall: I smashed it against the window – the pot broke, the window didn't. Then I heard the door next door opening, someone coming into the garden. Shit, I thought.

She was old, fragile, white-haired, in slippers and an apron. She looked at me uncertainly over the garden fence.

'I don't know if it's Thursday or Friday,' she said. 'Tell me, dear, is it Thursday or Friday?'

'It's Friday,' I said. 'Look – I'm afraid I have to break in.'

'Oh,' she said.

'There's a girl in there – I have to get to her,' I said.

'Oh,' she said again.

'Don't worry if you hear the window breaking,' I said.

She looked at me doubtfully.

'I thought it must be Thursday,' she said. She turned and went back into her house.

I took one of the bricks that edged the flower bed, smashed it into the window, shielding my face with my arm. The sound of shattering made my pulse race, even though it was me who'd thrown the brick. I took out some of the glass, reached through to the back of the door. Ben had left the key in the lock, thank God, I wouldn't have to climb in through the broken glass. I took the key out, pulled it through. I saw that I was bleeding, a deep cut across the back of my hand, but I couldn't feel it. I unlocked the door and went in.

I ran upstairs through the hush and darkness of the house, pushed open the door of the main bedroom where I'd never been. She was in the big bed, lying down, the duvet wrapped round and under her like a sleeping bag. She seemed tiny in the vast bed, her face framed in a messy halo of hair. With the curtains drawn, it was very dim. There was a smell of alcohol, sickly in the morning: an empty bottle of brandy on its side, the carpet dark with wet: some of it at least had been spilled, she couldn't have drunk it all. She looked like she was asleep, peaceful almost, seemingly not disturbed by all the noise I'd made, the shattering glass. Her face was white as wax.

I grabbed her. 'Nita.'

She opened her eyes a little, stared at me, as though she didn't recognize me. Her pupils were widely dilated, her breath smelt of brandy.

I pushed down the duvet, shook her gently by the shoulders.

'Nita, it's me, Tessa. Can you hear me, Nita?'

She stared at me, nodded very slightly.

I had her face in my hands, forcing her to look into my eyes.

'Nita, what did you take?'

She tried to say something, gave up. She made the slightest movement of her head, indicating behind her. I looked under the bed. There was an empty bottle of Dothiapin, Ben's antidepressants that I'd seen in the bathroom. I remembered that he hadn't taken any.

'Was it full?'

She didn't reply, her head lolling forward like there was no muscle tone in her neck.

I had my mobile in my bag. I told them what she'd taken. They said the ambulance would be there in ten minutes.

I put her in the recovery position. I drew back the curtains, opened the window, let in some air and light. She flinched from the brightness, turned her face away, but I needed that clear light of day, the dust motes dancing. I hunted around to check if she'd taken anything else, but there was nothing. So I sat there beside her in Ben's bed, smoothing the hair back from her forehead, breathing in the brandy on her breath and the tangerine smell of her hair, sat through the long reaches of time till the ambulance arrived. Fighting down my fear, that wasn't any use, that would just get in the way, a luxury I couldn't permit myself, as I felt her slip down the smooth easy slope into coma. Everything contracted – there was only the shallowness of her breathing, and, as the muscles in her forearm twitched a little, the ephemeral music her silver bracelets made.

Chapter 34

They wanted me to go while they pumped her stomach. But when I told them I was a doctor they let me stay and I held her while she vomited. Afterwards she was absolutely white. They wheeled her to the ward, tucked her up in bed.

I was sitting by her bed when Ben came. I'd rung him from the ambulance. He looked as though he'd been beaten up. I was glad they'd pumped her stomach before he came. He leaned down into the bed and put his arms round her very gently. She opened her eyes, murmured something, shut them again and turned her head away. You couldn't tell if she was really asleep – or if keeping her eyes open was just too much effort.

The registrar came.

'You're Nita's father?' he said.

'Yes.'

'She'll be fine,' he said. 'She was found in time, thank goodness. She'll probably need to stay in a day or two: she'll need to see a psychiatrist and so on.'

Ben nodded: I wasn't sure if he was really hearing what he was being told. He turned back to Nita. But she had her eyes shut: he spoke to her a little but for now she couldn't be reached.

'Perhaps we could have a talk,' said the registrar. 'Perhaps you could tell me a bit about what's been happening in her life?'

'Sure,' said Ben. He followed the registrar into the sister's office.

I sat by Nita's bed for a while, but she was definitely sleeping now. I went off into the corridor, walked around a bit. Everything was blue or grey and rather shabby, with the usual children's pictures: 'Thank you to the doctors and nurses' and a stick figure with a bandaged leg. There was something about being there with Nita that distanced me a little – so I didn't see the place as a doctor, but as a relative or patient might. And I thought how as a child I'd loved hospitals: on the rare occasions I'd visited someone with my mother – taking some bananas to an elderly woman from the church choir perhaps – I'd loved the exciting antiseptic smells, the sense of drama: that had all been part of wanting to be a doctor. You can relish those things when you're nine and you think that everything can be mended.

Ben came out of the office. We sat on the tubular chairs in the grey corridor. I told him how the child had run into the road and suddenly I'd known.

We were still talking when Kam arrived. She was in her forties, formal in her business suit and silk shirt, with lots of gold jewellery, but I knew at once who she was: she had Nita's thin grace, her candid look. Ben hugged her and she clung to him – you knew they hadn't embraced like this since she'd left him. I watched, then felt I shouldn't, turned away, wondered why I was still there.

'Where's Richard?' he said.

'He's coming as soon as he can,' she said.

She turned to me.

'Tessa,' she said, knowing at once who I was, 'how can I thank you? We're so lucky. Aren't we?' she said, turning to Ben. 'That you were there for her. That you were a doctor. So so lucky.'

'Yes,' he said.

They went into the ward together – I could hear them talking quietly through the open door. Then he left her to sit by Nita's bed for a while, came back to me.

He sat down heavily beside me.

'How could I not have seen?' he said. 'I'll never forgive myself.'

'We neither of us saw. It isn't easy,' I said.

'I haven't had time for Nita for so long,' he said. 'I haven't really listened to her. Not for months.'

I murmured something.

'It's because of Alysson,' he said. 'I know that's no excuse. But it's how it happens. One terrible thing – and it all just goes on and on.'

'Yes, I know,' I said.

'I knew Nita was troubled – all this problem with her eating. I mean, it scared me. I just didn't have the strength to take it on. I expected Kam to do it all – to do too much.'

He drank his coffee. His face was shadowed, heavy.

'I need to move forward somehow,' he said. 'I know that. I've been trying to find a way. It isn't easy.'

I went to get him a coffee from the machine down the corridor. I had to give him something: he so badly needed comfort. Charlie Cavanagh flickered through my mind, but the anger I'd felt that morning seemed to belong somewhere else – in a far country. That was all for some other time. For now we were here for Nita.

The coffee had a bitter aftertaste. A man was wheeled past on a stretcher, his face twisted up.

'God, I hate these places,' said Ben.

'Sometimes I think I hate them too,' I said.

'Why can't life be ordinary?' he said. 'I just want life to be ordinary for a while.' There was such tiredness in his voice. 'Just getting on. You know – coping with all the day-to-day irritations, the traffic jams and minor aggravation. Going out for a drink and looking forward to Saturday. All that stuff.'

'Yes,' I said. 'That's what I want too.' I thought of the baby, all the urgent practical things, the messy demanding world I'd soon be living in – so different from the pure harsh place where I'd lived since Alysson's death. I needed to tell him, but I knew I couldn't: not here in the corridor with its walls the colour of fog, with all the uncertainty about what we were to each other, and the fear for Nita, and people passing through.

Kam came out.

'She's still asleep,' she said. 'I can't bear it. I wish she'd speak to me.'

She sat down beside me, grasped my wrist, her fingers tight, clutching. She was all tension, taut like wire: you might cut yourself on her. I put my hand on hers.

'Tessa, I can't forgive myself.' Her voice desperate, the words tumbling out. 'It's all my fault. She was so histrionic. I lost it, I didn't listen, I told her to pull herself together.'

'Of course it isn't your fault,' I said. I couldn't bear her need to explain, to justify herself to me.

'I made this happen: I feel so guilty,' she said.

'No,' I said. 'You mustn't feel those things. We can only do so much.' But I knew she wouldn't believe me.

She couldn't sit still. She walked up and down the corridor, twisting the sparkly rings round and round on her fingers. She kept looking into the ward where Nita was.

This wasn't my place anymore; it was for Kam and Ben.

'I'd better go,' I told him.

'I'll come to the door with you,' he said.

'No,' I said, 'I'm fine. You stay here.'

I longed to touch him, but somehow I couldn't. There was a sense of inhibition between us, of not knowing where we were with each other. And he didn't reach out to me. He looked uncertain, confused, didn't meet my eyes: as though, after all that had happened, he didn't have the energy or the clarity to hold me there. I had such a sense of his separateness – like I'd sometimes had even when we'd been together, in those untended lost gardens of the city, those places where we'd walked, when I'd felt as though the river was flowing between us.

'OK then,' I said, and half-turned to go. 'Give Nita my love when she wakes.'

And I walked off, down the bleak corridor and out through the sliding doors into the car park, and all the things I hadn't said were locked up inside me, so I had a dull heavy ache in my chest, just here under my heart.

It was cold. I was so tired I was shivering, and I didn't have my jacket. An ambulance screamed in; people drove round the car park, tapping their fingers crossly on their steering wheels, trying to find parking spaces. I had to move rapidly out of the way of a Southern Syringes Services lorry that was reversing rather recklessly. I felt disoriented: it was only now that I remembered that I'd come in the ambulance and I didn't have my car. I didn't even know quite where I was, how far from Ben's house. I hadn't noticed when we came, I'd been holding Nita's hand, hadn't seen anything apart from Nita.

The day ahead felt like a heap of sand dumped down in front of me, full of problems I had to work my way through – getting back to Ben's house to pick up my car, making my way back home: and later, of course, the things I'd have to tell Mac, those things he'd struggled so hard to stop me from saying. I felt weighed down with tiredness and the difficulty of everything, soaked through with it, like something drenched.

There were several people waiting at the taxi rank, and no taxis. I realized I was famished, and I knew the nausea would really get a grip if I didn't eat something. I briefly considered going back to the hospital and getting a sandwich from the

WRVS stall, but I knew that was impossible: I'd said goodbye, it was over.

I followed the signs to the way out, but I must have gone wrong somewhere because I seemed to come out round the back of the hospital. I turned left, walking randomly down the road in search of some place that might sell something to eat. It was a quiet road with big Edwardian houses with little front gardens. There were fallen berries like fruit pastilles on the pavement: a dusty pink dahlia, heavy-headed, nodded in someone's garden. Starlings swirled in the sky, making patterns like the movement of waves in water, and the wind blew the litter along the pavement and tugged at my hair. I passed a florist's, with tall rather ragged daisies in terracotta pots and primulas ready for bedding-out on tables on the pavement. The road was lined with pollarded chestnuts: big yellow leaves that had fallen slapped at the pavement in the wind, like someone walking by me with bare feet.

There was a newsagent's on the corner. I went in, picked up two bags of peanuts. By the till there was a local paper with a headline about a cutback in maternity services, a subject which I suddenly found rather interesting. I bought that too, to read in the taxi.

Outside the shop I stopped to open the peanuts, tipped a few into my mouth. I glanced at the newspaper. On the front, above the headline, where it told you the highlights from the inside pages, there was a little picture of Charlie Cavanagh. The familiar mugshot, the resolute smile, the shiny, sharply cut hair. I felt the thud of my heart. Page 11, it said. I turned to page 11.

It was a piece about the Hollies. I started to read, and found it wasn't at all her usual style: not punchy, but rather detailed and descriptive, beginning with a long and elaborate account of the place, the battered comfy sofas, the kitchen smelling of drinking chocolate, and the welcome she'd been given by the people she'd met there. And then she'd written, 'Ben Connelly, the partner of Alysson Gates, the woman tragically stabbed to death by a psychiatric patient, has pledged his support to the users and relatives who are trying to keep the Hollies open in the face of local opposition.' There was a quote from him: places like the Hollies have a central role in the lives of those who use them, he'd said, and the interests of the general public will never be served by reducing the help available to the most vulnerable members of our society. It all sounded stilted and formal, not like the way he'd normally talk: I knew he'd found it hard. There was a blurry photo of Clive Lewis as a boy, in his cub's uniform, and a picture of Angie Lewis, with her perm and her worn face and her smile and that look of hers, straight out of the paper and into your eyes.

I put the newspaper in my bag and I walked back up the hill, under the pollarded chestnuts, the wind drying my tears. I walked as fast as I could but I didn't need to hurry really: I knew he'd still be there, sitting with Kam in the long grey corridor, sipping another unwanted cup of coffee, waiting for Nita to wake. I thought how it would be: how I'd put my hand on his shoulder and say how sorry I was, how I hadn't understood; feeling a little embarrassed with Kam there looking curiously up at me, wondering what had happened; and maybe he'd get up and hold me close for a moment, restrained because Kam was there, putting his arms around me as you might hold a friend, yet still astonishing me with the tenderness of his touch. And I passed the florist's shop, with the primulas in their little polystyrene pots, all ready to bed out in people's gardens, and the daisies, that seemed at once both tatty and gorgeous, with their yellow hearts, their fringe of pink-tipped petals, like the ox-eye daisies he'd shown me at Morden Cemetery, that grow so beautifully in the very poorest ground.

Chapter 35

I drive there through the November countryside. There's cloud, no wind: a still grey day. The landscape is brown, like the hides of animals. There's a tractor ploughing a field, a white smoke of seagulls following after the tractor. It's so quiet, so empty. A man in wellingtons walks through a field and calls his dog: he's the only human thing in this brown land.

There are tall trees with rooks' nests in them – you can see the nests quite clearly, most of the leaves have fallen. I pass the old brick wall round an estate. There are tall beech trees. There's an imposing gateway in the wall – gates of curly wrought iron, pillars twice as tall as a man with stone lions on them. But the driveway is overgrown with high dying grasses and doesn't lead anywhere anymore.

The emptiness of it all after London is surprising: you forget that there's all this emptiness still in England. When I stop in a layby to eat my cheese sandwich and drink some coffee from my thermos flask, I wind my window right down in spite of the cold, and the silence comes in through the window and wraps itself around me.

I get there at three. The building is intimidating, as these places always are. Because I was her doctor, I am visiting as a professional, I don't have to go in visiting hours. But they still run their metal detectors over me and look into my bag.

Her psychiatrist comes to see me, a pleasant man with greying hair, a greying beard, a soothing voice. He has some questions he wants to ask me – about what she's told me about her childhood. I try to help. I'm glad he doesn't ask me why I've come because I wouldn't know what to say.

I'm shown to one of the little faceless rooms you always get in these places, with a table and four chairs round the table and bars across the windows. Someone has tried to brighten it up a little, there are dried flowers in an unbreakable plastic vase on the windowsill. It's very hot.

A warder brings her in. She's dressed as usual, in jeans and a t-shirt. Her hair is a bit longer and softer, it's grown below her ears now, curling around her face. There's colour in her skin, and her gaze is level, more open, less afraid. I can tell she is well again, as well as ever she is.

'Dr Craig.' She smiles, she's really pleased to see me. She doesn't seem at all surprised that I've come.

'I just wondered how you were,' I say.

She sits down opposite me, her elbows on the table, leaning towards me.

'I'm fine,' she says. 'It's not so bad in here really.'

The warder takes one of the chairs and puts it against the wall, so he isn't in our direct line of sight. He takes a paperback novel out of his pocket.

'They're treating you OK?'

'It's not so bad,' she says.

'Are you doing any art?' I say. 'Making things? D'you have a chance to do that?'

She nods. 'The art therapy's great,' she says. 'They really help you. There's this guy called Hugo. He's the chief art therapist: he's really good.'

I have a mental image of Hugo, a bit earnest perhaps, with a silver earring and a leather jacket, and thrilled with Paula, seeing the talent in her, loving to draw that out.

'I'm glad,' I say.

'The food's lousy though,' she says. 'Too much stodge. We all worry about putting on weight. Saffron, my friend, she's really pretty, she's put on half a stone since coming in here, she's really upset about it.'

'I can imagine,' I say.

I sense how she's making connections here: this is her world now. I feel I know what I needed to know: that she has friends, that she has someone professional to take an interest in her and appreciate her.

'It's nice to see you,' she says. 'I don't get many visitors.'

'Well, it's a long way to come,' I say.

There's a little silence.

'Anyway,' she says then, 'Liam's left me. Liam and me aren't together anymore.'

'Oh Paula.'

She shrugs. 'I can't say I blame him, quite honestly. He was good to me but it wasn't going anywhere.'

'I can see it would be hard to keep things going,' I say. 'I'm sorry, Paula.'

She shrugs again. 'It's one of those things,' she says. 'So. Is everyone at the hospital all right?'

'As far as I know,' I say. 'They all seemed OK when I left. I'm working somewhere different now. I've got this job with homeless people.'

'Oh,' she says. 'D'you like it?'

'Well, it's quite interesting,' I say.

'I still think about them all sometimes, at the hospital,' she says. 'Like Cassie. She was nice, wasn't she? Though she did have some seriously weird ideas.'

'I guess so,' I say.

Another silence.

'Dr Craig,' she says then, slightly pink, lowering her voice, though of course the warder could hear everything. 'I hope you don't mind me saying – but are you pregnant?'

'Yes,' I say. 'Four months. The baby's due in April.'

A real smile. She seems terribly pleased. 'How lovely,' she says. 'I'd love to have a baby. I don't suppose I will now.'

I don't know what to say.

'D'you know if it's a boy or a girl?' she says.

'No,' I say. 'We couldn't see on the scan. Sometimes you can see if it's a boy, but we couldn't tell.'

'That's nicer though, isn't it?' she says. 'To have a bit of a surprise. Surprises can be nice . . . I bet your husband's over the moon,' she says.

'Actually,' I say, 'we're not together anymore. We've split up. I've got a flat on my own now.'

'Oh,' she says. Then doesn't quite know what to say. Then she smiles. 'Well, that makes two of us then,' she says. 'In the same boat. You know – in a way.'

'Yes,' I say.

I hear the ticking of the clock, the whisper of paper as the warder turns a page of his book. We sit there quietly for a moment, both perhaps contemplating the gulf between our lives.

She gets up. I think she may be getting agitated: it happens with this illness, that people grow more anxious as you talk. I think how this must be hard for her – me coming to see her, with my life that carries on with all these hopes and possibilities. Perhaps she wants me to go.

I'm about to say goodbye when she says, 'Could you hang on just a moment?'

'Of course,' I say.

She speaks to the warder.

'We'll only be five minutes,' she tells me. 'Promise you won't go.'

I sit there in the stillness.

When she comes back with the warder, she has a plastic bag. She takes something out.

'I made this in OT,' she says.

It's a crocheted baby blanket, with a blue ribbon threaded through the border.

'I want you to have it: for the baby,' she says. 'I'd have made something specially if I'd known you were coming.'

'That's so sweet of you,' I say. 'It's very pretty.'

'If it's a girl you can just change the ribbon,' she says. 'I'll show you — it's just threaded through — it's easy to do.' And she showed me where it was stitched. 'But it might be a boy after all,' she says.

'It's lovely,' I tell her again. 'Thank you. It's nice to see you — I guess I just needed to know you were OK.'

'I'm fine,' she says. 'Don't worry about me, Dr Craig. You've got your baby to think of.'

And I say goodbye and leave her and drive home through the quiet November countryside, where night is falling, that dense country darkness that's impenetrable as smoke or fog, and clouds cover the stars, but when I drive through the villages the brightness where people haven't drawn their curtains spills out to lighten my journey through the dark.